MW01045990

THE CONFESSIONS
OF ST. ZACH

BY GENE O'NEILL

WWW.NETTIRW.COM

WWW.DARKREGIONS.COM

Published by Written Backwards, an imprint of Dark Regions Press

Cover artwork by Michael Bailey

Illustrations by Orion Zangara

Introduction by John R. Little

The Confessions of St. Zach first appeared as a novella in lettered hardback and trade paperback editions by Bad Moon Books, which included an introduction by Gord Rollo, an afterword by Brian Keene, and artwork by Steven Gilberts. Copyright © 2008, Gene O'Neill.

The original work received a Bram Stoker Award ® nomination for "Superior Achievement in Long Fiction" by the Horror Writers Association.

The Confessions of St. Zach also appeared in its original novella form in lettered (A-Z) deluxe hardcover, 100 signed/numbered hardcover, and trade paperback editions of *The Hitchhiking Effect*, a collection of fiction by Gene O'Neill, which included cover and interior artwork by Steven Gilberts. Copyright © 2015, Gene O'Neill.

All four books in The Cal Wild Chronicles, including *The Confessions of St. Zach, The Burden of Indigo, The Near Future,* and *The Far Future,* were released in special 65 numbered hardcover editions by Thunderstorm Books, which included cover artwork by GAK. Copyright © 2015, Gene O'Neill.

FIRST EDITION TRADE PAPERBACK

ISBN-13: 978.0.9961493.3.4

THE CONFESSIONS
OF ST. ZACH

BY GENE O'NEILL

[THE CAL WILD CHRONICLES: BOOK 1]

INTRODUCTION

BY JOHN R. LITTLE

In 2008, Gene O'Neill published an amazing novella. As with this book, the novella was titled *The Confessions of St. Zach*. Like many of Gene's fans, I waited patiently for the book to arrive in my mail box, and when it did, I devoured it in a single session.

You see, Gene O'Neill is one of those writers who just grabs you and won't let you leave until he's done with you. I always figure, "Why resist?" The story will just keep calling to me until I read it, so let's get it done!

Because of that ability to reel his readers in, I've always been amazed (and frankly, more than a little envious) of his talent.

The funny thing is, we've had a lot in common in our careers. Gene attended the Clarion West Writers Workshop in 1979 and it wasn't long after that his first story was published in 1981. That story was "The Burdon of Indigo," of which I'd have a lot more to say if I wasn't obligated to keep my mouth shut and leave that delightful task to Lisa Morton, who is writing the introduction to the second volume of this series.

My own first story was published only a year later, in 1982. Although it made me a lot of money, it was very forgettable, unlike

Gene's story, which continues to live for new readers today.

Since our almost co-incident starting point, we've both published lots of material over the years, both of us working in the fields of science fiction, dark fantasy, and horror.

Then came 2008.

As I mentioned before, that was when the original version of *St. Zach* was published by Bad Moon Books. That year, I had my own novella published by Bad Moon: *Miranda*. One could argue that these two books reignited both of our careers.

Both books were nominated for the Black Quill Award in the category of Best Small Press Chill, and both were nominated for the prestigious Bram Stoker Award in the category of Long Fiction, along with great works by Adam-Troy Castro and Weston Ochse. I remember how humbled I felt being included in that group, but being side-by-side with Gene was the part that amazed me.

Somehow I was fortunate enough to win the Stoker that year, but I always felt it should have been shared with Gene.

(Gene and I shared nominations again in 2011, so again our writing paths crossed. That year, Peter Straub carried home the award, and I suspect we were both cheering for Peter. Well, at least a little bit.)

All of which is to say that when Michael Bailey of Written Backwards asked if I'd be interested in writing an introduction to this book, it took me about a nanosecond to say, "Hell, yes!"

If the original edition of this story is a memorable novella, this new full-length version is a richer, more fulfilling read that demands your attention. As with all his work, Gene transports his readers, taking them inside his imagination and not letting them escape until *he* is ready to let them go.

I mentioned that Gene writes in several genres. Is this book science fiction? Horror? Dark fantasy? Well, I'll let smarter people than me debate that one. To me, it's not important. All that matters is Gene's ability to tell a story. And what a story this has become! I read the manuscript several months ago as I write this introduction, and I still feel the characters seared into my mind. I see the nightmare setup, the aftermath, the amazing story of the dyed people, and so many other things. I want to tell you all about them, but really, you need to take that journey on your own.

In this book, you'll trip across several references to Ray Bradbury. I have no doubt that Gene is a big fan (as am I). More, I suspect Bradbury was one of the earlier influences on Gene's own writing (again, as he was on me). The genre-mixing, the use of language to pull the reader in, the storytelling above all, the clear desire to populate the book with real life characters ... anyone who likes Bradbury (and really, is there anybody who doesn't?) will feel right at home in Gene's world.

You can probably tell pretty clearly that I admire Gene O'Neill, both as a writer, but equally important, as a human being. We occasionally meet up at conventions and he's always grinning and laughing and ready to offer a hand, not just to me, but to anybody. He's the guy that everyone loves.

One day perhaps we'll end up again on a future award ballot, and I'd love that vote to end up as a tie. As our careers continue to run along parallel paths, I'm honored to know Gene and to call him a close friend.

Enough of this! Flip the pages. You have people to meet and places to go, courtesy of one of the best storytellers we have.

THE CONFESSIONS
OF ST. ZACH

"An outstanding use of an epigraph and title, in my opinion, is by Somerset Maugham in his excellent novel of the search for meaning in life, *The Razor's Edge*: 'The sharp edge of a razor is difficult to pass over; thus the wise say the path to salvation is hard *(from Katha-Upanishad)*.'" – UC Berkeley unpublished lecture notes by Dr. Jacob Zachary, PhD

PROLOGUE

GOLD MINES UNDER THE CANOPY

Amazonia—In the last six months, tons of heavy equipment and materials have been shipped on huge barges from eastern Ecuador on the tributaries of the Upper Amazon River to the new ERA, Equatorial Republic of Amazonia, for deep gold mining excavation. From released records, it has been estimated that the recently discovered vein under the jungle canopy has a potential yearly yield one and a half times that of all the older South African mines.

NSA officials in Washington are concerned about the impact of this sudden wealth on the new State's foreign policy. It is feared that President Jose Ignacio's administration will follow the lead of the leftist anti-USA policies of their neighbors to the west and the north. The anti-American rhetoric of President Hugo Chavez II has been amped up in recent months, which is of growing concern to USA Administration officials. Venezuelan banks have funneled the bulk of venture capital to the newly established nation, much of it originating from oil allies in the Mid-East. But ERA has been oddly silent concerning its foreign policy, especially toward its giant neighbor to the far north. Ignacio recently invited Chavez to a forthcoming completion dedication in the late fall at the mine sites.

GENE O'NEILL

PART 1

THE BLUE ROCK SPRINGS JOURNAL

"Get busy living, or get busy dying."
– Stephen King, *Rita Hayworth and*
the Shawshank Redemption

GENE O'NEILL

1

SNOWED IN

After six and a half days of steady shoveling with the inefficient garden spades, Jacob Zachary and his seventeen-year-old son, Lucas, managed to finish clearing the heavily-drifted snow along a five-hundred-plus yard exposed stretch of the narrow, private road. Enough at least to get around the rocky windward side of Mt. George, and down into the more protected beginning of heavy tree cover. They could see patches of un-shoveled blacktop ahead as the road dropped down and curved out of sight into the dense oak and madrone forest. The two stood under the trees, caught their breaths, looked back toward the mostly snowbound cabin, and admired the results of their work.

"C'mon, kiddo," Jake said, and patted his son's shoulder, "let's see if your mom needs help packing the car." He led his son back to the cabin.

At the turn-around near the cabin, they stored the shovels in the back of the partially packed Lexus. Eight days earlier, they'd first dug the SUV out of a twelve-foot high drift, discovering they would have to clear a long stretch of the road before attempting to drive off the mountain.

"Lauren," Jake shouted as they slipped inside the cabin, "anything else to load up? The road's finally cleared all the way down into the tree cover. We're ready to try and get back to civilization."

The family had been trapped almost three weeks in their four-room vacation lodge on Mt. George by a series of freak snowstorms, the winds howling up the rocky canyons, piling snow higher and higher around the cabin for nine consecutive days.

"Damned global warming," Jake had sworn when they woke up that first morning and couldn't see out the picture windows overlooking the Napa Valley below them and San Francisco thirty-five or so miles to the distant south.

It *never* snowed in the Bay Area any time of the year, he'd thought, even on the highest spot on the eastern side of the famed Valley. And he'd been coming to his family's lodge for forty years. But the exposed cabin had been completely buried by the series of freak storms, as if they were trapped in an igloo deep in the Artic.

On the tenth day, the wind and storms ceased. They began to painstakingly dig their way out of the cabin with improvised equipment: an ice ladle, a big spatula, and a flattened cake pan.

They were able to squeeze out the partially cleared front door around noontime. After estimating the location, they scooped a tunnel to the shed at the edge of the exposed turn-around driveway, where they found more substantial tools, including two rusty spades—but unfortunately no snow shovels. That afternoon, they shoveled a wider walking path back to the cabin and completely cleared away the front entryway.

With a sigh, Lauren said, "Well, thank God. I bet folks at Kaiser are worried sick about me."

She was a Physician's Assistant in the emergency ward of the Kaiser-Permanente Hospital/Medical Complex in Vallejo, but had been unable to contact her work for the entire nineteen days of their confinement. Cell phones had been out from that first morning of the surprise storm and still didn't work. Jake was on a sabbatical from UC to work on a new book on humanism in science fiction and didn't have to report in to anyone. Luke was in his senior year at Berkeley High, a good student, who would probably miss the work in his calculus and honors chemistry courses, but he'd catch up quickly enough when they got back home. As far as his Creative Writing class, his dad had been helping him with a new SF story. In Jake's opinion, Luke's stuff was getting pretty darn close to being publishable.

Of course during those first nine claustrophobic shut-in days of mostly reading and playing board games they'd discussed several times the necessity of contacting their folks. Jake's widowed dad was a worrywart, a retired chemist who had worked for the DEA for years in San Diego; and Lauren's folks were both teachers at Carlsbad High, thirty-five miles north of San Diego near the Marine Corp's Camp Pendleton. Luke just wanted a chance to call Berkeley and talk to his new girlfriend, Suze.

2

TEN-POINT BUCK

They drove slowly in first or second gear most of the way along the mile and a half of the winding, narrow, private road down the leeward side of Mt. George, hitting only a few thick patches of snow and ice. The four-wheel-drive SUV made the negotiation fairly easy and very safe.

In less than ten minutes they were out onto two-laned Monticello Road/State Highway 121, the snow much lighter as they rapidly dropped elevation. They stopped only once to drag a dead oak branch off the road.

The ten-point buck stood about a hundred yards away at the edge of the forest, apparently not the least bit frightened, and in fact staring down at Jake with a curious tilt to its head. After a few more moments the buck turned and disappeared into the forest— something about its graceful but nonchalant, almost dismissive movement sticking in Jake's mind. Oddly, the buck had been the only creature they'd seen on their way out from the cabin. Usually the mountain forest and meadows below the cabin were alive with game, even this late in the day—deer, wild turkeys, quail, rabbits, fox, wild pigs, and even an occasional mountain lion. Must be the sudden weird weather making them all take cover, Jake decided.

"Okay, we're off to see the wizard," he said with a cheery lift in his voice.

It was Luke who voiced the second unexplained peculiarity. "Look at the funny snow, Dad." He pointed out the window at the melting patches they were passing. "It's all a dirty gray, not white."

"Yes, it sure is," Lauren agreed. "Looks almost like a blanket of black fine ashes on top of the snow, Jake."

In some places the layers of ash were stacked thick, really darkening the snow surface. As they dropped lower below the snowfall line, nearing the floor of the eastern side of the valley and outskirts of Napa, the ashes were drifted and stacked high in a few places, like banks of black snow. An unusual and unsettling sight.

"Must've been a huge fire somewhere," Jake said in a tentative voice. Almost everything was dusted with the fine dark ash. He knew that occasionally winds from big Bay Area fires blew residue into the valley—like during the devastating Oakland Hills conflagration forty or so years ago when he was a young boy—but rarely, if ever, dropping it this far northeast.

Jake was also more than a little curious that they hadn't seen even *one* other vehicle moving along the highway. Perhaps 121 was closed down farther south, which would account for the complete lack of traffic, but he was unable to completely dismiss this unusual observation. Most of his earlier cheerful disposition had slipped away, replaced by a sense of growing unsettled concern.

Soon after, they passed a BMW stopped in the middle of the other lane of the road...apparently abandoned.

"That's surprising, not even pulling off the highway like that," Jake said, shaking his head as they continued south.

Lauren added, "And a big hazard, too—"

"Jesus, Dad, look at that!" Luke shouted from the backseat, shaking Jake's shoulder and making him flinch.

They'd come around a curve and should have been looking at Bork's Country Grocery Store with its attached rear residence and off nearby the first of the farmhouses … There was nothing left standing of either structure, except for a pair of charred foundations and a coat of the ominous dark ash covering what was left.

Continuing south, 121 skirting around the less-populated, rural easternmost part of Napa, Jake downshifted and slowed, creeping by two more deserted cars, both headed northeast on the State Highway back up Mt. George. Originally headed for where—?

"What's happened, here, Jacob?" Lauren asked calmly, her use of his full name giving away the depth of her concern.

She was the unshakeable rock of the family. Never panicking, even that time when Luke had been knocked out cold after a fall from a cherry tree in their back yard on College Avenue in Berkeley when he was nine. Lauren had immediately called 911, covered the unconscious boy with a blanket, and bathed his forehead with a cold cloth, while her husband, who had been working inside, followed her back out after the phone call and did little more than silently stand by, as if a detached spectator at a sporting event. She'd finally sent him out front to guide the EMT crew into the backyard. Fortunately, Luke regained consciousness before the medical crew arrived, but he had suffered a moderate concussion. As a precaution, the boy had been taken to Kaiser Hospital in Oakland and kept overnight for observation.

Jake never forgot his wife's *calm competence* during the sudden medical emergency—and this had happened before she began attending PA medical school at UC Davis. She was solid, almost unshakeable.

But he didn't answer her question—of course he didn't know—only shook his head as the SUV passed a partially-standing blackened old brick farmhouse. All the windows were shattered.

"Where are the people?" the boy said, not trying to hide his unease. "Why'd they leave their cars parked like that? Where did they all disappear? And where were they coming from?"

"Maybe there's some explanation on the radio, Lauren," Jake suggested, as he grew more and more concerned.

She scanned the dial through the entire AM band, and then slowly back through the FM channels.

Nothing, not even static.

Unable to see around an upcoming curve, Jake swerved the Lexus off the road and onto the gravelly shoulder, passing an abandoned minivan stopped in their lane. He managed to pull the Lexus out of a mini-skid and back onto the road.

For a few moments no one said anything, all shaken by the near accident.

"I'm not sure what's happened," Jake said after clearing his throat. "And that van back there looked badly burned on our side, like it'd been involved in a fire that burned over this area, similar to the houses." He shook his head again, openly puzzled. "But I'm most confused by the cars headed up into the mountains though, and abandoned, none of them appearing to be burned or damaged from the outside anyhow, as if they'd traveled *after* the fires . . ."

They slowed and approached an empty Ford Ranger pickup on the other side of the highway, the vehicle looking new and undamaged. Jake hit the brake and pulled onto the shoulder.

"I'll be right back."

He got out of the Lexus, and went across the road to investigate. In a minute he climbed back in the SUV, feeling even more troubled by what he'd found.

Frowning, he explained, "Maybe some of the others were abandoned during the fire or whatever happened for some mechanical reason, but *that* Ford pickup apparently ran out of gas . . . and it still has the keys in the ignition—"

"Okay, but what about the driver, Jacob?" Lauren said, her voice slightly higher pitched than normal. "Where's he now? He just wandered off and disappeared?"

"Maybe it was an alien abduction," Luke said with a dry chuckle from the backseat, his tone not quite indicating he was joking. "Kinda like those on Channel 65's *Unexplained Mysteries*, you know."

Jake began to say something about the driver obviously leaving in a hurry, maybe hitching a ride with another vehicle; then, he changed his mind and only shrugged as he eased the SUV back onto the road. Down deep he was badly disturbed by what they'd seen coming down the mountain and into the rural outskirts of town, but decided to keep his deep concern to himself.

Awkward silence filled the Lexus, everyone dealing with their own anxious thoughts. Jake glanced down twice at the dead car radio, as if expecting it to suddenly start up and clarify the mystery. No such luck.

"Do you suppose there has been a major earthquake and subsequent massive fires?" Lauren finally suggested. "One we didn't feel on solid Mt. George all snowed in like we were? The people down here maybe evacuated to a shelter downtown or someplace nearby? That would certainly explain most of these odd mysteries we're finding—"

"Yeah, it must've been the *Big One* finally hit," Luke chimed in, grabbing onto his mother's logical explanation, his voice edgy with excitement.

"I'll just bet that's exactly what happened," Lauren said, glancing over at her husband for confirmation, smiling thinly.

He stared back at her, noticing that the crow's feet at the corners of her eyes were maybe a little more prominent than normal.

But Jake didn't answer, paying close attention to his driving as 121 merged with the larger multi-laned State Highway 29 south of Napa. There seemed to be quite a number more stalled or abandoned vehicles here, but they were *all* traveling in the northeasterly lanes across from them.

It was almost as if the driverless cars and pickups had minds of their own, Jake thought, escaping some great catastrophe to the south, something terrible that had happened in the Bay Area. But whatever it was had finally caught up to the escapees, wrung the life out of them. The cars were all *dead* now. He tried to hide a shudder and get a grip on his grim, overactive writer's imagination.

Jesus, he swore to himself, *cool it, man. Don't construct a worst-case scenario here just yet, bub.*

Still, they hadn't seen another living person as they continued toward Vallejo.

Not *one.*

That really bothered Jake the most, actually frightened him. No matter *what* had occurred, they should have seen a few people by now. He remembered being overcome by a similar eerie feeling during last summer's vacation on a trip to Guatemala and the Maya site at Tikal, when he first gazed upon the overgrown, magnificent stone ruins jutting from the jungle, and wondering: *My God, what made the people suddenly abandon all this?* There really hadn't been a good explanation for that mystery either. Not even Jared Diamond's learned explanation of a number of contributing factors happening all at once in his book, *Collapse.*

The book seemed to offer a bit of a coincidence cluster, too much of a stretch, way too neat for Jake.

Whatever happened here wasn't easily explained by what seemed plausible—earthquake and fires. He couldn't help mentally thumbing through a few science fiction scenarios.

3

INEXPLICABLE DEVASTATION

Lauren had insisted that Jake stop at the Kaiser-Permanente Hospital Complex when they reached the northern outskirts of Vallejo city limits.

"They'll know what's happened," she'd said confidently.

Jake suspected that his wife figured they might need her help at the hospital, if there had indeed been some kind of major area-wide catastrophic event. Also, he reminded himself, they should call their folks as soon as they stopped and could find a landline. Their cell phones were still not functioning. His dad would be half nuts with worry.

The outskirts of Vallejo resembled the rural eastern area of Napa they'd just passed by, but worse. Almost *all* of the buildings here seemed to be knocked flat, and what remained had been heavily burned over. The multi-storied, steel-framed, concrete, modern hospital, opened only eighteen or so years ago itself, was still partially standing, but the older complex around it was little more than collapsed ruins.

No one around here, either, that he could see.

Not one living soul.

Again the eerie mystery of the Tikal image of the Maya abandonment flashed into Jake's consciousness.

Jesus.

"Stop over there," Lauren said suddenly, pointing at the
northwest corner of the Hospital building, near where the emergency ward entrance and circular drive had been in the past. Jake
thought he could easily detect the growing distress now in her
normally relaxed expression. Something else, too, something much
harder to define, something a little darker ... something that he
shared with her—a kind of apprehensive sense of dread of discovering what had actually happened here. It was almost like neither of
them really wanted to know *what* had caused all this devastation.

The three sat silently for a long minute in the car, shocked by
the impact of the massive destruction.

Finally they got out, and Jake wandered cautiously, looking
around the emergency parking lot of empty vehicles. All of them
were covered with a thick layer of fine black ash. Overhead, the sky
was overcast, a dismal dark gray, and no planes to be seen anywhere. No birds either. In fact, not a trace of any living creature.

A dead world of black and white, the silence terrifying.

They strayed apart, shuffling carefully about the ruins, each
searching for *any* clue at all of what might have happened.

They were all obviously badly shaken.

Scared shitless was more like it, Jake thought.

Near where the emergency ward entryway into the building
used to be, Lauren found something and shouted, "Hey, come
quick and look at this."

It was a five-foot square section of plywood tied down to a
piece of cinderblock rubble, the wooden face neatly lettered in caps
with some kind of green felt-marking pen:

BLUE ROCK SPRINGS PARK

FRESH WATER

MEDICAL HELP

"Blue Rock Springs Park? Where the devil is that?" Jake asked after reading the sign.

Looking confused and her concern undisguised, Lauren shook her head and shrugged. This really bothered Jake more than anything they'd seen so far—his wife, the bedrock of the family, visibly shaken, her eyes moist and almost teary. She'd lost her normally unshakeable composure. He put his arm around her and squeezed her shoulder, hoping he conveyed some comfort. But it was a confidence he certainly didn't feel at all.

"I know Blue Rock Springs," Luke said.

Both stared at their smiling son, eyebrows raised.

"Sure, Mom used to drop me off at day camp there, during a summer when I was in middle school, early in the morning before she came here to work at the hospital. Remember? Seven or so years ago ...? He thought a moment, and pointed off generally to the east. "I think it's that way, on the other side of Interstate 80, maybe ten or fifteen miles from here, tucked back in some unusual bluish-craggy foothills. You go the opposite way of the turnoff for Discovery Kingdom off I-80 when traveling northeast. Oh, except back then I think the Kingdom might have been called something like ... Marine World Africa USA."

"I believe you're right, Lucas ..." Lauren said, nodding, regaining some of her poise. "I remember now. It was my first year working at Kaiser. The summer you were between fifth and sixth grades." Her smile broadened as her recall solidified and extended. "You really loved their orienteering classes ... and that's where you first got interested in archery."

She ruffled her son's hair, as if he were still that middle-school boy. Luke belonged to an adult archery club in Berkeley now, had even gone turkey hunting with a bow several times during last season up at the cabin on Mt. George. Along with soccer, it was one of his major extracurricular interests. His new girlfriend, Suze, a basketball player, was also an avid archery enthusiast.

"Yeah, it was a terrific camp, Mom," Luke said.

Mother and son had temporarily forgotten the present grim situation, lost in reliving the past.

Jake read the sign carefully once more.

Fresh water?

What exactly did that mean?

No good water in Vallejo, obviously.

But why?

Broken lines, polluted, or what?

And what about the dead radio and their cell phones? Why weren't they working?

And why were there no people left around?

Whatever had happened was more than some kind of localized earthquake and fire. More serious than the forecasted *Big One* they'd heard so much about on the Channel 2 News every time the Bay Area experienced major shaking along the San Andreas, Hayward, or another major fault line. No, Jake suspected something even more horribly devastating over a much greater area.

He had a rising suspicion, but suppressed admitting the horrible thought, even to himself. There was no need to alarm Luke and Lauren senselessly about his growing belief, which couldn't possibly be right. You've just been dredging up too many SF apocalyptic premises, bub, he chastised himself. He shook his head.

"You want to drive out there and try and find this park, Lauren?" Jake finally asked, forcing his bleak suspicion to the back of his mind.

"Yes, I think we should, because this sign was left by someone here at work, maybe even one of the emergency room doctors," Lauren said with an obvious degree of increasing optimism, leading them all back toward the SUV. Neither Jake nor Luke bothered to argue. They had no better suggestion of what to do next. Blue Rock Springs was a good destination for now.

Jake turned the SUV around, negotiated the nearby freeway cloverleaf, and headed the Lexus easterly.

4

SUSPICION CONFIRMED, BIG TIME

Forty-five minutes later, they pulled into the Blue Rock Springs Park parking lot next to a pair of pickups and a dark blue minivan. The vehicles were dirty, but *not* ash covered. The signed picnic area spread out in front of them for several acres. Instead of tables and benches, it was covered now with twelve strong-backed tents, looking a little like a temporary military encampment—except the tents were old, faded, even threadbare in spots, as if they had been folded up and stored, unused for many decades. The bluish-colored crags, giving the park its name, loomed ominously atop the hills beyond the grounds to the north and east, a small lake bordering the grounds to the south. There was a pair of Quonset huts by the lake, several people unloading boxes and plastic bags from a flatbed truck and storing them in the huts. Closer, a man and a woman, both wearing dirty aprons, were moving in and out of one of the bigger tents and dropping pans and utensils into a garbage can of water. Blue smoke curled up from the tent stovepipe.

Jake was overjoyed to see people as he slipped out of the Lexus with a bounce in his step.

Two men hurried out to greet them, both wearing holstered

handguns, the taller, serious-faced young man leading. With one hand resting on his weapon, the leader announced, "This is Ron Harvey, and I'm Mike Shaw; I'm in charge of camp security." He added suspiciously, "Are any of you carrying weapons?"

"No," Jake said, glad to finally talk to someone alive, even someone who appeared to be a little edgy and paranoid. "We aren't armed."

Blue Rock Springs Park had been converted into an emergency medical camp by Dr. Hang Ky, Lauren's old boss at Kaiser-Permanente. She had been the one who had lettered and left the green sign at the Kaiser complex.

In addition to Dr. Ky, there were two of Lauren's emergency ward RN friends, Robin Fisher and Will Skoroski, and a number of other familiar faces working in the big central medical tent where Shaw first escorted them. Everyone was overjoyed to see Lauren and her family safe.

"What's going on here?" Lauren asked after all the warm greetings, pointing around the medical tent. "What's happened to cause this makeshift medical facility to be set up here so far out in the boonies?"

No one said a word for a long moment.

"You don't know about the pre-emptive strikes?" Robin asked, her expression puzzled.

Lauren shook her head.

"We've been snowed in at a cabin on Mount George near Napa for the last three weeks," Jake explained. "But, surely, you don't mean some kind of…nuclear strikes?" he asked, his voice tight, his heart sinking.

Robin nodded, her features darkening.

Jesus.

The thought he'd been wrestling with for the last few hours

was finally confirmed. He felt like he'd taken a hard punch in the gut that knocked all the wind out of him.

Someone quickly brought over three folding chairs.

"You better all have a seat," Robin suggested, pointing at the chairs. After taking a deep breath and gathering her thoughts, she began to explain what had happened. "ICBMs rained down on the Bay Area three weeks ago. Before we lost all television contact with the outside world, we learned that other parts of the country— probably the entire USA—had also come under nuclear attack at roughly the same time—"

"But *who* could've done this?" Jake asked after clearing his throat, his voice remaining a shocked, scratchy whisper. The whole country? The scope of this was even worse than he'd imagined. Almost inconceivable.

Robin turned and gestured toward Will, who reluctantly stepped forward after she added, "Will is the only one in camp with even a passing clue."

The handsome young man smiled wryly. "Actually, I'm afraid I don't know many facts, if any. I was on break in the basement of the hospital, like most of the medical personnel survivors here, but I wasn't watching TV, which quit before any explanations of release site origin were televised. I was listening to KOIT from the City in my earpiece, when the music was interrupted by a barely audible public service announcement. Something like, '... the USA being under massive attack ... long range missiles launched from the distant south ... only seconds away now ...' and then crackling static, followed by absolute silence." He shrugged. "That's all I know for certain."

"South?" Jake said after a moment's thought, still feeling severely disoriented by the extent of the revelations. "You don't actually mean Mexico?" That didn't make much sense to him at all.

"No, I don't think they came from Mexico," Will said, shaking his head. "They said *distant* south, and I had the distinct feeling at that moment, and, believe even more strongly now that it was probably much farther south than Mexico or probably even Central America—"

"South America?" Luke interjected, his young face wrinkled into a scowl, which marred his boyish good looks, made him look much older.

"I don't know for sure of course, but I *think* they came from some place in South America, perhaps one of the northernmost countries," Will said, his tone and emphasis indicating the speculative nature of his claim. "My best guess, anyhow."

"Makes sense to me," Luke said, "especially with the relatively lengthy advance notice broadcast on the radio."

"But why would someone down there launch intercontinental ballistic missiles at us?" Jake said, feeling now that this was all indeed completely unreal, almost as if he were watching one of his apocalyptic science fiction films, only a detached but curious viewer in a darkened movie theater. "We haven't had any major problems with anyone in those South American countries for quite some time, since Hugo Chavez senior died many years ago—"

"Oh, c'mon, Dad," Luke said, his tone almost dismissive. He reached out and touched Jake's arm to get his attention. "How about Nuevo Venezuela, or Ecuador, or even Columbia," he said, a teacher admonishing a slow student. "No one really loves us in those countries. Haven't for years. Remember way back when they bounced us out of OAS in... I think it was 2012 or so?"

"Yes, one of those three countries or maybe somewhere close nearby, like the leftist new nation, ERA, would be my guess for the site origin of the ICBMs," Will said, nodding thoughtfully.

"But how could they actually get away with that?" the boy said as he turned back to question the male nurse, an incredulous frown on his face.

"What do you mean get away with it?" Will asked.

"Well ... they would've had to construct the necessary silos, then assemble and stack the missiles, all requiring transporting heavy equipment to the various sites, with *months* of construction time," Luke said thoughtfully, his frown easing a little. "How could they accomplish any of that without us seeing or hearing something? You know even Castro and Khrushchev with his resources tried and failed at something like that during the Cuban missile crisis last century? They couldn't sneak in the missiles and build the sites. We discovered it all in plenty of time to intervene, you know."

"Well, they were obviously able to conceal it all this time," Will said. He shrugged, then added, "We may never know for sure *who* and *how*, but . . ." Again he paused, and with a sterner and wrier expression clouding his features, he added, "But we can imply one thing for certain."

"What's that?" Luke asked, staring at the young RN.

"Wherever they were launched from no longer exists," Will said. "Our SAC bombers and our nuke subs for sure would've retaliated shortly after the initial launch locations were pinpointed. And you can bet they were. Possibly hitting a number of other places around the globe, too. This undoubtedly required sophisticated technological support, including foreign-trained personnel. For all we know, half the world or perhaps more may be covered with the tell-tale black ash by now."

That startling image of a completely blackened world, so gloomy and depressing, caused everyone in the tent to pause and grow silent.

Seconds ticked by.

"All that speculation makes little difference to us here, at this time," Dr. Ky finally intervened in a firm, authoritarian tone. "We have to do the best we can now. Live in the present. Leave all that speculating to someone else, much later on."

Even though numbed by the horrific possibility of what might have happened to the whole country, Jake thought about the Cuban missile crisis in 1962 that Luke had mentioned. His son was right. How could anyone in this day and age of increased alertness catch us sleeping with all the improved Spy-Sats and electronic surveillance and monitoring equipment in place? And didn't we have CIA people on the ground in New Venezuela ... even Ecuador? He was certain we used to last century in Columbia, fighting against the drug cartels.

Jesus. He shuddered again, feeling light-headed and nauseated.

During the lull after the grim revelations and speculations, Lauren had reached over and slipped her hand into Jake's. It was warm but dry, her face calm and more or less relaxed again.

Everyone talked at once then, describing their initial surprise and shock to the attack, and reactions immediately afterward— where they were, what happened. The words ran together in an indecipherable string. It was all too ... too unnerving and unreal. Jake glanced at Lauren, who smiled thinly at him and leaned her head against his shoulder for a moment. He guessed she'd already accepted Dr. Ky's probably practical dismissal of the importance of *who* and *how* for now ... Maybe it was undoubtedly wise advice. Still, he was having trouble grasping the enormity and process some of the obvious ramifications of the horrific revelations.

The talking finally tapered off, everyone staring at the three of them sitting on the folding chairs.

Jake cleared his throat, tried to shake off the icy sense of despair that now clutched his heart, and asked in a subdued voice, "What happens to us now? I mean the three of us, our immediate family?"

Dr. Ky intervened again at that point, sending everyone back to work, and suggesting a meeting with the Zachary family tomorrow morning after they had some time to eat, rest, and get over the initial shock of what they'd just learned.

"You sort things out, catch your breaths, and then we'll talk."

Mike Shaw, the security chief, led the stunned family past the mess tent with the stovepipe back to the smaller tent quarters, dropping

THE CONFESSIONS OF ST. ZACH

Luke at the single men's tent, and directing Jake and Lauren to one of the smaller couples' tents at the back of the camp. He stopped outside and tapped a neatly lettered sign beside the entrance to their new quarters.

"If you notice any of these symptoms now or any time in the near future, immediately report to Dr. Olafson at the med center. Okay? You share this tent with two other couples. Inside you'll find your empty spot, blankets, and cots. Good afternoon."

Obviously the security chief was dealing with only the immediate needs of here and now.

Still holding hands, Jake and Lauren read over the ominous message:

RADIATION SICKNESS SYMPTOMS

Nausea & vomiting
Diarrhea
Skin burns
Fatigue
Loss of appetite
Fainting
Dehydration
Inflammation
Bleeding from mouth, nose, gums, rectum
Low red blood cell count
Hair loss

5

THE TEN-POINT BUCK

That first night, after an hour or so of trying to get comfortable on his unfamiliar and uncomfortable camp cot, Jake fell into a restless sleep.

He dreamed that he was coming down Mt. George again—stopped and standing outside the SUV with Luke. Having seen no animals on the way out from the snowed-in cabin. Suddenly, they spotted the magnificent ten-point buck, which just stared at them almost nonchalantly. It began to snow heavily again, but a thick black snow. And it began to quickly pile up around the two of them. Just before they were completely buried in blackness, Jake looked up at the buck again ... who had turned its head, and, with a graceful movement of total distain, it turned around completely and ambled back into the oak and madrone forest. As if abandoning them to their fate ...

Jake awakened at around four or so in the morning, covered with a clammy sweat, the dream lingering in his thoughts. Unable to go back to sleep, he got up quietly, searched through his backpack and found one of the three new blank matching journals. They were bound in distinctive black leather, with his initials in silver on the front cover in the lower right corner: **JAZ**—a surprise birthday present from Luke last month.

Before dawn broke, he wanted to get down his feelings regarding the reaction to the description of the missile strikes ... and the drastic impact on their lives. He thought carefully about what he wanted to say, then wrote down his initial thoughts and reactions, not bothering to concern himself with style or anything else.

6

JOURNAL ENTRY

BLUE ROCK SPRINGS MEDICAL CAMP
PS: THREE WEEKS

The entire Bay Area has been destroyed by ICBMs, almost completely flattened.

Few survivors, many of those dying of radiation sickness.

No radio.

No TV.

No phones working.

No outside contact.

Perhaps the whole country devastated.

For now, this little medical camp is the hub of the known universe.

But there is still the written word to record and communicate.

And this is the new beginning, everything will be dated now in this journal: Post Strike (PS).

My name is Jacob Zachary, and I was an Associate Professor at UC Berkeley, teaching a few typical undergraduate classes in English, but mostly responsible in the last two years for establishing graduate seminars in my gen-

eral field of interest: Science Fiction from Pulp to Literature and Literary Speculative Fiction. Like most English professors, I'd tried my hand at fiction, sold some SF to literary journals and placed four stories and a novella at F & SF and Asimov's—even been a finalist for the novella Nebula last year. I'd published my dissertation four years ago, a biography on the great Kim Stanley Robinson. And, presently, I had just started my first sabbatical, mostly working on another nonfiction book in my specialized area of interest—Humanism in Science Fiction. Not much demand for any of that now.

But I can keep this chronicle, not to mourn the old way, but to detail what it is like here at this makeshift medical facility. Record my reactions, feelings. And also note down my feelings and plans for the future. Perhaps eventually write some new stories—there are always new stories to tell. I guess it's ironic that I'm a SF writer, because we're truly living science fiction now.

But who knows about readers? Are there many of them left to read anything now?

7

ONE DAY AT A TIME

The next morning, the haggard-looking family sat down with Dr. Ky around her tiny desk at the rear of the medical center tent. None of the three had slept well.

"I'll take you on a quick camp tour in a minute," the attractive Asian-American woman said. Jake and Lauren were good friends with Hang Ky, and had sampled her excellent Vietnamese home cooking at her Vallejo waterfront condo several times in the past. She had often visited their home in Berkeley.

"I know it's difficult to fully process what has happened," she began. "But it is time to face a harsh reality. Our world has changed ... drastically. There is absolutely nothing we can do about that right now. Everything for the foreseeable future is *day-to-day*. No long range plans. Only practical concerns of survival are important. In fact that is our focus here at camp: *Survival*. Do you all understand me?"

Jake and Luke nodded.

After a deep sigh, Lauren nodded tentatively, and said, "Yes, I think so. We're trying to come to terms with what's happened. It's difficult, almost unbelievable. But we all understand the world has changed. We know we must live day to day now. Still, we would like to find out something about our families. See if they're alive."

"Didn't they live somewhere in the Southern California area?" Hang asked.

"Carlsbad and San Diego proper," Jake said. "We've talked some early last night about maybe driving down there. But the McCarrons and Hopkins in our tent didn't think that was even remotely possible now."

The doctor shook her head, sighed, and said, "They're right, it isn't ..." She paused for a long moment, apparently weighing her words, then in a measured tone she continued. "San Diego and Carlsbad, with their surrounding active military bases and airfields, were undoubtedly prime direct missile targets and probably don't exist now." A heavy crease between her eyes marred her smooth skin. "I would guess fewer survivors than here in the Bay Area. So, I'm sorry to be so blunt, but your folks may not even be alive."

"That may be true, but we still have to hope, until we know for sure," Lauren said, a mixed look on her face—a kind of desperate, dogged defiance.

Hang nodded, then looked directly at Jake and shrugged.

"Even if they were alive down there, that would be an extremely hazardous seven hundred mile trip. Impossible by vehicle. Travelers on the highways will most likely be subject to constant attacks by bandits. We are here, too, maintaining constant armed guard. Careful when we leave camp, especially when driving anywhere on I-80. Nevertheless, a small marauding band surprised our foraging group recently, south across the Carquinez Bridge near Pinole. They were driven off by Mike Shaw and his people, who during the attack had to shoot one, capture another, before the two or three others fled on motorcycles. The captured bandit—Mike calls them Desperadoes—died last week of radiation sickness. But before then he told us that the Oakland, Berkeley, and Richmond ruins are Desperado strongholds now, several small, organized bands going out daily to raid from each place, then squabbling among themselves over their plunder." She stopped for a moment to allow the family to process what she'd said.

"Okay, you all with me?"

All three nodded.

Hang continued. "Seems logical that most city ruins would be extremely dangerous places now, including LA and San Diego—the surviving gangs marauding where it's most productive … And the logistics of just getting down south would be a major problem. We don't know the shape of highways outside of the Bay Area of course. But here in the North Bay and upper East Bay, I-80 is in pretty fair shape until you reach Richmond, then it's torn up and becomes heavily clogged with abandoned vehicles. Impassable directly. Other highways like 101, 580, 680, 880 and I-5 may be even worse, perhaps damaged directly by the strikes and probably also jammed with vehicles. Both the Bay Bridge and the Golden Gate are down. No direct access across the Bay until you get south to the Dumbarton Bridge, which is relatively intact and passable."

She shook her head, her face even grimmer now.

"And food? Nothing fresh. We've been lucky initially, but we may soon have a difficult time finding adequate additional supplies, perhaps forced to ration in the near future. And fuel? We're doing pretty well foraging for the gas and diesel we need now. We have several large pumps and siphons that work well with abandoned vehicles and especially at the undamaged large truck stop tanks we've discovered north of here in Dixon just off an I-80 frontage road. Unfortunately, those tanks are only about a third full. But even as close as the South Bay and peninsula, who knows where to find fuel and safe food? Perhaps it has all been destroyed, burned up, or scrounged by survivors. And farther down south …?"

She let her voice trail off, held her palms up, and shrugged, shaking her head sadly, before glancing back directly at Lauren.

Dr. Hang Ky concluded her grim assessment for the family: "Traveling by vehicle to San Diego is not really an option, I'm afraid."

Jake put his arm around his wife and hugged her. He cleared his throat and said, "We appreciate your frankness, Hang, thank you. We were just kind of hoping, you know."

"You're welcome to remain here. Maybe we'll learn more about what's happened in other parts of the State. Have a better idea of the condition of highways, the travel dangers, food and fuel supplies, and such. Until then, Lauren, I can sure use a good surgical assistant. Dr. Olafson is an Internist and can use your professional help, too. He has his hands full with the ten patients we have suffering from various degrees of radiation sickness. When our food scavenging crew goes out this afternoon, they may find even more. Most of the survivors brought in from the Bay Area have the sickness or will soon develop it after inhaling or ingesting contaminated dust or being exposed to contaminated food-water in those heavily-polluted areas."

"And Luke and me?" Jake asked with a quizzical look. "What can we do here to be useful? We don't have medical skills like Lauren. As you know, I'm an English professor, a science fiction writer. Luke's a senior in high school."

For the first time that morning the plainspoken doctor smiled, her dark eyes lighting up. "No problem, Jake. We need lots of help here, even outside the med center. I have some specific assignments in mind for each of you guys."

Hang stood.

"C'mon, I'll introduce you to the other twenty-three members of camp staff. We'll visit the four kids in our little improvised school, and then look around a bit." She led them from the big tent, pointing southerly. "We even have some fresh water bucket showers set up down at the lake—private, Lauren, but oh so cold. *Brrr.*" She turned and smiled at Luke. "I'm sure you'll enjoy meeting Tara, our camp teacher; she's only slightly older than you are, and quite lovely—"

"I met her at breakfast, Dr. Ky," Luke admitted, smiling thinly, his face flushing.

"There you go," Hang said, throwing up her hands and glancing knowingly at his parents, as if saying: *See, that's what I mean, life goes on.*

Seven of the camp staff were trained medical personnel—Dr. Ky and five others at Kaiser Hospital had been in or near the basement cafeteria, sheltered underground when the two closest strikes hit southwest of Vallejo at nearby Mare Island Naval Shipyard and northeast eighteen miles up I-80 at Travis Air Force Base. Dr. Olafson was from San Francisco, a personal friend who was visiting Dr. Ky at Kaiser, and was fortunately shielded in an elevator near the bottom floor when the strikes hit. Among this trained group were also two RNs, two medical techs, and one lab tech. They were caring for eighteen patients at the time—the ten with radiation sickness in a separate chronic patient tent on one side of the big med center, the others with assorted injuries, broken bones, or awaiting surgery in a sickbay tent on the other side.

There were four older non-medical people working in the mess tent. Jay McCarron, a pre-Strike chef from a restaurant in nearby Benicia, assisted by his wife, Becky, and Deanna Cordoza from a Vallejo rest home kitchen; and the most recent healthy survivor, a retired salesman named Evan Hatcher, who worked as the mess hall attendant and dishwasher.

Mike Shaw, an ex-Solano County Deputy Sheriff from Fairfield, was in charge of camp security, but led daily scavenging parties to look for food and medicine. If they ran into survivors needing medical attention, they brought them back to camp. It was some of his people that had been off-loading the flat bed at the Quonsets yesterday. Recently, they'd found a collapsed grocery supply warehouse off I-80, west of Vacaville, and were able to dig out several dozen cases of undamaged canned and packaged assorted goods. All of the healthy young people in camp, except for Tara, the teacher—four women and six men—worked for Mike Shaw. The security chief would be Luke's new boss.

"This way, Jake. I want you to meet Leroy Robinson," Hang

said after leaving Lauren at the lake showers, pointing at a pair of grayish sheds as they climbed away from the camp, uphill toward the looming blue crags to the east. The flatbed was parked there.

"Leroy is quite a guy. You'll enjoy working with him," Dr. Ky said to Jake.

"He started as a janitor with Kaiser Hospital twenty-five years ago and worked his way up to be head maintenance engineer. He can fix anything—I mean *anything* mechanical—and operate effectively every piece of equipment in a machine shop."

They paused in front of a shed.

"Leroy goes out and forages for parts and gas for our four vehicles. He brought in and got most of my diagnostic/monitoring equipment operating in the medical center just after we set up. And he found me a pair of portable generators to run my stuff, including the small refrigerator we need for medicine. He's a genius at anticipating our needs, scrounging up stuff to fulfill those needs—a lot of equipment, supplies, and things actually coming from the Kaiser Hospital ruins, which he knows well. But his helper is unfortunately down with radiation sickness. Leroy may be the most valuable member of the camp staff …" She paused again and smiled. "And he's an enthusiastic reader, accumulating books on a shelf in the supply shed. He calls it The Camp Library. You'll have someone intelligent to talk to about literature and things of that nature."

Behind the two adjoining sheds, Jake could see a cluster of ten or so fifty-five gallon drums, a hand pump sticking out of one. Probably gas or maybe some diesel, he thought.

Hang knocked, then opened the shed door when there was no answer, and invited Jake into a tiny machine shop, where a distinguished-looking older man with wiry, silver hair was doing something on a drill press powered by a small humming generator.

"Leroy," she shouted, waving and finally catching his attention. He shut off the drill press.

"I've found you a new assistant. This is Jacob Zachary, a University of California professor. He taught English, writes stories, and knows a lot about books."

The older man took off his safety glasses, removed his earplugs, and smiled broadly. "Well, now, I thank you kindly, Dr. H." He stuck out a large brown calloused hand. "I'm real pleased to make your acquaintance, Dr. J."

8

THE CAMP LIBRARY

The next morning, after an early breakfast at the mess tent, the family split up.

Lauren headed to the med center. She would be assisting Dr. Ky in an operation—a newly arrived young woman with severe internal injuries, including a ruptured spleen. Luke had gone off with Shaw and the young people in the pickup and the van to search for food near Fairfield, where there had been row-after-row of warehouses. The strikes on nearby Travis AFB had flattened most of the tilt-up concrete buildings, fires sweeping over the crushed buildings and supplies. But the scavengers were carefully checking each demolished building anyhow.

Leroy took Jake to the supply shed next to his machine shop.

He proudly showed him the small collection of books on four shelves.

"This is the official camp library," the older man said, "and I expand it whenever I find something good in decent reading shape. Dug out most of what you see here at a flattened bookstore in Crockett, other side of the Carquinez Bridge—good ones. Unfortunately a large number of other fine books in the store had been burnt up and too badly damaged to bring back and read."

Jake quickly scanned the bookshelf of a hundred or so books, which included mostly exceptional titles. He was quite taken aback to see several of Nelson Algren's books, and also two by Hubert Selby Jr. Both American writers were underrated and not well-known now in this country, but were hugely popular in Europe. He was surprised Leroy knew that they were good writers. On second thought, he realized that was a kind of snobby intellectual bigotry regarding Leroy. The old Black man might not be a college gradu-ate, a blue-collar worker, but he was obviously a very good read-er—possessing excellent taste.

"You can browse more and take out what you might want to read later this afternoon," Leroy said. "Right now we have a little chore to take care of on the other side of Vallejo near the ship-yard."

Books, Jake thought, focusing on the small collection at hand.

Oh, my God!

He hadn't thought specifically about books since learning about the missile attacks the day before yesterday, and the possible worldwide devastation. He'd spent his whole life surrounded by books—they were a significant part of the nourishment required for his spirit. Now they would be in short supply, real short supply. Each book in the camp library was a treasured gem. He sighed un-der his breath, gently squeezing one in his hand.

Hang Ky was right of course. Leroy and I will have a *lot* to talk about, Jake decided, as he carefully slid back *Requiem for a Dream* in its place, and reluctantly turned away from the valuable camp re-source to attend to the day's more pressing mundane business.

"This is standard operating procedure for everyone whenever leaving camp," Leroy said, pointing at a pair of wide cabinets on a bench across from the books on the other side of the doorway. He selected what looked like a highway worker jumpsuit minus the orange vest from the freshly laundered stack in the first cabinet.

"You always need to bundle up, wearing both a roll-down cap

and facemask." He selected a black ski cap from a pile next to the jumpsuits, and a particle facemask from an opened box in the other cabinet.

"Even though we haven't been exposed directly to radiation here," he explained, "we can still become sick from inhaling contaminated dust or ashes we stir up. We strip off this protective stuff as soon as we get back and scrub off at the first bucket-showers down at the lake ..." Leroy paused as they pulled on their overalls. "And every time a person leaves camp, he also takes one of these." He shook out a pill from a white bottle in a cluster sitting next to the particle masks. "Potassium Iodide will protect us from at least thyroid cancer if we're exposed for a prolonged time to something really hot out there."

Leroy selected a badge from a long gray box next to the white medicine bottles, and hooked it on Jake's collar.

"This has self-developing film, the bands of color matching your level of exposure. We'll always check each other frequently when we're out working. You can develop symptoms from as little as a hundred Rem exposure, so we don't want to see anything over fifty Rems on our badges, you understand." A mixed grim expression crept onto his experienced features—sadness with a trace of guilt or regret.

He sighed deeply and shook his steely-gray head. "That's what happened to my previous helper, Lenny. I let him go off by himself last week when we were close to the Bay, near where we're going today. Didn't check his badge often enough. Exposed to at least three hundred Rems for some time when he was digging out a small hoist from some rubble dusted with fine ash, which must've been highly contaminated. Unfortunately, we don't have a Geiger counter or any other warning devices to take out with us. Wish we did. I haven't been able to locate one or even think where best to look. Maybe someplace over on Mare Island, but it's still too hot over there around the nearest ground zero."

They walked downhill through the camp toward the remaining

pickup, and Leroy grinned wryly, as he pulled something else from his jumpsuit pocket, saying, "Here, this isn't mandatory, but you'll probably want to use some of this in your nose, as we head through Vallejo."

It was a small blue jar of Vicks VapoRub.

Jake must've looked puzzled, holding and staring down at the jar of mentholated salve. He couldn't imagine what they would use it for—

"It masks the overwhelming smell of the dead bodies," Leroy explained, a serious expression now on his lined dark features. "We're just doing a little recon today. Looking for a big generator to service the entire camp. I think I know exactly where to find one. But we have to drive clear across Vallejo proper to get there—the whole area still pretty smelly."

They wove their way across the Vallejo ruins, recently a city of about 135,000 people, bordered on the west by the North Bay and decommissioned Mare Island Naval Shipyard—the site of the closest missile strike. Only on the far eastern side of the city were a few buildings still standing, heavily charred. But the bulk of the city was completely destroyed, homes blown apart and scattered, even most of the foundations, a surreal, pocked, colorless landscape. Nothing apparently left alive—not a person, tree, or plant. Only piles of scorched debris left in the wake of the terrible blast. It had a horrific nightmare feel.

Jake remembered the startling black and white photos of Hiroshima and Nagasaki, which had once seemed so unreal to him. Almost a SF movie. This looked much worse. And too real. He again recalled the abandoned feel and uncanny nature of the Maya ruins in Tikal—

The reality hit him like a hammer between the eyes, and he felt a slow sinking sensation in his stomach: Civilization as they knew it was gone, all gone, perhaps forever.

It was a spirit-bruising, depressing ride across the leveled city.

As they neared the waterfront and finally stopped, Jake soon discovered why he needed the Vicks lining the inside of his nose. The air was heavily laden with the oppressive, sickening-sweet stench of massive death. An unmistakable smell. The medicated salve helped only a little, but it was better than no protection at all against the pervasive stink.

They got out and looked around.

It was eerily quiet, no signs of birds, animals, or even insects. The dead zone, for sure. Jake couldn't suppress a slight shudder.

"Over here," the older man said, his voice muffled by the particle mask. He led Jake across the street and to a once-standing sign lying face up and still readable: ERNIE'S HEAVY EQUIPMENT RENTALS. The business was located in front of a slight hill that obstructed any view of Mare Island Naval Shipyard, and probably partially protected the place, deflecting some of the shattering effects of the direct blast. Leroy knew his way around the area. The yard's office building and nearby sheds were flattened, like a giant had been playing and tossing large vehicles and pieces of equipment into the air and letting them land willy-nilly, the heat of the blast charring many of the discarded pieces, some of the stuff lying crushed under rubble. The older man stopped near a still-standing cinderblock wall that had screened a partially-collapsed, steel-framed shed. He gestured, indicating this was the location.

"Buried treasure," he said with a grin.

Leroy and Jake worked together for half an hour or so, clearing the roofing and rubble away, finally exposing three large generators resting on special wooden skids. Leroy explained that the attached skids made the big pieces of equipment easier to move around with a heavy-duty forklift.

"Yes, this here is the one I want for Dr. Ky, over one thousand KWs, and plenty of voltage," he said, lovingly patting the side of the biggest one in the middle.

"It uses what—diesel fuel?" Jake asked, buoyed slightly now by the old man's cheerful enthusiasm over the useful discovery.

"Yeah," Leroy said absently, walking around and carefully inspecting the generator for signs of serious damage. "Looks pretty good to me. Only nicked up a little on the outside. But we'll have to remember to bring a can of diesel back and see how it runs next time. Remind me, okay?"

Jake nodded.

He estimated the generator to be about twenty feet long by five feet wide and about four feet high. He had no idea how much it weighed, but guessed well over a ton, maybe closer to two. He wondered how the hell they'd get it back to camp. Lift it onto the flatbed? He spotted a big forklift nearby on its side, a large I-beam resting across it, the rear engine area collapsed in. They sure wouldn't be able to use that one to lift anything, he thought, shaking his head.

Leroy cleared up the problem before Jake had a chance to ask.

"We'll need some help making a path through that mess," the older man said, pointing back at the rubble and debris between them and the pickup on the street. "Then ease the flatbed in here. We'll use some jacks and rigging to get the generator high enough, so we can just back the bed of the truck under it."

Leroy grinned broadly at Jake, as if they'd together figured out an intricate puzzle.

"I got a pair of jacks we might use back at camp. But let's check around in those collapsed sheds over there and see if we can find something even bigger and better."

After digging through the debris, they found four heavy-duty hydraulic jacks and some eight-by-eight timber rigging that would be useful for raising the generator and getting it off the flatbed.

The older man looked pleased, Jake hitchhiking on his glee.

"We'll get back over here in the next few days with some of the young people," Leroy said. "But tomorrow you and I need to go up to Dixon and pick up some more fifty-five gallon drums and fill them with gas. We're going to need lots more diesel now to run this big boy, too."

He nodded thoughtfully. "Probably need to think soon about checking the truck stops farther north for an additional supply source of both gas and diesel before we run out—"

Howling, yapping, growling.

The startling sounds not far away.

"Freeze," Leroy said and slowly withdrew a 9mm automatic out of his coverall pocket. Jake hadn't even known the older man was carrying a weapon.

"Dog pack coming," Leroy explained in a low voice, staring intently at the empty intersection just beyond their pickup.

Sure enough, two skinny mutts came into sight, wide-eyed and with their tongues lolling; they turned the corner and dashed past them, running along the drive parallel to the waterfront. They were chased closely by a tight pack of six bigger, mean-looking dogs— three pit bulls, two German shepherds, and a Rottweiler.

"Keep perfectly still, son, they probably won't notice us," Leroy warned in his low voice, as they watched the pack race by and soon disappear out of sight. "That pack will kill those two strays if they can catch them. Competing for food, you understand what I'm saying." Leroy frowned, a sad expression in his eyes. "Most of the poor buggers are going to get radiation sickness soon enough as it is from the other stuff that they've been digging up and eating."

Jake grimaced under his particle mask, knowing the older man probably meant dead bodies—the dogs were scavenging carrion in the ruins. They had to. The realization punctured the brief gleeful respite from his nagging sense of despair. His heart sank again.

"Yeah, a few stray dead dogs are turning up everywhere we go now, some of *them* even chewed on," Leroy added in his normal voice. For a moment he stared in the direction of the dog pack.

"C'mon, we can leave safely now," Leroy said, slipping his handgun back into his overalls pocket.

9

JOURNAL ENTRY

BLUE ROCK SPRINGS MEDICAL CAMP
PS: SIX WEEKS

We have adjusted to camp life here. Blue Rock Springs is home for all three of us now.

Lauren is busy and relatively content with her medical duties. She's a highly valued member of Dr. Ky's medical staff.

Remarkably, I am actually of some use to Leroy, working mostly with my hands. Helping find gas, diesel, and pieces of equipment he puts to good use. He's teaching me to run various pieces of equipment in the shop and actually use hand tools.

And we constantly talk about books—he's sincerely interested in what I taught as an English professor. He's indeed a treasure, a true renaissance man. A real life Leonardo!

But Lauren and I still miss our own home in Berkeley on College Avenue, our old friends, and especially our relatives down south—it's terrible not knowing for sure what happened to her parents or my dad.

Luke has adjusted the most quickly and accepts life as it is now. Apparently not reflecting back much on the past, if at all. The work with Mike Shaw and the young people has made him tougher, but coarsened his spirit . . . and perhaps made him more cynical. He's not a naive teenager anymore. No, he's grown up quickly . . . maybe too quickly.

In his free time, he has no interest outside his circle of young cohorts. Not sure what they talk about. But they consume all the alcohol they find. I know he infrequently visits the camp library, or the little school, or actually spends any time with his mother and me.

He's suddenly lost his teen years.

I worry about him.

On an upbeat note, Leroy and I found six more paperback books last week, all in relatively good condition, at a partially standing office near a freeway rest stop by the Woodland turn-off. Two are really notable, both award-winning books. Where I'm Calling From *by Raymond Carver, and* The Road *by Cormac McCarthy. Someone in that office had good literary taste— maybe reading during their lunchtime.*

Leroy has never read either writer. He will be starting The Road *soon. Be interesting to hear his take on this famous book, a critically applauded post-apocalyptic speculation that won the Pulitzer Prize in 2007 or 2008, sometime way back then—ironic because McCarthy's general post-apocalyptic premise has actually come true.*

That's not all the book is really about. But perhaps more on that later.

10

THREE SPECIAL SURVIVORS

Leroy had cleverly rigged an electric pump to one of the larger portable gas-run generators, and they had a much easier time now bringing up diesel and gas from the underground tanks at the Dixon truck stop. Not so much laborious hand cranking now. Easier, but it was still a slow and arduous process.

As they began filling the first fifty-five gallon drum, Leroy started talking about *The Road*, which he'd finished the night before. Jake always enjoyed their discussions of any book; but he'd been especially interested in Leroy's take on this particular one.

"As I told you, Dr. J, I haven't read much SF, with the exception of maybe a few short stories, Ray Bradbury of course, like everyone else, and a little Kurt Vonnegut—actually, this book will be my first post-apocalyptic novel ..." He scratched his nose and nodded slowly, as if weighing his thoughts before he continued, "It's a bleak, depressing book, isn't it? With kind of a cynical, pessimistic view of mankind."

"Yes, I guess the point of a lot of post-apocalyptic fiction is to focus on the fall and decline of the human race. By nature a depressing undertaking. This type of literary material is often bleak."

"But not all?"

"No, not all."

The older man was quiet for another few moments. He rubbed his nose again, cleared his throat, and asked, "What's up with all the peculiar punctuation of this book ... or the lack of punctuation, you know, like the missing quotation marks?"

Jake smiled, almost apologetically for Cormac McCarthy.

"Well, I guess he does this much of the time in his work. And it's not done much in regular mainstream fiction, almost never in SF, but there is a long tradition for this kind of thing in literary fiction. I don't know, maybe McCarthy's suggesting this isn't just a novel but more like a prose poem in structure—"

"That's a pretty vague academic argument or justification for doing it, and all I care about is reading the dang story," Leroy said, his tone cranky. "Common readers are used to normal punctuation, and we don't care much about all that extra literary fluff, you see."

"Yes, of course I understand, and I have to admit that even many good science fiction writers feel McCarthy's eccentric punctuation is a little ... well, a little pretentious. They also think this book contains material covered long ago in SF ... And perhaps the story itself is a little thin compared to most classic post-apocalyptic work—the work done by established SF writers considered to be better stories. But there *may* be a slight bit of jealousy harbored in that consensus judgment. SF writers feeling irritated that a mainstream writer like Cormac McCarthy can venture into the genre ghetto, then write a pretty slim book with some ancient genre ideas, and suddenly, lo and behold, the NYC literary establishment applauds it. Hoorah! Hoorah! Wins the Pulitzer Prize."

He made a kind of shrugging gesture with a quizzical face, and threw up his palms. "But who knows what is an honest reaction to it now?"

The older man chuckled during Jake's explanation of the general dismissive consensus of many SF writers' reaction to a mainstream writer like McCarthy delving into their genre—an obvious interloper. But then he was thoughtful for a few moments before he made another comment.

"Okay, good enough," he finally said, "the jury's out here on all that literary merit. But, you know, I also think that at the book's core, McCarthy expresses an unfair view of man's *basic* nature. Much too negative."

"Negative view? How do you mean?"

"Everyone seems completely out for themselves. Almost like the boy and his papa are against *all* the other survivors … Stealing from each other. Some even catching people, penning them up like animals, and then eating them. Cannibalism, right? I realize this can happen under extreme circumstances … like with that Donner party caught in the snow of the Sierras in the old days. But it seems almost here like … I don't know, almost like a too displayed basic evil. Not a necessary spontaneous occurrence, but instead a premeditated, almost preferred thing. If that makes sense."

He glanced at Jake, a skeptical frown on his wrinkled features. "Only at the very end is there even a glimmer of outside human kindness expressed and shared by anyone. But those last two paragraphs, man, they are indeed grand … even if I'm not exactly sure what they mean relative to the rest of the story. Something that appeals directly to my heart rather than to my intellect."

"So, I take it that you don't agree with this basic view of humankind?" Jake said, trying to stimulate the older man to further elaborate on his implied criticism, as if Leroy were a grad student in one of Jake's graduate seminars at Cal that needed some nudging. At the same time he was in agreement with much of the old man's feelings of the story, especially the book's ending—a concise, precise, and absolutely correct reaction.

After a moment's reflection, Leroy shook his head.

"Nah, I don't agree with the basic philosophy at the heart of this bleak novel. I feel that man is generally more humane than what is written here. I'm willing to bet that some of those *good* SF writers you admire so much have written stuff that would disagree strongly with this viewpoint, too. Some of those writers you call humanists. Am I right?" The older man peered intently and a little slyly at Jake.

Jake couldn't help smiling to himself.

Leroy, who had probably never heard of a graduate seminar in say: *Humanism Explored in American Post-Apocalyptic Novels,* still offered up a pretty well-reasoned out opinion. He made a well-educated accurate guess about possible written support for his opinion, even though he had read none of the classic post-apocalyptic SF novels. But still, Jake shrugged slightly, remaining silent, hoping the older man would volunteer some more of his measured and insightful thoughts.

After a moment or so, the older man kind of smiled wryly and said, "Ultimately, all BS-ing aside, the proof is in the pudding, isn't it, Dr. J.?"

"How so?"

"Look around at our own post-apocalyptic situation. Our medical camp. What's our motivation for helping others? No money is being exchanged. Obviously no medical insurance processed. No bartering of goods. No favors exchanged of any kind that I've seen. What's our material gain or motivation for helping the injured and sick, other than some kind of—what would you college guys call it … Altruism, is that the word?" He looked at Jake with his eyebrows arched, his body language almost challenging any disagreement of his assessment.

When Jake didn't immediately respond, he answered the series of rhetorical questions in a heavily judgmental tone, "*Nothing.* The people here are not benefiting in any tangible way from volunteering their services, you understand. They could let the patients die and save the resources for themselves, but they haven't reacted that way. I suspect there are others who would act this same way if given the opportunity."

Jake chuckled. Altruism, eh?

He shook his head thoughtfully.

"Well, I guess you've got me there, Leroy. The proof is indeed in the pudding. And you're correct in your guess that there are quite a number of excellent post-apocalyptic novels that aren't necessarily quite so relentlessly cynical and bleak. Let's see … *Earth Abides* by George R. Stewart is one—and, by the way, Stewart knew a little about cannibalism, as he wrote a fine nonfiction book about the Donner Party, *Ordeal by Hunger*. And of course there's the excellent *Alas, Babalon* by Pat Frank. But I guess my favorite of the more or less optimistic post-apocalyptic books is *A Canticle for Leibowitz* by Walter M. Miller. It's actually based on a humorous premise, and is indeed funny in parts."

Leroy nodded, smiling, his expression slightly wry.

"Okay, son, you been working me pretty good up till now, drawing out my opinion. Didn't guess I'd notice? What do you think of *The Road*? What's your more learned reaction? Is the pessimism about human nature justified under the circumstances? Is it a good book? Give me your take on *The Road*."

"Well, actually, I think it is a pretty good book. It won lots of critical praise and awards, too—"

He broke off and held up his hands in the stop gesture to ward off the older man's dismissal of that kind of literary argument based on expert opinion—most of it originating on the East Coast anyhow.

"Bear with me, please. Perhaps there is some more or less difficult thematic and legitimate other literary issues resonating here, something requiring a little more effort and thought to uncover than just the surface story. Which, by the way, you've done an excellent job of criticizing."

"Okay, thanks," Leroy said, smiling. "But what would those thematic and extra literary issues be, professor?"

Jake smiled at the sarcastic jab, nodded, thought a moment, and then continued, his expression serious.

"The title itself, *The Road*, suggests a journey. One might think it is the journey a father and son must take, the road a symbol for time. The father aging, growing sick, eventually dying, the son maturing, getting stronger, taking over responsibility for his father by the end. And perhaps what is happening around them in the story is characteristic of the many moral temptations that we all struggle with during life. In this context, the son may be a kind of an ethical register, keeping them on a narrow moral track, especially at the end. A recurring clue here that this interpretation might've been the intent of the author is the boy's constant questioning of his father: 'We're still the good guys, Papa'? And the father agrees that they are indeed carrying the flame of righteousness."

Jake stopped for a moment, but Leroy stared back at him with a non-committal, perhaps even slightly unsympathetic expression.

"And I'll admit that the potentially completely atavistic regression of mankind during a post-apocalyptic catastrophe is possibly handled a little too heavy handed here by Mc—"

"Whoa, whoa, too many big words there for me, Dr. J."

Jake laughed.

"I guess you and I mostly agree about most literary aspects of this book, Leroy. This is definitely a novel to discuss more though, if you want. As my students used to say: 'Lotsa stuff here.'" Then he added a personal comment, "You're really a perceptive reader, Leroy, you know that? And analytical, too? You might have made an excellent grad student if given the opportunity."

The old man's eyes narrowed, then he grinned when he realized Jake wasn't poking fun at him, and that the questions were rhetorical and followed by a generous compliment.

Leroy's good-natured expression was back on his face, his tone normal again.

"All of the stuff you talk about, in addition to story, sounds pretty interesting, son. Never thought too much about those kinds of things like that when reading before. Yes, we definitely need to talk some more about this book. I'd like that, son."

They had almost filled three of the four fifty-five gallon drums on the flatbed while they'd talked literature. But at that point, the older man said, "I want to check something out. You can watch the pump for a while, okay?"

"Yes."

Leroy wandered to the completely-leveled building of the truck stop, climbing up and checking out the nearby crushed trailer of a wrecked big rig.

Left alone, Jake daydreamed, feeling a little sorry for himself as the third drum finally topped. He prepared to switch the hose to the fourth and final drum filling—

He clumsily reached for the handgun in his overalls after seeing two pairs of brown eyes staring back at him from under a nearby abandoned Cadillac.

Kids.

The eyes belonged to a pair of skinny, malnourished children.

"Leroy, come back here," he shouted hoarsely, summoning the older man back to where Jake stood by the flatbed, drums, and the humming generator.

A slender young woman stepped around the Cad and into clear view. She held a small wrecking bar in her hands like a baseball bat.

"We don't want any trouble, mister," she said, shaking the wrecking bar for effect. "We're just hungry. Do you have anything you can spare for us, please?"

Her name was MacKenzie Ross, and her twins were Janey and Jimmy. They'd been living on an isolated horse ranch in Green Valley in the Coastal Mountains to the west of Fairfield. But the Ross family had only recently moved into their place just before the strikes hit. They had run out of food over a month ago, waiting in vain for MacKenzie's husband, a lawyer, to come back from a pre-Strike trip to Sacramento. But Denny never returned, and they were indeed hungry.

After the three new survivors were fed back at camp and cleaned up, Jake introduced the six-year-olds to Tara, their camp school-teacher.

She grinned broadly at her new and youngest students, and immediately took them in to join the others in the tent classroom.

Despite some noticeable general camp pessimism among staff, Tara was always upbeat and often said optimistically that her kids were the future; but she hadn't added a new child to her four regular students since before Jake and his family joined the camp almost three months ago. So the young school teacher would obviously treasure and nurture her newest charges.

11

JOURNAL ENTRY

BLUE ROCK SPRINGS MEDICAL CAMP
PS: FOUR MONTHS

Two more camp members died of radiation sickness yesterday.

Shaw and his young people have discovered no significant hordes of food supplies in several weeks.

Rationing is now necessary at the mess tent—only two meals served daily.

No new fuel dumps discovered, even though Leroy and I have spent several days a week searching both north and south along the I-80 corridor for undamaged buried tanks at truck stops and gas stations. The tanks at Dixon are down below a fourth full.

We have the huge camp generator in place, but must run electricity only one hour nightly to conserve valuable diesel.

Our shrinking supply of medicine is allocated on high priority need. Shaw and his people spend as much time scavenging for medical supplies as he does for food, especially looking for antibiotics in ruined medical offices and buildings.

Morale of staff is beginning to slide, despite the enthusiasm of Dr. Ky and Lauren and Tara.

On a brighter note, Leroy has carefully read one of my favorite main-stream American writers, Nelson Algren. In the last week we have discussed the merits of The Man with the Golden Arm *and* A Walk on the Wild Side, *Algren's best two novels. We've talked in-depth about the humanism reflected in this street-savvy Chicago writer's books, his compassion and love of the common man, and his genuine concern for the underclass.*

I'm convinced that Leroy is a humanist, himself, which of course brings a smile to my face.

12

THE HARSH REALITY OF CAMP LIFE

It was late at night and Jake was awake, lying on his back, listening to the Hopkins having sex on the other side of one of the flimsy partitions in their quarters. Debbie, a med tech colleague of Lauren's, was making tiny gasping moans, and finally whispering, "Oh, oh, oh …" while Darren, a security guy, was breathing loudly, accompanied by skin-on-skin sticky slapping sounds.

Lauren breathed evenly, fast asleep. She was shy about this aspect of communal life, and would have been embarrassed, perhaps annoyed, by the public sounds of her friends' lovemaking. But Jake didn't find it annoying at all; instead he was semi-aroused. When they weren't both exhausted, they usually waited for the heavy-set Jay McCarron to start snoring in the tent; then they'd try to make surreptitious love under public radar. The skinny cots made it difficult—a clumsy affair at best—and the semi-public nature of the intimacy usually dampened Lauren's interest. They much preferred to take a day off, scrounge food if possible, hike to the springs area in the blue crags above camp, and have a skimpy evening picnic. They'd make love leisurely on a spread blanket while listening to the fresh water bubble up and spill from the rocks, the stream eventually feeding the lake down below. Watching the sun as it set. But the romantic interludes could only be arranged infrequently during their grinding schedules seven days a week.

Jake bit his lip and tried to sleep.

Communal living, the constant presence of someone else around, limited even the intimacy of spontaneous discussions between Jake and Lauren. They often found themselves in a corner of their quarters or off by themselves in the mess hall, restrained and whispering back and forth. It was a practice Jake found especially constrictive when they wanted to talk about Luke. The only private conversations he now had with anyone were with his mentor, Leroy, when the two were out working away from the camp by themselves somewhere. They talked about books mostly, but sometimes about love and other aspects of life. More frequently Jake admitted his concerns about the hardening of Luke and all the other young people. These conversations were often illuminating and intellectually gratifying in their own limited way. Leroy was a walking Jungian archetype—the *wise old man*. Jake knew he was extremely fortunate with his work assignment.

Dr. Ky was a *wise young woman*.

Thank you, Hang.

13

JOURNAL ENTRY

BLUE ROCK SPRINGS MEDICAL CAMP
PS: SIX MONTHS

Two more horrible radiation sickness deaths, including one of the security people. Going out from camp is always high risk. And it's easy not to observe all the safety precautions. Fortunately, Leroy never allows a lapse.

Dixon tanks are nearing empty.

Leroy and I go out daily, find, and siphon gas and diesel from individual wrecked vehicles—takes at least twelve to fourteen hours a day to meet minimal needs.

The young people went off again at dusk last week, dressed in dark cams, coming back sometime late at night. They got into a skirmish with a small band of Desperadoes. Something that occurs fairly often now. One of our people slightly wounded. They brought back no new survivors, only a few captured items. Several AK-47s, a shotgun, ammunition, and, remarkably, three horses. Dr. Ky thinks that they don't need to go out after dark to scavenge—she said that it was an unnecessary risk. Of course she's right.

But Shaw disagrees strongly. Leroy has gotten into serious arguments with Mike Shaw about the priority use of gas or diesel—the security chief wanting to just roam at night, not believing he should be accountable to Leroy or anyone else for his fuel use.

After a group discussion, the use of camp vehicles and precious fuel is being tightly controlled now, used only to scavenge during daytime—most days the security people coming back empty-handed.

After some suspected unauthorized fuel use, Leroy has locked up all the hand pumps used to transfer fuel from the 55-gallon drums into vehicles.

This has irritated Shaw, and his feelings have become an ongoing source of friction with Leroy.

The young people have built a corral down by the lake.

MacKenzie Ross guided a pair of expeditions into the horse ranching country near her old home in Green Valley, and they've rounded up and brought back nine more horses that had been fending for themselves. She is teaching everyone how to ride and care for the horses, which will eventually reduce the use of gas-eating vehicles. Like Leroy, she too is a prime camp asset.

Luke has been training all the young people in the use of bows and arrows—sharp, deadly looking hunting arrows. Sometimes, the best riders practice shooting at targets off horseback. He doesn't offer much of an explanation to me or his mother for this type of training, only suggesting rather ominously that the bow is the best silent assault weapon.

Lauren has commented several times that all the young people, except Tara, wear a rather serious, somber expression now—they don't seem to be having any fun, or enjoying life.

She is very worried about Luke. So am I.

We've talked to Hang recently about perhaps having some dances for the young people at night . . . or even some athletic events when it's still light. Seems like a good idea. Hang is considering it.

14

BLACK SNOW NIGHTMARES

Jake still experienced the recurring dream about the ten-point buck, but it had turned into a nightmare. In the most recent one, the buck looked down on him and Luke as the black snow fell. The bizarre snow eventually trapped them, piling higher and higher. Until finally Jake couldn't see his son anymore. Nothing. And Luke's cold fingers had suddenly slipped from his hand. And the snow kept piling deeper, as he searched frantically for the boy's hand ... And then icy fingers touched his hand, just as he was beginning to experience the frightening sensation of smothering in the black snow. Standing on his tiptoes on a rock, he pulled Luke up next to him, and looked anxiously at his red-faced son gasping for air.

At the edge of the forest—

Nothing.

The big buck had abandoned them.

Jake awoke, soaked in clammy wetness, trembling.

He didn't care to bother Lauren about the nightmare ... or anyone else in camp. He couldn't even bring himself to mention the dreams to Leroy when they were alone.

15

A DISTURBING DISCUSSION

Of all the people in camp, Jake had the most difficult time getting to know Mike Shaw, the security chief. The young man seemed to be always on the go. When he stopped to eat or to attend a camp meeting, he was unusually preoccupied and taciturn. Jake had talked several times to Luke about his boss, who the boy—and in fact all the young people in camp—looked up to because of his perceived disciplined toughness. But Luke never mentioned much about the man's life before the pre-strikes.

So, one afternoon, after he and the security chief returned to camp, Jake made a point of malingering at the showers, waiting to walk back to camp with Shaw—a personal moment.

As they toweled off, Jake said, "I've been wanting to talk to you for some time now, Mike."

The young security chief glanced up as he finished drying his legs. "That right, Dr. Zachary?" He had the habit of using a person's formal title if he knew it. He asked all his young people to call him Chief Shaw or just plain Chief. He was dressing quickly.

Jake nodded, trying to keep up. "Yes, do you mind if we walk back to camp together and have a private conversation?"

"Suit yourself."

As he finished pulling on his boots, Jake said, "I was wondering if you might be interested in talking about some type of camp recreation for the young people for their off hours. You know, maybe play some sports together. Softball? Volleyball? Or soccer? Maybe organize some music and have dances on some nights. A party of sorts—maybe celebrate birthdays or something like that. What do you think?"

"With training and work, they are busy fourteen or fifteen hours a day now, and don't have spare time for such frivolous activities," Shaw said in a flat tone, diminishing and dismissing Jake's recreation suggestions.

"Yeah, I know," Jake said, keeping his tone cordial, "but I was hoping that maybe you could cut back on some of your late afternoon and evening training sessions, you know, just for an evening or two each week devoted to rest and relaxation—"

Shaw abruptly stopped walking and looked directly at Jake, his gaze overtly unyielding and cold.

"No, I don't see how we could possibly arrange that."

Jake suppressed the flair of angry reaction from his voice. "I've already discussed this briefly several times with Dr. Ky and a few of the older people around camp," he said, forcing a thin smile. "And, you know, they all seem to *think* it might be a pretty good idea."

Still the security chief didn't move. He stared intently at Jake in silence for a long moment, his pale cheeks reddening ever so slightly. Then he shook his head.

"It's not their responsibility."

Feeling more uncomfortable now, Jake cleared his throat and forged ahead: "They are mostly teenagers. And they don't seem to ever do anything fun—what is normal for most young people. We rarely see them laugh or smile. They are way too serious ..." He noticed Shaw's frown deepen, and debated whether to continue along this line; then he decided to throw diplomacy to the wind, to speak his mind.

"And, frankly, Mike, you seem to almost purposely lead them out looking for violent confrontations with Desperadoes, and then train them relentlessly for that specific purpose, you know—"

Shaw held up his hand.

"These aren't normal times, Dr. Zachary," he said, shaking his head and sucking in a deep breath. "We are only doing what's necessary to protect this camp." His tone was polite, but also authoritative, like a veteran combat officer lecturing a young replacement lieutenant. "If we don't attack these marauders wherever we find them, they will eventually attack us here. That is a fact of life, a piece of hard reality. It's a kind of preemptive security, you see. My people need to be on their toes ... always alert, ready. Well trained. So this requires us to be at tip top military readiness at all times—"

"Military?" Jake interrupted, frowning, unable to keep the judgmental sharpness out of his voice. "My God, man, they aren't in the Marines here. Most of them are barely old enough to have enlisted without parental permission, if there were an army left to join. They should be enjoying their teen years, not stalking and mercilessly killing people. Training every spare moment. Heck, even the military used to have R and R, you know—"

"See, that's your problem, Dr. Zachary, right there," Shaw said, his voice tighter and strained now, his face more flushed. "You've spent way too much time in an academic ivory tower. Not enough time learning about life, about practical matters. You have no idea about reality unless it's forced on you. Hell, even before the strike, it was tough out here on the street in most California towns and cities—racial gangs ripping and running, strong-arm robberies at convenience stores, rape ... and who knows what else." The security chief made a kind of all-encompassing, sweeping gesture with his arm. "Lots of really bad people were operating out there. People who intended to do you bodily harm. Now it's even worse. There is no semblance of law and order—the strong rule the weak. We can't be too vigilant, too strong. My people stand between the camp and being consumed by the surrounding violent chaos. Alert, trained, and ready to react. That is my responsibility. Whether you agree or not, I don't care. We don't have time for grab-ass." He sucked in another deep breath, his forehead wrinkles etched deeply, and peered intently at Jake for a response.

"You're absolutely right. That isn't close to my view of mankind either before the strike or even now. And I know it isn't Leroy's view either—"

"That old man spends way too much time with his nose in books. His view about most things is a little too ... I guess *soft* for my taste. Too interested in continuing his way-out liberal political philosophy and agenda before the strike, like worrying about ... oh, affirmative action and all that kind of nonsense. Problem was that we spent way too much time and money listening politely to people like Leroy Robinson in the past—that was one of the major flaws in this country's supposed leadership. Listening to weak-kneed, liberal knuckleheads, like that Black President in the old days."

Jake was shocked by the young man's skewed viewpoint of free speech and civil rights in a democracy. Especially his view of Barack Obama—an exceptional President, regardless of his skin color.

No question Shaw was referring to all Black leaders even if he hadn't specifically said the words. He'd known that Mike Shaw had been in the military, been deployed a number of times to Afghanistan/Pakistan, and then been on the Solano County Sheriff's department for several years after his military discharge. Probably seen some pretty terrible things when he was in the military, maybe even some serious and violent stuff, including protests after his return. But Shaw's judgmental rant reminded Jake a little of a PBS special he'd seen years ago on the Oklahoma City bombing. In fact, Shaw almost shared the same facial expression and general attitude of Timothy McVeigh. To be so cynical, so harsh, and so obviously wrong in his opinion ... infecting all the young people in camp with this skewed and biased viewpoint ...

Maybe it was more than prejudice and racism. White supremacy? Or maybe Security Chief Mike Shaw enjoyed the physical violence. Jake shuddered at that thought.

Luke had mentioned that Shaw wasn't on active duty at the Sheriff's Department when the strikes hit. He'd been suspended over some kind of a physical altercation and was on unpaid administrative leave awaiting civil and perhaps criminal proceedings. Yet Luke had been sympathetic to his boss's position.

The young security chief's expression softened.

"I've seen what people are capable of doing, Dr. Zachary. Horrible, hideous things. In the war over in Afghan/Pak. But even back here. Each and every day when I was a deputy sheriff during the last six years, I experienced—"

"You weren't an on-duty law enforcement officer when the strikes hit, were you?"

Shaw's facial expression hardened again. After a moment, he shook his head.

Jake kept his tone neutral now and asked, "What exactly happened...if you don't mind talking about it?"

The young man sighed, shrugged, and then shook his head again. "Roughed up a Black dude after a brawl in a bar. He'd tried to slice another person with a straight razor. My partner and me responded to a 911, arrived at the bar, took him down, cuffed him, and escorted him to jail...but only after quite a little donnybrook."

"And you were formally suspended for just doing that?" Jake couldn't restrain the skepticism.

Shaw gazed off to the west, apparently lost deep in thought.

"The guy and his lawyers claimed police brutality, filed some paperwork." He glanced at Jake, shrugged again and made a *what-are-you-going-to-do* face. "And that's typical bullshit for those people."

Those people?

Jake prodded: "But what actually happened, Mike?"

Shaw stared absently at Jake, rubbed his chin, and then began slowly moving toward the tents before he spoke again.

"He'd resisted strenuously, like I said, kicked my partner square in the balls, bloodied my nose; so we did a pretty good number on him after we got him cuffed and down. You know, a little payback."

"Payback? Ah, I see." Jake was unable to suppress the harsh judgmental tone that had crept into the end of his response.

They'd drifted back into the residential area and stopped at the entry to the single men's tent.

"No," Shaw said, his voice sharp and bitter, "I don't think you do see, Dr. Zachary. Everything my partner and I did was completely justified. Maybe not by the Black do-gooders like your friend here, Leroy, who all raised holy hell about the guy's minor bumps and bruises. But that's okay." He was glancing off again to the west, a smirk on his face. "Because our union's legal beagles told me that I'd be reinstated, with full pay, and the criminal charges dropped, and that I'd—"

Shaw caught himself mentally drifting at that point, stopped talking, shook his head, and grinned kind of sheepishly. "I guess none of that means do-diddly-squat now, does it? All water under the bridge, as they say."

This was the first time Jake had engaged Shaw in any conversation, and heard him talk with any emotion about his life prior to the strike or anything else other than camp security.

They stood for a few moments in silence.

"The Black prick walked about a week later after being released from the hospital, *no* charges filed against him by the County Prosecutor, either. Can you fucking believe it? We should've wasted the shithead on the street outside of that bar when we had the opportunity."

16

SUDDEN LOSS

Early in the evening, Jake sat on his cot trying to re-read a well-wrinkled paperback of *The Stranger* by Camus. Lauren was gone, assisting Dr. Ky with an emergency appendectomy on Deanna Cordoza, one of the cooks, who had been diagnosed shortly after dinner.

He recalled that Camus was occasionally described as a humanist in addition to being linked with Sartre and the Existentialists. But maybe Camus read better in French, because the English translation flattened out and drained the subtle emotional nature of some of the prose. Jake remembered having that same reaction before, when he'd first read a translation of *The Plague*. He sat the paperback aside, realizing that he hadn't thought too much about his academic specialty or partially finished book in ... My God, the last six months, except for an occasional philosophical conversation of humanistic issues in literature with Leroy—

The tent light bulb blinked out, and Jake was plunged into darkness ... Too soon for the normal one-hour lights out to conserve fuel.

After a moment, he went to the door of the tent and looked

out. This happened sometimes, usually a falling limb knocking down a line.

The whole camp, including the med tent, was dark.

They'd have their backup portable gas generator going in a minute, he thought, at least be able to finish their emergency operation. But maybe he'd go up to the big generator and see if Leroy needed some help. He didn't think it could be out of fuel. They'd filled it with diesel this afternoon. Maybe a clogged fuel line again? That had happened twice before, even though Leroy had added extra filters in the main fuel line.

His eyes adjusted to the darkness of the camp before he'd hiked even a quarter of the way to the generator site next to the fuel dump.

A number of footsteps pounded somewhere not far below. People running.

Crack, crack, crack shattered the stillness—the firing of an AK-47 somewhere near the center of camp.

Several flashes of gunfire in the direction of the med tent.

Loud but incoherent shouting. A number of shadowy figures darting off from the med center in the direction of the lake.

Rapid gunfire from the departing figures ... singular flashes from shadows near the med tent.

Jake stood on the hill, stunned.

Lauren was in the medical center.

Jesus, he thought, fear jumpstarting him into action. He ran downhill toward the central area, his heart thumping, pulse racing. He needed to get to Lauren.

Muzzle flashes and gunfire.

As he raced down the hill, several more figures ran from the center of the tent area.

Jake slowed as he neared the big med tent, some of the shadows around him now taking recognizable shape, young people from the camp, all armed ... and Mike Shaw, shouting and signaling wildly with his handgun in the direction of the lake. "That way!

They're escaping! Get them!"

A figure suddenly rose directly in his path from a dark clump on the ground.

Swinging something at him—

Pain exploded in Jake's head.

Struck numb, he lost his balance and fell to his knees.

Icy darkness closed in around him as he lost consciousness.

"Dad, Dad," came shouts from far away—a figure leaning over him.

Wet coolness against his forehead.

He blinked.

A fuzzy face leaning in close—Luke.

His son's face scrunched into a mask of pain.

"Dad, are you okay?"

The boy was washing his face with a damp cloth.

"She's gone, Dad, she's gone," Luke muttered through clenched teeth.

Jake tried to focus, to understand, and to talk, his throat dry and scratchy-hoarse, and he only stammered dryly: "W-w-who...?"

He blinked again, looking around.

Light glowed around him...

He was on a gurney in the operating area of the med center.

Jake could now see his son's reddened face wasn't convulsed with pain; no, he was angry, enraged.

Another face appeared over his son's shoulder—Hang Ky.

"I'm sorry, Jacob," she said softly, leaning closer, patting his shoulder.

He closed his eyes and tried to grasp what exactly was going on, but his head pounded unmercifully. Extreme pain. Again he blinked, touched his forehead, and looked at his sticky-red fingers.

"What happened to me, Hang?"

THE CONFESSIONS OF ST. ZACH

Dr. Ky answered, "You were apparently struck in the head with a rifle butt by one of the fleeing bandits. Not too bad though, a glancing blow, only a bad bruise, one deep cut, and probably a slight—"

"She's *gone*," the boy interrupted, his tone high-pitched and sad, as he wildly gestured to the other gurney, beside his father.

Jake pushed up on a shaky elbow and looked over.

"Jesus Chr—" he started to say; his throat tightened and cut off his air.

Lauren was lying on her back, partially covered by a sheet, her green scrubs ripped open down the front, her breasts exposed. But it was her eyes, her glazed dark eyes staring off into eternity ... and her throat, slashed and bloody.

"What—?" Jake frantically reached a hand toward his son.

"The leader of the Desperadoes did it, Dad," the boy explained. "I saw him leaving. He tried to rape her, but she fought back. So he cut her throat and left her to bleed to death. I saw him leaving. Tall and thin with a ponytail, and an odd scar high on his left cheek—shaped like a check mark."

Luke glanced out of the med tent into the night and said, "Mike's rounding up the others, we're going after them. I'm going to kill him."

Stunned, Jake didn't say anything for a few seconds, only stared at his son's contorted, red face. With effort, he pushed himself up to a shaky, sitting position on the edge of the gurney.

"I-I'm coming, t-too," he said, his voice shaky.

"No you're not, Jacob," Dr. Ky said, gently but forcibly pushing him back down. "You can't go anyplace right now. I need to stitch your head and dress it; and I think you may have a slight concussion, but it could be worse. Not sure yet. In any case, you can't go chasing off into the night on horseback with your injuries. Just take it easy for now."

Jake swallowed his nausea and glanced over at the doorway.

Luke was gone.

Overwhelmed and grief-stricken, Jake tried to concentrate to piece together what had happened from Ky's short clips of explanation as she slowly stitched him.

A band of Desperadoes, perhaps as many as ten, had come in quietly by the lake, on horseback to that point. Near the parking lot, they'd cut the lone security guard's throat. They'd entered the med tent, threatening the emergency operating staff with AK-47s, demanding drugs and medical supplies. Sometime during the ensuing confusion of the armed robbery, the leader managed to drag Lauren outside, about the time one of the Desperadoes cut the main transmission line from the generator. He had wrestled her to the ground and attempted to rape her, but in the dark Dr. Olafson stumbled onto them and intervened. The internist was cut down by a blast from the Desperado's AK-47 as all hell broke loose in the camp. Luke and a few security people arrived at the med tent about then as most of the Desperadoes were making their escape toward the lake.

In addition to Lauren, Dr. Olafson, and the parking lot security guard, the Desperadoes had killed two other young people, and a stray round had struck and killed one of the Ross twins, the little boy, Jimmy. The Desperadoes had made off with all the drugs from the med tent fridge and some assorted medical supplies. During their escape, they'd opened the corral, trying to round up and steal the horses; but in their haste they only managed to scatter them.

Luke and Mike Shaw's people returned to camp empty-handed at 3:00 A.M.

17

JOURNAL ENTRY

BLUE ROCK SPRINGS MEDICAL CAMP
PS: EIGHT MONTHS

At the end of each day I climb up to Lauren's grave, a rocky cairn above the springs.

I whisper a prayer for her, as I imagine her face when she was young, right before Luke was born. Of course she is stunningly beautiful—full, sensuous lips, high rosy cheekbones, almond-shaped, exotic mahogany eyes. But more memorable than her features is her general attitude and bearing, an inner sense of strength, which conveys a glowing confidence, poise, and, yes, even a measure of bravery.

What a waste. How could the bandits do this? For what: A few drugs? Is Mike Shaw correct about his views of most of the strike survivors? Animals? Was Cormac McCarthy's cynicism justified?

I'm unsure now.

There is an empty hole in my heart.

I miss Lauren terribly. It will be difficult, almost unbearable in the future without her love and strength of character for support.

Whatever, I can never fully escape my English professor mindset though when thinking of Lauren. So, sometimes I imagine a silly metaphor of her.

A long-term relationship is a little like having a beautiful pair of high-quality, fine leather boots. At first you admire their beauty, the quality crafts-manship, handling them in a gingerly, respectful way. But the boots are a little stiff, taking time to grow accustomed to. You shine them, thankful for the high quality, the comfortable fit, even muttering under your breath your gratefulness. As time goes by you still recognize and enjoy the fine boots, but you only shine them for special occasions; and eventually the day comes when you take the old-er, slightly worn, but still exquisite boots completely for granted.

It was like that with Lauren. I took her completely for granted. Over twenty years had gone by, and there were so many things I could have, should have, said to her. But I never really took the time.

And then, in a finger snap, she is gone. Too late for me to say any of those things now. The realization chokes me up.

Luke has never come up to the springs since the day after the murder, when he helped me stack the rocks over her.

He prays for no one now, not even himself.

The admission causes me great concern, and I remember the recurring dream of the ten-point buck.

No more talk of special sports or dances being arranged for the young peo-ple since Lauren has gone. No one pursues it; and I have lost interest.

Sadness has me in its firm, unrelenting grip.

18

THE CONFRONTATION OF SELF

In an extremely vivid dream, Jake slowly cut the throat of the man with the checked scar on his cheek. Slowly, ever so slowly, enjoying the frantic, contorted agony frozen on the Desperado's face. And afterwards, when Jake finally awakened, he felt not a twinge of remorse. In fact, he enjoyed the vindictive, regressive behavior. He should be shamed by this self-admission, but he's not.

What's happening to him?

It was dark, no moon, very quiet.

MacKenzie held the reins of all eleven horses, the blindfolds keeping them relatively quiet. Jake, armed with a pump shotgun, stood guard over the nervous mounts and the young woman. He glanced over the serious expression marring her pretty features, certain she could hear his heart thumping loudly out of control. His blood raced, his throat felt dry, his vision tunneled, as he sweated heavily and stared out into the muggy night. Jesus.

What was taking them so long?

Mike Shaw and eight others had set up an ambush along a frontage road paralleling I-80 near the University Avenue turnoff to Berkeley, based on information from a captured Desperado. A band would be returning tonight to their encampment after several days of marauding in the Oakland hills. The security chief thought—from information obtained before the prisoner died— that this group might be the same one that had attacked the med camp several months ago.

Jake hoped so. He could make out Luke's team of three archers crouched in the drainage ditch beyond the row of cedar trees screening the horses from the frontage road. They were supposed to silently hit the mounted advance guards leading a heavily-armed band back to camp near Emeryville. The Desperados would apparently be protecting a large horse-driven wagon laden with several days' plunder. Shaw would seal off an escape to the rear, while the main assault group of four, armed with AK-47s, attacked the wagon and the larger number of guards—ten or more.

The Desperadoes were late, the crescent moon rising behind Jake, MacKenzie, and the horses, making it difficult for Shaw's young people to remain hidden from sight. Jake wondered if the others were feeling as antsy and terribly frightened—

A horse whinnied someplace in the night.

But it was *not* one of their eleven mounts, each still blindfolded and kept calm and quiet by MacKenzie, who kept whispering soothingly into the ears of each of them.

Luke and his people filled the air with deadly arrows.

An uproar of shouting and automatic gunfire ensued, something exploding with a brilliant flash and lighting the western sky.

Jake edged himself forward a few feet into the cedars, trying to get a better view of the action. It was truly a confusing mess. He knelt, trying to see below the thick tree branches—

"Jacob, Jacob!"

He stood and jerked around, the frightened urgency in MacKenzie's cry making the breath catch in his throat.

THE CONFESSIONS OF ST. ZACH

Jesus, he thought, frozen in place.

A giant of a man came crashing through the stand of trees, his bare face a pale and terrified mask in the dim moonlight, his breathing labored. An arrow shaft was lodged in the back of his bloody right hip. Gasping, he shuffled toward MacKenzie, lifting the glinting blade of a Bowie knife. He gestured with his other hand toward his hip and the lodged arrow. Apparently he hadn't seen Jake standing in the shadows of the thick tree stand, for his stumbling path toward the woman led him almost close enough for Jake to reach out and touch him.

Stiffly, without thinking, Jake chambered a round instead of lashing out with the shotgun barrel—

The giant startled at the sound and turned. Before Jake could get off a shot, the Desperado moved in with surprising speed and flexibility, considering his hip wound, reached out with his free hand, and ripped the weapon from Jake's hand.

The tall man followed, lunging with the knife at Jake's face.

Jake twisted away and partially deflected the thrust. The sharp blade sliced through the meaty part of his palm below his thumb. But he ignored the pain, sucked in a deep breath, instinctively dropped down, and rammed his head into the midsection of the big Desperado.

Driven backwards by the force of the blow, the giant grunted as his lungs expelled air; but he maintained his balance, and with an angry, hoarse yell, he swung the long knife blade at Jake's face, as if it were a machete.

The knife narrowly missed his throat, its tip nicking the point of Jake's chin. Blood dribbled onto his chest as he backed up, frantically glancing about to locate the shotgun.

Not far from the horses ... twenty or so feet away. But not too far to make a successful move without the giant sticking him.

Jake made a feinting maneuver, as if to dive toward the shotgun, but set down on a wide left hook, and caught the Desperado a solid blow on the side of the chin.

The man should have gone down, but he didn't...only blinked and expelled a loud grunt.

Jake crowded in close and pulled the big man to the ground, attempted to wrench the Bowie knife from the Desperado's grasp.

But the giant was too strong, jerking his arm loose, scrambling backwards a foot or two in the dust, and finally struggling up to his knees. In an offensive position now, he was getting ready to lunge and slash out again, the blade now red and slippery—

Ughhhh.

The giant pitched forward with pain and a surprised look on his face, releasing the Bowie knife as he reached back and clutched at his thigh with both freed hands.

Still miraculously holding the horse reins, MacKenzie had managed to somehow inch forward, closer to the wrestling men; she had apparently kicked out at the arrow shaft, driving it deeper into his thigh.

Jake reached down and snatched the blade, lashed out horizontally in one continuous motion.

The man fell backwards, clutching his throat, blood spurting from between his fingers. He made an odd gurgling, drowning sound...his lungs filling. The giant's face contorted, his gaze distant and already beginning to glaze over.

It was a horrifying sight ... causing a flashback of Lauren's slashed throat and dead eyes staring into eternity.

He shouted in a panic, squeezing his eyes shut.

Then he scrambled wildly to the horses and retrieved the dislodged shotgun.

A round still in the chamber.

He jammed the shotgun into the dying Desperado's face and pulled the trigger.

Boom!

Blood splattered in all directions as the man's features disappeared.

Jake was gripped by an uncontrollable blind fury.

He jacked another round into the chamber and fired—

Boom!

And again—

Boom!

And again—

Boom!

He would've continued firing until the shotgun was empty if MacKenzie hadn't intervened.

"He's dead, Jacob, he's dead!" she shouted over the hubbub around them, still tightly clutching the reins of the now wildly nervous and rearing-up horses. "For God's sake help me with these horses!"

Jake blinked, his ears ringing. He first looked at MacKenzie, and then stared down at the bandit with a growing realization of what he'd done.

The Desperado lay twisted on the ground. No face, just a bloody mask. A scarlet flower growing on his chest. He'd even been shot in the groin. Only arms and legs remained undamaged, signaling the bloody pile of minced flesh had once been a man.

Jesus.

Sickened, Jake quickly turned away.

On the way back to Blue Rock Springs with the captured wagon, Shaw rode up and congratulated Jake in an almost warm, cordial tone. "MacKenzie told me about the Desperado. You did real good, Dr. Zachary, wasting that shithead."

Jake nodded, not feeling exactly elated by his first combat venture or Shaw's praise, but nauseated.

It had all been in vain.

These Desperados hadn't killed Lauren.

Jake should have felt devastated for killing a man so brutally, but he wasn't, not really. At least not yet. No, he just felt a kind of numb detachment from it all, even from himself, almost like the first-person narrator in *The Stranger* who, after killing the Arab on the beach, had fired dispassionately *four* more times into the still body. He understood better what Camus was writing about there: the detached nature of the violent act by the stranger—an inhuman, unfeeling moment.

As they bounced along on horseback, Jake's thoughts drifted; he tried to visualize Lauren's face ... But it was a blur. All he could see clearly was her red, slashed throat.

MacKenzie guided Jake to her tent, where her surviving twin, Janey, was fast asleep—the camp teacher, Tara, had baby-sat during the ambush.

The young woman made the be-quiet sign to Jake, gestured for him to sit in the one camp chair. She heated tea on a camp stove—a luxury item only a few in Blue Rock Springs owned. When the tea was ready, they took their mugs outside.

Neither spoke for a while, Jake unable to shake the violent encounter from his mind. It played back in slow motion, causing a tremor in his hands. But strangely he wasn't horrified by the bloody ending of it. No, he knew he should feel overwhelmed by guilt and remorse for what he'd done; but he wasn't experiencing a twinge of regret. Nothing at all, even the nausea gone now, and that dispassionate reaction was unnerving him, apparently causing the tremor.

Clutching his mug in his trembling hands, he absently blew on his steaming tea.

They sat in silence, sipping.

MacKenzie cleared her throat.

"You seem unusually preoccupied, Jacob. Do you want to talk about what happened tonight?"

He shrugged and sighed. He had nothing to say.

The two of them sat like a relaxed, older married couple in

front of her tent, casually finishing their tea and gazing off into the still night at the twinkling stars over the lake. Both comfortable with the silent sharing of themselves.

Hard to believe that he'd just killed a man, a complete stranger, only two hours ago. Even now he wasn't sure how he felt; he was pretty much numb.

Eventually MacKenzie stood and took Jake's empty teacup, but then she abruptly sat down.

"I'm sorry, Jacob," she said. "Sorry for *all* the death. My Jimmy. Your Lauren. And now this so personal violent confrontation with a stranger. It's horrifying, I know. But it wasn't your fault, you understand..." She let her voice trail off, as she too shrugged and let out a deep sigh.

He nodded, and in a barely audible tone he mouthed, "Yes, it was terrible, almost like a nightmare. And I should be more horrified, but..."

"But life goes on, doesn't it?"

He swallowed, his throat a little tighter, and he nodded.

"Yes, I guess it really does."

After another few moments of silence, MacKenzie slowly unbound her hair, which had been braided in two thick pigtails and pinned to the back of her head. She slowly combed it down around her shoulders with her spread fingers, a feminine, graceful movement Jake found to be startlingly sensual ... almost seductive, the young woman's thin smile and expression complementing the unsettling moment.

"You know, Jacob, we all need someone now. More than ever. The customs of courtship have changed. There are no elaborate rituals or rules." She reached over with her right hand and brushed her fingers along his cheek, a light, gentle, almost loving, but definitely sensuous touch.

His cheek felt warm, and almost tingled from her touch. But for a long moment he wasn't able to react or respond in any manner at all.

Then a chill swept over him.

Jake coughed and managed to stand, even though his knees were weak. He smiled at the young woman and whispered gratefully, "Thank you for the tea, and everything, MacKenzie. It helped. But I really have to go now and...get some rest, you know."

She smiled and nodded.

Awkwardly, he turned and headed to the single men's tent.

When he slipped in between the covers on his cot, he couldn't sleep for a long time. The events of the evening spun over and over through his mind. The bitter taste of nausea returned to his mouth.

19

YES, A VERY ATTRACTIVE WOMAN

Jake effectively avoided being alone with MacKenzie for the next few days, but he couldn't ignore her completely. The camp population was just too small, and there were too many communal activities. Deep in his gut, he didn't really want to avoid her.

He found her attention toward him—this younger, attractive woman to an older man—well, very flattering. And it wasn't like she was callous toward his feelings, ignoring his personal loss. He knew she missed her own son a lot.

Still, he couldn't kick the sense that if he spent any private time with MacKenzie, he was somehow betraying his dead wife's trust. Irrational, of course. Lauren was gone. All the accepted conventions had changed, as Hang had indicated to them that second day in camp. People accepted terrible personal loss now and immediately moved on with their lives—as best they could anyhow.

That was the new reality.

He understood all that.

Still, Jake felt conflicted by his feelings.

"Can we sit and eat with you?" MacKenzie and her daughter stood with their trays in hand across the table from where Jake sat alone in the mess tent.

"Sure," he said, smiling and perhaps blushing.

"You've been busy," MacKenzie said, cutting Janey's egg, cheese, and potato baked dish—the powdered eggs giving the modest serving of casserole a slightly green, unappetizing cast.

He nodded, took a sip of his weak tea. "You, too?"

"The crew brought in two more horses the first of the week, half-starved and completely wild. I've been working with them at the corral. Full time job."

They ate in silence until the young woman chuckled self-consciously and said, "I've debated back and forth about saying this for two days now. But I'll go ahead anyhow. Janey and I are going to take a hike up into the blue rocks this coming Saturday morning, clear up to the springs. Maybe have a picnic, if anything can be spared from the kitchen. I'd like to invite you to come along, Jacob."

He felt a sense of blind panic, his pulse accelerating. Closing his eyes, he sucked in a long, deep breath, let it trickle across his lips, and then looked down at his plate. He swallowed, trying to clear the lump, before he uttered hoarsely, "You know I buried Lauren in a spot up there near the springs a couple months ago?"

MacKenzie peered at him with her head cocked, and said in a tentative voice, "Yes, of course I do know, Jacob. It was such a quick and private thing with you and your son. We never really had a chance to say the goodbye to her she deserved—no one in camp did, none of her many friends…"

She paused a moment, then continued in a much more confident tone, "Lauren was a fine woman, Jacob. We don't mean to desecrate her grave on Saturday in any way, you know. We just want to get away from camp for some private time. And I would like *you* to come share that special time with us. Perhaps, if you think it's okay, we can send a belated prayer along for Lauren at her

THE CONFESSIONS OF ST. ZACH

grave. That's all I intend."

There was an awkward silence.

"Well, sure ... I guess that would be fine," he said, his throat still tight, his voice hoarse. He wasn't sure how he felt. He knew he was messed up, torn by his awakening feelings toward Mackenzie that were conflicting with his memory of Lauren.

"Good, then that's all settled, it's a *date*," the young woman said, rising to her feet, trays in hand. "C'mon, Janey."

20

JOURNAL ENTRY

BLUE ROCK SPRINGS MEDICAL CAMP
PS: TEN MONTHS

I miss Lauren. Everything about her. Think about her every day.

But I also miss the comforting touch of a living woman. The loving intimacy. It's the closest connection between two people—when they make love. I try to remember that last time with Lauren. It must have been at the springs … but the memory has somehow dimmed out.

MacKenzie is an attractive, wonderful woman, a good mother, an asset in the camp. And I'm strongly attracted to her—perhaps even falling in love with her. Is that really possible so soon after Lauren's death?

Before the strikes, I would have answered a confident no. It's just lust … all the philosophical rambling about loving intimacy only a rationalization for having desired sex. But now I'm not so sure. These are difficult times, and like MacKenzie has said: There are new rules.

Of course it's possible I'm just trying to trick and soothe my overactive conscience.

But, I'm not really fooling myself.

No.

And I know that MacKenzie has special feelings for me, and will accept any suggestion that I care to make about the specific direction of our relationship. She's almost said as much. She's here when I'm ready.

Still, I hesitate.

Maybe it's time to talk to Leroy about this. He's often talked about his wife, grown children, and three grandchildren—all lost in the strikes. How he misses them so much. How he loved them.

But my much younger wife with our relatively active sex life, was, I think, a very different situation from Leroy's—he and his wife had been married for over 55 years. He had prostate surgery years ago and may have been rendered impotent. So, was there even an intimate, sexual component to their relationship? I doubt it, but I'm not sure. But I'm sure he'll understand my feelings, perhaps suggest something.

The weird thing is that recently I've been having trouble visualizing Lauren's face. I have no photos to remember her by. But I still occasionally dream about her terrible murder.

My feelings about Lauren and now MacKenzie are really mixed up.

21

HE-SHE STORIES

They were in the maintenance shed by the generator, Jake handing Leroy tools as he worked on one of the small portable generators they used in the med center. Jake had delayed bringing up his developing relationship with MacKenzie and his conflicted feelings. And he said nothing now. The older man had just finished reading the camp's only collection of Raymond Carver stories: *Where I'm Calling From*. He had kind of a mixed reaction.

"I liked some of them a lot," Leroy said. "But some of the others seem to end … well, much too abruptly, just dropping off. Maybe I'm missing the point with these stories? I do think his style is consistently interesting though, the way he writes. Kind of simple like, you know. For sure, he's not overwriting anything. Reminds me a little of Ernest Hemingway, except the subject matter is so very different. Does that make sense?"

"Yes, it sure does," Jake said. "Early on that style was called minimalism, and it was copied by graduate students as university MFA programs in writing were exploding across the country in the 70s and early 80s. But Carver himself never liked the term— thought his style was misunderstood. I guess the style can fool a casual reader, making him think that the stories themselves are very simple. When, in fact, he's definitely like Hemingway, who he admired greatly. Both wrote anything but simple stories."

"How do you mean, Dr. J?" Leroy asked, with a kind of exaggerated quizzical look, poking fun at Jake who was sounding about ready to go into his English-professor-mode of explaining.

Jake chuckled, acknowledging he understood Leroy was poking fun at him. And it was okay. Nevertheless, he was going to have his say about Raymond Carver—professorial lecturing or not.

Jake sucked in a deep breath and slowly let it trickle back out across his lips, gathering his thoughts—man, he was getting a little bit rusty at this analytical stuff. No canned talks or snappy reactions left in his head anymore.

"Well, like Hemingway, what Carver leaves out is just as important as what's included, perhaps more so. You often have the feeling he explained something that really isn't there on the page at all. 'Why Don't You Dance?' is one of my favorite Carver stories in that book. You know the one where the older guy has stacked all his furniture and stuff out on the lawn, apparently for something like a garage sale?"

Leroy nodded. "I remember the story."

"Well, in that story we get the definite sense that the guy's dysfunctional married life has finally come unglued, that his wife has probably left, and all this is probably related to a drinking problem. The stuff on the lawn is all that remains of their shared but shattered life. But there is really nothing much ever stated about the wife, or a destroyed relationship, or even anything about his excessive drinking."

"That's the similar sense I got from the story, too," Leroy said, nodding thoughtfully. "But none of that is really spelled out, is it?" He looked up at Jake and smiled, his expression perhaps suggesting an impression of unspoken admiration for the technical accomplishment of Carver's writing.

Jake shook his head, and continued: "No, but it's all implied very subtly. Once at the end when the old man tells the girl that the neighbors have seen a lot over here, but nothing like him dancing out on the front lawn with her, right in the middle of all his discarded household belongings. That suggests quite a bit about what went on between him and his wife right there at home, I think."

"Sure, I get all that, and it's really good stuff ... But then the story kind of slips away after the dancing with the young girl, doesn't it? The kids buy a lot of the stuff real cheap, leave, and that's about all there is to it?"

"Well, not quite ..." Jake said, pausing until Leroy looked up at him directly.

"I think if you read it again carefully, it contains what I like to call a *slingshot effect* in the last page or two, the girl figuring out that the old guy was clearing out much more than just furniture and stuff. He was throwing away an entire past and there was quite a bit of unstated pain in him. Remember she says something to him when they're dancing like: 'You must be really desperate'."

"I think I remember that line," Leroy said. "And I suppose it tells a lot that he's practically giving all this stuff away free to the young couple who are just beginning their new life."

"Yes, I think that is a pretty astute observation."

Leroy worked on the generator in silence, and then he chuckled dryly. "I think I read somewhere, maybe in the book's introduction, that Carver was considered the poet of the working class? If so, it was only the *White* working class. My people had lots of his kind of problems, and then a heap more piled on, man."

Jake laughed, and after a moment he said, "It may have said that in the book. But, it's not a good characterization of his situation. He really wasn't a member of the working class for most of his life. Even though working class folks raised him in the northwest. But during most of their marriage, his first wife supported them, while he mostly drank and struggled with his writing. Sure they were always poor because of that—kind of a self-inflicted poverty—and he even declared bankruptcy twice, I think."

Leroy finished his work and wiped his hands. "How would you describe what it was he specifically wrote about in the stories, Dr. J?" The question reflected not even a hint of sarcasm.

Jake considered the question carefully, then said, "Well, he called them *He-She* stories. You know, stories about male-female relationships, usually married couples. Most of his stories anyhow. And often there is alcohol involved in a progressively dysfunctional relationship. And a juggling act to keep everything economically afloat, too. I know his plots are hard to describe to someone— because there is really minimal plotting. You have to carefully read his stories to gain a grasp of the emotional undertone running through them—and that's the key element, I think. He conveyed an emotional undertone of the intense struggles: with alcohol, failed love, infidelity, paying bills, and the whole sense of being impoverished in America in the 60s and 70s. He may be one of our finest short story writers, at least for the latter quarter of the 20th century—"

Jake broke off with a laugh, then added, "Perhaps even better than some of my favorite science fiction short story writers, who I love so dearly, as you know."

Leroy ignored Jake's dismissive and self-derisive throwaway line about his general literary preference. The older man's face had taken on a serious, pondering expression. He rubbed his nose thoughtfully.

"Interesting, son, mighty interesting. Maybe we'll find some more of his work, if we keep our eyes open. I'd like to try some more of his stuff… And maybe some of your top notch SF writers, too. Bet you can talk a little bit about them, too."

Jake said, "I do hope we run across some work by Kim Stanley Robinson and maybe Lucius Shepard sometime, and hopefully a copy of *Flowers for Algernon*. You know how I feel about that book." He'd described a number of times to Leroy about the merits of half a dozen favorite SF writers, the group he lumped together as humanists, and how much he admired Daniel Keyes' great book. Jake knew Leroy would intuitively understand and grasp all these writers' work. No question, the old man was indeed a humanist himself. They just needed to find the right SF books.

Jake frowned, wondering if somewhere in the Bay Area there was still a library left undamaged.

He hoped so. Yes, he truly hoped to find it.

22

JOURNAL ENTRY

BLUE ROCK SPRINGS MEDICAL CAMP
PS: ELEVEN MONTHS

Another recent radiation sickness death—one of Shaw's young persons. Small horde of medicine and food, all tightly rationed now.

The camp focus has slowly shifted to a mode of seeking vengeance for the Desperado attack and murders. Even Dr. Ky has been adversely affected, locked into a kind of taciturn moodiness—rarely talking about anything but current patients and medicine. She still administers top medical aid, having taken on the responsibility of Dr. Olafson's patients in chronic care, but with a little less cheery enthusiasm than before. She appears tired.

Most everyone in camp has volunteered on occasion to accompany the security people, who have unsuccessfully tried to locate the specific band that hit the camp several months ago. They hunt the hunters nightly, trying to capture more prisoners to interrogate.

I admit that I occasionally accompany the hunters. But I still have difficulty with the killing and looting.

23

CHANGES

Several months after the ambush and Jake's life and death struggle with the giant Desperado, Leroy abruptly turned off the lathe and came over to the bench, where the younger man was working with a file on a piece of metal tubing in a vise.

"You have a minute to talk, son?"

"Sure," Jake said, setting down the file. A glance at Leroy's face indicated that the older man wasn't interested in talking about books or discussing literary philosophy this time. "What's on your mind?"

"I'm kinda worried about you and especially all of our young people here in Dr. Ky's medical camp ..." Leroy rubbed the silver stubble on his chin.

"In fact, I guess all of the people here in camp. I see some truly negative changes occurring lately. The changes I see are directly affecting peoples' spiritual well-being. Seems like we are turning into nothing more than a mob of vigilantes or even something worse, if that's possible. Kinda like some of those *bad guys* in *The Road* the boy and his papa always worried so much about, you know what I'm saying ...?"

He stopped and reflected for a long moment, then coughed and cleared his throat. "What did you call it back during our discussions of *The Road*—some kinda regressive behavior, and ata ... ata, something?" His expression and especially his dark eyes reflected his concern even stronger than his words. Leroy almost looked to be in physical pain.

Jake pulled out a folding chair, indicating it was for the older man. He patted his shoulder.

Leroy nodded his thanks, sat, and gathered himself.

Peering directly at Jake, he said in a heavier, more judgmental tone, "Going out and seeking vengeance against others, committing violent acts without a trace of remorse. Now, I'm sorry about your wife, you know that, son." He shook his head sadly. "But I just can't condone what's going on here. I firmly believe the soul or spirit is at the heart of a person's humanity. It can be enhanced or it can be diminished ... not just by your behavior alone, but even by your thoughts and will, which may be more important. You folks are damaging your humanity, diminishing your spirits. You're becoming ..."

He paused again, shook his head, lifted his palms in a sort of surrendering gesture, and looked away from Jake, a frown deepening his etched dark forehead, pulling his silver bushy eyebrows into a *V*. His eyes were slightly moist.

Nodding back at his friend, Jake said in a concerned voice, "I know, and I can't disagree with you at all, Leroy. That's what my humanistic philosophy tells me anyhow. That's what I always believed so solidly ... And yet, here—" He tapped the left side of his chest. "—my heart tells me I have to go out until we find Lauren's killer. I have to do it for her. Can you understand that at all?"

The old man stared at him, but didn't answer the question. Instead, he raised his eyebrows and asked, "Really for her, son ...?" He continued in a voice so soft and gentle that Jake could barely hear. "And what happens if you find this man, son? You kill him? Then, what happens to you, or perhaps more importantly, what happens to your son? What will finding and killing this man accomplish? And finally: Will it be too late for you to seek redemption…? Because you will have to do that, you know."

A lump in his throat choked off Jake's immediate response.

He didn't have any answers to the old man's obviously heartfelt concern for his welfare.

Of course he was aware of the change in the nature of the camp's young people. They seemed to be enthusiastic and enjoying hunting Desperadoes more than their stated camp mission of searching for food and medicine. No, *enjoy* wasn't quite the right word. If you asked them, they would say they were only doing what they had to do—following Shaw's stated philosophy: being proactive, pre-emptive, and just protecting the camp. So maybe most of them weren't really enjoying the killing of Desperadoes, but felt duty-bound to Shaw's leadership and goals.

They all definitely had hard edges now, and facial expressions lacking any real affect, including his son, Luke—especially Luke. Almost a sociopathic cast. And their eyes? Oh, their cold eyes. He shivered thinking about their dead eyes.

Jake knew Leroy was absolutely right. They were all on a path of no return…even him.

And he also knew that Leroy was also right about salvation. At some point in the near future he would have to seek redemption.

24

JOURNAL ENTRIES

BLUE ROCK SPRINGS MEDICAL CAMP

PS: ONE YEAR

We've regressed into little more than a pack of thoughtless, unfeeling at-tack dogs.

We go out nightly now, robbing and killing Desperadoes, only half-heartedly trying to take prisoners, the young people having lost sight of that part of the newest goals. It is almost impossible to keep survivors alive after most of our ferocious attacks and ambushes.

But last night, with Shaw's intervention, I managed to get a badly wound-ed prisoner back to camp.

He's told us where to find the leader of the band who attacked our med camp many months ago.

The Iron Triangle in Richmond!

Maybe we can end this obsessive and soul crippling drive for revenge soon.

Closure for me?

I hope so. I am weary—my spirit diminished as Leroy has observed.

I am trapped in a vicious downward spiral.

25

A BOY AND HIS PAPA

Jake and Luke ate together, then lingered at the table in the mess hall—an unusual occurrence. Luke normally gulped his food down and left quickly with the other security people, anxious to go out on another of their nightly training exercises or death patrols.

"I've been wanting to talk to you for some time now," Jake said uneasily, reaching over and gripping his son's forearm before he could stand.

"Okay." Luke sat back down.

"You know that Mike Shaw and you young people have kind of lost sight of what Dr. Ky wants you to do? The camp mission?"

Luke didn't say anything, his face more or less a dead pan.

Jake continued: "I understand wanting to find Mom's killer, the people who raided our camp and caused so much misery for all of us. I want to find them, too. Bring them to justice for their act. But you see that doesn't have much to do with what's been going on lately…"

He looked away, his son's penetrating stare disturbing his train of thought.

Jake remembered Leroy's words of concern for him.

He was able to continue, but in an almost apologetic voice said, "Yes, I go out sometimes with you hoping to catch the man responsible and avenge Lauren's murder. That's my intent. But the killing of everyone we come into contact with is just not, not the right, you see…"

He shook his head, his gaze locking again with his son's.

"No, it's just not right, son. And you young folks are caught up in it, almost seeming to be relishing all the unnecessary bloodshed—"

"What do you mean?" Luke said sharply, sitting up straighter and leaning across the table closer to his father, and almost poking him in the chest with a probing finger. "What are *you* saying to me here? Who are you to make any kind of archaic moral judgments of what we do, what's right and wrong now?"

Jake was dumfounded by the intensity of his son's accusative tone and the expressed cold anger.

"I-I … well," he stammered and frowned. "I-I admit I go along on some of the hunts, but I never participate in any of the executions, never—"

"I'm not talking about *that*," Luke said, his glare almost hateful.

Jake took a deep breath and asked, "What are you talking about then?"

"How long has Mother been dead?"

"Let's see," Jake began to answer, initially taken aback by the question and it's bitter tone. "It's been about three or I guess actually four—"

"That's right, only a few months."

"I don't understand what you're driving at."

The young man nodded, a forced smile on his face. "Oh, you don't, huh?"

"What is it, Luke? What's bothering you about me? What have I done?"

"My mother has been dead only a few months and my father is repeatedly going to her grave with another woman and … and—"

His words suddenly choked off, with almost a sob, but the full implication of the unspoken words lingered, and were crystal clear.

Jake couldn't believe it … His son was suggesting that he and MacKenzie were having sex up at Blue Rock Springs, the act so near to Lauren's grave a desecration. More than just suggesting, he was accusing—

"No," Jake said, shaking his head emphatically, a rush of anger washing over him. "That is not true."

"Yes, it is," Luke said, leaning closer and peering intently into his father's eyes. "Yes, you *are*. And it isn't just me who knows that either. Almost everyone in camp knows what's going on up there at my mother's gravesite. You and that woman are fooling no one. You understand me? No one."

Jake was astonished, speechless, unable to verbally defend himself. All he could do was vigorously shake his head.

Luke poked his father twice in the chest, as if it were a sharply punishing blade of steel.

"So, man, don't you be doing any preaching to me about morality or my behavior or my friends' behavior. Do you get it?" He leaned back, withdrawing his finger, but maintaining a painful, steely-eyed look on his face.

There was an awkward silence.

Jake weakly shook his head.

What could he say? Had Luke peered deep into the dark corners of his soul, perhaps uncovering the lustful intent at the heart of his feelings for MacKenzie? What he might soon do? What he wanted to do?

He had no defense. Guilty as charged.

The young man finally stood. "I have nothing more to say to you," he said, his voice heavy with distaste, as if he'd rendered a guilty verdict. "Ever again."

The conclusiveness of the last two words echoed silently.

Jake remained sitting at the table and watched his son get up, dump his tray, and walk out of the mess tent without looking back.

Everyone in camp knows? he thought, his conscience stirring.

Knows what? Even if it was true deep in his thoughts, his sexual fantasies? And maybe in MacKenzie's, too? They'd done nothing … But was it so obvious the direction they were headed? Perhaps, more importantly, were they wrong? Was it indeed too soon? How long before it was right?

After a minute or two still sitting and pondering at the table, Jake sucked in a deep breath and stood. None of this was really fair, he decided. MacKenzie and him were guilty of nothing more than being human. Who had the right to judge them for that? Shaw? His security people? Luke?

He snorted, realizing the answer was apparently *the entire camp*.

Jake carried his tray to the garbage can of soapy hot water, feeling a tight, dull knot in his chest.

Just at that moment, he recalled that his friend, Leroy, had never said a word to him about MacKenzie, not once—his friend, the true moral compass of the community, hadn't condemned him for what everyone considered was such an obvious, glaring impropriety.

No, indeed, not the entire camp. Not Leroy.

His heavy heart lightened as he exited the mess tent into the breezy night air.

26

ATAVISM

They crossed silently into the area bordered by three rusty merging railroad lines on mounts wearing burlap socks. They dismounted and moved cautiously in the night, Luke and three other archers leading the way. Ahead, in the darkness, they could just make out the single boxcar... and a lone shadowy figure.

Luke stopped and let fly a notched arrow, hitting the single sentry, who slumped against the back of the car. The entire group efficiently fanned out silently, weapons at the ready.

But there was no one else outside to confront them, only the dead sentry.

Shaw and Jake led the squad to the closed boxcar, each taking a position on either side of the door. Shaw signaled a young man to slide open the door.

He did it with a jerk, the door crashing against the stop and the *bang* echoing loudly in the night.

But there was no sudden gunfire or any resistance of any kind coming from inside.

And outside, the iron triangle was as quiet as a graveyard at midnight.

Cautiously looking in, they found only one man lying on some filthy bedding, attended by an older woman apparently frightened out of her wits.

Shaw covered Jake as he hopped into the boxcar and carefully approached the couple. Keeping his shotgun trained on them, Jake gestured with his head for the woman to move away. She scooted clumsily toward the opened door.

He then stood over the man, who stared back up at Jake. From his son's previous description, Jake barely recognized the bald man; for he was thin, hallow-eyed, and obviously sick. Only the check mark scar on his cheek confirmed the identification. Jake kneeled, pulled out his Bowie knife and placed the tip at the Desperado's throat. His hand trembled. "You cut my wife's throat. An eye for an eye."

"Go ahead, man," the Desperado said feebly, "you'd be doing me a favor." He stared back at Jake, his face expressionless, his eyes cold, flat, and already dead.

For a moment or two, Jake hesitated, remembering his recurring dream of revenge; but then, almost at the same time, he heard Leroy's voice clearly in his head: *What happens to you then ...?*

And he breathed in the man's sour, sweaty stench.

He shuddered.

Abruptly, Jake withdrew the knife blade and stood back up.

"No, I'm not like you," he said to the supine man, shaking his head. "Not at all. Your spirit shriveled up as your humanity died long ago—"

Swish—Thunk.

The man gasped wetly, gurgling blood, an arrow buried deep in his throat.

Stunned, Jake managed to turn, staring out the boxcar door, where Luke stood silhouetted, with his bow in hand. The young man's pale face lacked any affect at all; his eyes, too, were stone cold, flat, and dead.

27

MORE LOSS

When Jake rode back into camp and dismounted, Will, the nurse, was waiting for him at the corral gate.

"You need to come with me right now," the young man said to Jake, leading him quickly over to the main med tent.

At the entryway, Jake paused and looked into the lighted area and saw his friend, Leroy, lying on his back on a gurney, Dr. Ky at his side.

She quickly stepped outside to meet Jake. In a barely audible voice she said, "I'm sorry, Jacob, but Leroy doesn't look good at all. He's had a serious heart attack. I'm pretty sure he requires immediate bypass surgery to even hope to survive this—"

"And?" Jake said, looking at her with raised eyebrows.

She shook her head sadly. "We aren't equipped for that kind of operation. I'm not qualified either."

He looked over at his friend, who appeared to be asleep, but even with an oxygen mask, his breathing was heavily labored.

"I've given him morphine," Dr. Ky said. "Despite his serious pain, when they brought him into the center, he asked for you, Jacob. But you were unfortunately gone with the security people. I told him you would visit him shortly."

With a guilty twinge, Jake swallowed, and asked, "How long does he have?"

"I'm not sure," Hang said. "This initial attack should've killed him. He's a tough old guy, but barely hanging on now. He'll go anytime, sooner rather than later. Could be a few hours."

Jake nodded, and left the doctor at the tent entrance. He made his way over to his friend's side, feeling terrible and put his hand gently atop the older man's rough, dark hand.

Leroy's eyes fluttered open.

With an obvious effort, he reached up and pulled down the oxygen mask.

"Son," he said hoarsely with a thin smile, his eyes and face tired. "Find him?"

"Yes," Jake said.

The smile slowly stiffened on Leroy's face. He pulled up the mask and closed his eyes as if he were going back to sleep. But Jake knew he was still listening.

Jake sucked in a deep breath and described the epiphany he experienced while holding the knife to the Desperado's throat. How he stood up, and what he'd said...

The old man's eyes fluttered open, his gaze clear.

"But then Luke shot him with an arrow," Jake said sadly, taking Leroy's hand. He squeezed. "For me it's over now. And you were right, I feel nothing but a sense of deep remorse ... For both the death of the nameless Desperado, but more importantly for the death of something in my own son. His loss of something deep inside himself there at that train..."

He paused, his eyes wet and full now.

In a soft voice, Jake continued: "Maybe I can make amends for my part in all this. Start my redemption. I hope so. There is much good to be done here for Dr. Ky. And you have to get well quickly, because I need a supervisor ... and a good friend to guide me. Maybe you can help me earn some, some kind of ... salvation?"

Leroy pulled down the oxygen mask again.

For a few moments it was quiet in the tent, only the sound of Leroy's labored breathing.

Jake watched his friend fight for his life. The older man's lips quivered slightly, wanted to say something more.

What?

Jake leaned over and bent close.

"And your boy?" Leroy murmured ever so softly. "What about Luke ... his ... heart ... and his redemption ... his path to ...?"

The question faded off before the old man could complete the sentence. But Jake understood what was unsaid.

Dr. Ky touched Jake's shoulder, shaking her head. "Enough for now, Jacob; let him rest," she advised sternly.

Jake squeezed Leroy's hand again before he said, "I'll see you in the morning, my friend."

≈ – ≈

Leroy died an hour and a half later.

≈ – ≈

The next morning Jake buried his respected friend in the blue crags, close to his wife. H prayed over them both for forgiveness.

28

THE TEN-POINT BUCK

For three nights in a row, Jake had the old dream again about the big buck curiously staring down at them when they stopped on Highway 121 northeast of Napa.

Only each time now, as the black snow began piling higher and higher around him and Luke, he again lost the boy's icy hand. But despite a frantic search, he could never find the hand again. The boy was gone ... And the snow piled up around Jake until he began to suffocate. He stretched up on tiptoes to try and keep his nose clear, but it was no use—

At that point he would awaken. Soaked in a cold, clammy sweat, and gasping for his breath.

A nightmare that always left him terribly shaken.

But it helped him make his decision.

29

JOURNAL ENTRY

BLUE ROCK SPRINGS MEDICAL CAMP
PS: ONE YEAR, TWO MONTHS

I have lost my wife.
I have lost my son.
I have lost my best friend.
Perhaps, I have even lost a large share of my own humanity.
All I have left is a remembered potential epigraph for my unfinished book: When a man loses the ability to love and care about others, he has lost everything of value.
I don't want that.

Tomorrow, I will abandon this camp of sorrow, begin a long journey east and perhaps south, and search for whatever redemption may be possible for me out there in the wasteland.
I know it will be difficult, but I must try.

30

THE ATTEMPT TO CROSS OVER A RAZOR'S EDGE

Although he left a brief note of explanation and apologetic statement of his feelings for MacKenzie, Jacob Zachary mysteriously
disappeared from the Med camp at Blue Rock Springs, and was not
heard from again around the Bay Area Ruins for many years.

But two plus decades later, shortly after the end of the Food Wars,
it was told around the campfires among the growing numbers of
herders and farmers in and around the Great Central Desert of a
legendary figure, a man they sometimes reverentially called St.
Zach, who wandered the desert in a plain brown cloak, teaching
children to read and keeping the cultural flame of humanity alive,
preaching moral lessons from the olden times, carrying his large
journals in his backpack, and telling stories ... oh, such sad glorious
tales of the developing history of the place known by then as Cal
Wild.

PART 2

THE CRIMSON MAN

[TWENTY-FIVE YEARS LATER]

"He thought that in the history of the world it might even be that there was more punishment than crime but he took small comfort from it."
– Cormac McCarthy, *The Road*

1

SAN JO TRADE-OFF

The Bay Area fog had quickly settled to ground level like a rapidly deflating cloud, but dispelling none of the early evening mugginess that had clung to the San Jo Trade-off all day. The blanketed humidity did little to smother the enthusiasm of the vocal buyers and sellers though. It was only 8:00 P.M., and already many bartered with tired, red faces and scratchy, hoarse voices ... but still loudly.

At the remote northern edge of the trade-off, just beyond the smoky barbeque pit area, a solitary tall figure stood, quietly watching the active trading scene. The shadows dancing from the flaring light cast by the fire of the closest fifty-five gallon drum did little to mask his bared facial features. The man would have been easily described by a stranger as fairly young and good-looking, *if* not for the facial disfigurement, which still left him ruggedly handsome, but scary and dangerous appearing. The scar—a razor-thin, white welt—began at the corner of his right eyebrow and trailed down his right cheek and ended at his square jaw line. Even with the ugly scar and his hard-edged, no nonsense expression, he appeared somewhat younger than his forty-three years.

Pulled down as if shading his gaze, he wore a ragged black

baseball cap with an almost completely faded orange *SF* logo. A long duster clung to his robust build, the black and tan stripes also faded and covered with dust. Bunched around his throat was a pale blue and green bandanna, the bright colors contrasting sharply with his attire's drabness and his severe expression.

The tall man had an elegant sounding name, Lucas Zachary; but no one here at the trade-off and few, perhaps only two or three of the people back at the nearby Raiders' stronghold, had ever heard him use that name.

Twenty-five years earlier, Mike Shaw, the Raiders' chief, had led a group of ten young security people away from Blue Rock Springs Med Camp, down to the present location in the San Jo Ruins below old Silicon Valley. A huge bunker-like sturdy basement and garage hidden under the fallen ruins of a warehouse, with individual comfortable living cubicles, a common cooking/eating area, and even an outside but walled private courtyard that also contained a small infirmary and access to adjoining horse stables. The compound was accessed by either one of two maze-like dark tunnels, the outside entrances concealed among the stacked and burnt-over rubble of the old industrial site—red skull and crossbones signs prominently displayed all around the sector to scare off potential scavengers. Over the last twenty-five years, at this secret, sheltered base, Shaw had gradually increased the size of his warrior band to around fifty strong. He'd led them out on carefully selected lightning raids against other usually larger groups, but most successfully during the sixteen- or eighteen-year span of the Food Wars.

All of the original Raider members, except for Mike Shaw, Lucas Zachary, and MacKenzie Ross were gone now, dead or replaced by newer recruits. In private, MacKenzie would often call the younger man Luke or Lucas, and she always thought of him in those terms; but for a long time now, he had been known to his colleagues as *Big Cat* or more commonly as just *Cat*. During a raid, the gifted bowman and rugged warrior was indeed as quick, as stealthily quiet, and every bit as deadly as his namesake; some even said only half-jokingly that he possessed the mythical feline nine lives because he'd survived numerous severe wounds, as his badly scarred face attested.

Nearby to where Cat stood, a vendor held up a steaming kebob from his jury-rigged grill and asked loudly, "Hungry, Brother?"

Cat closed his eyes momentarily, savoring the tantalizing smell of the seller's spicy roasted meat. He was tempted, but he didn't want to barter away for food any of the five cigarillos in his sealed package of Invasors. So, he blinked, reluctantly shook his head, and looked out again around the acre or so of crowded, noisy activity beyond the barbequing area set-off on the northern perimeter of the trading area.

The trade-off occupied the faded, broken asphalt of the northwestern end of Runway 3, once an integral part of San Jose International Airport—its name all but forgotten. The surrounding buildings and the other runways were heavily damaged during the Strikes and subsequent fires, most of the useable debris long gone now. For the weekend trade-off, vendors had setup an array of pre-cooked food, fresh produce, and dry goods on the dusty, broken blacktop. The merchandise was displayed on simple blanket layouts on the ground, along shelves in gaily painted semi-permanent plywood booths, at scarred tables in temporary stalls hastily assembled from building scraps, and some even remained in bundled stacks and piles in the beds of a few parked wagons. At the far southeastern end of the runway remnant was a thick stand of young eucalyptus, their distinctive strong medicinal smell lingering in the mist, which was beginning to slowly drift northerly. The fast growing gum trees had become the dominant species around most of the Bay Area Ruins in the last quarter century, quickly replacing the oak, pine, cypress, madrone, and other native growth flattened by the Strikes or burnt over shortly thereafter by the devastating series of fires that raged across the entire area.

Cat smiled wryly after looking over the general attire of the buyers and sellers at the trade-off.

After twenty some years it appeared everyone had finally received the message: *It is extremely hazardous to move about outside in the wasteland unprotected.* All here in this trade-off crowd of maybe seventy-five to a hundred people were appropriately bundled-up in the now traditional survivor mode: some kind of buttoned-down or zipped-up long coat completely covering body and legs; sturdy footwear, preferably high-topped; a cap, helmet, or brimmed hat of some type usually pulled down around the ears; and at least half in the crowd wore their neck bandannas or scarves pulled up to protect their lower face and nose. Everyone ... *except* for a few thin youngsters, who were wasteland defectives wearing little more than rags, their skinny arms and legs covered only with open sores. During his careful survey of the crowd, Cat had spotted a pair of chuckleheads, a quasimodo, and two gargoyles, all five defective youngsters roaming about the trade-off and begging aggressively.

Most survivors, even those heavily bundled-up, wisely avoided the known local *hot* areas—the most infamous, the L'More Groundstar, east and inland eight or ten miles from the South Bay—a meltdown still heavily contaminated this long after the Strikes. But there were also massive amounts of dangerous secondary pollutants lurking in or around the factories, laboratories, and warehouse ruins, some of it hidden under debris—especially up around the Silicon Valley area just a few miles to the north. Even before the Strikes, the Bay Area atmosphere had been heavily polluted and beginning to remain permanently altered; so that now, U.V. poisoning from the sun was another added major hazard to any skin foolishly exposed for even short periods of time when moving about outside.

One of the defective beggars, a chucklehead, not more than seven or eight years old, had wandered over closer to where Cat stood, and made a feeding motion with his hand to his drooling mouth, grunting: "Ugh, ugh, ugh."

Cat shook his head, sternly shooing away the rail-thin child.

He was sympathetic to their hopeless plight, but he knew from past experience that if he offered even one of the youngsters a scrap of meat, he'd have all five of the defectives closely following him about the trade-off. Tonight he didn't have extra time to deal with that sort of nuisance.

Curious, he made his way slowly nearer to the closest stalls, booths, wagons, and blankets, keeping a rough mental inventory of the kinds and quantity of produce and other foodstuffs, as he worked his way through the crowd, which was mostly circling clockwise. There seemed to be a little more and better variety of produce available since he'd last visited the site about two weeks ago, he thought, even a few luxury items like hothouse berries. For quite some time now, Cat had realized that survivors were finding more safe places in the wastelands to grow produce, even outside of hothouses, and safely raise their livestock, although finding ample clean, unpolluted water remained a major issue. Fresh food was becoming, if not plentiful, at least available for barter.

He stopped abruptly, staring at something that caught his eye.

A pair of sellers, both wearing clean and blue dusters heavily decorated with their own crafted specialty items, had a table well-stocked with an array of colorful charms, talismans, and amulets. The male seller was loudly hawking one of the more gaudy items made of flesh-colored plastic and glass backing an almond-shaped polished azure rock: "... Yes, and additionally these *Eyes* have been found very effective in warding off not only bad luck in general, but as protection against Jake's Shakes." Cat knew the seller referred to a kind of neurological affliction, which was found among some farmers, herders, and shepherds staying in proximity for long periods of time around hot places like the Groundstar.

He looked over the group of ten or twelve potential customers, all of them wearing some kind of long coat heavily decorated with various good luck charms—some even rough duplicates of those for sale on the table.

Cat sighed to himself skeptically, reminded that many folks believed that not only could a special charm ward off evil, but some of the more elaborate—and naturally the more expensive—amulets, if worn during pregnancy, protected babies against birth defects. Of course that was all ridiculous superstition, but it was not unlike the commonly held belief that parents of defective children were being punished for some past sin. There was, in fact, a popular religious cult leader in the Oakland Hills, Ezekiel Sun, who regularly preached to large crowds that not strictly observing the Sabbath and the Ten Commandments could result in a number of maladies, including giving birth to defective babies.

Strike survivors were now plagued as much by their own irrational fears and beliefs as by real environmental hazards.

Cat didn't say anything, only smiled. These two sellers were doing a creditable business, trading a finely-crafted brightly-feathered charm for two dozen eggs, a polished green rock amulet for several large bunches of carrots, and an *Eye* for a pound bag of dried kidney beans and two pounds of fresh onions. This was the first time he'd seen the long coat charms—usually homemade and traded privately—offered publically at a trade-off. Good for them and their free enterprise.

In due course, he turned away and let his gaze casually wander across the blacktop to several pens and a pair of small corrals near the trees, where sellers were offering a little livestock, including chickens, ducks, and even a few small pigs, two swayback horses, and an old milk cow. Times had indeed changed, he thought. For years after the Strikes and all through the long and bloody Food Wars, everyone hoarded all foodstuffs they could secure in hand. No one raised or grew anything.

"Hey, man, you holdin' salt, alky, or 'bacca to trade?" asked a sharp-eyed vendor seated nearby with a blanket display offering what appeared to be strings of dried jerky. He obviously suspected that Cat was a well-heeled Desperado, probably in possession of good exchange items for trade—salt, any kind of bottled liquor or moonshine, and even the poorest-grade tobacco were common prime barter items. Cat absently shook his head, pushing his expensive box of Invasors deeper down in his duster pocket, and beginning to wander again. The blended tobacco and marijuana cigarillos came across the border from the Latin Confederation—a very expensive and a highly prized but rarely available barter item over most of the central and northern wasteland.

Ahead a few paces, he stopped and glanced down at a table served by a bare-faced, attractive young woman offering what appeared to be some kind of rich cream-colored, processed food laid out and covered with a clean white cloth ... On closer inspection, he realized it was some type of fresh cheese—generous slices or a whole quarter round available for trade. How long had it been since he'd seen any of that?

He hadn't tasted freshly made cheese since ... Holy shit! Maybe *once* early on at the med camp at Blue Rock Springs at least twenty-six years ago, but for sure not since back before the Strikes at his home in Berkeley. The ripe, pungent smell made Cat's mouth water. But again, he shook his head. He'd actually eaten an early dinner in the late afternoon back at camp table.

In a few hours Cat and his cohorts would be part of a raiding party heading up to the lower East Bay to hit The Fist, one of the largest Desperado bands, who had a heavily fortified cave stronghold in the foothills near the Milpitas Ruins east off old I-680—the band reputed to be sitting on over a hundred pounds of high grade salt. A midnight attack had been carefully planned and rehearsed during the past week. Cat, and all of the other Raiders, were prohibited from eating or drinking alcohol four hours prior to such an attack by Shaw's long list of posted rules entitled *Raider Discipline*—the eating part rarely, if ever, enforced though. Nevertheless, he was hoarding his Invasors, not trading them away for any food, no matter how savory, when he wasn't hungry.

Cat had hiked a mile down the trade-off to work off a little nervous energy before mounting up for the ride and raid around the South Bay, an hour and a half from now; but he was also curious to take a good look at what was now being offered for trade and especially the various quantities of foodstuffs.

Trade-offs had begun springing up all around the wasteland like weeds in the last few years, including several smaller ones on the fringe of the Great Central Valley Desert to the east. He found it more than curiously interesting that people all over the wasteland were growing and raising enough fresh food that they now had a little surplus for trade. There were even a few hothouses being erected, most of those close around the San Jo Ruins. Almost all past food supplies—canned, packaged, or preserved—had been violently fought over and controlled during the eighteen or so years of the Food Wars by the Desperadoes. Only five of these bands— disciplined militia units—had survived the Wars, and now, six or seven years later, still called the greater Bay Area home. Shaw's Raiders, probably the smallest in number of actual warriors, had in recent years been forced to roam and raid as far south as the Gilroy and Salinas Ruins, to the east along the I-680 corridor and up to the once prosperous communities of Concord and Walnut Creek— nothing but a burnt-over part of the wasteland remaining there. In the past, they'd made a few forays much farther north, even as far as the Sacto Ruins, where a small but fierce group had been formed from mostly gang banger crew remnants after the Strikes. Sacramento, with its two nearby air bases and the State Capitol, had been a prime Strike target and was not a very lucrative raiding area—not much left to fight over after the Strikes and a series of recurring fires. Not enough anyhow to face the fanatic ferocity of *Hermanos de Sangre*.

Cat continued to wander like most of the other buyers into the heaviest congested prime produce area, his eye attracted to the attractive colorful displays of vegetables and fresh fruit, including bright crimson strawberries, indigo plums, yellow pears, orange carrots, scarlet tomatoes, and a few golden apricots.

This small San Jo Trade-off did not compare to the much larger San Fran Trade-off thirty-five miles to the north that sprung into

THE CONFESSIONS OF ST. ZACH

existence about five years ago, when the Company first appeared in the San Fran Ruins and began erecting the Shield.

He'd been up to the San Fran Trade-off at least a dozen times during the last several years, where they offered a much greater variety of produce and even fresh and dried meat, including a bounty of safe to consume seafood. There were also all kinds of games of chance, staged prizefights, and other kinds of duels, many finely crafted goods, fishing gear, comfortable leather footwear, a wide selection of ordinance, and usually at night at least one musical or dramatic performance staged—a spectator-packed event. By now, the San Fran Trade-off had become permanent and sprawled out over at least four or five acres, with evening crowds seven nights a week ranging from four to five hundred and fifty visitors. An exciting place to go—people coming from as far as the foothills of the Sierra-Nevada Mountains on the other side of the Great Central Valley Desert to visit the San Fran Trade-off.

Cat, MacKenzie, Shaw, and a few other senior Raiders had first gone up to the San Fran Ruins about four years ago to see the progress of the domed city. Up until that time, no one had seen much of anything above a thirty-five foot high plasteel restraining wall except for the tops of operating cranes, only able to hear the myriad sounds of various heavy equipment working around the clock, as the mass of construction workers and engineers laid out the great foundation base and massive first level. But on subsequent trips, Cat watched the curved plasteel ribs of the gigantic structure slowly rise above the wall and into clear view. Up, up, and up the intricate skeleton rose. And on his last trip around nine months ago, the scope of the finished project hit him, almost stealing his breath away. A gigantic ebony half dome, glistening in the sun, and rising at least six stories above the San Fran Ruins, perhaps rivaled in architectural magnificence only by the memory of the legendary Golden Gate Bridge—broken in half now, badly burned over, and in rusty ruins.

Nearly as impressive as the marvelous Shield, but in an ominous more personal way, was the size of the highly disciplined security force that had manned the restraining wall and effectively patrolled its perimeter—the black-clad and -masked Companymen. They were heavily armed with modern laser-guided automatic weapons and RPGs, some manning machinegun and rocket emplacements at strategic gun ports along the plasteel wall; and it was reported that they even had access to SSMs and SAMs, even though throughout the Bay Area wasteland only the Company itself had functioning armored vehicles or aircraft—including their impressive dark hummers. And at their belts, each dreaded Companyman carried a coiled come-along-stun, which would become feared throughout the wasteland as the years passed—the symbol of Company oppression, used to silently stun, completely overcome, subdue, and help lead inside the Shield the occasional hapless wastelander. Usually one who had run afoul of a Shield Resident in some way or another at a trade-off.

The spectacular project had been conceived, designed, funded, and built by the Company, a mysterious organization that had suddenly appeared unannounced in the Ruins and off-loaded tons and tons of heavy equipment, building supplies, and construction specialists from a seemingly endless number of hummers shuttling loads from at least a half dozen huge transport ships anchored in the Bay.

Naturally, rumors immediately circulated among wastelanders about the true nature of the Company. The most bizarre speculation was that elements of Company management came from the stars, the leadership composed entirely of humanoid aliens; and the masters were served by the Companymen, an army of ruthless, inhuman androids lurking behind their black uniforms and facemasks. But after a time the more logical, reasoned out, and widely held belief was that the Company was a very rich multi-national conglomerate of Canadian-Quebecois and Japanese interests. Over the last fifteen or so years reports had eventually begun trickling back to the Bay Area from travelers—mostly from the Latin Confederation to the south or Canada from the north—that confirmed that at least two countries, Canada and Japan, had almost completely escaped massive damage by the initial missile Strikes or the subsequent rounds of retaliatory Strikes that had leveled most of the U.S., the northern two thirds of South America, all of the Mid-East, and done serious damage to the remainder of the mid-21st Century industrial world, including Europe, China, and Russia.

Whatever was true about the post-holocaust state of the world, Cat knew that the omnipotent Company was now involved in erection of four more—much smaller—Shields up and down the west coast of North America: one right in the heart of the San Diego Ruins on the southern border, another a mile southwest of the Santa Barbara Ruins, a very small one inland of the once coastal town of Mendocino, and a final one way to the north at Vancouver near the Canadian border.

After confronting the much superior force of Companymen, Desperado band activity had immediately ceased in and around the San Fran Ruins. It was claimed in the Ruins that the finished Shield was a completely contained city now, accommodating hundreds of thousands of well-healed residents. Probably the bulk coming from Canada and Japan, but also significant numbers of wealthy immigrants coming from heavily damaged industrial countries around the world. There were even a few Bay Area wastelanders who possessed the necessary gold, silver, or jewels to barter for one of the very expensive lifetime habitation contracts. They probably most resembled pre-Strike wealthy time-sharers initially looking for some exotic, out of the way locations. But now, over twenty-six years post-Strike, residents probably desired a safe, secure, and unpolluted environment with lots of amenities. And apparently inside San Fran Shield was just that kind of wonderful place to live.

Cat kept moving around the trade-off as he thought about a life of opulent ease and excitement inside San Fran or one of the other Shields.

He stopped suddenly at a small card table display of books,

maybe fifteen or twenty total, all carefully wrapped in protective plastic. Both he and MacKenzie enjoyed reading books and picked them up whenever possible, but they were scarce items now, most libraries and bookstores consumed long ago in the old raging fires. They had been lucky to some extent. Although he wasn't aware of it at the time, MacKenzie had rescued at least a dozen good quality books from the Blue Rock Springs library and had packed them along with her other stuff during the exodus from the Med Camp to the San Jo Ruins compound—

There, at the right corner of the vendor's table, he saw an un-covered, larger book.

Scuffed-up black leather with three small silver initials were stamped across the bottom: **JAZ**. Cat thought he recognized the journal for sure, and especially the initials—it looked like one of the three he had given his father for his birthday in their life before the Strikes. He'd almost forgotten that time.

He pointed at the journal, and the vendor handed it to him.

"Sell it cheap," the seller said with a big fake smile.

Cat ran his hands over the worn cover, then opened the jour-nal and flipped through the first couple of pages. No question, it was his father's handwriting. For a few minutes, he continued flip-ping through the pages, realizing the entire book was filled with dated accounts. The entries were recorded during the year they'd lived up at Blue Rock Springs Med Camp … *except* for the last third or so. These entries were written at various small survivor's camps somewhere east of the Bay Area and then much farther south in what was now being called The Southern Dry. Cat *had* to have and read this journal, especially the last forty-five or fifty pages.

His father had suddenly disappeared from the Med Camp, about three or four months before Shaw decided to lead his securi-ty people to the South Bay, shortly after Dr. Ky had died unexpect-edly, apparently contracting a virus from a patient that proved to be deadly.

Cat stared at the seller and asked casually, "How much?"

THE CONFESSIONS OF ST. ZACH

"What do you have to trade?" the vendor said, eyeing Cat with a guarded expression.

"Hmm," Cat mumbled, fingering the box of five cigarillos and debating.

He could just *take* the journal, give the vendor some blood on the end of his nose for trade if he resisted. And maybe he would have done that sometime in the past. But he'd gradually changed in some respects since he and MacKenzie began living together. Over the last eighteen years, her gentle and loving nature had gradually mellowed him out and even had an impact on his interpersonal relations a little … except during raids. So he gave the seller a silent pass for now—no strawberry jam on the end of his nose.

"How about an Invasor?"

The seller's eyes suddenly widened and brightened, before he got a grip on his avaricious emotions. He coughed, clearing his throat.

"Ah … three would work much better for me, Brother," he said with a sly wink. "That diary is a valuable historical document, you know—"

"Okay, two," Cat interrupted, his tone growing brittle, his negotiating patience quickly wearing thin.

The vendor stared momentarily at Cat's intimidating, scarred features; then he said in an ingratiating tone, "Show me the box, please, Brother. I have to get genuine cigarillos, you know, no fakes." A wide greedy smile was plastered to his face.

Cat removed the box from his duster pocket. He held it up for view, slowly tore open the still sealed packet in front of the seller, and pulled two of the thick, brown cigarillos out of the long, narrow package. Before he handed them over to the vendor, he held them under his own nose for a brief moment, inhaled, nodded, and smiled thinly. "Ahhh …"

The seller greedily took the cigarillos and duplicated Cat's appreciative maneuver, holding them under his own uncovered nose for several seconds. He closed his eyes and inhaled even more deeply. He finally blinked, then grinned almost lasciviously and nodded vigorously. "You gotta deal, Brother. They's the genuine article all right! The book is all yours. And if you want to trade any of those three others in that package, I'll make you a super deal on anything I have here at my table. Any of these books at all. You name which ones."

Cat picked up the black journal he'd momentarily set on the edge of the table when he'd first dug out the Invasors. He didn't respond to the vendor's additional offer, only shook his head and walked away with his purchase tucked firmly under his arm. He felt elated, almost giddy by the surprising find of one of his father's journals and its purchase. He stopped and returned to the table.

"I don't know who you bought this journal from. But there are two others just like it. You find them, save them for me, and I'll trade you an entire package of Invasors for the pair."

The vendor nodded enthusiastically. "I remember the trader… Came from the south, I think. You bet I'll watch for him. Get them other journals, if he has them in his possession."

Again Cat walked away, holding the journal in his hands.

2

A DP

A few minutes later, he'd left the crowded trade-off proper, anxious to return to the Raider bunker with perhaps an hour free reading time to get a less rushed look at the journal; hurrying along, he'd advanced to the outer edge of the shadows cast by the light from the last of the lit fifty-five gallon drums—

Cat stopped dead in his tracks, just short of running into a quiet figure lurking under a tree in the darkness, almost causing him to drop his father's journal.

It was a man.

But like no man Cat had ever seen before. Oh, no.

The lurker was not bundled-up; instead he was dressed surprisingly in the old-fashion, pre-Strike manner—a raggedy gray sweatshirt with cut off sleeves and well-worn tan shorts, his head, lower arms, lower legs, and face all bare and readily exposed to the dangerous environment. But, no doubt, the most distinctive, startling aspect of his appearance was that every inch of his exposed skin, including all of his uncovered arms, legs, and face, appeared to have been bathed in fresh thick blood.

Dumbfounded, Cat stared, his pulse speeding up.

The figure was indeed a scary… crimson apparition.

But he couldn't be a ghost, Cat decided. Could he?

No! Of course not.

This was a living, breathing man of relatively small stature.

Cat felt unnerved staring at the stained man, retaining a thick lump in his throat.

The Crimson Man stared back at Cat, who remained too taken aback to even utter a delayed gasp of shock—forget offering a greeting of some kind. He let his held breath ease quietly across his lips. He was surprised by the man's appearance, but Cat soon regained control of himself, and by taking several slow breaths he managed to calm his elevated pulse…

And at that point, it dawned on Cat exactly what he was actually looking at, so amazed.

This had to be one of the *Dyed People* he'd heard so much about the last time he and Shaw had visited the San Fran Ruins. Someone had told them that the Company was punishing residents who broke the law or were malcontents by first rendering a formal Judgment of Color; next, the offender was dyed a specific color; then, they were programmed in sensory deprivation tanks; and finally, the Dyed Person—a *DP*—was banned from the Shield to wander the wasteland for the rest of his or her life as a pariah, permanently stained with a distinctive, telling color.

Color-coded, so to speak.

The reds were the various types of violent offenders, the greens included thieves, burglars, and embezzlers, and the blues were different kinds of sex criminals, and so forth through the visible spectrum. The increasing dark intensity of each color denoted the increasing severity of the crime. By this time, only a handful of criminals had been banned as exiles in the first year of the Shield's completed existence, and the Crimson Man had to be one of those first dozen or so.

Crimson?

An intense shade of red to be sure, Cat thought. Obviously

one of the major violent crimes. Murder or perhaps some kind of other lethal assault? Cat wasn't sure of the specific nature of the crime, but it had to have been seriously violent—

An unsettling sense of personal alarm and concern spread through him, an unusual sensation felt by Cat only very rarely; perhaps something like it occasionally surfacing to consciousness before a major Raider attack. The much smaller Crimson Man, sensing potential aggression on Cat's part, readily offered his palms in a kind of gesture of supplication … He slowly backed away, intently watching Cat; and finally, he turned and moved off swiftly, disappearing from sight into the depths of darkness.

Cat remained in place, slightly embarrassed, not by his initial startled reaction, but for freezing inactive in place for so long. So vulnerable. It could have cost you dearly, he told himself, if the Crimson Man had decided to attack during those two or three seconds. Despite his self-chastisement, he remained unsettled by what he'd seen, trying to recall other details of what he'd heard about Judgments of Color and the DPs…

Not too much really.

He recalled that the Company considered the variations of amber, the yellows, the most heinous of Shield crimes—treason, subversion, and sedition against the Company. So far no one knew if any wastelander had ever been taken in and rendered a Judgment of Color. It was believed that only Shield Residents had received Judgments during the last year of the San Fran Shield's full operation. Cat ventured to guess that most of these first DPs had probably been only *temporary* residents, most likely tradesmen and skilled workers brought inside after the completion of the outside dome. Surely wealthy newcomer residents settling in would not initially cause trouble—they had paid dearly to be there. But it was only a guess on his part.

Cat sucked in a deep breath.

This was a pretty terrible kind of punishment, he thought, even compared to some of the more irrational and brutal punishments meted out by Desperado chieftains to their members who violated the bands' codes: lashings, amputations of fingers, even complete hands, blindings, other facial disfigurements, and public death by garrote.

But to be permanently dyed a color and cast out to wander as a pariah, a complete isolate forever shunned by Shield Resident and probably wastelanders, too ...?

Cat had a difficult time imagining himself in that kind of circumstance.

He finally shifted from his reflections on DPs, glanced down at the black journal, and started back to the compound.

3

THE FIRST JOURNAL

Cat calculated the last entries by his father to be at least nineteen or twenty years old, the whole journal begun over twenty-six years ago. But they were of course new and intriguing to him, as were all the previous pages of entries. Most of the last third of the journal was about his father's wanderings. And really no clue to what had happened to him at the end, or why he'd somehow lost the journal. Disconcerting, Cat thought re-reading the very last piece.

But there were some good clues to where he'd been headed.

Journal Entry
Santee Camp
PS: 6 years 11 months

The devastation, flattening of Greater San Diego, almost completely wiped out the inhabitants of the heavily populated County—perhaps only several hundred survivors after the terrible wave of radiation deaths finally subsided. I was unable to find out anything about my father or Lauren's parents. But I'm almost certain they never survived the Strikes. Their neighborhoods were completely leveled and heavily burned over.

I've been living here at this sheepherders' camp twenty miles northeast of San Diego for over three months now. Several small springs feed a watering hole nearby. It will slowly dry up as summer approaches. Then the herders will move north and east thirty-five miles into the mountains where fresh water and some limited pasture are said to be available. I may move and live with them. At least for a while.

So soon after the Strikes, but there are now 10- even 12-year-old young-sters here and other places I've visited who are losing the ability to read. Most younger children don't remember ever seeing a book, hearing a story, or knowing what the written word actually looks like. No adults I've met read anything much. So there is a real danger of people here in the outlands soon becoming functionally illiterate. Perhaps I've found a useful calling, even my path to a kind of partial redemption? Is that really possible?

I have eight students ranging in age from 6 to 13. I've recently obtained a hand chalkboard and a small supply of chalk, scrounged up in the recent past by some of the mothers salvaging items from the rubble of a school near the eastern edge of the Carlsbad Ruins. Also they found a 3rd grade and a 6th grade reader, both only slightly damaged by fire. We are all learning our letters! Two of the older students can already read a few simple sentences! And of course I tell stories—many of the same old ones my boy once loved. But a few new ones I've made up, too.

I've gained some ground convincing the adults of the value of teaching their children to read, gaining some respect for the cultural merit of stories and books and literacy. Recently, I was helped greatly in my cause, when one of the shep-herds traded some wool up north and brought back two books for me. Alca-traz Angel by Gord Rollo and Machu Picchu by Michael McBride, two longtime NY Times best-selling authors from back when I was just beginning graduate school almost three decades ago. The pages of the books are yellow and brittle, but I handle them very carefully, reading lengthy excerpts nightly by firelight to a small but growing group of avid adult listeners. I think I've gained a place of respect with these hardened, tough-minded survivors.

I've reinforced a slight reputation earned in the last three or so years of wandering around here in the South, trying to be of service to others. The twenty-five or so herders look up to me as a kind of healer/teacher/professor and even sit still for my lectures from the past—about carefully protecting yourself and children against pollution, practicing humanism and tolerance, good will toward all, even strangers, the importance of observing the Golden Rule, and perhaps most importantly keeping alive the ability to read.

But the adults are much slower and more difficult students than their children.

A week ago, three of the men tracked down and beat to death a pair of hapless scrawny teenagers who had rustled and slaughtered one small lamb. They only wanted to feed their widowed mother and three starving younger siblings.

Sometimes the work is daunting, but I must struggle on.
My cross to bear for my past sins.

That last line grated on Cat's mind. He recalled his final conversation with his father in the mess tent up at Blue Rock Springs, over twenty-five years ago. He'd been so full of hate, and had condemned his dad harshly, believing he had disrespected Cat's dead mother by being intimate at that time with MacKenzie. But he'd been dreadfully mistaken. MacKenzie was a member of Shaw's Raiders, leaving the Med Camp with the original other nine—an invaluable handler of horses. At first Cat refused to speak to her, avoided her as if she were contaminated. But eventually she cornered him, and told him what had not happened. Even though his father and her were separated by a fairly significant age difference, they recognized their mutual loneliness, an attraction, and had begun to fall in love at Blue Rock Springs. But they had never slept together. Jacob had been too consumed by mourning his wife's death, and felt guilty about the timing of his developing feelings for MacKenzie. He'd disappeared from the Med Camp bearing that burden, but also a heavy remorse about participating in raids to look for Lauren's killer, and most of all he felt a deep guilt for not being a better parent and role model for his only son.

Those last impressions by MacKenzie stuck in his head. Perhaps the ultimate irony was that now Cat and MacKenzie lived together, even though there was a noticeable age gap between them. He'd help raise Janey, MacKenzie's daughter, who now lived with a young goat herder up in the San Fran Ruins.

There was so much Cat wanted to know about his father. The journal was too brief a beginning. He intended to carefully read the entire memoir. But the ending was a real concern. What had happened? Was his father even alive? And what about the two other journals? Where were they? He would remember to check in with the book vendor—those journals might show up yet.

Back at the bunker encampment in the cubicle Cat shared with MacKenzie, he'd just turned back to the first page of the journal, when a Raider knocked at the door interrupted him.

"It's time, Cat."

It was time to mount up for the raid into the East Bay hills along I-680.

Regretfully, Cat tucked his dad's journal under his pillow to read later.

He had to get his game face on now; it was time to fight.

4

SHAW'S RAIDERS

As usual in early summer of the years since the Strikes, the night sky remained overcast, and the Raiders rode in and out of pockets of heavy fog as they traveled around the southern end of the Bay— the mist doing nothing to relieve the heavy mugginess. They were headed for a rendezvous spot, a thick grove of eucalyptus near the ruins of the Tesla Automobile Assembly Plant about a quarter mile south of The Fist stronghold.

Cat's bowmen team would already be there waiting after carefully reconnoitering the cave fortress—pinpointing listening outposts, if any, counting sentries on the walls outside the cave, identifying locations of wall gun ports, charting the going and coming of the enemy into their compound, and such; MacKenzie would also be there at the rendezvous in the woods tending the bowmen's three horses. Later, with only one Raider helper—a teenager not quite old enough to fight—she'd be in charge of all the mounts not directly involved in the attack on the stronghold.

They rode into the heart of the thick stand of eucalyptus and dismounted, MacKenzie and her helper gathering reins together and gentling each of the horses in their charge.

She wouldn't have to hobble any of them tonight. But she did slip a modified sack blindfold over twenty of the horses' heads. The remaining thirty uncovered mounts, tended by riders, would be needed shortly for the cavalry charge part of the attack plan.

After dismounting, Cat met with his three bowmen, Oscar doing the talking.

"There are no manned outposts at all, which is not really too unusual if there is just a skeleton crew guarding the cave," Oscar reported. "And we spotted only one guard patrolling around the entire north and south walls fortifying the cave mouth. No relief for him during the hour we watched. Four large machinegun emplacements along each wall side and eight additional gun ports, none of them manned. Absolutely no movement in and out of the cave during this surveillance time at all. It seemed to be dead quiet inside their fortification, too."

"What about the entrance through the wall?" Cat asked. The formidable twelve-foot high rock wall was built in the shape of a horseshoe extending out from the cave, a pair of metal gates located at the top of the shoe, opening wide enough for a pair of heavy-duty wagons to easily pass side-by-side.

"Left wide open," Oscar said. "They've grown arrogant, obviously believing no one would dare attack them anymore."

Cat digested the recon without registering any reactions...

"So, nothing really unexpected to report?" he finally said with a slight edge in his tone. "The deserter's story checks out as best you can determine?"

A little over a week ago, a deserter from The Fist had offered information in exchange for a full backpack of supplies.

This was a rare occurrence up until the last year, but something happening more frequently now, with growing numbers of Desperadoes becoming disenchanted with dwindling plunder splits, opting to desert, and going it on their own. This Black man had sworn to Shaw and Cat that the gate to the cave compound would be left wide open, the stronghold guarded by only a token force of maybe half a dozen fighters at most. The main body of The Fist would be marauding through four small fishing villages along the coast south of the Monterey Bay Desalinization Plant ruins, looking to land a big haul of dried sardines and whatever else they could plunder from the fishing camps—they'd taken along two empty wagons anticipating a highly successful raid.

The informant thought the main body of The Fist would be gone at least until sometime late tomorrow afternoon.

"Yeah, I do think the place looks like they are off on a major raid," Oscar said, but he didn't smile, and he was wearing a slight frown as he finished talking.

Cat detected something in his voice … perhaps a lack of self-assurance. Oscar was his most trusted colleague, and his best bowman, for sure. But more importantly, tonight he was one of the top recon scouts among all of Shaw's Raiders—he seemed to exercise an uncanny sixth sense during recon patrols.

"But what…?"

"I don't like the gates left open like that. Arrogant or not, it seems too convenient. But there's something else even more troubling. I'm not sure it's really anything specific though…"

"I know it's nothing I can actually pinpoint," the bowman added after a short pause, shrugging. "But I just developed this kind of gut feeling in the hour or so while we were out there re-conning the cave—uncomfortable, and a little unsettling."

"A gut feeling, you say?"

Oscar nodded. "You know, a kind of vague intuitive thing, an undefined itch really, as if something wasn't quite right, something I was seeing, or maybe something I wasn't seeing but should…"

After another longer pause, he added, "It all just looked too, well, too good to be true. Especially those gates left unlocked and flung wide open like that."

"You don't think the majority of The Fist have gone south on the raid of those fishing villages?"

For a moment the young man said and did nothing, then he

smiled wryly and shrugged almost apologetically.

"Cat, I just don't know for sure."

"Well, I guess your gut feeling is good enough for me," Cat said. "We're going back out there to take a second look before we sign off on this attack."

The plan was that after a positive recon, thirty of Shaw's Raiders on horseback, including Shaw himself, all armed with the Raiders' arsenal of assault rifles, would make a frontal V cavalry charge, hopefully catching the skeleton force by surprise, while the remaining eighteen Raiders on foot—including Cat and his bowmen would follow up closely, executing a supporting double pincer maneuver, coming in tightly along both sides of the fence line and eventually over-running and securing The Fist cave stronghold. They would be responsible for packing out the bags of salt and whatever else worthwhile was stored in there.

After listening to Oscar though, Cat met with Shaw, who was standing with reins in hand by his mount near the head of the cavalry V—their horses beginning to stir and paw the ground, picking up on the conspicuous tension palpable in the muggy air.

MacKenzie and her helper had their hands full trying to gentle their charges by stroking, scratching, and whispering names softly into twitching ears. But they were only moderately successful.

"I need to go up to the cave again before we initiate the attack," Cat told the leader. "Something may not be right up there."

"Oscar spotted something wrong?"

Cat shook his head. "Felt something wrong."

"Felt?" Shaw said, his annoyance obvious, but then he added, "Okay, but get back here as soon as possible."

Cat took off with Oscar on foot.

⌖ – ⌖

As the two bowmen gradually approached to within a hundred twenty-five or so yards of the cave stronghold, Cat signaled for

Oscar to stop. The air was heavy, muggy, and still, not even the briefest hint of a breeze.

Sweating heavily under his duster, Cat stood silently in the smothering darkness and stared out toward the fenced cave compound, as if he possessed X-ray vision, and then for a few moments longer with his eyes closed, his other senses keenly alert ... Nothing seemed amiss.

The two crept twenty or twenty-five yards closer and stopped again.

Cat dropped prone and carefully scanned the top of the horseshoe-shaped wall against the skyline backdrop, which was dimly highlighted by a mist-shrouded half-moon rising above the nearby eastern foothills. Okay ... good, he thought, after checking all around the horseshoe. Only one sentry silhouetted along the catwalk, just as Oscar had reported before getting up, Cat squeezed his nose tightly, blew hard, and popped his ear canals; then he cocked his head and listened intently for almost a full thirty seconds ... He heard no one talking, nothing moving around near the mouth of the cave.

Slowly, Cat stood and they crept a few steps closer, stopping a third time and kneeling. Careful not to make a sound, he repeatedly sniffed the air ... Yes, he could detect smoke from a wood fire, but much too faint, nothing like what might be necessary to cook for a large force. And he smelled no tobacco smoke either. If the whole group were in there, surely someone would be smoking.

Moving as close as they dared, they both squatted and watched the sentry pace along the catwalk—about seventy-five yards away. The guard abruptly stopped when a night owl made a *whoo* sound, swooping down and over where Cat and Oscar squatted ... After a tense moment, the sentry continued on his patrol around the top of the rocky horseshoe.

Both Raiders sucked in a deep breath and smiled at each other.

From where they squatted in front of the opened gates, Cat spotted no shadowy figures manning the entry to the cave proper, and not even the glimmer of a lit candle. Everything seemed exactly as had been spelled out by the deserter. The Fist appeared to be gone from their walled cave stronghold. It looked vulnerable, guarded only by the band's fierce-some reputation, easy pickings for the Raiders.

But Cat shared Oscar's disturbing feeling that he was missing something important, something not quite right with the situation. He wished he had a pair of night vision goggles. He'd love to peer deeper into that cave, make sure there were indeed only three or four other Desperadoes in there. But the last pair of working NVG owned by the Raiders had been lost in a recent night raid up the Peninsula. Replacements were almost impossible to find nowadays, a highly prized item with lots of other folks in the wasteland.

Cat stood and let a deep sigh trickle out. After a moment, he signaled to Oscar that they were returning to the rendezvous point.

Back at the grove, Cat reported to Shaw and gave his approval to initiate the raid.

Shaw looped a small silver whistle on a cord around his neck—he always wore it on a raid as if it were a good-luck talisman. His cavalry of thirty was already roughly in their V attack formation; they were mounted up, their horses' hoofs shod with heavy burlap. The Raiders on foot quietly grouped along each flank of the V. Cat sent two of his bowmen ahead on foot to the northern side of the wall; Oscar would man the south wall by himself. Whoever spotted the lone sentry first would take him out with a silent arrow to the throat, before he could alert those few others down in the cave. The bowmen would shoot any of The Fist who decided to climb up and man one of the gun ports or four machineguns mounted but unmanned along each wall during the Raider attack.

With a cooling breeze now blowing at their backs, the cavalry and their mounts waited nervously, the supporting foot troops watching Mike Shaw expectantly for the signal to begin the attack—

The leader dropped his arm, everyone moving forward as quietly as possible, as the breeze stiffened, almost pushing them forward.

Advancing on the compound a hundred yards away with the skirmish line of seven other foot troops on the southern right flank, Cat noticed the wind whipping the flag atop the pole near the open gates—a black-gloved, clenched fist extended on a dark arm against a white background—

That was it, what he and Oscar both should've noticed.

The damn flag had been there, but hanging limply from the flagpole during both his and Oscar's recon; it must have only registered deep in their sub-consciousness—an undefined unsettling effect. Everyone knew The Fist never mounted an attack without taking along and flying their colors. Cat should have spotted it before, even though the wind had just made the flag flap—

The inference hit him like a blow to the gut: an elaborate set-up. A fucking trap! The Fist—all hundred or so—were probably in that cave lurking in the dark, prepared to counterattack and slaughter the unsuspecting Raiders.

Cat groaned to himself.

He instantly recovered his poise and shouted, "Wait, Oscar!"

The bowman, who was about twenty-five yards ahead of Cat, acknowledged Cat's frantic beckoning signal, and the rapid pumping of his leader's arm—double-time back.

Oscar began to run—

It was a moment too late to halt the main attack; the horsemen were already racing forward, the Raiders behind them on foot dashing ahead of both flanks, spreading out in a pair of diagonal skirmish lines.

On the wall behind the retreating Oscar, several figures popped up into view, the first two cranking off their automatic weapons at the bowman—the twin muzzle blasts flashing out in the dimness like thin fingers of deadly fire.

An extended finger touched him, and Oscar tumbled head over heels.

None of the Raiders on foot had yet squeezed off a single round when Cat heard to his far left a trio of slightly separated but extremely menacing sounds: *plunk...plunk...plunk...*

And the unmistakable metallic echo of mortar rounds being dropped into firing tubes.

The three plunks dropped close together meant the firing crew must already be triangulated in on a forward spot, probably directly in front of those opened gates. An obvious ruse designed to draw and bunch the attacking cavalry, which was indeed hell-bent at that moment for that very spot.

Momentarily frozen in place, Cat watched the scene unfolding before him with horror, hoping for some kind of a miracle to intervene.

And fate did indeed smile.

Fortunately for the Raider cavalry, The Fist had been a touch too impatient in the execution of their mortar trap.

Boom...boom...boom!

The first three explosions were fifteen to twenty yards short of the charging horses, throwing debris and a little shrapnel into the main body of the *V*—only the lead horsemen on the point were hit hard. All three went down with their mounts...one rider-less horse immediately struggling back to its feet in the cloud of dust and dashing off to the north.

RPGs exploded near the Raiders on the right flank closest to Cat, jarring him out of his trance.

Cat charged the wall of gunmen, but kept low while searching through the dust and smoke. He spotted Oscar, not more than twenty-five yards from the wall, but lying still. Cat closed in, zig-zagging the last few yards, hoping to avoid being hit by any of the gunmen firing down on him from their superior positions along the rock wall.

Oscar was alive, breathing evenly, and his eyes were open and alert. There was no one nearby able to help him, but his closeness to the wall protected them somewhat from direct fire. All around them the Raider attack had stalled out under the rain of Desperado fire, as if they'd run into an invisible wall.

To his credit, Shaw had reacted almost immediately after the first trio of mortar rounds dropped short and The Fist gunmen lining the horseshoe began firing their AK-47s at the cavalry. He blew a loud retreat on the silver whistle dangling from his neck— the high-pitched shrill distinct over the deeper-pitched *rat-tat-tatting*, *booming*, and *blasting*. He finished his signal moments before a horde of seventy or eighty gunmen streamed out of the cave mouth and toward the fence gates like a swarm of angry bees attacking from their darkened hive.

The air was alive around Cat with the confusion of the battle-field: gunfire, explosions, shouting, shrieking, the acrid smell of burning gunpowder, dust, fire, smoke, and the whinnying of fright-ened horses. In the disordered hubbub, he shouldered the wound-ed bowman, and began running back with the other retreating Raiders.

Only the Raiders' superior training and discipline saved them from a total massacre at the hands of the overwhelming numbers of ambushers.

As Cat struggled with his load, both flanks of infantry quickly doubled back twenty-five or so yards at a time, the one on the left dropping prone, laying down a hail of covering fire, as the horse-men pulled themselves together and along with the right flank con-tinued an orderly retreat.

Then the right flank dropped prone and lay down their cover-ing fire.

Back and forth it went between flanks as the Raiders staged a classic military battlefield infantry retreat.

The Fist's main counter-assault was slowed by disciplined bursts of covering fire.

By now, the cavalry that still remained mounted had tightened up and was participating in the staggered withdrawal, laying down a heavy barrage of automatic fire. Both infantry flanks simultaneously *zigged* and *zagged,* effectively drawing closer to the rendezvous point.

The undisciplined wild charge of the main body of The Fist gunmen had momentarily stalled out, as individuals in the lead had to drop down to seek cover from their own colleagues' withering friendly fire directly behind them.

Completely soaked with sweat, Cat lugged the wounded Oscar in the fireman's carry over his shoulders. Ahead, he could now see through the mist the first trees of the eucalyptus stand.

The band of superior force behind them managed to gather into several effective small fighting groups and begin pursuing again, discharging weapons, including several RPGs ... One grenade burst within yards of Cat and other members of the retreating right flank.

Miraculously, he wasn't hit by any of the grenade shrapnel or the accompanying small arms fire.

Hurry, hurry, he urged weary legs vigorously protesting the sustained effort.

Under the load of dead weight, Cat stumbled twice; but he managed somehow to recover each time and struggle forward with Oscar draped safely across his shoulders.

Gasping raggedly for breath, Cat made it to the shelter of the trees, MacKenzie, and the mounts.

The Fist attack had petered out forty yards short of the thick eucalyptus grove, twenty cavalry members forming an arc and executing short, disciplined accurate bursts of automatic fire back at their pursuers, forcing them to hunker down and seek cover.

Desperadoes continued to pot shot randomly into the dark woods.

As Cat approached MacKenzie and eased his wounded colleague across a horse, he saw the woman shudder as if she'd been suddenly chilled. He only had time to help her keep control of the horses milling about that were terrified by the gunfire and dust, until they could successfully match mounts to returning Raiders fleeing on foot—some of the latest returning were laboriously helping carry wounded to safety like Cat.

In a few more minutes, most of the Raiders were back in the heart of the woods, only four remaining at the edge of the trees to lay down bursts of automatic fire with their AK-47s. Shaw whistled two short and one long blast, and one-by-one the four peeled back. Everyone, including the wounded, were finally mounted on horseback.

The Raiders made their successful escape out of the westerly back end of the eucalyptus stand, headed for their secret stronghold in the industrial Ruins.

Some laughed as they safely rode away—hysterical gallows humor, giggling actually—for they still heard sporadic loud gunfire firing into the easterly but empty side of the woods they'd left far behind.

Back at camp, Shaw and Cat assessed the damage.

Ten Raiders for sure had been killed, two of the cavalry members on V point blown up back near the gate opening. Eight others were wounded, two seriously. And there were another three Raiders unaccounted for—probably dead or captured by The Fist. Thirteen horses had been lost.

Twenty-one human casualties!

Only twenty-nine Raiders had escaped the firefight completely unharmed.

MacKenzie and Cat helped Oscar—he had what appeared to be a gunshot flesh wound in his upper left thigh—and the other wounded over to the busy infirmary in the courtyard. Only then did Cat have a chance to catch his breath as he put his arm around MacKenzie and hugged her tightly.

"That was way too close for comfort, girl," he whispered hoarsely. "We must be living right, you know."

It was a wonder that any Raiders had escaped at all. The Fist should've waited perhaps for two or three seconds more, allowing the whole cavalry charge to enter the gates, and the accompanying flanking movement to get close to the wall line. Both their impatience and their undisciplined counterattack had allowed so many Raiders to escape death. Still, twenty-one casualties, almost *half* their fighting force was tragedy enough. But it could've been much worse, Cat thought, realizing he was thoroughly exhausted and dying of thirst.

His hand on MacKenzie's shoulder felt funny...wet and sticky.

He held it up and looked at his palm in the light; it was bloody, and the shoulder of her long coat was stained dark red.

"Hey, you've been hit!" he said, carefully turning the woman around to face him.

She shrugged and tried to smile...then her knees buckled.

Cat caught MacKenzie as she fainted into his arms. He eased her to the ground, and gently stripped away her long coat and shirt.

She'd been hit in the right shoulder, apparently back at the rendezvous—probably during the indiscriminate fire after he first reached her. That odd shudder? But she hadn't said anything, or complained. She was indeed a toughie.

He hustled MacKenzie into the infirmary to see one of the two healers.

Cat anxiously waited outside the medical tent for a prognosis.

Time crawled.

The attack on The Fist had been a fiasco, he thought, shaking his head.

About a half hour after he'd taken her into the infirmary, one of the healers told Cat he thought MacKenzie would completely recover. A bullet had passed cleanly through her shoulder, only nicking the small clavicle bone. She'd lost quite a bit of blood, required a few stitches, and a drain inserted. But the wound would soon heal—a couple of weeks at most, although she wouldn't have full range of motion in her shoulder for months, if at all.

All she needed now was sufficient rest to regain her strength. They would need to change her dressing and check the drain every three days for the next two weeks, watch for infection.

Cat sighed with relief and thanked the medical man.

The healer had also said that two of the other Raiders brought in wounded weren't so lucky—they'd died shortly after their arrival.

All Cat could think about while waiting that long half hour for MacKenzie's release was catching the fake deserter and making him pay for his treachery, and for the Raider's twenty-one casualties. He was probably well on his way back to The Fist stronghold at the very moment, with his ill-gotten backpack of Raider supplies. He deserved to die.

5

MACKENZIE

MacKenzie awakened late the following morning after the aborted raid, and ate the pear slices and two hard-boiled eggs Luke had left on the nightstand near their bedside. She washed it all down with the sweetened sun tea from the quart container he'd thoughtfully set out there, too.

She felt good, everything considered. Stiff and sore, part of her shoulder numb; and she was much too warm—actually sweaty. She wiped her face with the clean moist towel Luke had also put out for her. MacKenzie smiled, lit the candle, yawned and stretched.

She was normally an active person, but enjoyed reading when time permitted. Now, she had nothing but time on her hands. She picked up the well-thumbed book she was re-reading by Raymond Carver—one of the twelve hardbacks she'd brought with them twenty-five years ago from Leroy's camp library at Blue Rock Springs. She should have made room for more books from the old man's excellent collection, but she'd been in too big of a hurry, worried mostly about taking care of Janey and packing up all of her daughter's things. A year later, when they finally were able to get back to the abandoned med camp, all the books were gone. Everything else of value had been looted or burned.

She carefully flipped through the brittle and yellowing pages of *Where I'm Calling From*. She'd read all the stories at least a half a dozen times. At first she'd considered the stories irrelevant to the post-Strike time, the point in time some people were now starting to call the Collapse. Much like being back in her high school days and reading a Victorian novel of manners by someone like Jane Austin—so far removed from her life it was almost a total fantasy. The people in a Carver story were usually considered 20th Century working class, but compared to now they were all relatively rich. No material reasons to be so essentially unhappy. The stories initially struck her as unrealistic and depressing, but she didn't think that about most of them now.

Over the years, after careful re-readings, she'd eventually come to the conclusion that the stories were emotionally rich and guessed they would be eternally relevant.

In some ways the tales reminded her of certain aspects of their life together—Luke and her. The couples in the stories, despite their freedom and relative material comfort, were struggling emotionally to survive, often victims of themselves. Perhaps a little like Luke in the past.

He'd been so hurt and angry after his mother had been killed in the Desperado attack at Blue Rock Springs Med Camp twenty-five years ago. Mad at everyone, his head empty of everything except for revenge. Almost obsessive-compulsive in his desire to hunt down and kill Desperadoes. With the help of others, he'd finally tracked down and killed his mother's murderer in the Iron Triangle in Richmond, but it hadn't helped him much. Something inside Luke, something vital to being a human, had been critically damaged during his coping with all the Collapse aftermath, including his relationship with his father. Even after they'd moved here to the safety of the hidden bunker in the San Jo Ruins, she'd thought the damage was permanent. Nothing anyone could do to help Luke.

There were no splints for a broken heart, or ice for a bruised soul.

Back then she thought he was like all the other Raiders. Most of them tap-danced along a shifting thin line between observing a no-holds-barred warrior code of honor and being ruthlessly barbaric. After a foray, they rarely expressed even the slightest remorse for their brutal actions, which occasionally included the killing and maiming of women and children. She'd heard Shaw more than once justify these non-combatant casualties as being the "unfortunate victims" of collateral damage. Accidental deaths, with no one responsible. She found the really disturbing thing was something chilling revealed in the Raiders' hard-edged unguarded expressions. It was something in their eyes—a total lack of affect, a kind of deadness—that always made MacKenzie wince. She suspected many were sociopaths. Not too surprising. That's the type of person Shaw began actively recruiting after they'd first settled into their new stronghold. Ruthless and violent with no conscience. He only retained her in the band because of her exceptional abilities of handling the horses, certainly not for any fierce warrior-like nature.

She'd have left the compound in the early days if it hadn't been for Janey. She'd often reminded herself that she needed the security the group provided to safely raise her daughter. But she'd spent the first few years at the compound in the San Jo Ruins bringing up her daughter by herself. That unnerving look in the eyes of the men chilled her and prevented any fleeting romantic attraction MacKenzie might've entertained. She remained single and celibate by choice. And Luke seemed to be exactly like the others, perhaps even more so. The young man was the most merciless of Shaw's Raiders, completely fearless and relentless during a skirmish with other Desperadoes. More than respected, he was actually feared by even the most ferocious of the Raiders. He gave and asked no quarter, took no prisoners; part of the stern warrior code he'd adopted from Shaw, whom he apparently looked up to and greatly admired.

For a long time MacKenzie had known that Mike Shaw was a pathologically egotistical leader, most likely even disturbed, and a very dangerous man to cross. Just before he'd disappeared from Blue Rock Springs, Jacob Zachary had warned her that Shaw was also a hardcore bigot, especially toward Blacks; true racists, in one way or another, infected others around them with their intolerance. But she'd ignored Jacob's warning and followed Mike Shaw and the others to the San Jo Ruins. She'd pushed her concerns about the Raiders and especially their racist chief to the back of her mind, rationalizing that she required an immediate safe haven for Janey. The Raider bunker fulfilled that need. Yet from that very first day in the San Jo Ruins, she distrusted the leader of the Raiders, and warily avoided contact with him as much as possible. Luke was an apparent carbon copy of Shaw and his ruthless and bigoted code, so she avoided him, too.

Over twenty years ago, she'd been surprised by Luke's actions. He'd risked his life in the middle of a furious firefight in the Iron Triangle to save two crippled infants trapped on the battlefield. He'd scurried forward, placing himself at risk of fire from both sides. And a ricocheting piece of RPG shrapnel opened up a deep gash in his face. Despite his serious injury, and while bleeding heavily, he'd managed to drag the shocked children back to safety.

From that point, MacKenzie watched him closely, knowing that Luke was without a doubt much different from most of his cohorts. Few—if any—of the other Raiders would've risked their lives for two defective children, especially Black kids. Luke had indeed demonstrated he wasn't a bigoted racist at all, and he had also inadvertently revealed a degree of something else … maybe real compassion.

She knew Luke held a number of the other Raiders in high regard—Oscar for sure and probably the other pair of bowmen. But many of the Raiders respected each other—their warrior skills. After he got his damaged face sewed up, she wondered if Luke was capable of other, perhaps deeper, positive, sensitive feelings. It wasn't long before she noticed he was *often* kind to her Janey and the other Raider mothers and especially the children running around in the compound. Occasionally, he'd go out of his way to play games with them. He never tried to hide his inner warmth with the children. She felt a growing attraction to the young man.

So after four plus lonely years, MacKenzie had finally found someone to love again; ironically, it was Jacob's son. They'd lived together now for almost nineteen years. Essentially he'd been Janey's father—the only she'd ever known.

She stretched again and smiled. Their relationship had not been perfect by a long shot. Like many couples in the Raymond Carver stories, they infrequently, if ever, verbalized and shared their deepest thoughts, reactions, and feelings—at least Luke never did.

Rarely did anyone in the stories ever address the dysfunctional aspects of a relationship, which often led to disaster. She thought of the subtle and sadly compelling story "Why Don't You Dance?" What exactly had happened to the older man's wife? Had she left him, or perhaps died? Obviously the relationship was over, but had they talked it over before the end? Probably not, she guessed. He was definitely making an unspoken statement of his feelings though by selling off everything cheaply—getting rid of all of their things scattered around the front yard, shrugging off all the touch points of an entire life in a quick, cheap yard sale.

Sighing to herself, MacKenzie drank the rest of her cold tea.

She was still thirsty after having finally drained the entire quart container … which may have had something to do with the blood loss the day before. And her shoulder ached. The healer had given her four Vicodin to use, but only when absolutely necessary—that much painkiller was hard to come by, even the Desperadoes having rare access to these types of drugs, and usually small quantities. The painkillers traded their way up from the Latin Confederation, often arriving old and outdated, which reduced their effectiveness. She had taken one of the four dated pills an hour ago, wondering if it retained any punch at all.

She now realized the medication was working almost too well, numbing her pain but also making her feel a bit drifty, which perhaps contributed to her maudlin feelings about her past relationship with Luke.

She tried to focus her thoughts and get back to her reading, running her finger down the index of stories in Carver's collection.

She paused for a moment at "What We Talk About When We Talk About Love." The title was intentionally ironic, the people in the story didn't talk about love at all. It was a story about the fragile relationships of a pair of dysfunctional couples. She continued along the index, finally stopping and smiling, deciding to re-read "Cathedral," one of her favorites, an unusual Carver story about a developing positive interpersonal relationship. With a sort of upbeat ending.

Just what she needed.

~ – ~

Later that evening, Luke brought her more tea and food. She wasn't the least hungry, but quickly gulped down almost the whole quart container of tea.

"You're really thirsty."

She nodded. "Think I may have a little bit of a fever."

He felt her head, looking slightly concerned. "I don't know for sure, but you may be right. Maybe you should have your dressing and drain checked a day or so early at the infirmary, like tomorrow morning."

She nodded. "Probably a good idea," she said, then hedged, "but I'll see how I feel in the morning. They're still pretty busy there with all the other more severely wounded, you know."

Luke looked off absently out the doorway, obviously thinking about something other than her injured shoulder. He glanced back down at her, smiled thinly, and said, "You up to talking about something I've been thinking about for quite some time now?

About a different kind of future for us?"

This was an unusual request from Luke. He rarely initiated a conversation about any of his deep thoughts. Wasn't a big discussion kind of guy, either. In that way, at least, he was definitely a character from a Raymond Carver story.

"Sure I am," she said with an enthusiastic voice, turning and fluffing her pillow with her good arm, sitting up straighter. She peered back at him curiously. She'd known for some time that something was up, something really bothering him. But, typically, he hadn't volunteered anything, until this very moment.

Before explaining, he sucked in a deep breath, and then he fingered the scar near his eyebrow—a giveaway tell indicating his nervousness or deep concern.

"Well, I think it's about time to approach Shaw about leaving the Raiders and this compound. You and I, and whoever else wants to go along with us. Oscar for sure. Maybe the other two bowmen will want to come, too. I'm not sure yet." He stared back at her, obviously waiting for some kind of initial reaction.

"Where do you want to go?"

He shrugged and glanced away again, slowly shaking his head.

"Not really sure," he said, after some consideration. "But it's time to seek out a different life. The raiding lifestyle, at least with large groups of others, is going to disappear soon. It's already a rapidly disappearing way of living. Only five bands left in the whole Bay Area. Ten years ago there must've been forty-five or fifty. And these last large groups are beginning to lose strength. Members are deserting and going it alone. Big bands are too large to support—they are functionally obsolete. At the heart of this change, I think, is something that is happening all around us—has been going on for quite some time. Wastelanders are successfully growing their own food, raising animals for fresh meat, eggs, and milk, some with enough surplus for trade. Many are not even marginally dependent anymore on Desperadoes for the canned or packaged foodstuff stockpiled from raids. And, in fact, the big bands have no large stores of anything much left anyhow. As you know, the Raiders haven't made a big score of anything in almost a year. The Fist stockpile of salt might've been nothing more than rumor. We'll never know for sure. And we're probably fighting other big bands now for nothing. Stupid..."

As his last judgment trailed off, he peered directly at her again for her considered reaction, apparently anticipating some arguments for why they must stay in the safety of the compound.

From his expression though, she must've surprised him when she quickly nodded and said, "I think you're absolutely right, Luke. It's time for us to leave. Whether anyone else wants to come along with us or not."

Silence for a moment.

"Shaw won't like it," he said, absently trailing his forefinger the length of his scar. "I hope not, but I might have to formally challenge him, win the right to leave the Raiders, and take along whoever else is willing to go."

"We couldn't just peacefully leave without saying anything to anyone? You know, take along the bare minimum of what we will need and slip away unannounced some night?"

He frowned and slowly shook his head, like she'd suspected he probably would.

"I can't do it that way."

"What will we do if we do leave ... become farmers or maybe animal herders like Janey and her husband?" Her daughter and husband had a small herd of dairy goats up in old Golden Gate Park in the San Fran Ruins and were beginning a cheese making operation there with a partner.

"No, I don't think I'm quite cut out for that kind of daily repetitive routine. But I've been thinking some about that specific question, too. Got a couple of ideas. You could surely do something with horses—perhaps start a business training or even trading them. The outlying farmers and ranchers will need many more horses. A well-trained horse will probably sell for a premium ...

And maybe a person with my skills could make a living in another way besides helping you with your wrangling. Capitalize on my special abilities."

"How?"

He shrugged and said in a slightly more tentative voice, "I don't know for sure, but it's possible that in the near future groups of farmers in the Great Central Valley, or perhaps the larger herders, would be willing to pay for a security service. When the bands break up completely, there will no doubt be small gangs and even individual Desperadoes still trying to plunder others and take what they want."

She nodded thoughtfully, and then chuckled. "It sounds similar to something attempted a long time ago by the Samurai in Japan, when the feudal era came to an end in the mid-1800's. The great bands of warriors were forced to disband. Eventually, the individual Ronin cast adrift in the breakup began renting out their swords for protection against marauding bandits to rice farmers or others wanting their services." She'd been fascinated with Japanese culture so long ago.

"I guess it's a lot like being a knight freelancer in the old days in Great Britain," he suggested, his tone a little more confident. "You know, I just might be able to rent out my knightly services for protection."

"Uh-huh, knightly services. I don't think so, pal."

Luke laughed.

MacKenzie thought seriously about his idea and she smiled encouragingly.

"Hey, seriously I think it probably could work out nicely for us. I love the wrangling possibilities for myself. And some kind of security work for you is probably a natural, too. At any rate, it would be a much better, more honorable life than raiding, looting, and killing innocent people. Healthier lifestyle, too, I bet. I'm willing to give it a try."

After her declaration of positive support, she stared at him for a long time before asking in a voice more weighted with concern, "When are you actually going to approach Shaw and tell him that you've decided to leave the Raiders? Maybe even take along some of his key personnel?"

He blinked and flicked at his facial scar, cleared his throat and said, "As soon as possible. Maybe tomorrow morning. If I have to formally challenge him, then we have to be ready to leave immediately. We won't be able to safely stay here, you know. You up for that kind of abrupt total disruption in your life—?"

MacKenzie grimaced with pain, her hand jerking toward her injured shoulder.

Gritting her teeth, she carefully shrugged off half of her sweatshirt, exposing the right shoulder bandage. He gently peeled off the bloody wrap. The wound around the stitches was puffy and red and perhaps inflamed. She eased her breath out, relaxing a little.

He gingerly touched around the perimeter of the wound with his fingertips.

"That hurt at all?"

"A little," she whispered hoarsely

"Your skin there seems warm to me."

"Does it look infected?"

He again rubbed at his scar before he responded. "I hope not, but while I'm talking to Shaw in the morning, you should definitely check in with that healer. Forget about how busy they might still be with others. Get the dressing and drain changed, and ask him about the possibility of an infection."

"I will," she readily agreed.

They both knew the seriousness of an infection. Although the good healers used effective herbal and sulfur-based ointments, not even the largest bands had stored antibiotics. Some crossed the southern border, but rarely made its way this far north. Young children in the Bay Area routinely died from infection—what would have been considered minor and easily treated pre-Collapse. Even the remote possibility of an infection was a major concern.

6

A ONE-SIDED DISCUSSION

Early the next morning, MacKenzie went directly to the courtyard infirmary and waited in line, while Cat accompanied her and then eventually wandered off looking for the Raider Chief, Mike Shaw.

"To test the waters," he'd said to her over his shoulder, making a slight grimace.

∂◦ – ∽

Even after the dust-up with all the recent casualties, there was already an armed guard in a clean long coat manning the door of the cubicle Shaw called The War Room. It contained little more than old green USGS maps of the greater Bay Area stuck up on the walls—some of them heavily creased and faded from use, but it was where Shaw liked to meet and plan out their raids; and it was also where Cat could usually find him when he needed to talk about something important.

Mike Shaw hadn't changed much since twenty-six years ago

when Cat first saw him striding across the parking lot at Blue Rock Springs Park. His hairline had receded slightly back from his forehead, and his short-trimmed hair was nearly all gray—even though he was only forty-eight or possibly forty-nine. But the facial expression was exactly the same. Serious and preoccupied, with perhaps a faint hint that Shaw was wound too tight, his dark intelligent eyes peering back intently and complementing his physical impression when he talked. Cat had never met a high-ranking army officer in the old days, but he suspected that Mike Shaw exhibited what books had sometimes described in a character that possessed military bearing or command presence.

The leader of the Raiders waved Cat into his den, indicating one of the two large red leather chairs pulled up to the big table in the center of the map-lined room. The once elegant seats were well-worn and patched in several places with silver duct tape.

"What's on your mind?" he asked, skipping small talk, as was his normal custom. An obvious afterthought, Shaw asked, "Oh, how's MacKenzie doing?"

Cat sunk down deep in the comfortable old chair and enjoyed its luxurious feel for a second or two before answering.

"She's actually at the healer's this moment getting her wound dressing and drains changed. She may have a little fever, but hopefully no infection…at least not yet."

The chief nodded, his expression not really softening to anything vaguely resembling sympathetic concern. "I see." He glanced down at the bare table in front of him, as if searching for guidance there. In his matter-of-fact monotone he said, "Well, you need to keep an eye on that. She would be impossible for me to replace, you know. Never met anyone, man or woman, who handles horses any better than MacKenzie."

Cat was weighing how Shaw's statements fit into what he had in mind discussing: about leaving the Raiders and taking along MacKenzie…

Shaw looked up and extended his previous line of thought:

"We do need to seek replacements though for our Raider casualties, immediately."

"That will be difficult—"

"Difficult or not, it needs to be done as soon as possible," Shaw said, his tone slightly higher pitched than normal. The interruption was unusual, too, as he was normally polite and formal almost to a fault in any discussion.

Cat rubbed at the scar on his cheek.

"And we have to get them trained quickly. In days rather than weeks."

"Why the big hurry—?"

"Why?" Shaw interrupted again, his expression changing. He looked angry now—something else quite extraordinary for him.

"We can't let any time at all pass before we hit back at those Black motherfuckers." He jerked his head from side to side, as if to clear his thoughts or discourage an insect buzzing around his ears.

Shaw was a bundle of nervous contradictions this morning, Cat thought. He rarely swore or used street slang, and had never looked this upset, as far back as Cat could remember. Might be some kind of post-raid stress. They'd never lost so many Raiders so quickly.

"They're sitting in that cave fort, congratulating themselves on kicking our White asses … No way, Cat, we can't let this pass unanswered. We need to hit them again, soon. And *hard*. The bastards have to pay for Raider losses with Black blood."

Cat was fully aware of Shaw's increasing White supremacist attitude, but it hadn't made too much of an impact on him in the past, until the chief recently settled on The Fist as a target. Cat had tried to talk Shaw out of attempting to hit such a large and well-armed group—an assembly of mostly Black Desperadoes from around the Bay Area, but particularly survivors from the tougher neighborhoods in Oakland and Richmond. Shaw had rolled over and ignored all his past arguments against attacking the Black band. A practical opportunity hadn't presented itself to Shaw until the fake deserter had shown up in the San Jo Ruins. Told them about

The Fist hoarding bags of salt, and the band's planned marauding expedition through the fishing villages south of Monterey. In the final analysis, at least in Cat's mind, it hadn't been a Black/White issue at all, but a good opportunity for a successful raid. Those had been in too short supply for over a year. The kicker had been the rumored extra-large salt stash left virtually unguarded by The Fist—worth a fortune. So he had gone along with the plans, ignoring as unnecessary and irrelevant Shaw's obvious White supremacist arguments justifying the proposed raid.

The usually taciturn Shaw went on and on about recruiting candidates from the other three major Bay Area bands, picking up quality White recruits. No question the Chief was preoccupied with his racist thoughts.

Cat decided he'd pick a better time and come back to approach Shaw about leaving the Raiders. This morning wasn't the ideal moment. Besides, he needed to give both MacKenzie and Oscar a little more time to heal—at least a few more days. Because he suspected down deep it would come to a long knives challenge with Shaw. The chief wasn't going to agree to letting his top lieutenant walk away from the Raiders and take along others vital to the functioning of the unit. Especially now after the embarrassing defeat and losses at the hands of the Black Desperadoes. No way. Best everyone was in good health before they had to abruptly pick up and depart.

After enduring a few more minutes of the wild harangue, Cat politely excused himself and got up to go.

"I need to check on MacKenzie. See what the healer had to say."

"Tell her to get well," Shaw said as Cat was leaving the War Room. "We'll need her wrangling skills for the next assault."

Cat didn't respond, but the last statement left him feeling more than a little apprehensive about the future. The scar near his eye itched now.

7

JANEY'S NOTE

MacKenzie was walking back to their cubicle, considering the distressing news from the healer, when one of Luke's bowmen stopped her.

Paul handed her a folded note and explained, "This came down sometime late yesterday afternoon from the San Fran Ruins for you. Sorry I got busy and forgot to deliver it last night. I hope it's good news."

She flicked her fingers and smiled, dismissing his unnecessary apology.

"Thank you, Paul."

As suspected, it was from Janey. MacKenzie continued on to their cubicle, sat down on the end of the bed, collected herself, before she completely unfolded, smoothed out the note on the bed, and read it:

Dear Mom:

We are doing well, except for a developing problem with a dog pack. One has been picking off goats from our herd at night. It's the birthing season, and we've lost two newborn kids in the last ten days. Of course we can't allow this to go on, and expect to survive. I was hoping Cat would agree to coming up for a visit, and perhaps bring along one of his bowmen, maybe even all three. We hope they will be able to discourage this pack, which has cleverly avoided all our efforts to date to trap or poison them. If Cat would come we'd be grateful for sure, but we could also make it well worth his time. We'd give him two small wheels of our newest batch of high-grade cheese. A valued high trade item at the nearby San Fran Trade-off. Please ask him to consider this as strictly a business proposal. But it would be great if you could come with him for a quick visit, too.

Love,
Janey

MacKenzie read through the short note again, frowning the second time through. Janey was obviously having some serious trouble with these wild dogs. She knew that dog packs around some of the various city ruins were a hazard. More so than Desperadoes. The dogs that survived until now had become exceptionally smart and crafty. Never eating anything dead or possibly polluted by radiation or anything else, and therefore a deadly hazard to them. The successful surviving packs had adopted an eat-only-fresh-kill policy. This included healthy game of all kinds and obviously domesticated herd animals like Janey's goats. She'd heard that the packs were constant pests to others trying to raise livestock around the fringes of both the San Fran Ruins and at the nearby San Jo Ruins, too. And she knew that local packs even stalked the occasional man or woman foolish enough to wander alone and unarmed into the older areas of the local Ruins where the dogs apparently had several hidden dens. The dog packs were lean, hungry, mean, fierce, and very clever.

MacKenzie's frown gradually began to disappear.

This could be a good opportunity, she thought. Luke might be able to secure antibiotics at the San Fran Trade-off, which she was probably going to need soon. The healer had said he thought she was developing a low-grade infection, which could easily get much worse in the near future. He had carefully cleaned the wound and drains, generously applied some smelly salve, but he wasn't overly optimistic about stemming off a major infection.

So this morning he hadn't been ready to render a positive prognosis, give her a total clean bill of health. In their brief conversation, the healer had mentioned that if antibiotics were available and administered soon, it would be a big plus in her speedy recovery from the shoulder wound. In her note, Janey said she was willing to pay two wheels of cheese. Maybe that would be special enough as a barter item to secure the necessary expensive antibiotics MacKenzie needed.

She smiled, thinking maybe all this getting shot in the shoulder wasn't so devastating after all. This might be the kind of opportunity Luke was seeking if they left the Raiders soon. Kind of a chance to develop his skills against a dangerous dog pack. Perhaps he could even freelance for a while around the Bay Area, protecting other herders and wranglers having similar trouble with dog packs. A post-Collapse pest control agent, she thought, her smile broadening. It might not be a permanent employment solution—how many surviving dogs were there after all? But it could give them a good start making it on their own. They'd be able to accumulate a little something to allow her ample time to get established in her wrangling operation, time to build a place, get some horses together, take their time and train them properly, establish their reputation at trade-offs, and such.

The more she thought about it, the more certain she was that protecting Janey's goat herd would be a good trial run for Luke. She'd discuss it with him as soon as he got back from his meeting with Shaw.

Luke was disturbed by MacKenzie's news about her possibly developing a major infection, but he was intrigued—even excited—by her idea about possibly obtaining antibiotics at the San Fran Trade-off.

He carefully read the note from Janey...

After finishing, he glanced up, handed MacKenzie the note back, and said, "Okay. I totally agree, this is probably our best shot. Maybe I should take along some Invasors though, in case the cheese isn't sufficient to swing the trade. No idea what antibiotics go for, but I'm guessing they're a prime trade item."

A warm feeling spread through her.

"I was holding my breath, hoping you'd agree to take the time and go up to the San Fran Ruins. I know Janey and Coby will love seeing you. And it might be a perfect opportunity to broaden your bowmen's skills when we decide to part company with the Raiders. If dog packs are really major pests to some folks trying to raise animals now, then there should be lots of pest control jobs in the near future."

He'd already admitted to her that he hadn't been successful this morning in broaching the departure subject with Shaw. He'd suggested it best to let her and Oscar heal a little more before he confronted Shaw with his decision. Now, after finding out about her likely potential of developing a major infection, he thought it was fortunate he'd waited.

"Yes, I can see it as a good opportunity for us to develop our abilities in a different way," he said, smiling thoughtfully back at MacKenzie. "I hadn't even considered using our bowmen skills for protection against dog packs. But, *if* we can successfully knock out that pack for Janey, who knows how many other assignments might be available out there..." His voice tapered off as he developed an absent gaze in his eyes.

MacKenzie guessed he was mentally working on the goat predator problem, the best way of hunting, discouraging the pests, and so forth.

Luke looked up and said, "You know, I'd better talk to Casey and Paul this evening after dinner." He was referring to his two uninjured bowmen. Oscar obviously wouldn't be available for a dog hunting expedition at Golden Gate Park. "Make sure they're available."

"Maybe you can give Coby a few quick archery lessons when you arrive up there," MacKenzie suggested. "He's bright and handy. He might be able to fill in as the fourth bowman if you need one more in your plan."

She knew Luke and the other bowmen were accustomed and most comfortable working as a tightly knit team of four.

"That's a really good idea," he said, nodding.

After he returned from meeting with Paul and Casey, Luke informed MacKenzie: "The boys are eager to try and help at Janey's. I revealed our plans to permanently leave the Raiders soon, inviting them along, and the importance of this as a kind of trial run for a new way of making a legitimate living. They're definitely interested in leaving with us. Oscar is onboard, too."

"When are you going to head north?"

"Tomorrow morning, early. Sooner we obtain those antibiotics and get back with them, the better for you, right?"

MacKenzie agreed.

"I'll talk to Shaw about us sometime shortly after I return. We should be back in thirty-six hours at the most if all goes well."

"It really sounds like it's going to work out just fine for us," MacKenzie said, but knew she'd be anxious until Luke returned from the quick trip—everyone safe and sound.

8

GHOST DOGS

Fog blew in from the nearby Pacific Ocean, slowly spreading across old Golden Gate Park, clinging in clumps to the top branches of the eucalyptus trees like misty gauze; then, gradually breaking loose and continuing to drift on the slight breeze, eventually thickening and settling to ground level.

Janey and Coby lived in a small stone hut with a slanted corrugated metal roof, built next to a large milking shed and a fenced corral, all located back in the thick cluster of a eucalyptus stand. The pungent medicinal smell of the bark-shedding trees hung in the misty air around the goat-herder's place, masking the usual sharp barnyard odors. A line of gum trees led away from the thick grove several hundred yards to a concrete walled ramp that dropped steeply down to a group of old leveled ball and soccer fields.

This large, mostly treeless area was heavily overgrown around the perimeter, but the bulk of the flat playing areas provided a grassy meadow for the goats. Just after daybreak each morning, the two herders led their thirty-five goats out of the corral and down the ramp, turning them loose to graze. Coby and Janey took turns as shepherd sentinels for the rest of the day, keeping a watchful eye on their valuable milking herd.

Late at night, at least twice recently, individual members of a dog pack lurking around the park were able to silently dig or slip their way under/through parts of the split-log corral fence and make off with newborn kids, the adult goats unable to protect their babies. The following mornings, Coby found footprints left by the dog pack—always eight dogs total. To date, the herders hadn't been able to sufficiently plug all possible gaps in the rough log fence, which had been put together with the primary purpose in mind to keep the herd gathered in one place, not to secure it from outside predators. They'd also tried setting out poison bait and traps and staying up several nights to guard, all their efforts to no avail.

Cat had carefully looked over the entire goat dairy operation before developing his plan for that night. One of the bowmen spent the majority of the day teaching Coby basic archery fundamentals—how to correctly notch an arrow, effectively pull back and hold steady while controlling breathing, then aim, and accurately unleash an arrow at a target; then, they practiced at both stationary and moving targets. To his credit, Coby was a quick study.

As MacKenzie had recommended, Cat had Janey round up and launder four dark wool blankets in warm, clear water, along with sufficient undergarments for all his team members. In the afternoon he walked down the concrete ramp and closely examined the ball fields and overgrown perimeter abutting the surrounding eucalyptus forest. He had his plan firmly in mind now.

By early that evening, as the fog reappeared, all four bowmen had bathed in clean, clear water, dressed in freshly laundered undergarments, and pull-tested their bows a dozen times. After a hearty vegetable and rice meal with slices of delicious goat cheese, they were ready to set up their dog pack trap.

An hour after sunset, they staked out a live older male goat at the foot of the concrete field ramp. Janey had prepared a nosebag of favorite grain feed for it to keep the animal quiet. On either side of the lead-up from the pasture to the ramp, two bowmen were placed ten to twenty yards apart, and staggered so no archer endangered the bowman angled across from him. After the goat was settled, busy chewing on the special crunchy treat, the bowmen also settled, slipping under their spread-out blanket cover. Cat hoped their freshly laundered camouflage helped mask whatever remained of their human scent. In a minute they were all resting in place, each archer peeking out from under his blanket, out toward the pasture and surrounding woods. Four fields of fire.

The fog thickened as time passed.

Cat had slightly tented his blanket in front of his face and had a fair ninety-plus degree view out across the meadow and to the surrounding trees ... except the fog was beginning to shorten his range depth. Drastically. The trees gradually disappearing now.

As time crawled by, Cat figured he could only see out about fifty or sixty feet at the most. Easing himself forward a foot or so and glancing behind him at the staked goat—less than thirty-five feet away—he saw that even its outline was fuzzy, slightly obscured by the fog. The thickening ocean mist was growing colder, too.

It's a good thing we have the blankets over us, Cat thought; without them, and not being able to move around, we'd freeze our asses off.

More time slowly passed ...

It must be nine, maybe later, he estimated, the big toe on his right foot itching now.

Back behind Cat, the goat suddenly bleated.

The wavering, mournful sound startled him. He'd been dozing.

A distant bleating answered, apparently from the corral in the eucalyptus stand. One of the creatures probably trying to send comfort to its hobbled and lonely comrade?

Would that bleating scare off the dog pack, or attract it?

All they could do was wait. Cat smiled wryly, suspecting the goats crying out loudly was at least keeping everyone awake and alert under their camouflaged blankets.

The goats stopped bleating after a few more minutes.

In the silence, time continued to drag by...

10 o'clock...

10:30...

11:00...

∂ ‒ ∽

Eight fuzzy blobs appeared out of the fog directly to the far left of Cat's field of view, slowly fanning out in a *V* and advancing toward the staked goat, appearing to float forward silently over the ground. Drifting on the rolling fog ever so closer ... and taking on more defined shapes...Dog shapes, but still misty apparitions.

Ghost dogs.

He shivered with the weird thought, even though he realized it was nothing more than the expected dog pack predators.

Cat sucked in a deep breath, continuing to peer out at the dogs. His pulse elevated with anticipation.

The leader crept forward at the tip of the *V*. He was huge with a wide head like an alligator, and swiveled his reptilian head back and forth, sniffing the chilled air.

As if on some silent signal, the entire pack stopped as one.

The leader sensing something awry? Another dog back in the pack? How had they communicated? The eight dogs were only about twenty-five yards away. Fuzzy, frozen statues. But well within effective arrow range. He suppressed the immediate impulse to leap up, deciding to let them creep a little closer to the goat, making sure all strung-out eight dogs were better targets for the four bowmen.

If the damned things would just move.

C'mon, c'mon, he silently urged.

The eight ghost dogs remained frozen in place. Wary. Patient. Extremely patient. Waiting, waiting. For what?

Easing his breath back across his dried lips, Cat wiped his moist hands carefully on the sides of his duster; then again touched the bow resting at his side—before lying down earlier, he'd notched an arrow.

The leader, a mix of some kind of tan, thick-chested mastiff and pit bull, seemed to stare directly at him—the closest bowmen. Only the monster's nose moved, twitching ever so slightly, suggesting that, yes, he was a living creature.

Was it smelling him, or perhaps sensing one of the other camouflaged bowmen?

Hopefully not, Cat mouthed under his breath, keyed up, ready.

The standoff went on for at least another full minute—seeming like an eternity to Cat and probably the rest of the concealed bowmen.

With a degree of flexible grace, the pack leader slowly shifted his gaze to the goat, which had begun to bleat again. It must have sensed the ghost dogs in the mist.

Several other distant *bleats* came back through the eucalyptus-scented fog, sounding equally fearful.

The huge leader began to edge forward, but cautiously, one careful step at a time, almost daintily, as if he were tiptoeing through an active minefield.

The pack was almost completely inside the staggered bowmen trap. Five steps closer to the goat and Cat was going to jump up and unleash an arrow, shouting simultaneously to his three cohorts.

One...

Two...

Three...

Four...

Five.

Cat exploded to his feet, shedding the blanket with a backward flip of his head and shoulders, and pulled back on his bowstring—

Before he could get off a shot at the leader, the massive dog veered sharply to his left, darting away from Cat in the direction of where Paul hid under his blanket on the opposite side of the pack.

Cat aimed at the next dog in the V and shot, shouting, "Now!"

The three other bowmen rose and unleashed their arrows.

Two dogs dropped, but the others in the pack growled fiercely and darted in all directions, several headed toward a standing bowmen. All were in the process of notching and aiming second shots, except for Coby, who looked to be having some trouble … fumbling, dropping his second arrow on the ground.

As Cat notched his next shot and aimed, a charging black dog leapt and knocked Coby off his feet before the goat herdsman could get off his defending shot.

Paul, next on that side and closer to the ramp than the herder, turned, assessed the situation, and shot at the side of the leaping black dog, catching it solidly in the side of the throat.

Hubbub for a moment … then dogs fleeing in all directions.

The sprung trap was only partially successful: three dogs shot and down. But the majority of the pack was quickly escaping off into the fog and most were safely into the distant covering wood.

All except for the leader.

Where was he?

Cat scanned about. Had he made cover, too—?

The monster had circled widely back to Cat's right, momentarily out of sight; and then, after apparently identifying Cat as the leader of the ambush, the dog pack leader charged him, like a ghost dog materializing from the fog.

Closing the distance in giant bounds of ten or more feet …

Closer.

Closer.

Closer.

Cat lifted his bow, pulled the bowstring firmly back, and took aim—

The ghost dog soared high into the air, snarling, giant fangs bared, and hurtled through the damp air to an apex about eight feet in front and above Cat's position.

The bowstring whizzed by Cat's ear—

Thunk!

The arrow buried a foot deep into the great dog's chest—an instantly deadly heart shot, he hoped.

As if hit by an invisible sledgehammer, the thickheaded monster dropped to the ground with a final enraged growl lodged deep in its throat.

The magnificent creature died lying on his side, the lethal arrow shaft deep in his chest, his front legs making a last feeble fleeing motion, as if he were a dog dreaming of running—the creature's last dream.

Casey ran up to Cat's side. "You okay, boss?"

"Yes," Cat said hoarsely, shaken by the monster's unexpected attack.

Too close for comfort, he thought.

He sighed deeply, and looked around the clearing.

Across from them, Paul assisted Coby to his feet. In the area between the four bowmen, three dogs were stretched out dead, and a fourth, their leader, lay silent at Cat's feet.

The remainder of the pack, with perhaps some wounded, had escaped into the foggy night.

Cat suspected this particular dog pack would never prey on the goatherd again. No way. So in that vein, the experiment's outcome was a total success.

⌒ – ⌒

It was too late now to take the two great-smelling wheels of goat cheese into the San Fran Trade-off. Cat would go over first thing in the morning to find someone who had/could get antibiotics.

⌒ – ⌒

The next morning, Cat was directed to a vendor who displayed nothing on his small card table.

"You the Medicine Man?" asked Cat.

The barefaced, slender guy eyed him for a moment from under a wide-brimmed black Stetson, then said, "That's right. You need something in my line?"

"A good general antibiotic for infection … nothing requiring refrigeration, pills probably best, you know."

The vendor nodded, bent down, and opened one of three small polished boxes under the table. He came up with an unmarked brown plastic vial. "Amoxicillin pills. They should be kept cool and dry, but do not actually require refrigeration. Okay?"

Cat held out his hand.

The sharp-eyed Medicine Man shook his head and smiled.

"These six pills are very difficult to acquire here in the wasteland, and are very expensive. What do you have to trade?"

Cat opened his backpack and produced the two small wheels of pungent cheese. The vendor took one wheel in hand, smelled it, and smiled broadly. He accepted the other wheel.

"Okay, very good. That'll get you half the pills. Got more cheese or anything else in your knapsack to trade for the other three pills?"

Cat produced a full package of Invasors from the pocket of his duster.

The seller's eyes opened slightly wider and he nodded. "You just bought yourself a bottle of six Amoxicillin pills, pal."

Cat handed over the Invasors.

Time to head for home.

9

BACK HOME

MacKenzie felt a rush of joy catch in her throat when she first saw Luke standing there and grinning in their cubicle doorway early the next afternoon. She spread her arms wide and in a sexy-hoarse voice said, "I'm so glad you're back safe, Lucas. C'mon here to me."

He moved closer, hugged and kissed her, and rattled the small brown vial next to her ear.

"Brought you a little present, girl."

"I guess your hunting expedition was a success," she said, accepting the pill bottle. "Thank you kindly, sir."

"Two a day until gone," Luke said, repeating the trade-off Medicine Man's instructions for properly taking the Amoxicillin. He handed MacKenzie a water bottle from the end table. "Might as well start right now. You're also supposed to drink lots of water with each one of them."

She took a pill, washed it down with a big drink, and then asked, "How did it go up there with the kids?"

"Janey and Coby are doing real well, but miss you," he said, smiling. "They have an experienced partner who is helping them turn all their goat milk into these high quality cheese wheels—about the size of a pie plate. And I can confirm that their cheese tastes great and is readily sought after at the nearby big trade-off. If all goes well, they have plans to double the size of their dairy herd operation by the middle of next year, make a lot more cheese, market it around at a number of various trade-offs, and perhaps eventually make several different kinds, including extra sharp and real mild. I think your daughter and her husband are going to be very successful in their new venture."

That is all very gratifying to hear, Mackenzie thought, looking pleased as Luke finished explaining more of the personal stuff...

"And the dog pack?" she asked, her tone and expression a little more somber. "Your pest elimination plan must have gone well, too? No one injured on your end?"

He shook his head, shrugged, and sighed. "It was only partially successful. Although I don't think that specific dog pack will be bothering Janey and her goatherd again. But we only took out half of the predators, four dead dogs. Fortunately none of the crew was hurt during the process..."

He paused a moment before nodding thoughtfully. "Still, I guess we learned quite a bit. Things we may be able to use in the future, you know."

"Like what kinds of things?" MacKenzie asked, lifting her eyebrows.

Luke brushed at his scar.

"Well, the dog pack was very wary and smart, like we anticipated... They advanced ever so cautiously into our trap. And it was indeed important, I think, that we followed your suggestion and washed our clothes and the blankets we hid under, eliminating our man scent as much as possible. But at the last minute, even though they didn't seem to smell us, the pack somehow sensed our presence, and perhaps the trap. They all froze at the exact same moment. Canine group intuition or something? I don't know. It was an eerie moment."

"That's interesting behavior," she said thoughtfully.

"We didn't anticipate how fast they would adjust to our attack. I guess I thought they'd be disoriented and freeze, at least momentarily. When I first jumped up, they immediately bolted as if understanding it was a trap. Surprisingly, some of the dogs tried to mount an instant counterattack, including the pack leader, who attempted to circle back around, momentarily disappear in the fog, and then come charging out of the mist directly at me."

"Hmmm... What do you think you can do about that in the future?"

"Well, we knew there were eight dogs total in the pack. Coby had determined that from paw prints. I should've assigned each of the four bowmen, including myself, two definite targets by potential pack position... It probably wouldn't have done much good on this particular hunt—we didn't have enough lead time to even get off a second shot before the dogs bolted. And, in the future, I'm guessing we still may not be able to unleash multiple required shots with a large dog pack attacking us across level ground. But I'm thinking it might be smart to establish a similar kind of trap, except in a depression, gully, or shallow ravine, the sides rising to where the bowmen would be hidden from the dog pack. The incline will slow them down for a second or two—enough time to get off required secondary shots. Might be wise to include some gunmen in our ambush party."

MacKenzie made a slightly disapproving face. She knew that Luke could notch and get off a second arrow almost as fast as a rifleman could get off a second shot.

"Well, maybe..." she offered, her tone tentative. "But I'd worry with everyone so close together and the confusion with dogs flying about that guns would more likely introduce friendly fire, either directly or from ricochets."

Luke thought a moment, then continued, "Sure, I guess that's possible ... But maybe we could have the extra gunmen stationed back away from the initial trap, somewhere along the most likely escape routes? Take advantage of their longer shooting range. Probably be safer, too."

She nodded, her expression easing.

"In any event, a good count of the potential size of any future pack will be an essential part of effective planning. The critical things we learned yesterday were that a dog pack is not only clever and extremely wary, but very aggressive—not the least afraid of counterattacking humans. We'll have to account for at least all three of these characteristics in future planning."

"Sounds like you learned more than enough to warrant pursuing this kind of work when we leave the Raiders. Right?"

"I think it could be worthwhile. Both Coby and Janey thought it was a good business idea, too. They mentioned several other herders or ranchers just east and one north of the San Fran Ruins who might be able to use us and pay well for our special pest control services—gave me a couple of names to contact."

MacKenzie smiled deeply. "Seems like you did very well to me, Luke."

He smiled back, generally pleased with how it had all gone.

She shifted her thoughts, her tone sobering again, as she asked him, "When are you going to tell Shaw we're leaving with your three bowmen?"

Luke rubbed his scar. "Soon as you finish your Amoxicillin. Oscar should be in fair shape by then, too. He only has a little bit of a limp."

10

NO OPTIONS

Three days later, in the early evening, the big red leather chair in The War Room did not feel quite so comfortable to Cat.

Mike Shaw was in a good mood, almost talkative, briefly describing three new recruits he'd interviewed in the last few days. White recruits. And that afternoon two of the Raiders who had received minor wounds were cleared by the healers and released back to full duty. The Raider Chief even smiled as he described these positive personnel events.

Despite Shaw's good mood, Cat felt ill at ease, apprehensive of the suspected reaction to what he wanted to say.

"Okay, what's on your mind?" the Raider Chief asked abruptly.

Cat sucked in a breath and let it trickle across his lips. He rubbed the scar near his eye before steeling himself to answer.

"I think we need to talk about how things have been developing in the wasteland lately. And the eventual impact on us."

Shaw nodded. "Okay," he said, his smile gone, his features inexpressive. "What specifically do you mean by *developing?*"

"Well, there are no longer any large hordes of packaged or preserved foodstuffs remaining in old warehouses or controlled by any of the bands. Wastelanders are mostly growing or raising their own food now. Some of them even have enough surplus to trade. Which has given rise to the proliferation of these trade-offs you see springing up all over the place, including the one expanding weekly right next door to us on the runway at the San Jo Airport Ruins…"

Cat paused to allow Shaw to offer some kind of a reaction.

The chief of the Raiders didn't respond, only acknowledged he was listening.

"So," Cat continued, "life in the wasteland is changing. Especially for the large bands of Desperadoes."

"What exactly do you mean by *changing*?"

"Well, there is no real need anymore for such large, well-armed groups," Cat explained, speaking more slowly now. "Basically, there is nothing much left to fight over and control. Large bands of Desperados are not functional, can't be supported by this kind of environment. They will soon be obsolete, if they aren't already. That's why we're seeing so many deserters from other Bay Area groups."

Cat stared silently at his chief.

"I get the point you're trying to make here," Shaw said. "But I don't agree with that last obsolete judgment at all. The Raiders exist not only to hit other bands of Desperadoes for their stores of stolen supplies, but as a tight brotherhood, dedicated to fighting and protecting the honor of the White race…" He paused, his features hardening. "Why is it so important we discuss this now? Are you suggesting we need to change something immediately?"

"I think it is time to disband the Raiders—"

"Whoa," Shaw said, interrupting Cat and holding up the palms of both hands. "That isn't going to happen anytime soon, period." He paused, his thick eyebrows drawn down into a V over his nose, and shook his head.

There was a long moment of awkward silence.

"Got anything else you want to add?" Shaw finally asked, his tone brittle and confrontational.

"Yes, I guess there is one more important thing," Cat said, flicking at his scar again. "Whether you elect to disband the Raiders, MacKenzie and I are leaving, and I think the other three bowmen will elect to go along—"

Shaw slammed his hand down and reached across the table, clutched Cat's wrist, and said, "Absolutely not." His face was almost completely flushed, a large blue vein in his neck protruding.

Cat had never seen Mike Shaw so angry.

"You and MacKenzie are not going anywhere, you understand. I forbid it!"

He sucked in a deep breath and noisily let it out, releasing Cat's wrist, and then pushed away from the table, as if distancing himself from such a ridiculous proposal. But he kept his unwavering dark eyes locked on Cat's gaze.

Ever so slowly, he shook his head from side to side, and he added in a raspy but clear voice, "Those three bowmen of yours, they're not going anywhere. Not while I'm chief of the Raiders. Is that clear?"

It was quiet for a long spell—at least a full minute; neither man spoke or moved.

Cat cleared his throat and said in a coldly determined voice, "Oh, I understand you all right. But I can't abide your decision. You need to give what I've said more thought."

"It's more than just an arbitrary decision pulled out of my ass, Cat," Shaw said in a throaty voice, barely audible but ominous. "I've built the Raiders into what they are today. And no one, I mean *no* one, is going to take that apart while I'm alive and kicking. You understand that?"

Cat leaned back in his big sagging chair and nodded. "Well, I guess that leaves me no real option, Mike ... I have to formally challenge you because of your decision. You understand *that?*"

"A long knives face-off?" the Raider Chief said, his shocked expression mixed with surprise, disappointment, and perhaps even some dread. "You and me going at it, Cat?"

"That's right."

For a moment Shaw looked troubled, almost distraught, as if he might break down emotionally. Then he slowly shook his head, visually regaining his poise, and said, "You know, I never thought of you as a son, of course, because of the closeness of our ages…" With a sincere sadness creeping into his tone, he added, "But, you *always* seemed to be like a…well, a little brother I never had."

Cat sucked in a breath and shrugged. "I'm sorry it's come to this, Mike. But MacKenzie and I are leaving, and soon. Of course we'd prefer to go with your full blessing, but if it means you and I must fight in a long knives challenge before we can go, then so be it. Make the announcement."

"I see," Shaw said. "Well, so be it then. Tomorrow morning at 7:00 in the courtyard. Billy Joe will be my second. And yours?"

"Oscar."

He hadn't thought the challenge would be so soon.

"I'll make sure the formal announcement is circulated tonight to all Raiders," Shaw said, his hardened features inexpressive again.

Cat had mixed feelings; a certain sense of relief. He'd finally said what he had to say to Shaw, but in a way he felt remorse. He'd bitterly disappointed—perhaps even badly hurt—Shaw by what he'd said. He rose stiffly from his seat, as if he'd instantly aged ten years.

Before he could leave, Shaw offered his hand, adding, "Lucas Zachary, you were a good Raider, perhaps the best to ever serve under me. I'm going to miss you."

Cat shook the chief's hand, but remained silent, turned away toward the doorway, and left. He felt a heavy sadness in his chest.

11

LONG KNIVES CHALLENGE

During the decade and a half of the Food Wars, the Desperado bands had all grown in size, authoritarian leaders taking over and leading the then undisciplined militias. All strong, ruthless, ambitious, and very bright men. But after a while a kind of semi-egalitarian custom developed among the bands. Someone widely respected in the group, usually a high-placed lieutenant, could rise to publicly challenge either an official edict—or more commonly the leader himself—for his position. These dramatic but infrequent confrontations became highly structured affairs, formally called *challenges*, and they were always settled with long blades—Bowie knives or K-Bars the two most popular weapons. Participants were bound together with a six-foot length of rope tied to the participants' wrists. The existing leader usually possessed a distinct benefit, exercising his right of deciding which side of the wrists to bind. Obviously he chose his non-dominant side. If both competitors were right handed, the existing leader then had the huge advantage of binding the dominant hand of his challenger—a benefit almost impossible to overcome in the quickly concluded duels. Challenge matches were settled in *two* possible ways: death, or if one of the participants—usually badly wounded and bleeding—elected to cut the rope from his wrist to his winning opponent's.

Fortunately for Cat, who was right-handed, Mike Shaw was left-handed, meaning that both would have their dominant hands free. A basically fair match.

A ring roughly thirty feet in diameter was chalked on level ground in the Raider courtyard. The ground was then carefully raked and sprinkled with water, offering as smooth and good a footing as possible, free of dust. The match would be fought with no time limit in this chalked, dry, level ring.

At 7:00 A.M. a thin mist hovered several feet over the compound courtyard, but threatened to quickly dissipate as the sun rose over the coastal range and the air gradually warmed. All the Raiders stood around the chalked circle, even the recently wounded, except for one who was unable to leave the infirmary. The tension was palpable in the misty morning air, like the electric tingling that raised goose bumps on a muggy day moments before a thunderstorm. The bundled-up crowd was sweating heavily, but remaining absolutely quiet, standing still, as if they were attending a graveside funeral and awaiting the arrival of the deceased's wooden coffin— and in a way that was almost true. In a few minutes either Luke or Mike Shaw would probably be deceased, needing a coffin.

For moral support, MacKenzie stood between Casey and Paul, the uninjured bowmen, her heart thumping, her pulse racing, a lump in her throat making it impossible for her to talk. She dug into her right long coat pocket, her fingers touching and taking some small comfort from the fully loaded .357 revolver she'd brought along in the event there was trouble after the match. She had convinced herself that Luke would win, but she worried about the immediate reaction of several of Shaw's closest and wildest sociopathic supporters. She feared she might need the handgun to force a safe exit after the contest—at least to wave as a visual threat.

MacKenzie stared helplessly across the chalked circle at a path opening between the spectators. Luke would soon appear, being led along that path through the Raiders by his second, Oscar...

A nervous shuffling at the rear of the crowd, and then the wounded bowman limped into view. Close behind him, Luke followed.

No one in the crowd said a word as the two made their way through the silent Raiders, stopping only when they reached the center of the chalked circle.

A few moments later, Mike Shaw appeared, led by his second, Billy Joe.

Both challenge opponents were dressed exactly alike, neither in traditional protective garb. No, they were exposed, barefoot and bare-chested, each wearing old-time athletic shorts that were cinched up neatly by a length of rope at the waist.

Luke's scarred face bore no expression as an announcer of sorts entered the center of the ring beside him and spoke loudly in a high-pitched, brittle voice.

"Ladies and Gentlemen, this challenge is now declared official and on schedule. Seconds, arm your participants."

Both seconds handed their principal a weapon—duplicate Bowie knives glistening in the morning sun that was just now beginning to burn off the thin mist. Huge blades of polished steel—sharp and lethal-appearing.

Underneath her long coat, MacKenzie shivered, even though the air was starting to grow hot. She uselessly squeezed the .357, knowing that for now everything was completely out of her hands. Luke was essentially on his own in the ring.

"Seconds, any questions or problems?" asked the announcer.

Both grim-faced men shook their heads, the seconds remaining quiet.

"All right, tie them off," the announcer instructed.

Oscar and Billy Joe carefully bound their participant's wrist with an end of the six-foot length of clean white rope. They exchanged places for a moment and carefully checked knots.

Both seconds nodded, signaling to the announcer that all was in order. They were ready.

He nodded back, before hesitating and glancing about the chalked circle at the unsmiling crowd. No one moved. It was time for someone to die.

Straightening himself, the announcer said, "Attention."

And he slowly stretched his right arm above his head. "May the best man remain standing. Let the challenge, commence—"

With that last word the announcer simultaneously dropped his arm and exited the chalked ring.

MacKenzie tried but couldn't swallow the thick lump in her throat. Her mouth was too dry and parched.

Last night Luke had described to her two previous long knife challenges involving the Raider Chief, which she'd elected not to attend. Mike Shaw had been a little younger then, thinner, and probably much faster. He'd also been skillful with a Bowie knife, managing to kill one opponent and severely disable the other, both matches ending quickly—under a minute. But he'd depended on the same trick each time, which Luke had described to MacKenzie. He'd be on his guard, and had a clever plan for countering Shaw's special move if he relied on it again.

The two opponents circled each other slowly, clockwise, moving in tandem, the umbilical rope stretched loosely and keeping each well within easy closing range of the other's sharp weapon.

Luke stopped circling, leaned in slightly, and poked out with his blade, a sort of weak fencing maneuver, little more than a token feint. Shaw reacted with a lazy but effective shuffling lateral move, easily remaining well out of range. Even though he was older and heavier since his last long knives challenge, he still seemed agile on his feet.

They began to circle again—

With a lightning-fast forward skipping movement, Shaw closed the short gap between them, slashing with his Bowie knife, a kind of wide sweeping scythe-like movement.

Luke's reaction was equally quick. He dodged backwards to the end of the binding rope that was immediately stretched bowstring tight, only the tip of Shaw's Bowie knife reaching and nicking Luke's chest. The injury was a slash about an eighth of an inch long and barely skin deep. Blood oozed from the wound, streaking the right half of Luke's chest with several bright scarlet trickles.

The crowd gasped collectively at the sudden sight of blood, and moved in lockstep a foot closer.

MacKenzie recoiled, and then she dug in, resisting the jostling push forward from behind.

Oh no, she mouthed, unable to resist squeezing her eyes tightly shut. But she blinked, and immediately realized Luke wasn't seriously hurt. No, not at all, she thought, releasing a quiet sigh of relief. The blood streaking his chest momentarily looked grave.

They circled each other like a pair of wary fighting dogs, looking for an opponent's lapse in concentration, anything allowing an opening for them to dart in and finish off the other combatant.

But for at least a full minute no opportunity presented itself—not the slightest. Both opponents were too alert, too wary, and too focused. Around and around they shuffled, a lack of grace marring the barefoot ballet of death, a slight clumsiness introduced by the restraining rope tethering them together.

As they circled, MacKenzie recalled Luke's words from last night: *He always tries the same trick within the first two minutes. I'll be ready.* Then, he'd described Shaw's maneuver and his unusual planned countermove, smiling confidently back at MacKenzie. She wasn't quite so confident it would work. But she trusted Luke's judgment.

She waited, watching carefully, anticipating Shaw's trick.

Luke made another short fencing probe with his long blade.

This time Shaw didn't bother to acknowledge the half-hearted effort. He continued circling, peering at Luke, watching intensely, like a snake turning and tracking a victim, waiting for its moment to successfully strike.

Slowly, they circled.

MacKenzie noticed Shaw's bound right hand open ever so slightly and begin to edge down slowly—a fraction of an inch— finally slipping around and nonchalantly touching the rope with his fingertips. The beginning of the trick.

She held her breath.

The Raider Chief grabbed the rope, forcefully jerking it toward himself, and stepped backwards a full stride, pulling stoutly—

Instead of lunging forward off-balance, arms flailing and caught completely off-guard as Shaw had anticipated, Luke dropped forward onto his knees and drove his glistening blade down, burying it into the middle of Shaw's bared right foot.

Shaw froze, a silent grimace of pain paralyzing his expression.

In his opponent's complete immobilization, Luke sprang upward with his bloody Bowie knife—reversed now in his hand—and drove the blade under the Raider Chief's chin, sinking it deep into his throat.

Shaw's weapon slipped from his right hand, and he sagged to his knees, his left hand reaching up to clutch and stem the crimson flood gushing from his throat.

A large wet circle of black stained the dry, raked dirt.

The Raider Chief lay prone in the center.

The challenge was over.

One or two spectators with incredulous expressions moved forward to the edge of the ring, but the majority of the crowd stood silently in place, too shocked to even take a measured gasp of breath.

Mike Shaw, the feared long-time Chief of the Raiders, was dead.

Along with Casey and Paul, MacKenzie hurried forward to Luke's side, and as Oscar limped ahead of them, they shouldered their way through the stunned, silent crowd. MacKenzie clutched the grip of the handgun in her pocket, but didn't need to brandish it. No one bothered to confront them as they cleared the ring and exited the courtyard.

They made their way back to MacKenzie's cubicle, picked up their backpacks and other gear left neatly stacked; and a brief few moments later they were back in the stable off the courtyard, each mounting a saddled horse ... And all were soon riding safely out of the Raider's sanctuary.

So ended the brief—two and a half minutes—last Raiders' long knives challenge.

12

THE BEST OF TIMES

The next three and a half years were the best of times in Cat and MacKenzie's shared life.

For the first half of that period they roamed the greater Bay Area, working their challenging pest control service—themselves and the three bowmen.

They would camp for a week or so near a large herd of cows, goats, sheep, and even two or three times by penned chicken coups or large turkey flocks. Once they'd spent most of a week near an isolated hog ranch in the Oakland Hills.

After considering the specific problem and circumstances, they would usually set a baited trap of some kind, wait for the predators to be lured in close, and then eliminate them. Most often it was the wild dog packs, but once, near the L'More Groundstar, they killed a kind of mutant bigheaded coyote that was slaughtering turkeys. In the case of the hog farm, it had taken three days of assessment, but then only a day to actually track down, corner, and shoot an old mountain lion.

They usually lived in tents, MacKenzie and Cat intensely happy with their positive lifestyle away from the dangerous world of the Desperado bands. Doing something socially constructive. And the venture proved moderately lucrative. They bartered for their fees, always converting a large portion of their earnings to some kind of easily-stored, non-perishable goods, like tiny amounts of gold or silver or packaged high grade tobacco, or occasionally unopened packs of Invasors.

During this time they often spent their evenings in front of campfires discussing plans for the development of MacKenzie's horse ranch dream. They knew they would need substantial start-up costs to locate a good spot near a supply of wild horses and to actually build the spread. They would also need savings to carry themselves until they broke even—they estimated about six months.

But after almost two years, before they thought they really had enough saved for the ranch, the assignments came a little less frequently. Ranchers and farmers were growing larger with more hired help, some able to adequately provide their own protection. At the same time, the outdoor, rugged, and nomadic lifestyle seemed to be wearing heavily on MacKenzie's fragile health, which had never been robust since her gunshot and infection. She'd never regained a full range of motion in her right shoulder. When the climate was exceptionally damp or the air thick with allergens, she was subject to various respiratory problems, often ending up with a dry, rasping cough that sometimes lasted for weeks. She regularly took several herbs, but they were only marginally successful strengthening her weakened immune system or controlling the coughing spells. Still, she suffered stoically without complaining.

In the middle of winter, despite not quite reaching their savings goal, they were forced to make a decision. MacKenzie had been temporarily bedridden for a day, and after the two-week long severe dry hacking spell she was really run down physically. They talked it over and decided it was a good time to give up their nomadic lifestyle, start the ranch, and finally settle down in one place.

So, after twenty-two months of battling the predators preying on farmers and ranchers in the Greater Bay Area, the pest control team ceased operation. Two of the bowmen, Casey and Paul, headed back to the busy San Fran Trade-off to look for possible opportunities. Oscar stayed on with Cat and MacKenzie, and the three close friends ventured east into what had once been the Great Central Valley, but was now a hotter and semi-arid Great Central Desert. They wanted to get closer to the great mustang herds roaming the Sierra Foothills, and also hoped the drier climate would help reduce MacKenzie's recurring respiratory problems.

They traveled out beyond the eastern remnant of the Pre-Collapse great freeway system, the once green belts of irrigated agricultural land paralleling old I-680 scorched a golden brown now, and continued on past a few operating dry farms. They encountered only isolated nomadic herders as they moved deeper east into the most desolate region. The land in the barren wasteland was priced right, with no existing landowners preventing them from squatting for free almost anywhere they pleased. A year-round fresh water source was in short supply in the high desert.

It took almost four weeks of searching and a few days of carefully observing several larger desert critters before they pinpointed a good year-round source of sweet water. A clear spring in a shallow cave, located about thirty-five miles due east of the sprawling Stockton Ruins, just at the beginning of the rising Sierra Foothills.

Taking their time, the three spent the next five months boxing in the spring, constructing two solid rock dwellings with sloping tin roofs, and three large horse corrals with open-sided, wood-framed sheds. Using gravity flow, they piped water in tiled conduits to both houses, the corrals, and even had enough piping left to cap a line near two acres they cleared of rocks, where they eventually intended to plant irrigated alfalfa, hay, and maybe a vegetable garden. During the waning days of summer they established physical contact with three different groups of wranglers capturing wild horses: the largest operation in the high desert twenty miles to the north, another ten miles deeper in the nearby foothills, and the smallest located a full day's ride up in a meadow in the distant Sierras. They advised the wranglers of their new ranch location, and their need for a constant supply of healthy, unbroken stock. They promised to pay well and immediately did so, bringing back to the ranch three wild but handsome mustangs.

MacKenzie was an absolute marvel at breaking and training even the most unmanageable horse, only slightly hampered by her disabled right shoulder.

Still, the size of the ranch operation slowly grew and was an ongoing drain on their dwindling hoard of valuable trade items. They'd experienced a relative high cost buying and hauling building materials and supplies out to the isolated site. And there was no inexpensive available feed for their animals, neither hay, alfalfa, or grain grown anywhere near them in the high desert. They wouldn't be able to supply their own feed until the following late spring. They estimated it would take at least until then before they were breaking even and not burning up their meager savings. Fortunately, Oscar had chipped in with most of his own savings.

MacKenzie usually stayed back at the ranch, working at their spread full time with the new stock, while twice a month Luke, or sometimes Oscar, took the newly trained horses in to the closest trade-offs and picked up supplies—usually a four to six day round trip away from the spread. After six months of selling off their horses, the ranch was beginning to gain a solid reputation with their farmer, rancher, and herdsmen customers. They were confident they were going to make it to late spring and their first alfalfa harvest.

During these bi-weekly expeditions back to semi-civilization, Luke noticed significant change. There were small Desperado gangs or individuals still leading the plundering lifestyle, but basically only on the fringe of society now—true wild west outlaws. More farmers and ranchers were producing more foodstuff and many other kinds of goods for trade. More weekend trade-offs were springing up, usually somewhere near an old freeway. Many traders around the Greater Bay Area were now using printed scrip from San Fran Shield to facilitate commercial exchange—Shield credits even used at a number of the outlying trade-offs almost as commonly as straight barter. In conversation the wasteland was often referred to as Cal Wild, and all those who lived outside the Shields were called Freemen, partly to distinguish themselves from the slowly increasing numbers of wandering DPs.

It was becoming rare to hear anyone refer to the time before or after the missile attacks as pre- or post-Strike. It was more common for a Freemen to just say: Pre-Collapse or Post-Collapse. This recognized that even though Cal Wild still had a number of dangerous hotspots, there were also many other environmental hazards, some—like UV poisoning—set in motion a long time back, way before the missile strikes had been launched almost thirty years ago.

Times were indeed changing.

13

THE WORST OF TIMES

MacKenzie knew it was already after seven in the morning, and with Luke gone taking a string of four of their best horses to the big trade-off near the Stockton Ruins, she should be out helping Oscar with the early morning chores—a dozen other horses in various stages of training to feed, water, and groom, two coops of chickens to feed, eggs to gather, and the cow to milk. All this before any actual training commenced. But she was exhausted, could barely lift her head off her pillow, much less muster the energy to dress herself and struggle out to face the long day's demanding work. She'd been awake much of the night, coughing, and this time bringing up some nasty-looking green phlegm. Fever mixed with bouts of teeth-chattering chills all night long, her chest walls aching after the steady coughing. Early in the winter she'd had another long spell with the dry bronchitis, but this was something else.

Deep down, MacKenzie feared she was seriously sick this time.

She decided to rest her eyes for a few minutes more, and then she'd pull herself together and get up … But apparently she'd slipped back off to sleep. The wind-up clock on the end table read eight-thirty now. She sucked in a deep breath that made her gasp from the sharp pain stabbing deep into her chest—

Knock, knock.

Oscar stood politely with his knuckled hand still resting on her bedroom doorframe and respectfully holding his hat in his other hand.

"You feeling okay, MacKenzie?" he asked, the same slightly concerned expression on his face as last night at dinner, when she'd experienced a prolonged coughing fit. "It's getting kind of late, and since you hadn't showed up to begin training—"

She interrupted him with a rackety round of coughing…

After recovering and wiping her teary eyes, she shook her head.

"No, I'm not doing real well, Oscar. I've been up most of the night, and I'm running a fever now, I think. I hurt in here, too." She touched her hand gingerly to both sides of her chest. This was a lot of complaining for MacKenzie. She closed her eyes, as if the effort to whine about her symptoms had not only embarrassed but exhausted her.

"Want me to hook up the wagon, take you in to see the healer?" Oscar asked, looking more than just concerned and helpless.

She shook her head. No telling how long she'd be bouncing around in the back of that buckboard before they tracked down Serra. The healer was itinerant, roaming about over a thousand square mile area of The Great Central Desert, swinging by various permanent camps, large herds of goats and sheep, a few big cattle ranches way up north, and some of the weekly trade-offs strung up and down old multi-lane State Highway 99. No, she thought wryly, the damn ride by itself would probably do her in.

"Guess I'm not up for that kind of jarring trip, Oscar," she murmured in as strong a voice as she could muster, shrugging apologetically.

A frown spread across his face, then he jammed his hat back on his head.

"It must be pretty bad," he said, nodding. "And in that case, maybe I should head over to Lodi Camp by myself. That's Serra's home base, and they'll know where I can find her …" His hesitant voice trailed off as he peered at MacKenzie to agree with his suggestion.

She smiled and whispered, "That sounds like a good idea to me."

"You'll be okay alone until Cat gets back though, right?"

She nodded, even though she knew Luke probably wouldn't be back today. He could be gone at least another two days—probably not back until tomorrow evening or even the next morning at the earliest. Maybe three more days. It all depended on how long it took him to get a good price for the four horses. The three of them had recently decided they weren't selling their stock so cheap anymore, not taking first offers.

"Sure, I'll be fine," she said in a raspy voice, her throat feeling scratchy and dry now.

"Okay, but let me get some water and something to eat laid out handy there on your night stand."

Oscar disappeared from the bedroom doorway.

Lodi Camp was almost a full day's hard ride away and that much back … *if* Oscar was lucky enough to find the healer there. She could be anywhere, as much as another good two days ride away either to the north or south.

MacKenzie drifted off again with Oscar in the kitchen. She blinked when he came back into the bedroom and noisily set the water and cold dinner leftovers on her nightstand.

"Thanks," she said, smiling and trying to show more confidence than she felt.

He reached down and gently patted her shoulder. "You take care, MacKenzie. I'll be back as soon as I can with Serra in tow. You get some rest."

She sucked it up and in a slightly stronger voice she said, "Okay, Oscar. *You* be careful, you hear."

He grinned and shook his head. "Don't worry."

They'd heard reports of a gang of Desperadoes robbing small herders east of the Lodi Camp area.

MacKenzie smiled wryly to herself as Oscar left the house. Better be at least two or more outlaws try to jump him together, she thought, and they best be heavily armed and bring their A game. Oscar was bigger and heavier than Luke now, real handy with his bow, rifle, sidearm, and Bowie knife. And completely fearless despite still walking with a slight limp from his wound over four years ago at The Fist fiasco. He was a good friend and a top wrangler. They were lucky he stayed on with them, because he'd made no more than room and board in the last year. And he'd sunk most of his own life savings into the ranch, so he was heavily in the red, too.

MacKenzie dozed back off, too tired to even keep her eyes open.

14

A PRETTY GOOD RUN

Cat had been lucky, finally selling off all four horses for top prices, but not until his third night at the Stockton Ruins Trade-off.

The next day he was riding back hard to the ranch, anxious to return before the sun set at his back. He'd been gone not quite five days, and couldn't wait to tell MacKenzie and Oscar about their good fortune. He was carrying fifteen ounces of silver and another full ounce of gold. At these rates, the ranch would be operating at a profit sooner than they all thought—even before early spring planting. He couldn't suppress a slight grin.

But at dust, he slowed as he cautiously rode up to the larger stone house built nearest to the cave spring.

There was a strange horse tied up to the front hitching post…

No, it's not a strange horse at all, Cat decided, after dismounting, pulling the bandanna down from his face, and quickly brushing part of the dust from his long coat. He checked the mount up close, rubbing its head between the ears. The grayish roan with the neatly trimmed black mane belonged to the healer, Serra, from Lodi Camp southwest of Highway 99, not too far north from the trade-off. He smacked his dusty cap against his side before entering the front door, growing more concerned.

Why was Serra here?

He found Oscar and the healer standing and talking outside the closed door to the main bedroom.

Cat's pulse raced. Something must be wrong with MacKenzie!

He approached the two as they broke off their whispering

"What's happened?" he asked in a lowered voice, heavy with concern. "An accident?"

Oscar shook his head and said, "No, Cat. But MacKenzie's down pretty sick." He gestured his head at the healer. "I had to ride in and get Serra for her."

"She's actually quite ill," the healer said, kneeling to pick up her little canvass bag on the floor and snapping it open. "MacKenzie has pneumonia—"

"And how bad can that get?" Cat interrupted.

"Without antibiotics, pneumonia is always serious," the healer said, handing Cat a bottle of pills from her bag. "Unfortunately, I don't have any antibiotics. But I was just telling Oscar that these herbs *may* help boost her immune system. I hope so, anyhow."

He took the bottle from the healer, but paid little attention to it. MacKenzie already took all kinds of herbs, had since her injury five years ago.

"What do you exactly mean by serious?"

Serra looked him steadily in the eye, and then she glanced away at the closed door, noticeably frowning. She sucked in a deep breath before directly facing him again.

"I guess you want a realistic prognosis in plain language, right?" she whispered, nodding thoughtfully, as if answering her own question.

His throat felt tight, his heart thumping, and he dreaded what he was about to hear—he knew by that last statement it wasn't going to be good. With only a momentary hesitation, he replied, "Yes, of course, Serra. Please don't romance any of it. Give it to me straight up."

She took another deep breath and visibly sighed.

"Well, Cat … MacKenzie has all the most critical pneumonia symptoms. Even with a younger person in her condition, antibiotics at this point probably wouldn't help all that much. Her immune system is too compromised. So, she's really like a much older person, just struggling to survive. Not much anyone can do for her at this point. I realize this sounds downright pessimistic, but I'm afraid it's the truth, my best assessment, straight up."

Serra stared at Cat and then shrugged, her expression sympathetic. She knew Cat, Oscar, and MacKenzie fairly well, had even bought the young roan outside from them—one of their first sales. So Cat knew it was more than a detached, unemotional professional talking to him.

"I think I know some of what you must be experiencing, and I certainly feel for you …" She looked down at her bag, swallowing, and gathered her thoughts.

She looked back up at Cat. "Okay. So what can you do for MacKenzie, right? Give her those herbs from the bottle, four times a day. Keep her at an upright angle with pillows to help keep her lungs clear, even when she's sleeping. That's one of the major dangers right now, her lungs filling with fluid. Try to help her to keep water and maybe some thin soup down. Vomiting and diarrhea are also common symptoms at this stage. And dehydration is another deadly danger. Keep her comfortable, as cool as possible when she's feverish or warm when she's feeling chilled—"

The healer stopped suddenly, and then for a long time she looked sadly at a loss for more concrete suggestions. But finally, she shrugged and continued in a barely audible tone:

"It's really up to MacKenzie now, you know. She has to fight for her life. There's not anything more we can do for her than what I've just said."

"She's a tough one," Cat insisted, his voice a little too loud.

The healer raised her eyebrows, nodded, and smiled. "She is indeed."

There was an awkward silence then.

"Thanks, Serra," Oscar said, taking the healer's arm to lead her back to the front door. Cat knew he'd take care of whatever fee had to be paid for the visit.

He absently nodded his thanks, turned, and eased the bedroom door open. He stood inside the darkened room, letting his eyes adjust to the dimness.

At first he thought MacKenzie was sleeping comfortably propped up at a forty-five degree angle with a stack of pillows behind her ... but then he heard the ominous sound—a little like a slightly punctured bellows of wheezing air. Her breath labored. As he neared the side of the bed, MacKenzie's eyes popped open. Surprisingly, they appeared clear and alert, even in the dim moonlight coming through the window. But her face was pale, gaunt, and drawn, crow's feet and forehead wrinkles more pronounced. Not the same woman he'd left five days ago with just a dry hack. She had visibly aged.

She smiled broadly—the *ole MacKenzie special*, he called it.

He slipped her nearest hand into his, and held up the herbal pills with his other free hand. "Serra left these for you; she thinks they'll probably help you some." His voice sounded stiff, even to him, as if he didn't believe his own words. Self-consciously, he cleared his throat. "You're supposed to take them with lots of water."

MacKenzie motioned for him to put the pills on the nightstand, shaking her head almost dismissively, her smile thinning. In a fairly strong voice she said, "You're back later than we planned. Must've sold all the horses?"

"I did," he said with a trace of enthusiasm, but with a hard lump caught in his throat.

"Got a really top price for all of them, too—including that smallish chestnut you worried so much about. No problem, girl." He grinned sincerely at her.

Her broad smile quickly returned. "Ah ... that's my boy." She gave his hand a quick, firm squeeze.

During the subsequent silent lull, MacKenzie's expression grew darker, more serious.

In a weaker but still very measured tone she said, "Luke, we've never really kidded each other about anything important, right?"

He shook his head in agreement.

"Okay, so we're not about to start at this stage of the game. All the cards on the table, face up. Straight shooting. Okay...?"

Her voice trailed off, her expression serious and thoughtful as she peered intently back into his eyes.

She turned her head and coughed into a large handkerchief, which she quickly hid out of sight under her pillow. After catching her breath, MacKenzie continued in a slightly weaker voice, "I didn't need Serra's visit, you see. I fully understand what's happening to me here, Luke. And so do you, I think. So it's time for just plain talk, and some necessary planning. Right?"

Again, he agreed without commenting.

"When it's all over, which will be soon, I'd like you to go in to the San Fran Ruins and tell Janey in person. Even though you saw yourself as her big brother, she always looked up to you as her dad, you know. It's best she hear it from you." She closed her eyes for a moment then, her breathing grew even more labored, close to ragged.

MacKenzie visibly swallowed and blinked, the thin smile permanently etched on her gaunt, careworn features. She gestured and looked out the window.

"I'd like to be buried up on that little hill out there overlooking the corrals. Because it was a grand time for me here with you, getting the chance to do what I truly loved...Too short, I know, but a happy time."

"It was a happy time for me, too," he said, his voice hoarse and barely audible as he squeezed her hand. He didn't even try to dry his eyes.

She rested until she caught her breath again.

"And your plans, Lucas? I suppose you're not going to want to stay on here and keep the ranch?"

He shrugged, the ranch and its continued operation something he hadn't considered yet.

She chuckled wryly. "Okay, but after you do decide you're going, let Oscar take it over. He can pay you our share of it back over time. He's a good man, and I'm convinced he's going to be a top wrangler and eventually pretty successful. He's been a principal backer in the ranch's early tough development, both financially and with muscle. So he deserves the place if he wants it. And I'm pretty sure he will."

Cat nodded. "No problem from me there," he whispered, the lump still in his throat.

She locked onto his gaze then and shook her head ever so slowly. "And Luke, don't look so damn sad for me. Wipe your eyes." She clutched his hand more firmly, letting the smile broaden, and then after a moment's thought she slowly nodded.

"You and me, Luke, well, you know…"

Her hoarse whisper trailed off for a second or two before she added in a stronger, clearer, loving tone, "Thank you, Lucas Zachary, for sharing part of your life with me … We had a pretty good run, didn't we, boy."

He wiped his eyes then.

"We did indeed, girl," he whispered, his voice cracking, his eyes still moist.

Despite the alternating bouts of sweats and teeth-rattling shivers, Cat insisted on sleeping by her side that night in their bed. Not actually sleeping, but trying to rest, stretched out next to MacKenzie, slowly going over their life together in his head, like seeing a favorite old movie repeated, but slowed down … In the middle of the night, he decided she'd summed it up perfectly: *We had a pretty*

good run. Especially him. MacKenzie had made a positive impact on his life, causing some important attitude changes, and he would always be grateful. He turned to face her and mouthed: *Thank you, my sweet lady.* Then he kissed her cheek ever so lightly.

Finally, exhausted, he drifted off.

❧ – ❧

She died in her sleep around four-thirty in the morning, waking him with the ending dry rattle.

❧ – ❧

The next day, Cat, with the help of Oscar, buried her body up on the little hill in back of the corrals. They carefully stacked a rounded mound of rocks over her grave to keep away the varmints. For the next two days he mostly mourned her death, going through the other necessary motions of living. Then during the third day, he thought some about what he was going to do in the immediate future. Of course he was going to leave the ranch with Oscar. He didn't want to continue in the horse business here without MacKenzie. That had been *her* dream. He decided that on the fourth morning after Mackenzie died, he was going to leave permanently, head for the San Fran Ruins. He'd see Janey first like he'd promised, maybe reminisce some with her about her mother. Then...

Well, then he wasn't sure what he wanted to do. Perhaps he'd look up Paul and Casey while he was near the San Fran Shield, see what they were doing. He'd even considered using his dad's journal, head down south, and see if he could track and locate him. But after a little more consideration that didn't seem practical at this time...just a kind of long-term wish, which he pushed to the back of his thoughts.

❧ – ❧

Early the next morning, Cat watched the sun break over the rounded pile of rocks on the hill overlooking the ranch. He whispered a final goodbye to MacKenzie. "Adios, my best friend, my sweetheart."

Then he went down to where Oscar was milking the cow and told him his decision about the ranch.

Oscar readily agreed to the briefest of sale terms.

Cat shook hands and said goodbye to his friend before he rode off from the horse ranch for good.

15

A WINDSKIMMER

With the sun warming his back, Cat rode due west. Bouncing along, thinking mostly about MacKenzie, knowing he would never forget her signature broad, warm smile. She was a fine person. Kind, personable, generous. He'd been fortunate to have known and lived with her for over twenty years. No question, she'd made him a better man.

Cat rode on without stopping for most of the day, enjoying the waning coolness of the early desert morning, then the pink-streaked, wispy clouds drifting overhead in the faded denim sky in the late afternoon. Sunrise and sunset were always spectacular in this part of Cal Wild, he thought—something to do with the gradual changes in the atmosphere, but maybe because the air was a little thinner at this higher elevation, warmer, and of course much drier.

He arrived at the tangled old junction of north-south I-680 and east-west I-580 an hour or two before sunset. He began looking for a good place yo camp for the night, and to eat a couple hard boiled eggs, biscuits, and some dried fruit he'd packed at the ranch and stored in his saddlebags. He was thirsty, too.

A hundred yards ahead and running along the southern side of the freeway was a long knoll with a few live oaks intermingled in a taller stand of young eucalyptus. The thick woods stretched westerly for several hundred yards.

Elevated slightly, he could see almost a half-mile to the east and even further west along the old freeway.

Cat dismounted in the late afternoon shade, hobbled, fed, and watered his horse; and then he sat down with his back against one of the shedding gum trees. It was quiet and peaceful here, the highway stretching out toward the west in fairly decent shape, the asphalt lanes cleared of most of the old rusting vehicles and other post-Collapse debris that had once clogged the highways—stuff hauled off and stacked at rest stops. The highway a major east-west well-traveled trail now. He enjoyed his meal, washing bites down with sips of spring water from one of the three canteens he also carried in his saddlebags.

On the far side of the highway, Cat absently watched a small hawk hover in the air against the westerly wind current for a moment or two before swooping down on its prey—maybe a mouse or even a rabbit if the hawk were lucky. Animals were gradually growing in numbers, returning to Cal Wild, he thought, even out here on the western fringe of the barren Great Central Desert—

Cat sensed something coming.

He focused back a half mile away … and there, for a moment, he thought he was looking back out over a lake or a stream, because he saw a *sail* … actually three clustered small sails coming up over the horizon …

But not a boat.

No. It was a land craft moving rapidly along the outside northern lanes of the old freeway, I-580, in his direction. He watched it swing gracefully from one lane to another, easily avoiding potholes, some washouts, and the occasional standing obstacles: a rusting wheel-less truck, an abandoned auto, and other debris. Approaching rapidly … and in a few more seconds it was almost adjacent to his spot on the wooded knoll.

One of the windskimmers, a three-wheeled small craft that could sweep swiftly across flat land and deftly negotiate even partially cleared highways. But he'd never expected to see one way out here in the desert. He'd only heard about them from a horse trader at a recent trade-off up near Dublin Camp. The trader said that 'skimmers were beginning to appear now all over Cal Wild, but usually much closer in to the Bay Area where he thought they were being built and sold. The trader told him that the sailed land craft were most commonly seen out on cleared areas of the Black Desert—the asphalted north-south highway complex of multiple lanes that once led from the San Jo Ruins south under the LA Curtain— the permanently polluted dark cloud hanging over the highway—to the fabled metropolitan area's northern sprawling ruins—

Cat caught movement from the corner of his eye.

Two Freemen were darting out on mounts from the trees at the far western end of the eucalyptus stand from where he sat. He hadn't been aware of them until now.

Desperadoes!

They rode hard down the knoll to cut off the passing 'skimmer, handguns drawn … and they were taking aim and firing.

Bang, bang, bang.

But at the first sound of gunshots, the sleek craft veered sharply to the far northern lane of the highway, maneuvering nimbly between a pair of rusting autos, reminding Cat of a remembered sailboat in a long ago regatta on the Bay near Berkeley, gracefully negotiating around the buoys in one of those races. Only the 'skimmer was even faster on land than that trimmed sailboat on the water.

The Desperadoes rode hard, but as they gradually closed in to effective handgun range, the 'skimmer seemed to suddenly rocket forward, leaving the closing horsemen in its wake, like an expensive sports car shifting into a different gear, kicking on its turbocharger and then roaring off.

Cat squinted into the dropping golden sun, watching the craft easily distance itself from the two outlaws and soon disappear into the heat waves shimmering off the asphalt to the far west. He chuckled, remembering the trader who had first described a wind-skimmer to him had mentioned that he thought the land craft even had fairly sophisticated gear ratios for its three wheels.

At that point Cat grinned, thinking he'd witnessed a winning score for the home team.

With the two Desperadoes still fresh in mind, Cat decided not to build a fire and draw attention, despite the rapidly dropping temperature. He snuggled into his two blankets, and with a firm image of MacKenzie's special smile warming him, he quickly dropped off to sleep.

Early the next morning Cat rode west along the freeway in the trail of the speedy 'skimmer.

16

JANEY

Cat sat knee to knee, with Janey's hands clutched firmly in his, watching two tiny tears trickle down her cheeks. She reminded him of her mother. No question, she was a tough one, too. She even looked a lot like a younger version of MacKenzie.

He cleared his voice, briefly touched the old scar on his face, gripped her hands again, and continued, "That was definitely one of the last instructions she asked of me—see Janey and tell her personally."

Janey released one hand, sniffed, and wiped the back of her hand across her nose. She nodded and smiled apologetically. "Thank you. Sorry."

"She was a good woman, and during our time she made me a much better man," Cat said.

"Of course I loved her dearly…"

He smiled, shifted his thoughts somewhat, and said, "It was a good time for all of us, while you were growing up at the San Jo Raider compound. Lots of good memories, right?"

"Yes, that's true," the young woman agreed, wiping her wet cheeks and sniffing.

"I guess the only thing MacKenzie regretted way out at the new horse ranch during this last year was that we were too busy to get back here and see you and Coby. And your successful goat cheese business. I told her all about it, your future plans and everything, after taking care of the dog pack for you. She was so very proud of you."

Janey nodded. "I know," she whispered in a choked voice. "I really wish—"

She broke off and coughed, her voice choked up.

After regaining her poise, Janey said, "I just wish we hadn't been so busy that we couldn't have ridden out in the desert to see you guys. I know Mom had to have dearly loved that new horse ranch. It was her dream, as far back as our time at the medcamp at Blue Rock Springs."

"It sure was," Cat agreed. "Our friend Oscar is running the spread now. He'll take good care of it. The operation is going to be successful. Mackenzie liked Oscar. She would be happy for him."

Janey nodded, gathered herself, and then sat up straighter.

"What are you going to do now? Sounds like you've decided not to go back to the horse ranch." Just like her mother, Cat thought, smiling inwardly. Always thinking of others, even during the middle of such a shocking and heartrending time for her.

He shrugged, rubbed his scar, and thought for a few moments.

"Well, I'm not really sure…Maybe look up Paul and Casey in a day or two. I think they are probably living somewhere in the San Fran Ruins. They may have some suggestions."

She nodded thoughtfully.

"Are you hungry?" Janey asked, standing up suddenly, obviously wanting to just move around, do something physical.

Cat recognized her need, and realized he was hungry. "Sure, I could eat a bite."

She struck up the fire in the kitchen stove to heat up something in a big pot, cutting cheese and bread, and setting a plate and cup at the table.

"Hey, you remember that little kitten MacKenzie found after we moved down to San Jo? That mean little rascal that you finally tamed?"

"Yes, I sure do," Janey answered, a big smile easing back onto her face. "Peewee. I called him Peewee. Not very original." She laughed. "That little guy got into everything back then."

They began to reminisce more about the past: Janey's time growing up, about her mother, a little about Cat, but mostly about all the good times the three of them had shared together. And they continued on talking about the past, even as he enjoyed the delicious stew, cheese, and homemade bread...

In the early evening, with Coby at her side, Janey, with a kind of sly smile, made a startling announcement: "You're going to be a grandfather, Cat. We're expecting. Going to start our family real soon—about seven months from now."

"Well, that's terrific news!" Cat said, and he meant it, even though it caused a sharp twinge in his chest. MacKenzie would've been so excited, if she'd just been here to hear their good news. So excited—

"Wow, I'm going to be a grandpops. Now that's hard to believe. Who would've guessed I'd live so long?"

Janey corrected him, laughing loudly. "Oh, you're a very young grandfather!"

Before bedtime, Coby took Cat outside as he checked the goat corral and herd. "I've got a proposal for you," he said.

"Oh?"

"You know we sell our cheese at two other trade-offs in the Bay Area besides the big one at the San Fran Ruins. Been talking to

Janey about maybe expanding soon to some of the weekend trade-offs to the east off I-680, out there where you traded your horses. You probably know all of them pretty well. Anyhow, I think it's a potential untapped cheese market. There are goat herders, but no cheese makers out there. But we don't really have anyone extra to send out, especially with Janey pregnant now. Knowing the people out there, do you think you'd care to help set something like this up for us? Even for just a short-term period until we got someone out there permanent?"

Cat knew he wasn't interested in being a goat cheese salesman at trade-offs ... but it might be something to think about as a kind of temporary job until he decided what he really wanted to do. It'd sure help out Janey and Coby, too. Now that he was going to be a grandfather, he wanted to find something nearby. Maybe taking cheese out to the weekend trade-offs was a good opportunity, at least for now.

He shrugged and lifted his eyebrows, a kind of non-committal gesture. "I'll give it some serious thought, Coby. Thanks. But first I want to run down those two bowmen friends of mine at the San Fran ruins. See what they both have going on right now. I'll let you know real soon, okay?"

"No hurry, Cat."

17

SAN FRAN TRADE-OFF

Cat stood looking up at the awesome San Fran Shield late the next afternoon, the great half dome's light filters were darkened to a shiny ebony, screening out the sun's angled rays. The sight caused mixed feelings. No question the shielded city was an impressive sight, an engineering feat. But at the same time, even recognizing all that, gazing at the domed city stirred a vague sense of unease. Almost a portentous feeling. Like all those rich people are hiding away from view, he thought, planning to do something bad … not in the best interests of Freemen. And then there were the scary black-clad Companymen—reminding him of bogeymen from his childhood books. No question that the Company was an omnipotent force, surreptitiously reaching out from each of the five Shields, like tentacles from a giant octopus, gaining a measure of control over more and more aspects of the surrounding Cal Wild.

Cat shuddered.

He sucked in a deep breath, sighed, shook off the creepy feeling, and headed off toward the San Fran Ruins proper, soon arriving in the living area, which was near the great trade-off—a lantern and candle-lit maze of tents, metal shacks, wooden hovels, bare-sided lean-tos, and used-brick shanties intermingled with mounds of old building rubble. He began asking around about the location of his two bowmen friends...

Just before dusk, Cat was directed to a neat little stone hut set off in the ghetto from the surrounding cluster of leaning sheds and stacked debris.

He found Casey at home, getting ready for work. A kind of elaborate process. While Cat watched, Casey finished combing and patting down each stray hair, carefully trimmed his beard, and then pulled on his fresh undergarments and highly-polished boots.

Cat smiled, and joked, "No shaving lotion or cologne? You should get rid of that old lingering Desperado stink, you know."

Casey didn't defend himself. He made a dismissive shrug, as if saying: *What are you going to do?*

Mostly the two friends talked about what had happened to each of them in the last year and a half.

"That looks about right," he finally announced after slipping on an expensive black Stetson and matching duster. He carefully checking himself out in a wall mirror, brushing off a speck of dust from his chest. "Have to be ... ah, presentable for this kind of work, you know."

"*That's* presentable?"

He reminded Cat of a gambler gunfighter from a classic western movie DVD he'd seen long, long ago as a kid: *The Gunfight at O.K. Corral.*

Casey nodded, then directed Cat's attention out his open front door to shimmering glow from the nearby great trade-off. The fifty-five gallon drums had already been lit, and were flaring up and casting a wide umbrella of flickering light, easily visible in this section of the Ruins at least a quarter mile away.

"C'mon, we'll get something to eat first, and maybe have a

half hour or so to talk and explore around before I have to be over to work."

Casey had been evasive about exactly what he was doing at the trade-off. But he sure looked prosperous enough. Cat figured it had to be some kind of security work, because his friend had carefully checked out a .45 automatic, an extra pair of ammo clips, and his Bowie knife, concealing both weapons and the rounds under his high-quality long coat. Reinforced the Doc Holliday gunfighter image.

As they walked toward the dancing light, Casey deflected another of Cat's direct questions about the nature of his job with: "You just wait and see. I'm going to surprise you." He laughed. "But I guarantee you'll find it unusual and interesting. If I have a chance I'll introduce you to my boss, Mama Pajama, who is an intriguing character herself for sure. She might be able to use you. She's expanding her service soon again. We'll see."

He had told Cat, when he first asked about Paul, that their friend also worked for the same woman. Paul had recently been sent south to the smaller San Barboo Trade-off to help set up a new operation. In the course of the brief conversation, Casey had said that his boss was a Shield Resident who operated a similar but much less exotic business inside San Fran Shield—the enterprise operated illegally under the radar in the Shield. He implied that she had juice at the upper levels of the Company. Including access to some very specialized high-tech stuff. Equipment they needed and used every night in their work. But he wouldn't say anything more specific about the nature of the secretive operation. Or anything more about his mysterious boss.

Mama Pajama?

Who could she be with that kind of strikingly bizarre name? What did she do?

Cat knew it was illegal for a Shield Resident to even be outside in the Ruins, but the Company rarely enforced that. So the braver/wilder Shield Residents did wander out for brief illicit adventures. But running a business out here—and something that was apparently illegal in the Shield? Pretty gutsy. The vendors at the trade-off were all Freemen. Cat had never seen a Shield Resident selling anything—only buying. What had Casey stumbled into here? And just what kind of security could the two bowmen be providing for this intriguing Mama Pajama?

Exasperated by Casey's closed mouth, Cat shook his head and smiled. His friend had piqued his curiosity. He looked forward to meeting this woman, but he'd have to be patient.

The San Fran Trade-off had grown to at least twice as large from the last time Cat had visited almost two and a half years ago. With its noise, dozens of scattered, lit fifty-five gallon drums, hundreds of hanging methane or candle lanterns, a gray cloud of dust that lingered in the air like a bank of dirty fog, and a dizzying blur of hyperactive motion, it reminded Cat a little of the carnival at the State Fair his father had taken him to visit in Sacramento when he was around fifteen years old. Except the trade-off wasn't nearly as organized or neat. The *carnival* and various areas of interest weren't nicely separated as they were at the State Fair. No, here the stalls, stands, blanket ground presentations, wagon displays, and arenas offering every kind of conceivable foodstuff, dozens of services, hundreds of crafted goods, assorted games of chance, and other kinds of entertainments, were in an almost random mix. Arenas and stages were permanently established of course, but other sites were probably governed by the time of arrival and subsequent set-up of the vendor. First come, first pick of spots. Except for the half acre of sellers offering a wide assortment of cooked/cooking foods, which were grouped tightly together. Barbequed, boiled, deep fat fried, baked, roasted, stewed, or just plain raw—it was all offered from within the same congested area.

They stopped first in the barbeque meat section, and were immediately assaulted by hawking cries from the hoarse-voiced cooks/sellers, delicious sights of roasting meats and grilling fish, accompanied by the pervasive nose twitching and mouth-watering smells. After briefly sampling a number of delicious tidbits of various kinds of barbequed chicken, beef, pork, and lamb, most smothered in thick, rich, spicy, and hot sauces, they each settled for two barbequed chicken wraps—Cat picked one with a tasty green curry, and his other smothered in a sweet and sour sauce. They were both scrumptious. The two friends washed down the wraps with a lightly sweetened limeade drink, after Casey had declared, "No wine for me before work tonight. Maybe later."

Cat smiled to himself, wondering when his friend had become so conscientious about mixing drink and work. Must go with his fancy get-up.

They mingled in the noisy crowd next to the prepared food area, weaving by numerous colorful displays of a wide but haphazard assortment of vegetables, fruits, seafood, and meats, the muggy air tantalizing with the scents from open jars, baskets, and tubs of various distinctive sauces, spices, and condiments: including cinnamon, nutmeg, rosemary, pesto, horseradish, and even a sharp kind of dry mustard that made Cat pinch his nostrils.

Casey introduced Cat to the largest of the four wine vendors, who he said hired Freemen with Desperado experience for selling positions at his busy stall. But of course that type of thing didn't much appeal to Cat—too many periods of idle time standing around, trying to stay alert, and occasionally dealing with a belligerent drunk or a cantankerous customer. And the pay was pretty low. Not for him. Casey probably guessed as much, too, because he was grinning sardonically after glancing at the frown on Cat's face.

They moved along through the mob, making their way to the northern fringe of the crowded trade-off area proper.

"We're living dangerously now, going where questionable or sordid activities are rumored to take place," Casey announced with a sly, thin smile, leading Cat beyond the outer edge of light cast by the farthest of the fifty-five gallon drums, moving along into the shadowy perimeter surrounding the trade-off. The dimness added credibility to the area's unsavory reputation that Casey joked about so glibly.

"First, we'll swing by the fight pit, although it's dark now, nothing scheduled for tonight. They stage bare-knuckle, bare-chested fighting challenges three nights a week. Big crowds, lots of betting. Bloody. Pretty exciting." He glanced back at Cat.

"Where do the fighters come from?"

"Mostly Freemen, coming from...well, all over this part of Cal Wild. Some nights competitors come down even from as far away as Ocino Shield. Winners here can easily make 150-200 Shield credit purses for one three-round, six-minute fight, depending of course on the size of the paying crowd. Might even get a 50-credit bonus for a knockout. So there are never any shortages of potential competitors. Despite it usually being a pretty short-lived career choice. Lots of damage. Oh, and occasionally, we do see a snooty-ass Shield Resident come out slumming and sign up to fight. I admit they all have excellent training from probably mixed martial arts facilities inside the Shield. Highly skilled fighters, too..."

He paused briefly for effect, shook his head, and added, "But they never have as much heart or killer instinct as our rough and tumble Cal Wild lads." He chuckled as they passed by the darkened pit area surrounded by five rows of bleachers—an arena that appeared able to accommodate maybe four hundred or perhaps as many as five hundred spectators.

"The Saturday night bullwhip fights are an even bigger draw here, the place packed with standing room only back of that last row of bleacher benches," Casey said, as they moved along deeper into the shadows cloaking the area. "Now those are some rugged-ass contests. Usually no one getting out unscathed in one piece, you know. And some serious betting taking place, too."

They continued moving beyond the fight arena, into a sprinkling of trees...

Casey slowed and advised Cat in a lower voice, "Stop here and just watch for a few minutes."

He gestured at an isolated nondescript table sitting off by itself about hundred or so feet away, surrounded by three shadowy figures just visible in the dim light flickering from a hanging small lantern.

It was actually an empty table manned by a seated Freemen vendor flanked by a pair of rugged-looking bodyguards, both probably armed under their thin dusters.

"What's he selling way out here that's so damn valuable he needs that kind of muscle?" Cat asked, his voice a curious whisper.

"Recreational drugs," Casey said simply, restraining Cat by the arm from moving any closer. "Giggledust, Soar, Rush, Dream ... all special designer stuff originating from lab connections inside the Shield. This guy, who I think is a Shield Resident despite his Freemen dress, does a brisk trade out here—I'm guessing maybe as much as 2,500 to 3,000 credits a night. As you can see he needs some impressive strong-arm to protect all that scrip ... But I'm hoping we may spot something even more unusual about his operation. An unexpected Cal Wild drug supplier. This is the best time of the evening to catch them. A time when they can safely slip into the fringe of the trade-off and then back out again, before too many of the rowdy night crowd wander out here. A definite hazard to this special kind of supplier's personal safety. They usually steer clear of trade-offs in general—much too dangerous."

They watched for about ten minutes. Half a dozen Freemen customers came and went. For each transaction, the dealer reached under the table to a chest for the bagged various drugs, but carefully securing all the scrip receipts in an adjacent heavy strongbox.

It all seemed dully routine to Cat. Several times he glanced quizzically at Casey, who just smiled and lifted his palm: *Wait.*

And that's when Cat spotted him.

A Dyed Person!

A DP appeared, stepping out of the shadows, looking about

furtively, and then cautiously approaching the drug dealer's table. Even in the dim light, the DP's lack of Freemen protective clothing and his skin's dark green, oak leaf color were distinctive.

Cat and Casey edged closer.

The green man placed his hands on the table, leaned down close, talked for only a brief moment with the vendor.

After listening, the dealer shook his head, but still ducked under the table, and brought up some scrip from the strong box.

The green man stared at the credits for a long moment. Then he nodded with a reluctant expression, slipped off his backpack, dug through it carefully, and laid out three dark blue capsules on the drug dealer's table.

Then things moved at a rapid pace: the green man snatched up the paid scrip, slipped on his back pack, turned away, and quickly disappeared back into the darkness. Five additional seconds at most to finish the transaction after initial negotiations.

"What was that about?" Cat asked, turning to his friend. "What's in those blue capsules the DP sold to the dealer?"

"Smoke," Casey said hoarsely. "That's the most common name, although it's a drug occasionally called Blue, especially by DPs."

Cat shook his head. "Smoke or Blue? Never heard of it."

Casey cleared his voice, thought a moment, then explained, "DPs become addicted to Smoke soon after they're dyed, programmed, and released into Cal Wild from a Shield. They have direct access to the drug in the foodpaks stored at various Company hummerpad cache sites scattered about out in the boonies. Their addiction controls their wandering pattern, motivating them to find a new cache site every four days. That's also how the Company keeps easy track of each of them, their electronic palm prints required to open the cache site door. Anyhow, a few are able to somehow save part of their Smoke allotments. So, they come in here to trade the saved blue capsules to this dealer. Usually you can see one most nights, occasionally two or more. They may have a trade setup at the other four Shield trade-offs, too. Or maybe other

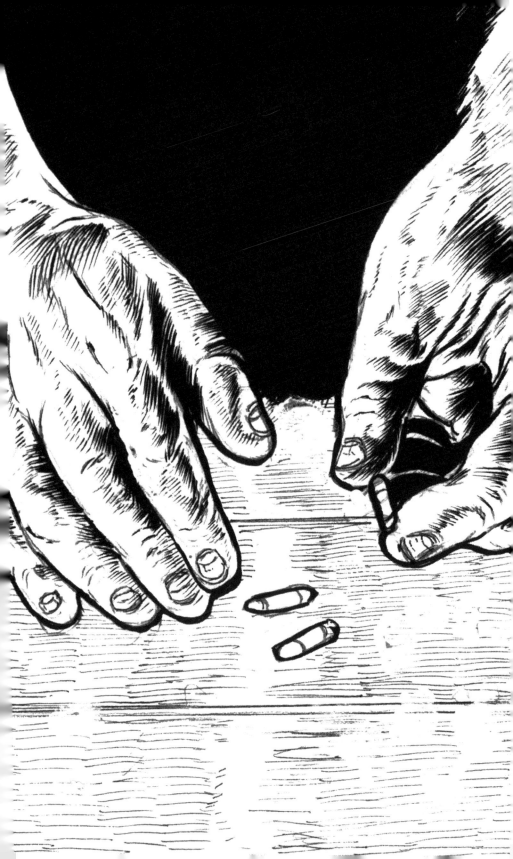

places in Cal Wild. I just don't know about that. But I do know it's the only item of trade value any of them carry in their backpacks. And Smoke has exceptional value here at this dealer's table. The most expensive drug by far. Normally costs you at least ten credits to buy one capsule of the stuff. I think this dealer probably pays DPs only one or two credits per capsule at most. Pretty good mark-up, eh?"

"That's fascinating," Cat said, watching the drug dealer finish with another Freemen customer, hoping to maybe spot another DP coming in to make a trade.

Casey continued spelling out another interesting revelation about DPs and Smoke: "I've heard that some enterprising Desperadoes have recently taken to robbing DPs near cache sites, snagging their whole four-day allotment of the drug or what they've saved up, even the little scrip they may have hoarded from sales in their backpacks. A new business opportunity, you see. Times are tough for the poor Desperadoes ... and even worse for the robbed DPs." He shrugged and made a fake sad face at Cat.

His curiosity was aroused, but after another ten minutes of anticipating, no other DPs appeared. Or anything else especially entertaining going on around the drug stand, even though business was beginning to pick up, a steady stream of customers trading. Cat wondered if Casey's estimate about nightly gross receipts were right. If so, maybe *he* should take up drug dealing.

"Okay, it's getting close to seven-thirty, and I should be getting over to work soon," Casey said, leading Cat away, continuing around the darkened perimeter of the trade-off.

"I work out here in Sleaze-City, myself ... just up there in that dense cluster of tall eucalyptus trees. He pointed ahead about hundred yards where the gum forest began to thicken, the light a little better, the area closer to the trade-off proper.

18

PAINTED LADIES

As they neared the edge of the deep forest, Casey eased up.

"Well, I hope some of my help have come to work on time. I see we have a pair of potential customers headed our way already."

From Cat's right, two Shield residents in silver and purple modtrend and matching funmasks were making their way toward them from the well-lit trade-off. But they both stopped short of the wide trail that led off into the darkened eucalyptus grove, ignored Cat and Casey, and glanced around as if looking for something or someone special—

Dazzling neon lights burst on overhead and momentarily blinded Cat.

While his vision gradually cleared, he thought that it might be some kind of carnival display suddenly coming to life ... like the glaring lights twirling around on a Ferris wheel, or maybe some other ride, or even the lights illuminating the brightly-colored canvass sideshow display ads ...

He sucked in a deep breath, still squinting, and was stunned by what he actually saw.

A writhing dragon!

Yes, it was a brightly lit-up dragon, twisting about ten or twelve feet in the air above them, its scales glistening silver and blue indigo, peering down with glittering red eyes at its potential victims—the two Shield Residents.

"Holy shit! What's going on here—?"

Casey touched his shoulder and pointed in the air to the left of the awesome dragon. A giant hummingbird had unexpectedly appeared like magic, hovering and shimmering with a lustrous brilliance of its own, its puffed-up chest a deep, shiny scarlet. Beside the humming bird a few seconds later appeared what seemed to be a huge luminescent green and blue … parrot. And in another moment a great dragonfly darted a little higher above the three dazzling creatures, its four wings glistening iridescently in the darkness like a patch of spilled oil on an asphalt stretch of highway on a rainy night.

The four creatures presented a breathtaking, glittering overhead display, much more astounding than any carnival exhibit.

"Magnificent," Cat whispered after catching his breath, completely awestruck by the surprising and spectacular display in the muggy night.

He had to be peering up at four holograms projected from somewhere at the edge of the grove of eucalyptus.

Cat continued to stare overhead, and one-by-one the holograms blinked off. The night air above them was dark, muggy, and still again.

Directly below the blanked-out neon display stood four gorgeous women dressed skimpily in bras, panties, sandals … and wearing some kind of thin belt with a pair of tiny instruments attached at either side of their shapely waists.

"Ah, I see some of my help is indeed working already," Casey said, laughing at Cat's stunned expression. "Pretty unusual, right?"

"Why are these women standing out here in the dark, almost totally exposed?"

"They're entertainers, personal service providers, attracting and entertaining customers with their holographic totems," Casey explained. "But let's wait a moment and see who they select for...ah, some additional individualized services."

Two Shield men advanced cautiously closer to the four near-nude women, who all became animated, smiling broadly, chattering, and seductively touching their potential customers. There were very brief discussions. Then, hand-in-hand, two of the women led the Shield men up the trail into the woods and disappeared out of sight.

Cat realized the women were going to do more than entertain the Shield men with their dazzling holograms—they were indeed full service providers. He turned again to his friend for a more detailed explanation.

"I think I know what the ladies actually do—the type of special personal services they provide. But how do you fit into all this?"

"Oh, I guess I'm kind of middle management," Casey said, and then laughed at his friend's still bemused expression. "I mostly keep an eye on the customers, making sure they conduct themselves as gentlemen," he added. "Also, I make sure the ladies have their holo-apparatus properly attached on their belts, power pack at the back hooked up, holo-cartridges seated, and insure the projectors are clean and functioning properly...Of course, I keep a close eye on Mama and her nightly receipts, which are probably as high as our drug dealer colleague's...And let's see...Oh, I usually walk the ladies home, back to the Ruins early in the morning after work is over for the night. Do whatever else Mama Pajama might require, you know. Every night is a little different. And never slow. Cat, I really like this job. Oh, and these Painted Ladies are indeed ladies, you know. Really exotic performers with their holograms and such. Not just common prostitutes. Nothing sleazy here."

Cat glanced again at the two nude women standing in the dim

light, watching for more early customers to dazzle with their holographic totems.

"C'mon, " Casey said, "I'll introduce you to Macaw and Dragonfly. Then I'll take you to meet our boss. I know she'll want to interview you for a possible job, after I finish talking you up."

19

MAMA PAJAMA

The Painted Ladies provided their specialized personal services in a half-moon cluster of six neat tents off the right side of the trail deep in the eucalyptus forest. Two of the tents were dimly candle-lit at the moment, as Dragon and Hummingbird entertained their Shield male guests. Female giggling and male laughter issued from the nearest tent ... And just moments later, the other tent went completely dark, and he could hear some muffled huffing and puff-ing.

Cat smiled to himself.

Closer to the trail was a solitary, well-lit smaller tent, its flaps rolled up and tied off to the strong-back framing to allow even a trifling of a breeze access to cool the apparently stuffy interior. Cat watched as Casey tapped on the frame near the entry and went in-side when beckoned by the strange-looking woman sitting behind a huge desk. They held a brief, low, animated conversation. The woman glanced out at Cat several times and kept nodding her head at Casey in agreement or understanding.

Casey turned and gestured for him to enter.

He did, remembering to take off his black and orange cap.

"Cat, this is my boss, Mama Pajama."

The woman stood, and shuffled around the desk to politely greet him.

Mama Pajama was as remarkable a sight as her odd name. She was nearly as broad as tall, her one-piece garment more loosely-fitting than other Shield residents' distinctive skin-tight attire, almost a small tent itself, but made of the same metallic modtrend material. The colors shifted and darkened as the heavy-set woman ambled forward: yellow, amber, orange, mocha, cinnamon. Her rusty-orange hair was frizzy, sticking out in every direction, still a relatively subdued frame for her heavily painted face, burnt-amber-shaded eyelids, and indigo-mascaraed eyes. Her harlequin appearance would have been almost a laughable caricature of a bizarre clown, except for her engaging and magnetic smile, dazzling white teeth, and the warm, charismatic aura she projected.

"Ah, M'sieur," she said in a husky French-Canadian accent. "Your friend speak most highly of you."

She held out her pudgy hand.

Cat shook it.

"Sit, please," she gestured him toward a foldout canvas seat, then waddled back around behind a desk, and dropped into her leather chair with a loud sigh.

She looked over at Casey as she gave him some brief instructions: "Please check the girls already entertaining and those out front; in a few minutes, Robin and Butterfly should be along before it get too busy. In meantime I will have a little talk here with M'sieur Cat, yes?"

Casey nodded to his boss, winked at Cat, turned, and left the well-lit tent.

"Your friend has describe your … ah, recent unusual pest control business," Mama Pajama said, gazing back steadily at Cat. "Very good. Daring. Ingenious."

Inwardly, he smiled at her thickly accented English sprinkled with odd pronunciations. Little, which she used a lot became *lee-tul*.

Pest almost sounded like *pissed*. But despite her funny looks and accent, Cat guessed the Tent City vendor didn't miss much with her shiny-bright mahogany eyes. Her quick appraisal reminded him a little of the shrewdness of Mike Shaw of the Raiders.

"Perhaps we have a spot for you, M'sieur, in our little business," she said, pushing a full package of Invasors across the desk.

He shook his head. "No, thank you. I usually like to keep my head clear when I'm talking about business. But, please, go ahead yourself."

The woman pushed the cigarillos aside, smiling almost approvingly.

"Well … We need to train someone to take M'sieur Casey's place soon. In maybe ten days he take away four Painted Ladies up to Ocino Ruins." She grinned even more broadly. "Little business expansion, yes?"

Cat nodded.

"Also, we need help next week. Fourth anniversary of Completion Day of the Shield. Very busy week, very busy."

"Oh, that's right," Cat said. He hadn't known the date was next week. But he remembered that the San Fran Trade-off had been flooded with Shield celebrants three years ago during the first Completion Eve celebration. It had been a big holiday celebration inside the Shield … and apparently it spilled over outside, too. The Freemen vendors had experienced an exceptionally boisterous day, but very profitable—one of their best.

"Your friend describe job responsibilities, yes?"

"Yes. He told me what he does, but only briefly."

"So, this kind of job fitting to you?" She was raising her pencil-thin black eyebrows.

Cat rubbed his scar and thought for a long moment. "Well, it's pretty different, I'll say that." He chuckled. "Might be interesting to give it a try."

"150 Shield credit per week, you supply own weapon," she said. "Most important part of job, you provide safety for our Painted Ladies. They all fine trained young women. Almost like daughter to me. So, not easy to replace, yes? Second, our scrip receipts must also be carefully guarded." Her smile faded slightly. She tapped a box at the corner of the table. A silver .38 revolver rested in plain sight next to the strongbox. "No problem yet, but a big temptation for some old friend, yes?"

Casey must've mentioned something about their past Desperado background.

He nodded. "I certainly understand the prime importance of both of those responsibilities."

"Ah, excellent," she said, her broad smile returning.

150 credits was good pay for a week's work, Cat thought. More than each of the bowmen had ever made when they were successfully hunting dog packs and other predators. He had no problem with that part of the deal. And Mama Pajama seemed like she'd be a decent sort to work for—eccentric looking maybe, but apparently considerate and polite to her employees. Casey seemed genuinely content. Paul must be okay with everything, too, if he accepted an assignment to travel and live down at the San Barboo Ruins.

So, after only another brief moment's consideration, Cat flicked at his scar and answered in an almost enthusiastic voice, "Sounds like a good opportunity for me. I'm in."

"This all very fine," the heavy lady said, standing and reaching out her hand again to seal the deal.

"Start tomorrow night. Seven-thirty. Work with friend for the next week and half. Then, he go to Ocino Ruins. You be my manager here, yes?"

"Sounds good...But what exactly do you like to be called? Not *boss*, right?"

"No, I'm Mama Pajama or just Mama to ever body, of course, dear boy," she said, grinning broadly at him.

Cat was quickly growing accustomed to her unsettling appearance. He rubbed his facial scar again and decided he liked this Mama Pajama. Yes, he did.

20

ON-THE-JOB TRAINING

Cat's OJT lasted five days, until the end of the Completion Eve celebration, which spilled over and encompassed three extra nights. Busy, hectic nights. Mama Pajama utilized the services of four additional women from inside the dome. Although they were well trained in the hands-on part of their entertainment package at Mama's place inside the Shield, they'd never operated holographic cameras like out here in Tent City ... or even been outside the Shield into the Ruins for any length of time.

The four of them were a little clumsy with the holo belts and cameras at first, but Casey and Cat helped them catch on, all ten Painted Ladies popular and busy with Shield Completion Eve celebrants. They needed to only briefly flash their holographic totems before quickly scurrying off with a new customer. Mostly Shield residents—some female, even a few couples. This went on for over three days and four nights, each of the Painted Ladies getting brief four-hour staggered respites from Tent City to rest and recharge their overworked libidos. Busy, busy, busy.

Surprisingly, Casey and Cat, although on the go almost constantly around the clock for ninety-six hours, dealt with few serious problems. One drunken Freemen made a half-hearted robbery attempt of Mama early the night before Completion Eve. He was sent limping off, his weapon hand bashed after a firm lecture on the error of his ways. And there were more than a few of the usual rough, drunken/loaded customers, mostly Shield Residents, who had crossed the line of acceptable behavior at Mama Pajama's Tent City. Cat and Casey easily handled even the most belligerent and physical cases, roughly escorting them out of Tent City, occasionally with a solid boot in the hindquarters or a little strawberry jam deposit on the end of their noses to remind them of their rude indiscretions. It was intense, but nothing that really overtaxed the capabilities of the two ex-bowmen.

Cat had pretty much experienced the compressed gamut of possible emergencies along with the normal nightly routine job requirements during those four nights of OJT, or so he thought.

Mama Pajama was satisfied with the performance of her newest middle manager, and decided to send Casey and four selected Painted Ladies off to Ocino Ruins several days early. Get the new operation up and running ahead of schedule. Start recouping a return on investment.

Early the next Monday morning, following the lingering Friday night Completion Eve celebration, Casey drove a wagon off with all the necessary tenting, cots, clothing, personal care items, supplies, and holo equipment his four Painted Ladies would need up north. Everyone was excited to begin the new venture.

That evening Cat was on his own with the remaining six Painted Ladies, working Tent City at the still busy San Fran Trade-off.

❧ – ❧

As time passed, Cat maintained a strictly professional relationship with his attractive charges, joking and enjoying their flirtatious behavior of course, but drawing the line there. He still mourned MacKenzie's passing, and was not interested in any intimate feminine company or romantic interests.

Off work, over at Casey's stone shack, he spent most of his time reading from the small library of books he was beginning to accumulate from several sellers located at stalls in the trade-off. But, he'd often stop reading, and stare off into the night, MacKenzie never completely out of his thoughts. When he was tired or feeling slightly depressed, he visualized her special smile, and the warm image never failed to lift his spirits. Cat missed Mackenzie terribly.

There came a lull of customers one Monday evening after a month of fairly busy nights at Tent City, and Mama Pajama summoned Cat into her tent.

"Sit down, please," the heavyset woman said.

When she'd sent word for him to come see her as the slow night wound down, he'd had a brief anxious moment, but her full-toothed wide smile and kindly expression dispersed any anticipation he had of bad news.

"Well, M'sieur Cat, we talk little business, yes?"

"Okay," he said cautiously, more than a bit curious now.

"Everything going fine here. Also down at San Barboo. And up at Ocino. Friend doing fine work. I'm happy. When Mama happy, Mama want ever one happy. Yes?"

"Glad to hear that, Mama."

"You doing real fine, too," she said. "M'sieur Casey and M'sieur Paul have more responsibility … so I give them nice raise last week. But you need a little something, too, yes?"

He didn't say anything, just continued grinning like a fool.

"You get 175 credits a week, begin tonight."

"Thank you, Mama. I appreciate it."

He was surprised and delighted with the unexpected raise. His only luxury was his books. And he'd been putting a good portion of his salary aside each week to do something for Janey's baby when it came. Maybe setup a trust fund like his folks had once set up for his college—all lost now. With a good raise, Cat could save even more for the baby.

"You welcome, dear boy," she said. "Very soon talk seriously about San D Ruins. They need Painted Ladies down there, yes?"

Cat sat up straighter in the canvas chair. Mama had mentioned several times perhaps expanding near the border.

"I hear that trade-off has grown to be almost as big as here," he said.

They were getting a fair number of far travelers interested in seeing the Painted Ladies of Tent City. Some of the recent ones had talked to Cat about the San D Ruins and the growing size of the trade-off there.

"Then, we think about moving down there very soon," Mama Pajama said, her face growing serious like it always did when she discussed any significant business decisions. "I want you to manage Painted Ladies there. Take along four, maybe five good Painted Ladies. You want to do that for Mama Pajama?"

Cat was taken aback, massaging his facial scar for a moment while he considered the offer. He hadn't anticipated having to make any decision like this so soon.

He wanted to stay at the San Fran Ruins to be near Janey for the upcoming birth of his grandchild, but at the same time knew this was a terrific opportunity. He wasn't quite sure, but he suspected both Casey and Paul were drawing salaries in the neighborhood of 250-300 credits a week, fast-accumulating what seemed to Cat like relative fortunes. And the San D Trade-off was much bigger, more exciting than either Ocino or San Barboo and growing rapidly—maybe eventually growing bigger than the San Fran Trade-off sometime soon. Managing the operation for Mama would be a big challenge, demanding, but an extremely lucrative opportunity. And he liked the work—something different every night.

The heavy-set woman smiled back at him, almost a twinkle in her heavily lined dark eyes. Mama Pajama knew he preferred to stay at the San Fran Ruins and why, but she also knew he was ambitious, always looking for a challenge. And she was sorely tempting him with the offer to go south. He'd do what was best for both himself and the new baby.

"Let me think about it, Mama. You know I truly appreciate your offer."

After work, as he walked back to Casey's stone hut in the San Fran Ruins, Cat thought everything was going well for him. The economic future looked very bright, whether he decided to go south or elected to stay to be near when the baby was born.

He glanced up at the almost full moon gleaming like an amber Japanese lantern in the slowly thickening mist. A good omen. He took a deep breath of the air heavily laden with the sharp medicinal smell of the surrounding eucalyptus grove. Yes, Cat decided, he did feel good tonight, real good.

And this contented state of wellbeing would last, too … for about another twenty-two hours.

21

BLOODY FLASHBACK

Business was relatively slow in Tent City the next evening.

During a lull in customers, Cat stepped into Mama's office tent to advise her that Macaw had gone home early a few minutes ago.

"Started her monthlies," he added as explanation to his boss.

Mama Pajama nodded. "Good timing, yes?"

He chuckled. "Yeah, I suspect it's going to be pretty slow the rest of the night. The entire trade-off has been quiet tonight. Probably be able to send another girl or two home early. If it's okay with you, Mama."

She nodded, then said, "Maybe we have time to talk San D a little, yes? You think it over?"

"Okay, sure, I have been thinking on it—"

Before Cat could unfold and slip down into one of the canvass chairs, a sharp, chilling cry burst from across the path in the direction of the Painted Ladies' half circle of tents.

"Cat! Cat, come quick."

He moved as fast as his namesake, darting outside.

It was Dragonfly, her unlined face frowning uncharacteristically, wrinkles marring her fine features. She pointed toward the farthest tent, which was completely dark. "It's B-B-Butterfly," she stammered, simultaneously trying to catch her breath, grab up Cat's hand, turn, and drag him along.

"Stop," he said to the frightened Painted Lady. "What's happened to Butterfly?"

Dragonfly sucked in a deep breath and shivered.

"A Shield customer couldn't perform, blamed his erection problem on Butterfly … you know. Probably he did too many drugs earlier, not used to the lingering effects …" She gasped for another deep breath before continuing. "But now he's hurting Butterfly real bad."

Cat broke away from Dragonfly and sprinted the thirty or so yards toward the darkened tent—

Outside the open tent flap, a completely naked Shield resident bent over a prostrate, nude, and very still Painted Lady.

Butterfly was hurt … maybe badly.

Cat grabbed the Shield man by his bare upper arms, pulled him upright, spun him around, and delivered a vicious head-butt solidly into his face. The man dropped to the ground on his knees … while groaning weakly in pain—

Cat spotted the weapon in his hand—a long bloody knife glittering in the moonlight.

He knocked the blade out of the customer's hand with an accurate kick, booting it over the tent and off somewhere into the darkness.

Cat dropped to a knee beside Butterfly.

For a second he thought she was unconscious, but then saw the gaping-wide neck wound, like a bizarre crimson grin, and underneath her head a spreading pool of black blood.

No! he shouted silently, rising to his feet, squeezing his eyes closed.

But it was too late.

He'd been hurled instantly back in time to Blue Rock Springs Med Camp, to that night over thirty years ago when he stared down in the darkness into his mother's unseeing eyes as she lay in a widening pool of her own blood—

He blinked and shook his head, as if trying to dislodge the vivid, hurtful memory.

"No!"

He stared down into the past: *Darkness ... bared breasts ... a slashed throat... black blood.*

He blinked again and tried to swallow, completely overcome now with an increasing choking rage.

A veil of red fury overwhelmed his vision—

Moaning snapped Cat out of his frozen trance-like state. The sound came from the man lying on the ground near his feet.

The murderer!

The man who slit his mother's throat.

"Ahhh, you, you filthy ..." Cat shrieked, as if stabbed with the missing knife.

Not the least concerned about anything other than exacting vengeance for his mother, Cat dropped a knee onto the killer's chest and brutally pummeled him, smashing his face with fists, elbows, and head butts. A steady cascade of damaging blows.

The man tried frantically to protect himself, shielding his head, and then he rolled up into a fetal ball and cried out under the violent rain of Cat's wild and ferocious strikes.

Soon he went silent and completely limp, lying helplessly with his arms flung astray, not even attempting to shield himself. He wasn't moving at all—not even a twitch of an eyelid. In fact, his eyes were open wide and glazed over.

Cat continued to pound the now unrecognizable face until he felt a hand grasp his shoulder, and heard a gruff voice in his ear.

"Enough, M'sieur, enough."

He stopped, and gasped for breath, finally glancing back over his shoulder.

Mama Pajama stood behind him, along with Dragonfly and the three Painted Ladies. All staring first at him, then down at Butterfly and finally at the bloody customer, with horrified expressions on their faces, too shocked to even cry.

Cat sucked in another deep breath, closed his eyes again, and then blinked. Still numb, he rose to his feet. He looked first at the dead young woman, and then down at the bloody mess at his feet. He was back in the present. The strength and rage had drained from his body.

He asked himself: What have I done?

The knife-wielding woman killer was obviously dead. The man's head had been crushed in and his face looked like it had been beaten to a pulp with a baseball bat. But Cat knew somewhere under that bloody mask was a Shield resident.

A murderer, yes, but a Shield resident.

The significance of this recognition slowly sank in.

Cat couldn't speak; he shuddered, as if suddenly chilled by a strong gust of wintry wind.

"Over," Mama said simply, interrupting his thoughts.

Cat nodded his understanding.

It was indeed over. And he had only a vague recollection of what he'd done to the woman murderer—the number of blows he'd thrown. His hands were barked, both sore and bleeding…the right one perhaps broken and beginning to swell. His forehead throbbed, bruised badly where he'd used it as a battering ram. He only remembered looking down and seeing his mother lying there, before rage overwhelmed his sensibilities, choking him with fury; and he only saw the Shield man at that moment through a fuzzy red veil. For the first time since he was a kid back at Blue Rock Springs, he'd lost it—lost complete control of himself.

Whether the Shield resident deserved it or not, Cat had beaten him to death.

He was still holding a knife when Cat attacked him.

Where was the long knife now—?

"You run," Mama advised sternly. "The Companymen come soon. Take you to Shield if you here."

"I must find the knife," Cat said hoarsely. "It's evidence in my favor."

She forcefully shook her head, looking very worried and concerned for him. "No evidence good for you... Must run, now!"

Cat said nothing more, only nodded, agreeing with her shrewd weighing of the situation.

The Companymen wouldn't care about evidence, or probably even listen to what had happened. A Shield resident had been beaten to death. Period.

"Come, office. Quick."

⌇ – ⌇

Mama Pajama gave Cat a large wad of Shield credits. He jammed the scrip into his long coat pocket.

"Maybe go south. See friend, Casey, yes?"

"Thanks, Mama," he said, grateful for the woman's generosity and sincere concern for his welfare. He wasn't sure where he was headed, except he knew he had to first say goodbye to Janey.

⌇ – ⌇

At the goat farm in Golden Gate Park, Janey made him fill his backpack with bread, cheese, some jerky, all wrapped up tightly in greased paper, and two full canteens of water. After filling his pack, he hugged both her and Coby.

Janey was round and large now. Her time was coming soon.

Cat felt a deep twinge of regret.

"I wish I could wait to see the baby," he said, feeling bad, knowing MacKenzie would've loved to have been able to see the newborn.

Coby said, "Maybe down the road some time, after this mess about the Shield resident hopefully blows over."

"Yes, but you must go quickly now," Janey said with tears in her eyes. "Take care of yourself, okay?"

He tightly hugged her roundness. She was all the family he had left since MacKenzie had died. He'd miss her, and the baby. He shook Coby's hand.

"Stop right there!"

Cat was only a few feet deep into the nearby grove of eucalyptus when the disembodied voice startled him.

Frozen, he watched shadows from deep within the forest take form into three shapes.

The dark apparitions slowly moved closer.

And he recognized them.

Dark-clad Companymen! They'd found him already.

They slowly spread out and circled around him, each reaching down to his waist … Suddenly, one flipped his come-along-stun. But the Companyman was too far away, giving Cat time to duck and dodge.

The nearest Companyman to that side cut him off, moved several steps closer and flipped his come-along-stun through the air—

Cat was caught around the neck, the come-along-stun biting coldly, like a violent electrical charge immediately coursing through his body, short-circuiting every one of his synapses … perhaps even those around his lungs.

He was stopped dead in his tracks.

Dumbfounded. Unable to see or to hear. Only able to hurt.

And he was suffocating, unable to breath.

He slowly crumbled to his knees.

Stunned and down, smothering.

Mercifully, the darkness descended.

22

ADRIFT

Disoriented. Awareness coming back, but slowly… still cloaked in darkness … but Cat had a vivid kinesthetic sense of floating, being adrift on water.

Yes, floating, yet unable to move.

Not too hot or cold, the temperature comfortable.

Unable to see, unable to hear.

Cat was adrift in a blackness darker than a starless night fallen in on itself, the silence of deep space.

But where exactly am I? he asked himself.

He had no idea—

Dead!

Was he dead?

The question was like an icicle of fear piercing his heart, fracturing his momentary relative calmness.

After a few moments, his heart pounding, his pulse racing, he finally managed to get a grip and collect himself, focusing and trying to think logically for a minute about the death question.

He wasn't one hundred percent sure, of course, but he felt that he couldn't be dead…yet, because he was at least able to think, and to feel fear. And there was still some minimal physical sensation. If he were dead, Cat suspected he probably wouldn't feel anything at all, or be afraid, or be able to examine his thoughts.

No, he decided he was probably still alive.

But floating

And, yes, like maybe off in deep space somewhere …

Was that possible?

He recalled a story from a book of science fiction he'd read in high school in Berkeley. The collection was by one of his dad's old-time favorites, Ray Bradbury. Spacemen, all wearing their suits, had been involved in a spaceship's terrible explosion, and had been blown free of their spacecraft, and were helplessly drifting farther and farther apart in the weightless vacuum of deep space. It was one of those simple—not much happening—but absolutely terrifying stories because they were completely helpless, only able to communicate with each other at first. And they would soon lose even that aural/vocal tether—or maybe they didn't, but he'd forgotten the actual ending. The helpless drifting apart was the vivid image in his head. He thought the story was called "Kaleidoscope."

Whatever.

That was what he felt like: adrift in a weightless vacuum.

Apart.

Alone.

He shivered.

What had happened?

How had he gotten here?

Cat concentrated and it slowly come back to him: what had taken place at Tent City, the attack on the Painted Lady, losing control and brutally beating to death the Shield resident, running to Janey's, attempting to leave there, the three Companymen confronting and taking him down with a come-along-stun. And then he'd completely blacked out.

Until now, finally regaining consciousness.

So he obviously wasn't dead.

No, the Companymen had him in their clutches.

They'd probably first brought him inside San Fran Shield, and then if the rumors he'd heard years ago were true, he was probably taken to a low sub-level of the dome. At this moment he was hooked up and floating in a sensory-deprivation tank.

Definitely alone and isolated from other prisoners.

Again he tried to move some part of himself, anything ... But he could only float and wait.

Wait for what? Cat thought.

No answers.

Of course he was wary of the unknown and, yes, even frightened. Scared shitless in fact.

Cat somehow called up MacKenzie's beautiful smiling face, and the image gradually calmed him. He held her firmly in mind as time passed...

How much time? he thought.

How long had he floated in this sen-dep tank?

He had no way of judging.

⤙ – ⤚

After what seemed an eternity since regaining full consciousness, the silence was suddenly disturbed by a strange voice.

Can you hear me clearly?

The voice was intrusive, jarring, grating, sounding almost mechanical, computer-like, no ... more like a tin echo from the end of a long tunnel.

But then he realized he hadn't heard a voice at all. No, it was more like what he heard was a vibration inside his head, as if it caused by a tuning fork placed against the back of his ear. The words formed from vibrations resonating inside his head.

He thought: *Yes, I can hear you.*

There was a humorless chuckle. *Good, because I am your conscience.*

Cat floated without saying anything.

The voice vibrated again: *You must listen carefully to your conscience. Do you understand?*

I think so.

Good. Because that means, if you listen carefully, you will not have to experience this: The Probe—

The words were followed by a searing sliver of incredible pain stabbing behind his right eye. Deep. Penetrating. Probing. Like a white-hot icepick—unbearable, excruciating, electric, all-consuming pain.

Then it was suddenly gone.

Instant relief.

So, no more Probe, if you listen carefully to your conscience, and then repeat your confession back correctly. Understood?

I'm not sure.

Let me refresh your memory of recent past events outside the Shield…

The voice was silent again for three or four seconds.

Then it said: *Just listen now carefully for a few moments. This is what happened last night in Tent City. You followed Philippe Marceau, the Shield's Assistant Controller, into the Painted Lady's tent. You attacked and struck him from behind. Then, you brutally pounded him to death. You did this because of your insane jealousy over the affections of the Painted Lady called Butterfly. Isn't that correct?*

Of course that wasn't correct.

No, it didn't happen like that at all—

Immediate searing pain: The Probe stabbing into his sinus cavities, more excruciating than a severely abscessed tooth. An eternity of horrible pain…then it was gone; turned off.

Let's try and reconstruct the events once again, but slowly, one true statement at a time, the voice echoed in his head.

He was barely able to concentrate, his thoughts scattered from the intense pain of The Probe, an effect that rippled across every synapse in his body.

You followed Philippe Marceau into Butterfly's tent.

No!

Agonizing pain again, on and on...

And then gone.

Let's try to remember correctly this time. You followed the Shield Resident into Butterfly's tent. Repeat.

There was a brief pause before he tried to wade back correctly through the lingering confusion.

Yes, I followed Butterfly into the—

The Probe: searing pain.

And then gone.

Incorrect. Let's try again.

And so it went on.

Pain.

And on.

Pain.

And on.

Until finally his thinking was completely scrambled by The Probe, or even the threat of it. Cat had a difficult time constructing any coherent thoughts on his own, even stringing together two correct phrases. He was like a slow student trying to learn a few simple phrases in a foreign language, with a strict taskmaster.

But the voice was now patient, very patient. The Probe was lurking nearby, always lurking. Cat's pulse raced at just the anticipation of the threat.

With much painful negative reinforcement and endless practice, he eventually managed to eliminate all his incorrect statements, and succeeded in describing the true sequence of events that had transpired at Tent City, which resulted in the Shield dignitary's bloody murder.

Finally, he had it right.

Cat repeated the true sequence over and over and over. A drone of correctness that made the unhappy voice happy, which also made Cat happy.

In subsequent sessions, clear headed, and with absolutely no prompting from The Probe, Cat repeated the sentences correctly... and convincingly, in the appropriate voice and with pitch-perfect tone.

After uncountable painful sessions, the time eventually came when the voice in his head said in a soothing, satisfied manner: *Very good. Now, we need to make a transcription of the truth, which will be your voluntary confession. Yes?*

Yes.

23

JUSTICE

Cat awoke with his hands planted like magnets to a cold metallic railing, a dark-clad and masked Companyman stationed in full view nearby to his right. The Companyman stood before a small computer stand, and manning a layout of switches, toggles, and buttons.

Click. Flip. Push…

The quiet room slowly darkened.

"The San Fran Shield Hall of Justice is officially in session," the Companyman said in a deep, confident voice. "All arise for JUSTICE."

The air in front and just above Cat's head shimmered, like heat waves dancing off old highway asphalt on a hot day. Gradually an apparition took definable shape…

It was a man, seated in the lotus position, but hovering off the floor as if suspended on a robust column of air. A thin, almost frail, delicate man, bare-chested, and wearing only a simple white loincloth. His hands were pressed together in front of his shaved forehead, the *wai* position signaling polite respect. A short queue dangled from the back of the man's head.

THE CONFESSIONS OF ST. ZACH

As the figure took more solid shape, he slowly looked up. His features were Asian and heavily lined. He wore a wisp of a goatee and mustache, almost totally gray. His expression, including his unwavering gaze, appeared kind. But his eyes were an unnatural milky white, the man obviously blind. As he hovered magically, he appeared to be some kind of an ancient, Japanese or Chinese holy man…or perhaps more likely a legendary wizened and aged wizard of indeterminate Asian origin.

A fine hologram.

The Companyman announced simply, "JUSTICE."

Blind JUSTICE asked, "Do we have a quorum of witnesses, Officer?"

"Yes, Sir, there are ten Shield residents presently in attendance," the Companyman replied.

"And the Defendant?"

"Standing at the Rail of Truth, Sir."

"He has a relative in attendance?"

"No, Sir, the Defendant is a Freemen, not a Shield resident, and no relatives were located Outside," the Companyman explained. Then he added, "I will act as his surrogate relative."

"That is acceptable."

JUSTICE appeared to look down at the Defendant with a benevolent gaze.

"And the offense, Officer."

"Heinous first-degree murder of a high-ranking Shield resident, Philippe Marceau, Assistant Controller for San Fran Shield."

"Does the Defendant understand the charge?" JUSTICE asked, still gazing down non-seeing at the Rail of Truth.

"Yes, Sir," Cat whispered hoarsely. His voice felt like it originated in the rail, traveled up through his fingers, into his head, and finally resonated in his larynx.

"And how does the Defendant plead?"

For a moment Cat hesitated, the Rail of Truth heating up…

"Guilty, Sir."

"Officer, as surrogate, do you wish to present a defense of any kind?"

"No, Sir. I've heard the transcription of the Defendant's confession, gone over it in detail with the Defendant, and we will present no actual defense. I agree completely with the guilty plea."

"Mitigating circumstances?"

"None to offer, Sir."

"I see," JUSTICE said, a slight frown further etching his forehead wrinkles. "May we hear the transcription of the confession, please?"

"Certainly, Sir."

The transcription played twice, a nervous or angry murmur developing in the attending witnesses by the end of the second play.

JUSTICE nodded thoughtfully.

"Does the Defendant agree that this is his correct and absolutely true confession?"

Another moment of slight pause, the Rail of Truth painfully hot.

"Yes, Sir."

"And not obtained under any kind of duress?"

Cat hesitated again, but the Rail of Truth became unbearably hot, and still he couldn't release his grip.

"Yes, Sir. No duress."

"I see."

The hologram floated silently for a few moments, then asked, "Officer, is there anything else to add, before I render a judgment?"

"No, Sir," the Companyman said, his tone sharp with finality.

"So be it."

JUSTICE bent forward, almost touching his forehead to his hands again, which were clasped near his chest.

Minutes slipped by ...

JUSTICE blindly looked up at him and spoke not unkindly to the Defendant.

"I have no choice other than to render a Judgment of Color. The Defendant will be dyed Crimson, the most serious shade of red for the stalking and murder of an unarmed Shield resident ..."

The hologram program paused, then added, "And cast out to roam Cal Wild as a Crimson Man. Officer?"

"Yes, Sir."

"I remand the Judged to your custody. You will see that he is exposed to sufficient aversive conditioning to rid him of his anger and potential future aggression, and also the deletion of his given name. He will be programmed with a mental map of all the Cal Wild cache site locations to insure he has sufficient supplies during his lifetime of wandering as an outcast. Finally, he will be dipped in the coloring pit, permanently dyed. After all these preliminary steps are completed, he will be cast forth from the Shield. Clear?"

"It will be done per your instructions, Sir."

The hologram became a shimmering ghost before gradually disappearing.

"The Hall of Justice is out of session, all witnesses released from duty," the Companyman announced, just before looping a come-along-stun over the head of the newly Judged.

Darkness, again.

24

A JUDGEMENT OF COLOR

Again, he awakened, and found himself floating in the sen-dep tank. The next week or so was a blur of mental activity: viewing various holographic scenes of brutality and death. Sometimes his reactions followed by severe pain from The Probe. But the length was nothing like before his judgment.

⁊ ~ ⁊

Cat was dipped naked into the coloring pit, his skin a mass of tiny stinging sensations; and he stepped from the pit permanently dyed the color of fresh blood—deep crimson.

⁊ ~ ⁊

Twenty-five days after his Judgment of Color, the Crimson Man emerged from San Fran Shield to begin wandering Cal Wild, equipped with an empty backpack, a bedroll covered with a poncho, and most importantly, an almost GPS-like ability to accurately pinpoint the exact location of various supply cache sites—each site number triggering a visual map of surrounding site locations within a four-day walk. Even though he retained a vivid recall of his past, he had no memories of his pre-Judgment name—it had been completely struck from his memory.

Now he thought of himself simply as the Crimson Man.

Spread out before the Crimson Man was the San Fran Ruins and the great San Fran Trade-off. It was all different now, because he was so very different.

With a deep sigh and resignation of his situation, the Crimson Man turned and hurried off southerly, eventually reaching old Highway 101.

PART 3

THE THIRD JOURNAL

[ONE YEAR LATER]

"Atonement was powerful; it was the lock
on the door you closed against the past."
– Stephen King, *The Green Mile*

"Are we still the good guys?" (Boy to Papa)
– Cormac McCarthy, *The Road*

GENE O'NEILL

1

CACHE SITE #12

San Fran Shield Cache Site #12 was located in the South Bay just off old State Highway 101, about sixteen miles northwest of the Raider's vacated stronghold.

Like most of the other supply sites designed to serve Dyed Persons, it was a large, flat hummerpad of concrete about four feet high, with a palm print sensor inset near the two-foot square plasteel door on the south side of the pad. Periodically, usually late at night, Company hummers landed on the pad and Companymen quickly serviced the cache. Site #12 sat in a cleared, flat spot near a thick stand of eucalyptus trees forming an elongated crescent atop a slight knoll, the area once the location of a pre-Collapse neighborhood park next to an elementary school—both long gone, victims of the Collapse.

The post-Collapse sky, as usual in the Bay Area during late summer, was heavily overcast and dark. No stars or even the moon visible. Sometime around midnight, thick fog from the South Bay slowly invaded the area, eventually cloaking the site in a wet, pale shroud. The fog had stilled the enthusiasm of chirping crickets; but a chorus of amorous bullfrogs continued to bellow from the marshy lake overgrown with cattails at the northern edge of the old park. No other creatures braved the foggy, dark scene.

But someone equipped with NVG and carefully scanning the perimeter of the cleared area might have stopped at the glaring silhouette of a figure standing under the cover of the darker forest shadows. A much closer look without the blinding luminescent glare of the NVG would reveal the immobile figure to be human. A big man, curiously not heavily bundled up like a Freemen, but dressed in the pre-Collapse way: baggy pants and a baggy sweatshirt with no facial covering of any kind, but wearing an old faded black and orange ball cap. Skimpy, unprotected attire for the environmentally hazardous Cal Wild.

An even closer inspection would reveal the man's most distinctive and startling characteristic: All of his exposed skin appeared to have been bathed in fresh blood. Of course he was a Dyed Person. In addition, the DP's no-nonsense expression was complemented by a thick, ragged scar extending from the corner of his right eyebrow, across his cheek, and down to the tip of his square chin, definitely reinforcing the unnerving effect on a voyeur of his crimson body color. He was indeed a scary, bloody apparition silently lurking under cover for some reason at the edge of the forest.

The Crimson Man had concealed himself under the eucalyptus stand shadows before the fog rolled in. He maintained a cautious reconnaissance mode, which included constantly scanning the perimeter of the cleared area, while at the same time listening ever so carefully, and then occasionally sucking in deep breaths to sample the air—pungent with the medicinal smell of the surrounding eucalyptus grove. He was alert for any sensory clue that might reveal the presence of Desperadoes lying in wait in the nearby vicinity. The bandits themselves would probably be hiding and patiently watching for an unsuspecting Dyed Person to palm the Site insert and trip the cache door; then they would sweep down and rob the careless DP.

Before his Judgment of Color, the Crimson Man had learned about this potential DP hazard from Casey, his bowman friend. So he always waited and watched at cache sites, sometimes for extended periods of time. Casey had said the thieves were mostly interested in the DP's four-day cache allotment of Smoke capsules—the drug having high trade value. They would plan on striking before the Dyed Person had time to consume the first of his four caps, something most DPs did immediately after breaking open the cache supply pack, which in addition to the drugs, contained food-paks and water for four days.

Dyed People were all heavily addicted to Smoke, the addiction forcing them to seek out the next cache location religiously every four days. This enabled the Company to accurately track and, to an extent, control their pattern of wandering.

DPs could only easily remove the top pack from a spring-loaded protective storage mechanism at each cache site. If they did manage somehow to jimmy the mechanism and take more than one pack from the trap, this would immediately trigger punitive conditioning—programmed by the Company into the psyche of every DP. All Cache Site locations within an eight-day radius would be blanked out from the foolish DP's programmed mental map of re-supply sites—the elaborate internal GPS system of portions of Cal Wild.

Naturally the attacking Desperadoes would take everything the DP might have of value, but they only had a quick shot at one new supply pack. Once closed, the DP's palm print would not re-open the present cache site door. The small-time bandits fearful of retaliation by the Company were interested in only a quick snatch and run.

The Crimson Man was remarkably not addicted to Smoke.

Even before release to Cal Wild, he was aware the drug was highly addictive, and in addition would be the only item of high trade value to which he would have regular access. From that first night after being cast out of San Fran Shield, he'd resisted the urge to break a capsule of Smoke and inhale the highly soothing drug. But, oh, he had been sorely tempted many times during this first year of wandering the wasteland—most strongly to help combat the loneliness, which was extremely depressing. But he never gave in to the temptation for temporary relief. Not once. No, he needed those caps for trade for a number of things that made his wandering life easier, including his books.

In his backpack he now carried nine light paperback books carefully wrapped in plastic—a mix of genre and literary, like *The Razor's Edge*, *Flowers for Algernon*, and *The Girl with the Dragon Tattoo* that were all published pre-Collapse. Paperback duplicates of favorite books that had once been part of his father's extensive hardback library in Berkeley. The acids in the paper were slowly breaking down and turning the pages brittle and yellowish brown. He was careful with the fragile books, because reading was his major source of relief at night around his solitary campfires—his relief from the enervating loneliness. Hours of escape. Much better than the brief few minutes of distraction offered by the disabling Smoke.

In addition to searching for good books to read, he hoped that by occasionally swinging by the bookseller he knew well at the San Jo Ruins, someday another one of his father's remaining two journals might turn up. A long shot of course, but he'd placed a special order with the bookseller, who often made trips to the nearby trade-offs looking for books. The vendor had promised to keep an eye out for the two journals—both black leather with a distinctive **JAZ** embossed in silver on the front cover. The vendor's payoff from the Crimson Man would be five caps of Smoke—worth even more than a full package of Invasors.

The Crimson Man shifted his backpack higher on his shoulders. As a ploy, he kept three Shield credits and two caps of Smoke in his backpack under his other things—to be easily discovered if he were ever attacked. The bulk of his stash—both drugs and scrip—he kept squirreled away in a small leather pouch he wore strapped to his back underneath his baggy pants. In his year of wandering, he'd never been assaulted by Desperadoes, or anyone else; but he was prepared to take a minor hit if he were robbed, hoping the thieves would overlook the concealed leather pouch after discovering the diversion in his backpack.

As the Crimson Man sat quietly and watched for any sudden revealing hint of hidden Desperadoes, he practiced a necessary form of self-abuse—something he did at least once every morning and evening.

Tonight the Crimson Man was visualizing the long knives challenge almost three years ago with Mike Shaw, the Raider's Chief. He played the duel back in his head like a favorite old-time movie, from the very beginning to the quick death scene. When he reached the part when he stabbed Shaw's foot, the Crimson Man experienced the anticipated clenching in his gut, followed by a kind of lingering stomachache—the mild pain lasting for about fifty or sixty seconds. Quite bearable relative to the excruciating pain he'd first experienced a year ago, right after being cast out from San Fran Shield. He'd started back then to methodically conjure up various past scenes in his head, where he'd acted in a violent or physically aggressive manner. Immediately, aversive conditioning was triggered by the vivid visual recall, a sudden clenching sensation in his gut doubling him over, bringing tears to his eyes, and at first lasting for as long as five or six minutes. An agonizing painful reaction that instead of avoiding, he daily initiated—twice.

During the last year since his release into Cal Wild, over the days, weeks, and months of calling up at least several hundred violent scenes, he'd gradually desensitized himself to the Company's aversive conditioning. The pain eventually became less intense and lasted for shorter and shorter periods of time. He believed the formal term in classical conditioning for what he was practicing was called extinction. He'd learned about it in an honors course in

Psychology at UC Berkeley Extension before the fateful snowing-in on Mt. George ended his formal education over thirty-one years ago.

The aversive conditioning programmed at the sen-dep tanks—the negative painful response to a stimulus of personal violence—had been expertly engrained by the Company, with the intention of lasting him a lifetime of wandering Cal Wild. A punishment almost as bad as his being dyed blood red, because at first he was rendered virtually incapable of defending himself against attack by anyone. He'd be doubled over in disabling pain before he could react and protect himself. But the Company bio-programmers had not anticipated someone with the intelligence, creative will, and dedication of the Crimson Man.

He figured in another month, at most, he would be completely free of any conditioned painful response, which was now slight.

The Crimson Man smiled wryly. His size, color, and scarred facial expression had been sufficient past protection against assault; because his appearance did not encourage arguments from Freemen, other DPs, or even most individual Desperadoes—who were mostly cowardly bullies anyhow. So even though in the first few months after Shield release, he was relatively defenseless against an attack, the Crimson Man managed to move about even around crowded trade-offs—which most DPs avoided—without experiencing serious physical confrontations. He'd regularly sold his Smoke capsules up at the San Fran Trade-off; and every month or two he returned to the San Jo Trade-off to select a few *luxury* supplies, look over the bookseller's current stock, and unsuccessfully check on the missing journals. Even now he could easily be the victim of an attack by a group of Freemen or Desperadoes, especially if they were armed. As the numbers of Dyed Persons released from the Shields increased, he'd noticed a recent growing hostility from Freemen toward all DPs, including himself. A dangerous trend, for sure.

He needed to secure a sidearm of some kind. There were rifles usually available at all but the smallest trade-offs, but the Company banned DPs from carrying *any* weapon—even a bow and arrows. He needed a good handgun, which he could conceal. It would probably deplete his horde of scrip and Smoke—if he could find a vendor at a bigger trade-off who would sell one to him. Unlikely, with the growing ill will toward his kind. Some time ago he had traded a Freemen for a K-bar, a military assault knife, which he carried on his hip back near his leather packet.

The Crimson Man was always cautiously alert and careful around potentially dangerous situations, like tonight at the cache site. He avoided all confrontations if possible, but he was able to vigorously defend himself if necessary.

Around 12:30 A.M., the romantic frogs croaking to the north abruptly ceased.

A minute or so later, he spotted a single, dark figure creeping in from the overgrown marsh directly toward the cache site.

The Crimson Man took a few steps forward, squinted, and focused intently.

As the figure neared the hummerpad, a sporadic breeze seemed to swirl and slightly thin the mist, providing a brief opportunity of much better visibility in the entire old park area, but especially around the hummerpad.

The solitary figure was a DP, as he'd suspected—

But a woman!

Yes, a woman of sleight but athletic build and dyed the shiny pale green of a cut lime.

She glanced about furtively for a few moments, then she bent down, palmed the inset, cracked open the heavy plasteel door, and withdrew one square supply pack. Per her programming, she immediately slammed shut the sturdy door before beginning to tear open the top of the supply pack.

Three riders thundered into view, emerging from where they'd been hiding in the northern end of the same thick forest crescent that sheltered the Crimson Man.

The Lime Woman didn't have a chance to run or cry out before the three Desperadoes swept down upon her, initially covering her with a thin film of gray dust when they reined up.

One man lassoed her before she could flee, dismounted, and ripped the supply pack out of her hands. Another bandit simultaneously jumped off his horse, and went through her backpack, scattering stuff on the ground...and eventually shouted victoriously while holding up what appeared to be two or three folded bills of Shield scrip.

The third rider, still wearing his bandana over his lower face, remained mounted, almost casually covering the bound Lime Woman with an old rifle, which looked like a small-bore .22.

The two Desperadoes ripped open the supply pack and dismissively flung away the container of water and four foodpaks— they were considered too bland and tasteless and an undesirable item to most Freemen in Cal Wild. The Desperado who had lassoed the woman held up his palm toward the mounted boss, showing off what he'd found at the bottom of the Lime Woman's supply pack.

"Ah, listen here, Jimbo!" he said almost gleefully, shaking the valuable four caps of Smoke in his hand as if they were dice.

Jimbo nodded, keeping his eye on the Lime Woman, who was lying on the ground on her side, and beginning to sob.

"Check her over closely, see if she's hidden any more credits or caps of Blue or anything else of value on herself. Best strip her down to her shorts."

The two Desperadoes untied the lasso, and roughly stripped away the old-time long pants, heavy sweater, and even the flimsy undergarments worn by the Lime Woman. They found nothing of value, and indicated this to their mounted boss.

The naked Lime Woman sat up, covered her bare breasts with

her crossed arms, shivered, and continued to sob a little more loudly in the mist, which was beginning to thicken back again.

The youngest of the Desperadoes, a skinny, hawk-faced teenager, reached down with his foot and forced the nude Lime Woman's knees apart, exposing her bushy triangle of secret hair, while he massaged his own crotch and smiled lasciviously. It was obvious what he had in mind.

The Crimson Man steeled himself at the realization, momentarily motivated to intervene; but for the time being, he forced himself to remain hidden in the forest shadows, keenly cognizant of the mounted rider's weapon—small-bore or not, it would be lethal if used properly.

"Okay, enough, Kid," Jimbo ordered in a sharp voice. "We don't have time for any of that. Company hummer could be along anytime to restock. Who knows? And we've got a pretty good ride left to get to the nearest cache site and find a good hiding spot before tomorrow evening. Mount up. Both of you."

"I'll just drag her back into the woods for a minute—"

"Now," Jimbo said impatiently, gesturing with his rifle at the two horses beside him.

Reluctantly, the two younger men obeyed, and climbed back upon their horses. For a few seconds, Kid looked down on the naked Lime Woman with a frustrated expression before he shook his head and pulled up his bandana.

The three Desperadoes turned their mounts and rode off to the east.

∽ – ∽

The Crimson Man remained in his sheltered spot, and watched carefully as the Lime Woman pulled herself together and began slowly picking up her clothes and the scattered foodpaks. She dressed quickly, then carefully repacked her gathered things into her backpack.

2

THE LIME WOMAN

Approaching her slowly from his shadowy hideaway on the forest perimeter, the Crimson Man said in a low, soft tone, "Hello, there—"

"Oh, no," the Lime Woman said in an alarmed voice, twisting about and pulling her backpack protectively in front of her chest.

"*Wait*... please, I mean you no harm," the Crimson Man said, shaking his head. "I, too, am only a Dyed Person, not a Desperado like those three who attacked you."

His words fell on semi-deaf ears; the poor woman had not yet recovered from the shock of the bandits' sudden attack, and was still badly frightened. She probably anticipated the rape she'd narrowly avoided.

She crumpled to the ground in a fetal position and sobbed again with renewed grief and self-pity.

"You're safe now," he said, trying to keep his tone as soft and non-threatening as possible. He also stood still, keeping both hands open and in plain sight at his sides. "Don't be afraid."

She forced herself to look up at him squarely, but with still fearful, tear-filled eyes.

Slowly, he kneeled, and reached out, gently brushing back her hair from her dusty face, and said, "It's getting very late, maybe we should build a fire to warm you up and heat our foodpaks. You'll feel better after you get cleaned up, eat, and—"

The Lime Woman scooted away from his outstretched hand, and interrupted him in a barely audible voice, "Please, don't hurt me."

"No, no, I won't harm you. It's okay, now. They're gone. You don't need to be afraid of me. I'm only a DP like yourself."

Her sobbing gradually ebbed.

He tentatively stroked her hand with his fingertips, as if she were a kitten.

"You're safe. Nothing more to fear. Do you understand?"

After another minute or so, even her sniffling tapered off, and she peered back at him, but obviously still suspicious of his intent.

"Get up, please, " he said, beckoning her to stand. "We'll find a more sheltered, safer spot back up in the trees. Build a good fire. Warm up. Get cleaned up. Eat, and then get some rest…"

He then added in a whisper, "You have absolutely nothing to fear from me. I won't steal your things … or assault you. If I wanted to do any of that, I could've already done it. But I'm not a thief." He smiled, holding his red-stained hands palms up in a gesture of supplication.

The Lime Woman nodded, and stood, but continued to wear a concerned expression on her face.

"Be right back."

He made a quick trip to the cache to claim his own supply.

Crackling flames leapt from a fire the Crimson Man had built under a tight cluster of smaller eucalyptus trees, the canopy of branches partially breaking up the rising smoke. They'd eaten in silence close to the comforting fire, but the woman maintained a constant wary frown on her features. She relaxed noticeably after the Crimson Man offered her one of his capsules of Smoke. She grabbed the capsule as if it were a lifesaver thrown to a drowning woman. Then she immediately cracked the cap and inhaled the bluish whiff of smoke ... and sighed with obvious deeply felt relief. She shuddered and visibly relaxed.

The Crimson Man had the opportunity to gaze at the Lime Woman more fully without further frightening her. Despite her lime green color, the woman was quite comely, with full lips, high cheekbones, and large hazel eyes. When the drug began taking effect, her frown slipped away and left her features in their natural wrinkle-free state. She was small, almost tiny, but her distance runner's build was contoured by feminine bumps and curves. Yes, a very attractive woman. The Crimson Man guessed she was young— maybe in her mid-to-late-twenties. He stared at her for a good ten minutes, sipping his weak tea. It had been a long time since he'd been so close to an attractive female for more than a fleeting moment. He'd always been moving quickly with purpose at trade-offs when he was forced to be around any Freemen men or women— not intending to rely on his scary appearance too long for protection from confrontation.

So, he really enjoyed the pleasing moments sitting near the fire, under the shelter of the aromatic trees, in the quiet night, in the company of this young, attractive woman.

After the better part of fifteen minutes, the Lime Woman finally blinked repeatedly, sucked in a deep breath, and began recovering from the initial effects of the strong drug that had left her body limp, her movements sluggish, and her expression slack. She cleared her throat, sighed, and stared steadily back at the Crimson Man. But now her expression was more than a little warmer; it was softer, and almost friendly. Her smile was engaging, her teeth straight and white. Before she'd been dyed, she had been a *stunningly* beautiful young woman.

The Crimson Man wondered what specific crime she'd committed to be dyed pale lime—obviously one of the categories of green crimes, but he didn't ask. It was considered extremely rude to do so in the unwritten DP code. You never asked another Dyed Person what they'd done to be dyed. Nor did you ask anything directly about their background before receiving a Judgment of Color. Or anything else of a strictly personal nature. He guessed she hadn't been a Freemen like him.

The woman reached out and shyly touched his hand.

"I appreciate your kindness, Crimson Man. I'm sorry I was so, so..."

She paused and shrugged apologetically.

He smiled back, shaking his head. "No problem. Of course I realize my appearance is frightening when you don't know me, perhaps even a bit gruesome." He fingered the rough scar along his cheek.

The woman took another deep breath, forced a slight frown, and with a bright twinkle in her hazel eyes she said, "Yes, you may be gruesome-looking, but probably *only* in the dark ... and to strangers." Then she coughed, cutting off a chuckle, unsure at her attempt to lighten the tenseness between them.

There remained an awkward long period of silence, as there usually was when DPs first met on the road. They were like strange teenagers meeting, ungainly, shy, and awkward; their brief conversations usually self-conscious and formally stilted.

"How long have you wandered with color?" he eventually said, disregarding his unsettling sense of being not quite sure of what questions to ask. He hadn't had a real personal conversation with anyone for over a year. Even the few DPs he'd met, barely more than a greeting exchanged or a snatch of rumor between them before they moved on. Just a sentence or two with Freemen, bartering with the vendors at trade-offs—few of them attractive women.

Her color, the pale lime green, in and of itself looked unnatural and a little unnerving.

After a briefer silence, she replied, "It's been almost three years. Three very long, rough years. This is the fifth time I've been robbed like this, and twice before I was—"

She broke off abruptly and quickly looked away; then followed in a diminished, obviously embarrassed voice, "Well … even worse things happened those two times."

He understood to what she alluded. He hadn't thought too much about the difficulties of being a female DP because she was the first dyed woman he'd seen during the last year. He knew that wandering with color must be especially difficult and dangerous for a woman. It was remarkable she'd survived so long and remained in such relative good shape—at least on the outside.

She interrupted his thoughts. "Where are you headed?"

"I intend to stop by the San Jo Trade-off in two or three nights, probably staying there overnight before continuing south-easterly five miles to San Fran Shield Cache Site #13. And you?" He took a long drink of water from his canteen.

"Well, I need to continue directly to that closest cache site myself," she replied. "They stole all my Smoke, as you know. But maybe we could at least walk together for the next couple of days?"

He nodded agreement.

She looked directly into his eyes, as if searching for something else, before adding, "And then after restocking, I'm going to continue on southeast for a distant hidden location in the Southern Big Dry—"

She stopped her sentence abruptly at that point to suck in a deep breath and clutch her hands together, which were trembling ever so slightly. As she continued her train of thought, her voice grew more emotionally charged, her tone edging higher in pitch.

"A secret place established not too long ago by a truly holy man. It's a place of freedom for our kind. It's a location where we are truly welcome, regardless of our skin color." She shook her head as if incredulous of her own words, but at the same time maintaining a positive, joyful expression.

"Do you know anything about it?" she asked him, her eyebrows lifted, as if hoping for a positive answer. "Have you heard any of the stories about this remarkable saintly man and his wonderful refuge?"

He shook his head. "No, I'm afraid I've heard nothing at all about this...holy man or a DP sanctuary in the desert. I'm sorry."

"It's a safe haven for many different kinds of people other than DPs, you know." She was still speaking in a voice elevated in pitch. "Freemen of all kinds. Even Cal Wild defectives. But especially young people, children, orphans, and such. It's said there is a place for everyone there who comes in peace with a loving heart. Actually it's a hidden refuge from the Company, a tiny, but growing, community of rebels, you see."

He nodded, caught up in her passionate, confident tone; but at the same time thinking the vague description of the place or founder sounded more like a fairy tale, a rumored place conjured from the wishful imagination of the minds of DP Smoke addicts.

"Crossing the Big Dry can be extremely dangerous," he said. "Do you know the exact location of this hidden sanctuary? The name of the founder?"

As soon as he finished saying it, he knew it was ill-advised.

The joy ebbed from her expression, her forehead growing deep lines, her smile fading, leaving her lips pinched in a thin, tight line.

After a long hesitation, she whispered, "No, that's a major problem I'm afraid. I don't know the exact location or the founder's name. It's kept a secret on purpose. I'll have to take my chances of finding it along the way. Surely someone, maybe one of the herders, farmers, or other people out there in the Big Dry will be able to direct me or at least tell me more about the holy man..."

By her expression and the way her voice faded, it was easy to see he'd seriously dampened some of her enthusiasm for reaching her goal. And he regretted doing so. Everyone, especially DPs, needed hope for a better life, or something to look forward to.

He coughed and added clumsily, "Well ... I'm sure you'll be

successful finding this holy man and his refuge. It sounds wonderful, too."

She didn't look at him squarely then, only nodded as she broke down her bedroll, which the three thieves fortunately hadn't taken. She'd apparently lost her poncho, perhaps in one of the previous attacks.

He got up and spread out his poncho over a thick bed of fresh-smelling leaves he'd scattered on the ground. "Spread your roll out on half of this poncho. It'll keep your back and bottom dry."

For a moment she hesitated, looking at him with a suspicious glance ... Then she slowly broke into another grin. "Ah, you're not really quite so gruesome tonight, my friend. Of course, it's not really too dark here near the fire."

"Oh, are you quite sure?" he said, making a fierce but silly face at her, as if he were trying to scare a young child.

They both laughed.

A few bullfrogs bellowed in unison from the distant cattails.

They made ready to bed down for the night, their bedrolls almost a foot apart on the wide poncho. The young woman was allowed to claim the preferential spot nearest the fire, which was beginning to die down.

Sometime in the early morning hours, the Crimson Man awakened.

The fire had died down considerably to a few ash-covered coals.

The young woman's back was pressed solidly against him, and in his sleep he'd doubled his arms around her in a spooning position, despite the clumsy separation by the two bedrolls. For a few minutes he lay there awake, enjoying the comfort of sharing the close body warmth of another person, and her female smell, which was not perfumed, but clean and sweet. It chased the cold loneliness from his heart off into the misty night. It had been a long time, he thought. A real long time. He inhaled her scent deeply.

Then he became painfully aware that his enjoyment of the close presence of this attractive, young woman was not exactly a completely platonic thing. He had a full erection, which he was surprised hadn't awakened the young woman, as it was poking obtrusively into the small of her back despite the bedrolls.

But the Lime Woman slept on, snoring ever so softly.

The Crimson Man grinned wryly to himself as he attempted to adjust and ignore his aroused state, while getting himself back into a more comfortable sleeping position.

Difficult, very difficult…

He found he even had trouble calling up MacKenzie's image, which usually helped him drift back off when he awakened at night. He suspected she would've thought his predicament tonight was pretty hilarious.

He sighed deeply.

3

TO TOUCH A SOUL

They walked together the next day, making good time, and he thoroughly enjoyed her company. She seemed to be a modest, good-spirited person in every sense of the word. Surprisingly, she was not psychologically beaten down much by her difficulty of wandering three years cloaked in color.

She gradually volunteered bits of her background, which he pieced together.

She had been a Shield resident before she'd received a color judgment, and like him, she'd been judged at San Fran Shield. Her family came from a small place in eastern Canada—Dunnville. A town between Toronto and Buffalo, an area that had received some serious damage during the major strikes around Buffalo. Although of relatively affluent means, her family, including a younger brother, had emigrated, her folks signing one of the first habitation contracts with the Company at Couver Shield. It became difficult for them financially—cut off from their Canadian business resources. She had been studying accounting at McGill University before emigrating. After considerable effort, she was able to secure an auditing position in the commercial contracts division of the Company's

Energy Department; but the entry-level job had required her to relocate to San Fran Shield. Months after she'd began working there, she was swept up by the Companymen in a bribery investigation. She was eventually judged, even though she was not really involved in the case—credits illegally transferred between some large Shield businesses to a number of staff members in her division. She had been aware of some suspicious contract alterations that a friend, a more senior auditor, should have reported. With no family at San Fran Shield to help or anyone important to intervene in her behalf, she was lumped in with the other complicit staff. She received a minor color judgment—lime green. Her friend and three others, all relatively low-level employees, received more severe black oak leaf-green judgments. The four were cast out of the Shield to roam as DPs.

"Yeah, I know, everyone is always innocent, but you see, it's true in my case," she'd said in a joking manner, with a thin smile, her eyes not laughing at all. "I never received one illegal credit."

The Crimson Man did not choose to go into any detail about his crime or judgment, nor did he insist on his own innocence. He had after all beaten an important Shield resident to death—deservedly or not. But it made no difference now. Nor did this innocent woman's story. He saw no real difference between wearing lime green or a more intense shade of green. All DPs were dyed for life. All were outcasts, treated as pariahs. All suffered equally despite the severity of their crimes.

In the early evening, they picked a good spot to camp near a spring and small pool by several huge live oaks. After they ate, and she'd recovered from using another cap of his Smoke, the woman graced him with her musical talent. She sang for the Crimson Man, a number of pre-Collapse classics, mostly sad, bluesy ballads, like "The House of the Rising Sun." Her voice, even without the accompaniment of a musical instrument, was quite distinctive, husky but pure and melodic. Seemed to be almost of professional quality.

"Did you have some voice training and maybe paid experience when you were living in Canada?"

"I did," she answered without elaborating.

She held up a finger. And then, with her eyes closed, she sang the most moving a cappella version of "Amazing Grace" he'd ever heard. The song had been written over three centuries ago by a captain on a ship bringing slaves to the new world ... the words still moving and relevant to both of them now.

It was a pleasant night at the dying campfire. The best he'd spent in over a year. For a few hours he'd completely forgotten he was dyed crimson.

It was again relatively late before they turned in, both having enjoyed the others' company.

Tonight the Lime Woman spread her bedroll next to the Crimson Man's. Before she turned in she gave him a glowing friendly smile, and it touched his heart, took his breath away, reminding him a little of a *MacKenzie Special.*

For a long time he had difficulty sleeping. The Lime Woman's easy deep breathing—a velvety snore—finally lulled him away.

Just after midnight, something startled the Crimson Man awake. He was instantly alert, sensing nearby danger.

The fire was little more than smoking coals.

He glanced around, trying to discover what was amiss—

Glowing red eyes stared back at him, not more than twenty-five yards away on the other side of the small spring pool.

Perhaps it's only some animal come to drink, he speculated.

He carefully slipped out of his bedroll and pulled on his clothes. Then he eased over and threw five or six broken-up oak branches onto the fire, keeping his gaze on the glowing eyes that peered back unblinking.

"What's wrong?" the woman asked sleepily from her bedroll.

He shook his head without looking at her directly.

"Just an animal drinking," he added in a barely audible whisper.

The red eyes seemed to move in closer. And at that moment he heard a vaguely familiar deep-throated cough/growl that raised the hair on the back of his neck and arms.

Whatever the thing was, it wanted to do more than drink.

"Is it dangerous?"

He didn't answer.

Instead, the Crimson Man eased over to his backpack and picked up his K-bar in one hand. He returned to the fire and grabbed the largest oak limb in his free hand. He stoked the fire, sending a shower of sparks high into the night air, and waited for another few seconds. Then he jerked the now burning limb from the coals. Holding it like a fiery lance, he charged into the night directly at whatever lurked there.

Red eyes hesitated only a second...

The creature growled loudly in protest before the eyes suddenly disappeared.

Stopping near the spring, the Crimson Man made out the sounds of the creature retreating into the night. He waited a minute or two, staring into the darkness, but no glaring eyes reappeared.

Back at the campsite, he piled more branches onto the fire, causing it to blaze higher than his head. Making a wide reconnoitering circle of the immediate area, he collected an armful of more dead wood. Returning to the crackling flames, he deposited his fresh load onto the remaining stack of broken branches.

Glancing again into the night, he sighed, then turned and stepped closer to where the woman was still lying on the poncho.

"You're brave," she said, the admiration obvious in her tone.

He shook his head in denial. "I think it may have been nothing more than a big dog," he said, staring off again into the night. He wasn't convinced that was true. Because of its odd cough/growl sound, the creature might have been a bigheaded coyote, a mutant much more aggressive and vicious than most post-Collapse dogs. The creatures were usually found further south and east, the closest he'd heard about down near the L'more Groundstar. And they were not so easily discouraged, either.

Whatever it was it'd been scared off for now.

"We'll keep a good fire going through the rest of the night," he said, directing his attention back to the woman. "It's safe for you to go back to sleep if you want. I'm going to stay up a little while longer."

When he looked down at her, she smiled in a sexy manner, licked her lips provocatively, and shook her head.

Still preoccupied by the possibility of a lurking dangerous animal, the Crimson Man ignored her seductive expression and returned to tend the fire. He stared into the darkness until the young woman demanded in an impatient whisper, "Come to bed, now."

He did.

By then it was quite warm where they'd spread their bedrolls too near the now raging, snapping fire. Flames leapt into the night. He was even sweating slightly. By the time he finally took off his outer clothes and climbed into his bedroll, the young woman had combined their blankets into one overlapping cover. She had also scooted to the middle under the common covers ... and was completely naked.

She made a sound like a hoarse chuckle from deep down in her chest, and with no apparent inhibitions, she pulled him close to her nudeness. She helped him slip off his undergarments.

Then he pressed his damp chest against her sweaty breasts, her right leg locked possessively over his left hip. Clutching him even tighter, as if to prevent him from sliding away from her slippery breasts, she kissed him firmly—not exactly a first date kiss either.

Oh, no. This was much more serious in intent: open mouth, wet tongue probing, sloppy, exciting. After she'd finished that arousing first kiss, she placed her finger to his lips and shook her head. Neither said another word as the fire slowly died down behind them.

They took their time, first exploring each other's bodies, fingers erotically slipping across slick skin, while they kissed, nibbled, and bit … before they finally conjoined. The woman was slippery wet and easily guided him into her. They both moaned with that first grand tactile moment of pleasure. They made love, but not like a frantic, impersonal, selfish first encounter or animals panting in heat. No, it was much more controlled and careful lovemaking—more like a naked tango practiced by two long-term partners, each completely aware and in sync with the other dancer's subtle moves.

Which was surprising, considering his self-enforced celibacy for so long—even before his Judgment of Color. It should have been over in a few frantic minutes of rapid huffing and puffing.

They stayed joined for a long time. There were periods of one or the other yo-yoing about, but both stopping often to rest, to savor the exquisite moments, each finally peaking to orgasm twice before they finally broke apart gasping.

Thoroughly exhausted.

Totally content.

When it finally ended, when he withdrew from her, he whispered against her cheek, "That was glorious!"

In a sexy-hoarse voice, she said, "Yes, it was … incredible!"

After her reaction, he lovingly nuzzled her face and head.

"Oh, that tickles," she said in a still slightly gravelly voice, pushing his nose away from her ear.

They both sighed deeply.

Neither said anything more as they separated, each rolling apart onto their backs—nothing more relevant needed to be added to what had been experienced and already said.

The woman fell asleep first, a smile locked on her full lips.

He lay on his back and thought of MacKenzie. He could almost see her looking down on him with her special smile and nodding her head, as if rendering her approval. So, he felt not the least twinge of guilt for making love to this attractive stranger.

Instead of drifting off, for some reason he was reminded of an old essay that his father had published somewhere. Maybe in one of the odd philosophical e-chapbooks circulated for free around the UC campus before mid-21st Century over thirty years ago. His father wrote that lovemaking—not just sex—but deep, caring lovemaking, was the closest two people could ever come together spiritually. A complete exposing of self to another, a mystical deep bonding of sorts. A religious experience. Something that people more and more infrequently attained during those hectic times back then just before the Collapse. It was kind of an encouraging, promotional how-to article. He smiled because his father had dedicated it to his mother, Lauren—sentimental, but the memory very touching, even now. And he thought his father had called the lyrical, and almost poetical essay "To Touch a Soul."

At the time—he must've been sixteen or maybe seventeen—he didn't understand any of it. His hormones were interfering with reading anything insightful about love or sex. He erroneously thought the essay was some kind of semi-theological tract; many of the circulating chapbooks seemed to be of that nature, people seeking something religious or metaphysical in nature to anchor their hectic lives and then share the discovery with friends.

Now he thought he understood his father's intention. A few moments ago, he'd touched this woman's soul.

His dad had been right about this belief, like so many other things.

Swallowing, he felt a lump stick in his throat. He missed his father. He wished their relationship hadn't ended on such a sour note back at the med camp. He wondered if the older man was still alive, and if so, where was he now? And then he frowned, wondering what his father would think seeing his son dyed crimson—a judged murderer.

He pushed these unsettling thoughts away as he spooned the woman, who responded in her sleep with a deep sigh.

Drawn completely back to the present circumstances, the Crimson Man's breath caught in his throat. He knew they probably had one more night together, at the most. One of the programmed Rules of DP Conduct: *No assembly with other DPs.* In fact, if they both palmed another insert at the next cache site too close to the same time, like had been the case back at #12, it would undoubtedly provoke a visit from the Companymen. Some form of discipline sure to follow. They both knew this, so they would probably drift permanently apart after they neared the San Jo Trade-off, each going their separate way. He might follow her a day or so later to Cache Site #13. But it was doubtful they would see each other again. She'd be immediately moving on, propelled by her addiction to the drug, Smoke. And perhaps to search for her dream refuge somewhere down in the Southern Big Dry.

The emotional reaction to the realization again caused a lump in his throat, and for a moment he was shaken with the deepest sense of regret. Just like at the end with MacKenzie. He would soon permanently lose another woman. A woman whose soul he'd touched, if just briefly. And sadly, he didn't even know her real name—another terrible Company prohibition.

The Crimson Man sucked in a deep breath, coughed, and finally cleared his throat.

☙ – ❧

He was able to force the depressing thoughts to the back of his mind and clung to the woman with a deep sense of gratitude as he eventually dropped off to sleep.

4

THE BOOK SELLER

The Crimson Man and the Lime Woman stopped walking together the next day sometime in the late afternoon as Highway 101 swung in close to the San Jo Ruins.

They hugged and kissed stiffly before saying goodbye, the Crimson Man holding back his emotions.

"Maybe our paths will cross down the road before I head off for the desert sanctuary, you know," she said, still standing on her tiptoes, pressed tightly against his chest. "Or maybe even sometime in the future at that refuge in the Big Dry?"

He nodded and replied, "Maybe."

They both knew it was highly unlikely they would ever see each other again. The system was designed to discourage that. And the woman, even though she couldn't admit it to herself, probably realized the sanctuary was little more than a pipe dream.

The Crimson Man released her, and quickly turned away to head off in the direction of the trade-off, looking back once before he disappeared down the steep shoulder of the old highway proper.

She stood in the same spot, waving, her beautiful features cloaked in pale lime green sadness.

About twenty minutes later, the Crimson Man cautiously approached the outskirts of the San Jo Trade-off. Even at this late afternoon hour, it was noisy and dusty, buyers and sellers moving about. He'd wait until after dark before venturing in—safer that way.

At dusk, he finally entered the busy trade-off, ignoring the Freemen stares, searching for the bookseller's set-up. Lots of new vendors since his last visit and more buyers too, he thought, standing about in the center of the busy place.

Ah, there he was ...

The crowd parted slightly for him, respecting his size and appearance, as the Crimson Man made his way across traffic to the bookseller's table.

The vendor spotted him coming, smiled thinly after glancing nervously at the nearby crowd. He reached under his display table and enthusiastically held up and waved a large black book.

The bookseller held a battered black log with a flaking silver **JAZ** embossed in the corner of the front cover. It could only be his father's journal.

"You found one!" the Crimson Man said, quite pleased.

"Spotted it over a month ago at a trade-off several days south of here near the ruins of the Monterey Bay Desalination Plant off Highway 1. Small bookseller there. Mostly old brown paperbacks, a few textbooks, and this old journal."

The Crimson Man took the frayed journal in hand carefully, as if he were worried about damaging it further. He fingered the faded initials, nodded, and then opened to the first page. He flicked through the entire journal quickly until he came to—

Pages were missing in the last section. They looked like they'd been carefully torn out.

He looked at the vendor quizzically, who was frowning and shaking his head.

"I know, I know, it's missing a few pages at the end," he said, a sheepish expression on his face.

"A few?"

"But it's the right journal, eh?"

The Crimson Man admitted, "One of them."

"And you have the … ah, ten capsules of Smoke for it as we agreed, if I found it, right?"

"Five," he said, frowning and touching his scar. "And that was presumably for a full journal. This is only a partial journal, the critical last part is missing. I think it's worth even less than the five—"

"Whoa there," the bookseller said, holding up his hands in the stop gesture. "I had to give up several Invasors to secure this journal for you, and I'm entitled to some profit for my efforts, you know…"

The vendor paused, then shifted the discussion away from the damaged condition of his merchandise. "And besides, you know the Company is taking an active interest in old books like this one."

"What do you mean, an active interest?"

"They've been rounding them up for quite some time at most of the farthest outlying trade-offs, and they appear to be working this way toward the bigger coastal ruins—"

"Why would they do that?"

The vendor shrugged. "Not sure, except booksellers out there say the Company is interested in several kinds of books: historical ones, academic texts about teaching reading, all children's books, and especially diaries, logs, and journals, anything else written since the Collapse. Some of these books may become scarcer, if the Company keeps this up. Who knows? Over time it might be difficult to find anything worthwhile left to read." He sighed sadly. "The bottom line is that books are becoming more expensive."

The Crimson Man remembered what his father had written in

the first journal about teaching others to read. How important that was in Cal Wild. Without books to read—especially children's books—Freemen would eventually become illiterate, uneducated, and ignorant of the past. No, this skill couldn't be allowed to die out. He shook his head.

"How did this other bookseller obtain the journal?"

"He traded for it from a stranger. A young Freemen, who offered a pair of children's textbooks and the journal. The bookseller made a good deal for them all."

"Where did the young Freemen get the journal?"

"The bookseller didn't ask the man how it had come into his possession. He just recognized the value after hearing about the Company's ongoing intent to round up all such post-Collapse diaries inland."

The Crimson Man dug out five caps of Smoke and handed them to the vendor. "There is one more of these black journals out there somewhere. If you can find it before the Company gets it, I'll pay you a bonus, say ten caps of Smoke total for it. But it has to be in fairly readable shape, not a lot of missing pages."

The vendor grinned. "You got a deal."

The Crimson Man turned and headed away from the center of the trade-off, anxious to look over what actually remained of this second journal.

Who knows, maybe his father was still alive. He might be able to figure out his recent movements from journal entries ... at least until the time of the last entry. And if he ever got his hands on that third journal, he hoped he'd be able to pinpoint his father's present location.

5

UNEXPECTED CONFRONTATION

The Crimson Man was looking down at the journal, lost in thought, when he barged into the four Freemen—all young men.

"Hey, watch where you're going," the small, skinny one said, puffed up and angry.

"Sorry," the Crimson Man murmured and tried to move on.

Another of the Freemen, a bigger, husky, tough-looking guy, firmly grabbed the Crimson Man's shoulder and restrained him as he attempted to continue his way peacefully from the trade-off.

"Where do you think you're going in such a fucking hurry anyhow, red man?" the Freemen said, his face sweaty and flushed, his expression challenging. "Running away from something you've done? Bet you've been bothering Freemen women ... maybe even some of the kids?"

At that last suggestion his three friends moved in slightly closer, completely circling him.

"I don't want any trouble," the Crimson Man said, trying to gently pull his shoulder out of the Freemen's firm grip.

"Yeah, what have you been up to?" another of the Freemen asked, his voice slurred.

He smelled alcohol on all of them now. They were all juiced up, reckless, and probably dangerous. He'd have to do something before this turned ugly.

"Maybe we ought to make sure he ain't hurting anyone else ever again," suggested the big, tough one—the obvious ringleader.

The Crimson Man jerked himself free from the man's grip. Then he touched his scar.

"I aim to walk away from all of you *right* now," he said in a low, precise voice. "And I strongly recommend that none of you try and stop me."

The leader smiled dismissively. "Noah, you got a rope on your horse?"

Noah, the youngest of the four Freemen, looked kind of puzzled back at the ringleader. "Yeah, of course, Matt, but you aren't aiming to do anything serious—"

"Get it," Matt said, and his angry expression suggested his intention was serious.

Noah took off for wherever they'd left their horses, and the three stirred-up Freemen edged in a little tighter.

He wasn't going to be able to avoid trouble this time. So, the Crimson Man sucked in a deep breath, let it out slowly, then slipped his hand around to his backside, firmly grasping his K-bar.

"It looks to me like someone here is fixing on getting hurt," he said, bringing the long knife into view. "I'm thinking you're going to be first, Matt." He bent over slightly in an aggressive crouch.

All three Freemen, including Matt, recoiled backward several steps at the sight of the glistening, sharp weapon, the two unnamed Freemen looking fearful now.

"Hang close," Matt said to them, pulling out a knife of his own from inside his duster and assuming a fighting posture. He held the weapon properly in hand like an experienced knife-fighter. "Noah will be back in a few minutes, and we'll string up this fucking murderer. And he ain't going anywhere until then."

Too bad.

The Crimson Man took a quick skip forward and slashed at Matt's bare face.

The ringleader caught the blow on his forearm, but the sharp K-bar had sliced through his long coat sleeve and cut deeply into his arm, perhaps hitting an artery or large vein. Blood quickly soaked through the lower sleeve and began dripping to the ground, near his dropped weapon.

The Crimson Man felt a sudden clenching sensation in the pit of his stomach, followed by a lingering dull ache, but the aversive conditioned response was only a minor annoyance.

All three Freemen froze aghast, staring at the leader's arm and the spreading pool of blood at his feet.

That was the opportunity the Crimson Man needed. He bolted through the loose circle, darting off into the crowd, flashing the bloody blade in front of him to discourage any ill-advised heroics. Someone, perhaps one of the three Freemen shouted, "Hey, hey, stop that red man."

No brave soul responded by trying to step in front of him or follow on his heels…not yet.

He soon reached the darkened edge of the trade-off, knowing exactly where he was heading to escape from possible pursuing Freemen, who he knew would soon be rounded to follow him.

∂ − ∂

The Crimson Man ran for over a mile, panting for breath, and finally stopped in a familiar industrial sector of the San Jo Ruins.

He found the mouth of one of the tunnels into the Raider's secret basement compound, which remained undisturbed, the general area still guarded by the red skull and crossbones warning signs. Inside the dark tunnel he spotted a pair of blurry small gray forms scurrying about…Rats, attracted by the litter left behind from what appeared to be a hasty abandonment, when the Raiders broke up, probably not long after he'd put Mike Shaw down for good.

Regardless of rats or any other animal squatters occupying the hideout, the Crimson Man thought it would be a good place to lie up and wait for the trade-off Freemen to tire of searching for him. He didn't think it would take too long—probably shortly after they began sobering up in a few hours.

Whatever happened outside, he'd stay right here at least for the night.

The Crimson Man searched around the basement area for any other danger, making sure no other people or wild animals were trespassing on the premises.

The place was empty.

Fortunately, he'd found a handful of unused candles in one of the last cubicles he checked.

He stood in the doorway of the old cubicle MacKenzie and he'd shared, and lit a candle. The room was damp and smelled of mildew, but looked just about like they'd left it, except for a few heavy spider webs in the corners. After setting the candle in a holder on the nightstand, he spread his bedroll on the old bed frame. He sat, ate a cold foodpak, and chased down the dry food with water from his canteen, thinking about the confrontation back at the San Jo Trade-off…

Matt, the bully ringleader, had gotten what he'd bargained for, and he felt absolutely no remorse for slashing him. But the confrontation had confirmed what he suspected about Freemen resentment building up against DPs. In the near future, he believed they'd present an even greater hazard than Desperado thieves. From now on, he'd have to be doubly careful around trade-offs.

He dug out the second journal from his backpack, and figured he'd read a few entries before slipping off to sleep.

6

THE SECOND JOURNAL

The Crimson Man opened his father's journal to the first entry.

Before he began reading, he dug out the first journal from his backpack and checked the final entry. The last entry was dated PS: 6 years 11 months—almost seven years Post Strike. He set the older journal down next to the lit candle on the nightstand. Again, he picked up the second journal.

This first entry was dated: PS: 7 years 2 months. He flicked to the second journal's last entry before the missing pages, PS: 22 years 6 months … Fifteen years of more concise entries, with much longer calendar gaps between those entries … and the journal was only missing its last nine pages. He flipped back and forth roughly estimating the amount of time usually covered in nine pages.

Holy crap!

If he were even close in his rough calculations, the missing last entry had to be fairly recent. No more than eighteen to twenty months ago at the most, probably even less.

His pulse sped up. It was possible his father was still alive! He would be … ah, seventy-three by now. Not terribly old by pre-Collapse standards.

He felt close, so very close to this man who he hadn't seen in over thirty years.

The Crimson Man squeezed his eyes closed for a few seconds, took a deep breath, and let it trickle back across his lips, getting a firmer grip on his emotions.

Calmer, he flipped back to the first entry in the second journal, and began to read, continuing through most of the rest of the night, unable to stop himself from devouring the entire book. He paused only twice to light fresh candles.

At first his father had continued his wandering, staying for longer periods of time with different groups of herders, and eventually with farmers at tiny settlements at what he then called the southern part of the arid Great Central Valley. He had been preoccupied with encouraging the adults to read from books he carried with him, listening to stories he read, but also concentrated on teaching children the reading basics wherever he went, often preaching about pre-Collapse values, like the Golden Rule.

He'd eventually developed a reputation as a saintly figure out in the desert. But in the last four or five years, he'd wandered closer back into the more populated southern coastal ruins after the San D and San Barboo Shields were well established, finding better op-portunities to teach and lecture larger, more receptive groups.

By then he'd became somewhat of a renowned figure all over Cal Wild, his readings and lectures well attended, his audiences fond of his own stories. Also by that time he'd begun teaching teachers—young people who he found to be fast learners and good readers, even finding a few older pre-Collapse professional teachers able and willing to help.

All this time, fourteen or fifteen years, he remained enthusiastic despite various difficulties. He was gradually encouraged by his efforts, judging that he was indeed having an impact keeping the flame of literacy and core values alive. Yet the itinerant life had apparently taken a toll on him physically as he aged. He had developed some lingering arthritic foot and joint problems—very painful. Something affecting his eyes, too. Nevertheless, he never faltered in his focus: teaching children, lecturing to adults, reading stories to groups of avid listeners. By necessity, he remained for longer periods of time in the same locations, forced to reduce his traveling.

Even though the night was almost gone, and his eyes were tired, the Crimson Man reached and carefully read the very last entry.

Journal Entry
Monterey Fishing Village
PS: 22 years 9 months

Finally, we have the next major school site selected and partially established. We will model it on the successful one down not far from here at the San Barboo Ruins. Siobhan O'Connell is doing a fine job down there as Head Mistress. All of her four teachers working hard, too. 106 students, from ages five to fifteen, most of the older ones good readers now. The younger ones enthusiastically progressing well.

Now, I must locate enough good books and teaching materials for the DeYoungs up here, who will make an excellent Head Master-Mistress team, both with some pre-Collapse college teaching experience. In fact, Ron was one of my young graduate assistants at Berkeley just before the Collapse. Books, blackboards, chalk, pencils, and all the other materials are in short supply here in this small, but rapidly growing fishing area. The sardine schools that disappeared early last century have returned in abundance in the last few years. This area's early 20th Century years well chronicled by one of my mainstream favorites, John Steinbeck.

I am delighted with the first month's progress here. Already 10 students permanently enrolled. Ron and Linda are also teaching a small group of adults to read at night. I read one of my stories to this group last evening after dinner—mostly fishermen and their wives—but they are indeed enthusiastic.

I hope I will be able to find and bring back ample supplies on my excursion north along old 101, lots of new trade-offs there between here and the San Fran Ruins. H, a famous old science teacher, book collector, and long-time friend, has been rounding up textbooks for me, maybe some of the other things we will need, too. Even with only one good eye, he is a great reader for kids—he dearly loved my SF stories, and often picks a couple of them from the old SF anthologies to read to groups.

I will rest tonight with a joyous heart, and hopefully return in less than a fortnight. Stay in the fishing village until the school is going well before heading back south for our new major project.

I am finally making a legitimate difference in Cal Wild!

My major concern is the recurring rumors of the negative influence of the Company. They seem to be intent on disrupting our teaching efforts, at least out in the Big Dry. There are reports of reading materials being confiscated out there by Companymen. And they even seem to be harassing teachers—picking them up in hummers and taking them into the nearest Shield for extensive interrogations. Discouraging them from returning to teaching. It's almost as if they were trying to reduce literacy in Cal Wild, and were intent on eliminating all awareness of post-Collapse history.

Why? What do they gain by doing that?

Only talked to three different teachers who'd been taken in for questioning and intimidation. All ex-teachers when I finally caught up and talked to them briefly. They said the Company intended on doing the teaching of Freemen children in the future, at only Company approved schools. That doesn't seem credible to me—they haven't demonstrated an interest in betterment of Freemen in general, much less their children's education.

So I still wonder about the motive for the Company in doing this.

Why indeed? the Crimson Man asked himself, but he knew from what he'd heard recently that his father's earlier suspicions four or five years ago about the Company's ominous intent was most likely accurate.

Had his father ever returned to the fishing village at Monterey with those teaching texts and supplies?

He must have. The journal eventually returned there. He'd even recorded a year or two of more entries. But then those nine or ten pages had been torn from the journal…

By whom? Why? And how had the young Freemen obtained the journal from the DeYoungs before he sold it to the bookseller?

Intriguing questions for sure.

The Crimson Man blew out the third candle and nodded to himself. A good place to start asking those questions would be at the trade-off and the Monterey Fishing Village, track down and talk to that bookseller, and then the two DeYoungs.

7

A VENUE OF BUZZARDS

At mid-afternoon the next day, the Crimson Man stopped to rest off the shoulder of 101 in the shade of a black oak. It was hot and muggy, and he was tired from not sleeping much the night before. Too caught up in his reading of the journal. But he wasn't sorry in the least about missing that rest. The journal had been truly enlightening. He knew he was getting close to discovering important information about his father, who he believed must still be alive. He could even be living at the Monterey fishing village. The thought caused a surge of excitement.

Taking a breath and glancing into the cloudless sky, the Crimson Man spotted five … no, six buzzards circling off to the south, near the location of Cache Site #13. The birds had repelled him as a boy in pre-Collapse times. Scary harbingers of death, with their ugly, bare, red heads. But now he saw the buzzards as a good sign. Scavengers, they required dead animal life to support them. There were more and more live animals appearing again in Cal Wild, especially throughout the expanding forested areas. The increase in numbers of flying scavengers indicated a gradual recovery of Cal Wild. Positive harbingers for sure.

He took a long drink of water and forced himself back onto his feet. He had over a mile and a half to go before reaching his destination at Cache Site #13.

The Crimson Man stopped as he neared the cache site, squatting in a stand of tall saw grass a hundred and fifty yards from the hummerpad. As he waited in hiding, to insure there were no bandits lurking about, he glanced again into the bright sky. Whatever the six circling buzzards had been attracted to was close. They were further south of the cache site. Probably something large had died there to attract so many scavengers.

A half an hour later, the Crimson Man decided it was safe to venture into the hummerpad and pick up his supply pack. He palmed the insert, withdrew his supply pack, and quickly closed the plasteel door. After storing the contents in his backpack, he headed south, curious to see what the buzzards had found.

A human body, he thought as he moved in closer, shooing away a pair of buzzards that had already landed near the corpse...

"Oh, no," he uttered, stunned.

The Lime Woman.

She was completely naked, lying on her shoulder in a ditch alongside Highway 101. Her back and legs were a dark purple mass of bad bruises, deep cuts, long scratches, and sores beginning to scab over. Her face was not even recognizable—only her skin color gave away her identity. Both of her ankles were severely bruised with shiny rope burns. He suspected she'd been tied and dragged from horseback ... But not before they'd taken more than her life. She'd been sodomized, probably with a large foreign object. He guessed she'd probably been vaginally raped also.

He eased her onto her back to inspect her battered face. This young woman had once been a stunning beauty. And she'd been totally ravaged. Drug along the rough, pot-holed highway. Then abandoned alongside in the ditch where she eventually died, like some kind of trampled mutt. Left as a useless piece of garbage.

A tightness had welled up in his chest when he first recognized her; and it'd grown into a big dry lump lodged in his throat, constricting his breathing. He tried to swallow, dryly, then dug out his canteen for a drink.

Who could have done this?

Why?

He blinked and wiped moist eyes ... and spotted what looked like three letters she'd scrawled in the dust in the ditch before she finally died:

K I D

Kid?

The three thieves!

They'd attacked her again, stealing her caps of Smoke from Cache Site #13 ... and then took her life.

The realization of who had committed this brutality sobered up his grief and replaced it with an immediate anger.

Hot, red anger.

Overwhelmed and shaking with rage, the Crimson Man closed his eyes and sucked in several deep breaths, swallowing, clearing his throat, and remembering the young woman's beautiful smile; gradually he gained back some control of himself ...

First, he must bury this woman.

He nodded to himself as he dragged her away from the road and up a slight ravine.

In an hour he'd scraped out a shallow site and stacked a pile of large rocks over her grave. No varmints could damage her body any more than it already was, he thought, satisfied by his burying efforts. For a moment, he again closed his eyes, and he gave thanks that he'd had the opportunity to briefly know this young woman before she'd died, and had touched her soul.

He stretched, looked off to the west at the sun beginning to sink down beyond the coastal hills; and he smiled thinly, visualizing the Lime Woman's wonderful smile.

"I promise you those three will pay dearly for what they took from you. They will *never* again have the opportunity to brutalize another woman."

And the Crimson Man aimed to fulfill that pledge as soon as possible.

8

VENGEANCE

The Crimson Man reached back into the recent past and called up some of the tracking skills he'd acquired when he'd headed the pest eliminating service. Seemed so long ago, now. But it really didn't take a lot of expertise to follow and catch up to the three horsemen. They'd traveled along the shoulder remnants of Highway 101 and stopped not far from their brutal crime—maybe two miles south at most.

The late summer night was unusual, clear, and with not a trace of fog. The stars twinkled brightly overhead. An almost full moon lit up the night like a large yellow paper lantern. It wasn't muggy, but unusually cold, the temperature dropping steadily. It was after dark when the Crimson Man tiptoed in close enough through the thick eucalyptus grove to listen to the three Desperadoes clustered in close around a campfire. The thieves were resting against their saddles, sharing a bottle of something, joking, laughing, and enjoying themselves. Not a trace of remorse on any of their bare faces for the horrible things they'd done to the Lime Woman. In fact, they were talking about her now, how surprised she'd been to see them after they'd robbed her only four nights earlier. The youngest one, the hawk-faced Kid, seemed proud. The other young one was bragging, too. He'd participated enthusiastically in the sexual depravity. Even the older man, Jimbo, was grinning, seeming to be enjoying the younger men's atrocious recollections.

The dropping temperature did little to cool the Crimson Man's smoldering anger. Nevertheless, he remained squatting patiently out of sight in the trees, watching alertly. These three cowards didn't deserve the warmth of the fire on a cold night or any other comforts—especially anything they'd stolen from the dead woman. But he'd wait until they went to sleep, take them one at a time, make sure each *knew* exactly why he was about to die.

They finally bedded down. The older man, Jimbo, was soon snoring loudly, sounding like a busted bellows. One of the younger men also bedded down, but Kid remained by the fire . . . soon pulling out, cracking open a capsule and deeply inhaling a wisp of blue Smoke.

The Crimson Man clenched his jaw at the sight, but remained in place waiting and watching.

Half an hour later, Kid recovered from the effects of the drug, struggled to his feet and shuffled off into the trees directly opposite where the Crimson Man hid. So he circled around, not making a sound as he crept up from behind the young Desperado, who stood next to a shedding pale tree, relieving himself.

Stealth-like, the Crimson Man reached out and clutched the Desperado's face, covering the young man's mouth, while at the same time kicking his legs forward and jerking him backwards off balance. He stuffed a wadded sock into the stunned Kid's mouth. The startled boy looked up wide-eyed at the Crimson Man with obvious terror, not even trying to resist. Probably unable to cry out even if he weren't gagged.

"This is for the woman you brutalized and left for dead," the Crimson Man whispered, making sure what he said registered, before he leaned down and slashed the thief's throat from ear-to-ear. He left him lying in a steaming pool of piss and blood.

The Crimson Man then crept back toward the dying fire and watched the other two sleeping Desperados. He looked around their saddles, hoping to spot Jimbo's single-shot rifle.

It was nowhere in sight. A troubling hidden danger. He'd incapacitate Jimbo first.

The Crimson Man tiptoed close, kneeled over the older man, and slammed a solid blow into his exposed left temple with the heel of the K-bar. Jimbo grunted and slumped over facedown.

The younger man, roused by the loud sound of pain from his chief, pushed up and out of his blanket on an elbow, blinking, his expression drowsy with sleep.

"Don't you dare move," the Crimson Man said, threatening the young thief and murderer with his bloody K-bar that glistened in the dying firelight.

The Desperado sat stone still, terror frozen on his face.

"Good," the Crimson Man said, edging closer. He stood over the frightened man, peering down, his own expression obviously grim and undoubtedly scary.

"You three robbed a young woman twice in the last four days, then brutally drug her to her death, after torturing her unmercifully," he said in the condemning voice of a pre-Collapse judge.

The boy began to shake his head in denial.

"No, you did it," the Crimson Man insisted. "You deserve no mercy, and for your terrible crime, you must die … tonight." He began to kneel, knife in hand, but the boy closed his eyes, sobbed, and like a little boy tried to cover his head with his blanket.

The Crimson Man stripped away the blanket, completely exposing the bandit, now curled into a fetal ball.

"No, please, don't, please…"

He grabbed the young man's long hair and jerked him onto his knees; then, he cut his throat. The boy slumped over onto his back, a wide crimson grin permanently etched across his neck.

Dropping down to cover the dying boy's bloody mess with his blanket, the Crimson Man heard a gunshot behind him, and felt a sudden stinging in his left ear.

He twisted about.

Jimbo was up and out of his bedroll, armed with the .22 rifle—which he must've had with him under the covers. His duster was wrapped around him for warmth, but the front was unbuttoned and exposed his gray hair-covered potbelly. The older man was clumsily fingering another small round into the weapon's single-shot chamber—

The Crimson Man was on him, slamming his forearm squarely into Jimbo's face…his elbow landing with a loud *crunch.*

Dropping his rifle, Jimbo bent over, trying to breathe through his mouth but making a gurgling, choking sound, his face smeared with blood from his nose.

The Crimson Man kicked away the .22, and waited for the murdering thief to partially catch his breath, blink his vision clear, and look up.

Jimbo carried a puzzled expression, as if silently asking: *Who are you?*

The Crimson Man said, "You allowed your two young sidekicks to brutally rape, torture, and murder an innocent woman. Drug her naked from horseback and left her to die alongside the road like a trodden animal."

Jimbo stared back with watery eyes, his badly broken nose streaming blood, and didn't even attempt to deny the charge.

"For this you will die like they both have."

The Crimson Man stepped forward, buried the long knife into

Jimbo's stomach, ripped the long blade upward, and withdrew.

The Desperado gasped and slumped to his knees, both hands laced across his potbelly, as if attempting to hold his guts in place. He gasped weakly again, and crumpled to the ground, dying.

He left the three bandits where they lay, like discarded offal, exactly like they'd done to the Lime Woman. Before leaving the campsite, the Crimson Man checked each Desperado's corpse, kicking each dismissively, and watching for a reaction … None. He wiped the blood of the dead men from his K-bar on Kid's long coat.

Then he headed south, not wanting to camp anywhere near the three pieces of crap he'd left behind.

The Crimson Man realized something ran down the left side of his neck. He reached up, and glanced at his bloody fingers. Only then did he feel the burning/aching sensation in his ear. It'd been numb since Jimbo shot him, but was now a little more than an annoying pain. He gingerly fingered the bleeding wound—

The lower quarter of his ear, including the entire lobe, was missing. He shrugged off his pack, then searched for something clean inside. Pressing an old handkerchief against the still bloody ear remnant, he soon stanched the trickle, but the ear continued to throb. Since he had nothing else, he was sorely tempted to use a cap of Smoke to quell the dull ache. But he knew it would only be temporary. So he sucked in a deep breath, steeled himself against the pain, and continued on.

As he walked along Highway 101, headed for the turnoff to old coastal Highway 1, he diverted his thoughts from his damaged, aching ear to his father.

He remembered his dad's stated regret about hunting and killing Desperadoes in those early days after the Collapse, when they still lived at the Blue Rock Springs Med Camp, his deeply sincere remorse, and the beginning of his apparent lifelong search for some kind of redemption or salvation. The Crimson Man examined his own feelings. Intellectually he knew his life had been ten or maybe a hundred times more reprehensible than his father's. He'd killed...? No clue how many. But they were never really innocents, he thought. Still, he knew, if anyone, he should be seeking some kind of salvation for his past violent acts. In all honesty, he felt not even a sliver of remorse for executing the Lime Woman's murderers. He felt only disgust for them, and a sense of deep satisfaction for settling the score. He'd reached maturity under much different conditions than his father. Different times, different ethical rules, perhaps even a different moral code. Hopefully, different final judgments, too. If there were such a thing.

The Crimson Man pushed the metaphysical speculation and his father's moral/ethical concerns to the back of his mind...

Glancing west, the Crimson Man saw the glowing moon sink lower, almost resting now on the coastal mountains, and he struck his path in that direction. He'd find a campsite along this old road. Tomorrow he'd be looking out over the Pacific Ocean.

9

MONTEREY BAY FISHING VILLAGE

Two nights later, the Crimson Man found the small trade-off near the old Monterey Desalinization Plant Ruins was busy, packed with maybe seventy-five to a hundred buyers and sellers—small by comparison to any of the five Shield trade-off standards, but a good crowd for most inland Cal Wild trade-offs. Cool, salt-laced mist blew in from the Pacific Ocean, the sound of the surf competing with the vendors hawking their merchandize. Scanning over the wagons, tables, stalls, and blanket layouts, it didn't appear that any of the vendors were selling books.

"May I ask you a question?" he said to a bundled-up Freemen offering wine and a few bottles of some other kind of spirit.

The wine seller glanced up from under a pulled-down old blue baseball cap, and apparently, after taking time to weigh options, he nodded and finally added, "We don't see many of your kind around here … In fact, I've never seen a red-dyed man anywhere." The vendor's speech was slightly indistinct, and his eyes appeared blood-shot. The Crimson Man wondered if the vendor was sampling his own wares? This would account for why he didn't appear to be the least frightened by the sudden specter of a giant scarred

DP missing the bottom part of his left ear.

The Crimson Man smiled thinly. "Your trade-off has been off the beaten track until only recently. Anyhow, didn't there used to be a bookseller with a table doing business here?"

The man frowned with concentration, then snapped his fingers loudly. "Sure, Julian, a regular for years, left the trade-off … oh, a month or so ago, couldn't get enough books to trade and make a living. But now, maybe twice a week, this tall, stooped, old Free-men with a black patch over his right eye sets up a blanket display with a handful of usually paperback books. At first he just wandered around here and down in the village, asking lots of funny questions about the Company and the school. Mostly now though, he reads these odd stories to the kids, after doing a science trick or two to draw them in and get their attention. They think he's some kind of a magician and the older ones call him The Wiz. I just think he's a weird old guy, maybe a little addled. Never seen him really trading any of his books."

The Crimson Man wondered if the strange guy was his dad's old friend, H? Sounded like it might be him, but right now he was more interested in that other bookseller, the one who'd bought and sold his dad's journal.

"Know where Julian went?"

"Might've gone back to fishing," the vendor said, gesturing with his head behind himself, and then pointing across the wide cove in the direction of the southern spit of land curving back out to sea—the southern boundary of Monterey Bay. "Boats still hauling in lots of 'dines when they're running, you know. Been running pretty regular lately … Or he might be working at one of the drying and packing sheds. Pretty good pay over there, too. Haven't seen him lately around the trade-off though." The man shrugged and turned away to help a customer, who was looking at the Crimson Man askance.

He thanked the vendor for answering his questions and stepped away.

With no reason to linger at the trade-off, the Crimson Man followed the shoreline around the cove to the fishing village—about a half an hour's walk. The village was obviously expanding, a number of new stone huts, sheds, well-maintained tents recently erected, and even a few wood-framed structures in various stages of completion, all springing up in the old town's cleared ruins.

He wandered about, searching for a building that looked like it might be a school, without any luck. Getting pretty late to start banging on doors and looking for the DeYoungs, he thought, rubbing his scar. His damaged ear was okay now, not hurting badly, but scabby and sensitive to the touch. He figured most folks here would probably not be quite so calm after checking out his hard-edged DP appearance, nothing like the laid-back wine seller, who had definitely been into his own stock. So, the Crimson Man decided to camp on the beach, clean himself up, dress the ear with some salve, get a good night's rest, and look for the teachers early tomorrow. Maybe even check on Julian, the bookseller-fisherman.

Just before sunrise, he ambled along the main street of the new village, candles and lanterns already lighting most of the huts, shanties, sheds, and tents. He knew almost everyone in this fishing village would be up early, some of the men probably already out on the boats searching for the sardine schools. But no one answered his knock or shouted greeting, even though he spotted pairs of eyes peeking back out at him from inside tent flaps and hut windows—

"Hello," said an unexpected voice from close behind him.

He turned about cautiously.

"Hey, mister, how come you aren't wearing a long coat?"

It was a young boy—maybe nine or ten—apparently the only person in the whole village not frightened by the Crimson Man's dyed, rugged appearance, although the lad was maintaining a wary six or eight feet of separation.

The Crimson Man smiled at the brave boy. "It's prohibited by the Company. DPs have to keep exposed as much of their color as possible—no long coats. I think the dye actually protects my skin against the dangerous environmental stuff, like UV poisoning. So it's a relief during hot, muggy weather, like most of the time, not to be heavily bundled up. You know what I mean?"

The boy, bundled and wearing an old batting helmet two sizes too big, was barefaced. He nodded, his expression bright and alert.

"And that red color of your skin means you … ah, killed somebody?" The pause was brief, the boy not embarrassed by the intrusive question "Probably not the guy who ripped off your ear. It's too scabby-looking and *fresh*. Right?" He pointed at the Crimson Man's long facial scar and raised his eyebrows questioningly.

The Crimson Man almost laughed. Truly gritty, perceptive kid, for sure. But he avoided a long explanation and nodded, confirming the boy's supposition. Before the inquisitive youngster continued his interrogation though, the Crimson Man asked, "You go to school?"

The kid nodded. "I did, but the school is closed down now…" He paused a moment and kind of puffed up a little. "But I know how to read. Best in my class. Mrs. D even give me a prize. An old book about a Lorax by that famous doctor guy."

"Dr. Seuss."

The boy smiled and nodded. "Hey, that's right, mister."

"What's your name?"

"Timmy."

"Well, Timmy, how come the school is closed?"

"Companymen came about three months ago, sealed it all up, and took Mr. And Mrs. D away."

"Picked them up, eh? Do you have any idea where they took them?"

He had a grim and painful memory of the sen-dep tanks at San

Fran Shield. He visualized an image of the two teachers wandering around now as DPs, wearing ... oh, maybe one of the yellow colors for political criminals.

The boy shrugged, then added with a smile, "But they're back home now. Been here over two months."

"Both of the DeYoungs?"

Timmy nodded. "They still can't teach us anymore though. Said the Company pro-hib-its that now ... just like you not being able to wear a duster, you see."

The Crimson Man nodded.

After a few moments he asked, "Where are the school and the DeYoungs's house located, Timmy?"

"Same place, mister," the boy said, hopping from one foot to the other and inching a little closer. "You want me to show you?"

"Yes, I'd appreciate that."

The boy led the Crimson Man on a worn footpath going south, and as they walked the DP learned that Mr. DeYoung was a fisherman now, and his wife worked in a packing shed. Timmy made it clear there would be no more teaching school by either of the DeYoungs here at the Monterey Fishing Village. He said that when Mr. DeYoung got back he looked like he'd had a tooth pulled or been drinking too much wine. Hurt, sad, darkened eyes. Changed. Not really much fun anymore.

Both had been worked over, the Crimson Man thought, probably in the sen-dep tanks. But at least they hadn't been dyed and cast out to wander.

The school was an old barn about a quarter mile out of town, the DeYoungs living nearby in a neat little wooden shed with a tin roof, what appeared to be newer than the original farmhouse.

One of the two doors of the barn hung open from a broken hinge. The Crimson Man poked his head inside and looked around.

It was a big mess, stuff scattered about, no real indication that it'd ever been a school ... until he spotted a pair of overturned chalkboards and several old-time school desks pushed into the far corner and partially covered by a tarp.

"Companymen didn't make all this mess," Timmy explained with a frown. "Thieves busted in the door after sneaking in at night after the school was closed, and stole a lot of stuff; then they tore up and left behind what they didn't want to carry off." He smiled slyly. "But an old man with a patch over his eye had come for a few books the Company missed, just before the thieves busted in."

Was it the guy the wine seller had mentioned?

He looked down at Timmy and asked, "No books left in the school now though?"

The boy shook his head, obviously saddened by the thought.

"You like to read?"

"Yes I do, mister. Read my Lorax book almost every night. Some of the pages loose now."

As the boy led him to the shed, the Crimson Man dug out a five credit note of Shield scrip. "Go over to the trade-off and check if there are any good books available for you over there—"

"Hey, thanks, mister," Timmy said, snagging the five credits.

"When does Mr. DeYoung get off from fishing?"

"Depends on if they find a 'dine school or not this morning," the boy said frowning. "If they are running, he won't be back until late this afternoon. My pops will be even later, because he always stops to see Mad Walter."

"Who's Mad Walter?"

"He sells wine over at the trade-off."

"I see," the Crimson Man said. "Well, Timmy, I appreciate your help. You know that Dr. Seuss wrote a lot of other books? I read most of them when I was a boy like you. If you can't find one around here, maybe someday at the San Jo Trade-off or up at San Fran. Have you ever been to either of those places?"

"Nah, we don't go any place, mister. Since Mom died, Dad just fishes, drinks wine, and sleeps mostly." He shook his head and smiled thinly. "Wasn't too bad around here when the Ds had the school going."

A huge yellow and black butterfly flitting near the side of the shed diverted the boy's attention. "Hey, look!"

The Crimson Man was sympathetic. If given any kind of opportunity, this bright, curious kid might someday be more than a drunk like his pop, possibly even make some kind of social contribution. But the immediate future didn't look too promising for young Timmy. Yet then again maybe someone would establish another school here or nearby someday in the near future—soon enough to do the boy some good.

"Well, I have to go do my chores," Timmy said, stepping close and offering to shake the Crimson Man's hand. "My dad will get after me if I don't wash up the dishes, feed the chickens and collect eggs, milk our cow, pull some weeds in our little garden, and pick a few vegetables for dinner this afternoon before he gets back…"

His voice trailed off kind of sadly, obviously reluctant to leave. The Crimson Man knew seeing a real live DP had brightened the inquisitive boy's day, no matter how briefly. He hoped the lad found some other books to read. The Lorax might soon fall completely apart.

"I'm going to hang around here, see Mr. DeYoung when he gets in. Bye, Timmy."

The lad waved, and then dashed off.

☞ – ☜

In mid-afternoon, a thin Freemen made his way toward the little shed home. The man slowed as the Crimson Man's features and skin color registered. He stopped between his shed and the DP, his eyes narrowed suspiciously, pulling a bandana down from his face.

"Mr. DeYoung?" the Crimson Man said, rising to his feet and keeping both empty hands in view. "I mean no harm. Timmy showed me where you live. I'd like to ask you some questions."

DeYoung remained where he stood, looking the DP over thoroughly. In a tentative voice he asked, "Questions about what?"

The Crimson Man stayed in place, not moving any closer. "About the school—"

"There is no school anymore," the ex-school teacher snapped.

"I know all about that. The Companymen. And the thieves. But I'm interested in the man who helped you start the school originally, secure all the books and supplies ..." He let his steady voice taper off as he slowly reached down into his backpack and withdrew the second journal. "Your old Cal professor, the man who wrote this journal—"

"Where'd you find that?" DeYoung said in a challenging voice.

"I didn't steal it," the Crimson Man said. "I bought it from a book dealer at the San Jo Trade-off a few days ago. He got it from a book dealer at your trade-off. A man named ... Julian? After I read it, I knew I had to come down and visit you."

"Why do you care about the man who wrote that journal?"

"I think he's my father—"

"You a DP, a ...?" The thin Freemen let his question trail off.

"I wasn't always a dyed person. I last saw my father over thirty years ago at a med-camp in the North Bay at a place called Blue Rock Springs near the Vallejo Ruins."

DeYoung still looked incredulous. He shook his head. "The man who wrote the journal didn't have a son."

"Well that's just *not* true. He once had a son, and a wife named Lauren. We lived in Berkeley on College Avenue before the Collapse. He was an English professor, teaching at the University." The Crimson Man stared at the ex-teacher, who now looked slightly taken aback by what had been said. "In fact, I think you were one of his graduate students before he took a sabbatical to write a book, and then the Collapse drastically changed all that."

DeYoung nodded absently, probably off in the past ... "Okay, he did have a son. What's your name?"

The Crimson Man shrugged. "The Company has erased my name. I'm prohibited from using or even thinking it. In fact, I can't hear it even if it's spoken aloud to me."

"I see," DeYoung said, and from his expression it was clear he still didn't believe the Crimson Man. "I don't know, you could've maybe dug up all that information from the journal or something else you might've read or someone you talked to."

The Crimson Man smiled and dug out the first journal from his backpack. "I probably could from one of these two journals. But why would I do that and take the trouble to look you up?"

The Freemen shook his head, looking puzzled.

The Crimson Man pulled out four of the paperbacks from his backpack and carefully unwrapped them. "I carry copies of some of my father's favorite books. You must remember how much he admired Nelson Algren." He held up *The Man with the Golden Arm*. "*Flowers for Algernon* and *The Razor's Edge* ..." He held up both books, moving a few steps closer. Finally he tapped *The Catcher in the Rye*. "The first thing he always asked his students when his classes had finished reading J.D. Salinger's famous novel was 'This is told in first person. Who is Holden Caulfield telling this story to?'"

DeYoung's expression relaxed and he almost smiled. "That's right! And those were indeed four of his top favorites. He lectured often from the ARM and Algren's other great book..." He paused and stared at the Crimson Man, gesturing c'mon with his hand.

"*Walk on the Wild Side*."

"What was your father's major academic interest?"

"Literary SF, but he obviously liked good mainstream work. Even well-written mysteries—like the turn of the century writer, James Lee Burke, or the Swede, Stieg Larsson."

"And that book he was working on?"

"*Humanism in SF*."

The ex-school teacher wasn't frowning anymore, obviously swayed by the accurate details. "Well, I do remember Dr. Zachary's son back in Berkeley, but you don't look anything like him—"

DeYoung broke off that thought and asked, "You had an unusual sport for a hobby back then. Something you'd learned at camp?"

"Archery."

DeYoung rubbed his mouth. "I'm just not completely sure. That bright boy, a…DP now? Hard to believe."

"I know something else from back then that may be even more compelling. A special electronic chapbook father wrote that was only circulated to a few of his friends, but all his grad students. Well received."

The tall man shrugged, apparently not recalling any special chapbook—

"To Touch a Soul."

"Oh, my God! You are [DeYoung's lips moved but the Crimson Man didn't hear his name], Zach and Lauren's boy. I'm so sorry about your mother." The thin Freemen was red-faced now, struggling to contain his excitement.

The Crimson Man shook his head. "Thanks. We lost her a long time ago at that med camp, you know."

DeYoung opened his shed door. "C'mon in. Linda didn't know your dad at Berkeley. She was a graduate TA at St. Mary's. We met after the Collapse…She was so impressed with what he'd been teaching and lecturing all around the Big Dry…and what he tried to do here. A truly inspiring, almost saintly man."

"You sure it's okay to come in?" the Crimson Man said tentatively, stopping in the doorway. "My gruesome appearance might give Linda a heart attack when she gets home."

DeYoung smiled broadly for the first time. "It's alright. I'll step out and prepare her for the shock. You're staying for dinner."

They ate a wonderful fish stew with homemade bread, the Crimson Man enjoying every bite. He listened to the DeYoungs talk about his father, how much they enjoyed working with him, setting up

the school here, but when either of them mentioned anything specific about the school, their speech would painfully trail off for a
moment, their voices choking-up.

After dinner, DeYoung went outside to smoke his pipe, inviting
the Crimson Man to join him.

"I know, it's a bad habit, very expensive now," he said, lighting
the pipe and puffing with obvious enjoyment.

"Neither you or Linda have mentioned when you saw my dad
last?"

DeYoung sighed and shook his head. "I'm sorry to say that the
Company may have him...or he may not even be alive."

"What do you mean?"

"Well, your father had left us that journal you have to help
teach current history, before he went off to work on another secret
project about two years ago. One night, maybe five months ago, he
came by and retrieved the journal from me and tore out the last
few pages. He'd heard rumors that the Company might shut down
the school at the San Barboo Ruins and was looking for him. He'd
apparently been anticipating that. Anyhow, he felt the last journal
pages would give them too many good clues about where to track
him. What he was working on. All that. He'd encouraged us to flee
if we heard that the school down south was actually closed by the
Company. But we heard nothing until several Companymen
showed up at our door here..." He paused and coughed, obviously
deeply affected by the memory.

They sat in silence for a few moments.

Then the Crimson Man asked, "You don't know where exactly
my father was headed, remember what those last ten or so pages
were about?"

"I'm sorry, we hadn't even used the journal by that time. Too
busy establishing the basic curriculum. The journal was stored in

the bottom drawer of my desk along with several other texts, everything buried under a pile of student writing papers. Neither of us had read it. Well, I'm not actually sorry we didn't read those last pages. When the Company suddenly picked up Linda and me, after closing the school here, they took us to San Fran Shield. Interrogated both of us in the sensory deprivation tanks. Lots of probing questions about your dad, what he was doing, where he was, and so forth. Over and over. Of course we had to tell them the little we knew. But neither of us were aware of his specific plans."

"Or where he is now?"

"No…" DeYoung paused, thinking.

"You know he has a colleague who we think came and rescued a few of the supplies and some books from our school. A Freemen—an older man. Timmy saw him at the vacant school just after the Company closed us down. Before the thieves vandalized the place. I'm hoping he was picking up those books for your dad. But I'm just not sure. Sorry."

"He's not an old science teacher my dad called H?"

DeYoung shrugged. "We didn't know his name or anything about him—probably another good thing. Nothing to really tell the Company." The ex-teacher puffed absently on his pipe, then added, "A couple weeks ago, Timmy spotted this same elderly Freemen at the trade-off, reading a story to a group of kids. An old, slump-shouldered guy with an eyepatch. Non-threatening. The Company's spies probably didn't pay any close attention to him."

"Spies?"

"Oh, yeah, they're all over this area now, you know," DeYoung said, with a wide-eyed, almost furtive expression of fear. "You don't know who to trust. Someone's spotted you by now, I'm sure, and will be relaying that information on…if they haven't already."

The Crimson Man nodded, staring off into the darkness. The Company already knew his approximate location anyhow—he'd palmed a sensor at a cache site off 101 before heading this way. Everyone in the village knew he was here for sure, but Company spies? DeYoung sounded paranoid … But maybe it was justified in his case.

Linda came out with three mugs of tea. "I had a little sugar saved for this special occasion," she said, smiling. She was an attractive woman in her late fifties, but her face was slightly gaunt and heavily lined, as if she suffered from a lingering painful memory. Probably the sen-dep tanks.

They sat and shared the wonderful sweetened tea together, but no one said much of anything more about the school, or teaching, or The Wiz, or the Crimson Man's father. The ex-teachers reminisced quietly of their life in pre-Collapse days, when they were grad students at Cal and St. Mary's.

The Crimson Man thanked them for the dinner, tea, and their help, and he left the DeYoungs in their little shed near the ex-school. He knew now that he needed to find the stooped, old science teacher with the patch over his right eye, who the Freemen—and his father—called H, and who the older kids called The Wiz.

10

THE WIZ

Mad Walter was about the only one at the trade-off near the desalinization plant ruins who would have much to do with the Crimson Man as he hung about the trade-off the next day. The spirit vendor may've been prone to sampling his own merchandize, but he was a much more crafty observer than one might have thought at first. And sharp. From their brief conversations, he'd managed to pull together that the Crimson Man was keenly interested in the shutdown school, the two ex-school teachers, and the old Freemen who'd established the school; Mad Walt guessed this was all somehow related to the DP's current interest in The Wiz.

The Crimson Man didn't elaborate any further on the wine vendor's perceptive speculations and questions. He tried to direct their conversations to more neutral matters: Mad Walter's trade-off business and the rapidly growing economy of the fishing village. The spirit stand was the community's locus for gossip, and the vendor was an enthusiastic participant in everyone's business.

The next morning, the Crimson Man wandered up from the beach into the trade-off, which wasn't busy yet, and stopped at Mad Walter's table. The wine-seller acknowledged his greeting, then winked conspiratorially and gestured with his head toward a Freemen standing at a nearby blanket display of six old paperback books, each little more than a collection of brittle brown pages held together with a pair of thin rawhide bands.

The book vendor was tall, stooped, wore a patch over an eye, and his weathered, experienced face was furrowed with deep lines.

It was H of course.

The Crimson Man took the new journal from his backpack and kneeled at the foot of the blanket display, as if perusing the meager offerings. He glanced up at the old man, who looked back down, his expression guarded. He pointed at the initials in the corner of the journal: **JAZ**.

"Have you ever seen a journal like this? And if so, may I ask you a question about this man?"

"JAZ? Don't think I know him," the Freemen said, his tone neutral and expression even more guarded. "Never seen a journal like that either."

The Crimson Man nodded, standing up and gazing sternly into the older man's face. "Oh, I think you do know him. You were good friends with him before and after the Collapse."

The ex-science teacher stared back silently with his good eye, apparently not really frightened or noticeably intimidated by the size, color, or rugged looks of the Crimson Man.

"I'm his son. You're H, his old friend."

The older man blinked, his good eye widening ever so slightly.

Then the Crimson Man basically repeated the step-by-step proof he'd laid out to Ron DeYoung to convince the ex-schoolteacher he was indeed Jacob Zachary's son. Either the Crimson Man was more convincing now, or the science teacher was apparently more open-minded, perceptive, or whatever. H smiled broadly when the Crimson Man was only partially into his argument, after he unwrapped and displayed a few of the books he carried in his backpack. "You remember these favorites—?"

H held up his hand, interrupting the argument.

"I'm convinced, I'm convinced. I once knew you. We'd actually met …" He shook his head as if to clear the fuzzy memory. "…when you were probably a sophomore in high school. My wife and I ate dinner at your folks' house. I was teaching at a posh private high school up in the Oakland Hills. Demonstrating science principles and experiments on a weekly local TV program. Your dad wanted me to encourage you to bear down on your science and math interests—figured I had the cachet of a celebrity. He believed you had real ability but were perhaps a little distracted, drawn more to other subjects that required less day-to-day structural work of math and science. Humanities, literature, and such. Do you remember that evening…?"

He remembered that dinner, but this man looked nothing like the KQED-TV super-star science teacher he remembered his dad inviting to their home. For one thing, back then he was not wearing a patch over a bad eye, and he was without most of the deep forehead wrinkles. The Crimson Man realized he didn't resemble that skinny, bright-eyed kid from long ago in any way either, except perhaps for his voice or speech pattern, which he knew were both pretty well formed by late adolescence, after a boy finally lost his higher-pitched bird squeak. That may have been what H first recognized about him—his voice.

"Well, [again the Crimson Man's conditioned hearing blanked out on his own name], why are you looking for me now?"

"I want to know about my father. When you saw him last, if he's alive…If so, where is he? Anything else you may be able to tell me about him."

The stooped, older man frowned, unable to keep a suspicious look of deep concern from flashing across his worn features.

"Well, I'm not sure where he is exactly," H said in an obviously guarded manner, looking away. "I'm not even sure he's still alive."

He glanced back indirectly at the Crimson Man and shrugged. His guarded tone, expression, and lack of eye contact made it perfectly clear that H wasn't completely forthcoming.

"I haven't seen my father in over thirty years," the Crimson Man explained. "If he is still alive, I'd like to talk with him. Perhaps make amends for how we separated. I'm not a Company spy or anything like that ... How could I be?" He pointed at his bared arm, the dyed crimson color. "Why would I volunteer to be an outcast with this permanent stain?"

H shrugged again, but remained silent.

"The DeYoungs didn't know much either, but they thought he might be working on a new project of some kind maybe down south somewhere in the Big Dry. Thought you might know something about it."

For almost a full half a minute it was awkwardly silent.

H finally nodded and admitted, "Yes, I think that after he helped out at the school in the village setting up the DeYoungs, he headed somewhere off in the remote Big Dry ... Of course you realize the Company is actively searching for him."

"Yes, the DeYoungs mentioned that."

H rubbed his chin and reflected for a few long moments, repeatedly glancing intently with his good eye at the Crimson Man, obviously debating with himself.

"Okay, I understand your personal need to see him ... I'm not sure about the complete accuracy of any of this information. But, there is a very small trade-off out in a distant part of the southeastern Big Dry. An old highway, I-15, comes up from San D, leading northeasterly out to there. The trade-off is just off that old freeway, several miles north of the ruins of a place once called Barstow, in pre-Collapse times. Mostly horses and other livestock, things like that traded out there. I think there may be a Freemen, who was a fairly decent pre-Collapse playwright your dad and I once knew at Berkeley, who occasionally drops in on that trade-off on weekends, looking for old books. Nowadays, he goes by the name Shakespeare. If your dad is alive, and working on a project anywhere down there near that area, I'm guessing this guy Shakespeare will know about it, perhaps even the exact location. But…"

As his voice tapered off, the old man reached out and gripped the Crimson Man's arm with surprising strength. "You mustn't lead the Company down there."

"I won't."

"Not even unintentionally, you understand," H said, his expression reinforcing the concern in his voice. "You won't be able to use whatever cache sites are out there that could leave a palm print trail for the Company, indicating your movements and recent approximate locations, you know."

"I understand that. I won't lead them anywhere near that trade-off. I won't use any cache sites after I leave the Black Desert for I-15. You can be assured of that. Thanks, H, I appreciate your help."

The old Freemen stared at the Crimson Man, and then smiled. "It's a long, dangerous trip on foot, so take care of yourself."

H shook his head.

"Back pre-Collapse, you know your pop always thought that besides being really good at science and math you were also developing into a very talented fiction writer. I suspect he was hoping you'd someday be a first rate science fiction novelist, surpassing his handful of published SF short stories and novellas. I guess the Collapse put an end to all that." He chuckled dryly and added in a sardonic tone, "Now we're all living in one of your dad's science fiction scenarios."

The ex-science teacher pulled out a scrap of clean paper and scribbled a brief note on it with a pen. "Give this to Shakespeare if you find him. It'll introduce you from me. He'll probably listen to you then. Help if he can."

The Crimson Man glanced at the note with the big *H* signature scrawled at the bottom, looked back up, nodded his gratitude, and then carefully stored it in his backpack.

They shook hands.

As an afterthought, H added, "Oh, when you ask about your dad out there in the Big Dry, they might not actually recognize his real name. Probably have better luck if you ask about The 'Teller."

"'Teller?"

"Yeah, short for The Storyteller, you know."

"Got it. Anything you want me to convey to my father, if I do catch up to him?"

"No, we've pretty much said everything to each other that's necessary for now," H said, kind of cryptically.

"Then, I'll be on my way. Hopefully I'll be able to hitch a lift on a windskimmer or a wagon after I reach the Black Desert ... if I come across someone I don't scare the life out of. If not it will be a long trek—figure at least two months before I see that trade-off near I-15."

"Good luck, son."

A half hour later, The Crimson Man headed back east toward old 101 on the other side of the coastal hills, his spirit uplifted, even though H had remained evasive with details about his father and did not appear overly optimistic about a successful search. He thought the old science teacher probably knew more about his dad and his exact location than he was willing to share with a DP, someone who depended on his everyday existence to the Company. And of course the Crimson Man understood that. He was hoping what H shared was accurate and would eventually lead him to his father. If not, he was off on a lengthy wild-goose chase.

11

MESHACH, SHADRACH, AND GRAMS

Two days later, the Crimson Man detoured wide around a huge pile of deteriorating concrete structures, the fallen and fractured remnants of a stack of merging freeways a few miles south of the greater San Jo Ruins.

He stopped and sucked in a deep breath, surveying the amazing sight sprawling out before him.

Stretching for as far as his eyes could see was a massive landing strip—an accommodation for giant alien spaceships, or so it appeared. Miles and miles of asphalt in three directions, heat waves shimmering off the blacktop in the near distance. Heat radiated from where he stood.

The Black Desert was a merger of all the north-south roads, state highways, and interstate freeways into one gigantic super freeway, the black corridor of multi-lanes finished about five years before the Collapse, much of it here in the north covering some of the finest farm/orchard land in the entire world.

Stretches of grayish dashes and a few Bot's dots, remnants of the white stripes and reflectors once separating the merging multi-lanes, remained like some kind of blurred Morse code, directing incoming spacecraft down onto the humongous landing strip. The Black Desert was in a sad state of repair: unfilled potholes, large craters, stretches along the far west shoulder completely washed out in places, and here and there wheel-less big rigs or other heavy equipment too large to be easily removed. Abandoned rusting artifacts cluttered entire lanes. To the south, the Crimson Man could barely make out the edge of the LA Curtain, shrouding the superhighway in a veil of heavy gray smog. The Curtain, originally created by the 24/7 exhaust pollution from thousands of thousands of internal combustion engines, was now maintained from a variety of lingering sources, including the continued smoking post-Collapse ruins of LA and other southern cities, burning garbage dumps, and stacks of rotted tires smoldering at many of the old rest stops—the current graveyards for stripped autos and pickups, some even flattened long ago and stacked high, as if tottering monuments to an unsustainable and irrational oil-dependent lifestyle.

The Crimson Man shook his head. It was unbelievable what they'd subjected themselves to before the Collapse. By the third decade of the 21st Century *one man, one car* was still the rule, not the exception, despite mass transit opportunities in the Bay Area and the Bullet Train option to LA.

During his Company programming and in the last year of his wandering about the Bay Area, he'd heard numerous warnings about the horrors of the Black Desert. An extremely hazardous place for DPs to wander, with only a few widely separated deep wells drilled along the median at some of the old rest stops—each well a green oasis of mostly willows breaking up the brown pattern off sun burnt weeds and field grass, even the once hearty oleanders long dead now. The DP cache sites along the super highway were almost as rare as the well sites, often spaced away from the highway and more than the standard four walking days apart—seven, sometimes eight or more days—the most distant, infrequently visited sites in the isolated southeast serviced irregularly by Company hummers from San Barboo and San D Shields. Not to mention the nomadic fierce bandits who often preyed on travelers. A DP took his life in his hands on the Black Desert.

Fortunately, the Crimson Man had stocked up, saving some of his easily packed foodpaks, eating mostly other things during his time since acquiring the second journal. The last day at the Monterey Trade-off, he'd stuffed his backpack with lightweight jerky, dried fruit, goat cheese, and nuts; and he'd filled two extra canteens, so he now carried four at his sides.

He'd ration himself, but he didn't plan on starving or going thirsty on the long two-month trek south.

The Crimson Man was fortunate that first half a day of travel—or so he thought—as he ambled along the cooler far shoulder of the southern bound lanes of the Black Desert.

A two-horse wagon stopped. At first he thought the bundled-up Freemen driving the wagon was a stout man, wearing a wide-brimmed, smudged-brown, battered hat, pulled down and partially obscuring his bare, beardless face.

But it was a woman—an older, weathered-faced, heavy-set woman.

"Hello, Red Man, you want to ride with us a spell?" the driver drawled loudly.

The Crimson Man looked up at the old woman, then asked, "You're not afraid being seen hauling around a DP?"

"Nope," the old woman said, and grinned, exposing a missing front upper tooth. "You'd be good insurance for us."

"Insurance?"

"Yep. Make bandits think twice about trying to rob us with a big, ugly, and mean-looking red devil like you aboard." She chuckled. "Course me and my grandsons are packing a little discouragement ourselves just in case." She indicated the revolver holstered at the hip of her long coat.

The two fifteen- or sixteen-year-old youngsters in the back of the wagon cradled rusty old shotguns between their legs.

Both boys were obviously quasimodos with noticeable humps on their shoulders, but their features were not badly twisted like most other defectives of their ilk. They each peered down at the Crimson Man curiously.

"That's Shadrach on the far side there, and Meshach right close to you. Call me, Grams. We're taking a load of hides down to the San Barboo Trade-off. You can ride to the turn-off if you're going down that far."

"I'm going that far."

But the Crimson Man hesitated, looking at the smallish mound of hides covered by a tarp behind where the boys sat.

"So, do you want to ride with us a spell or not?" Grams asked with a hint of growing impatience, patting the wide seat beside her on the wagon.

"Yes, I guess I do."

"Hop on."

The Crimson Man climbed onto the wagon and settled next to the older woman. Despite a sense of lingering unease, he told himself it was indeed his lucky day. The turnoff for San Barboo Trade-off was probably a good three and a half to four days' wagon ride down the Black Desert. A ride that far would reduce his walking time by almost a third—probably save him eighteen to twenty days.

They bounced along in the wagon for the rest of the afternoon.

Although Grams was a little vague on specifics, the Crimson Man learned a bit about the odd threesome. The boys were twins, born fourteen years ago somewhere up north. He thought maybe near the Sacramento Ruins, but wasn't sure. Their mother, Grams' daughter, died in childbirth, and the father died shortly after, afflicted with what she described as, "that shaking disease." She'd apparently raised the two quasimodos by herself. Neither spoke, but both were plenty sharp. She indicated the hides were mostly deer and elk, with a few cowhides they'd taken off of *lost* steers.

Grams and the boys were obviously survivors and handy with their guns, but the Crimson Man never understood why they were hauling the meager pile of hides so far to trade. San Fran or San Jo seemed much closer to way up north. Grams had mentioned they had "a good trading partner" for their hides down at San Barboo.

Around sunset, they stopped at a small rest stop with a ring of green willows drooping down and hovering over an old well.

"Good spot," Grams said, reining in her pair of tan plow horses. She turned and instructed Shadrach and Meshach to water and feed the horses.

After Grams and the Crimson Man dismounted the wagon, the two quasimodos jumped down spryly, unloaded supplies and bedrolls, and then led the horses and wagon toward the other side of the well to a tiny patch of fresh field grass.

"Boys are right helpful," Grams said, "and damn handy with them shotguns, too. You can bet on that."

They ate a savory stew Grams whipped up, the Crimson Man volunteering some of his horde of jerky to fortify the dried, spicy vegetables. Grams also had some thin rock-hard biscuits that were tasty and filling.

Before they turned in, Grams dug out a well-worn, black leather bible from her bedroll.

"Boys got to have a few verses from the Good Book before bed time," she explained, exposing her missing tooth again in her broad grin. She thumbed to an obviously familiar spot.

"Their favorite story: Daniel, Chapter Three," she announced to the Crimson Man, and cleared her throat before beginning to read from the Bible in a clear and melodic baritone voice.

It was the familiar Biblical tale of the Babylonian King Nebuchadnezzar II, who condemned three Jewish boys to be executed in a fiery furnace because they would not bend down before one of his Gods. Of course the three boys were quickly rescued by an Angel sent from their own Jehovah…

"…So Shadrach, Meshach and Abednego came out of the fire, and the satraps, prefects, governors and royal advisers crowded around them. They saw that the fire had not harmed their bodies, nor was a hair of their heads singed; their robes were not scorched, and there was no smell of fire on them."

As the old woman came to the dramatic ending, the two boys nodded and smiled widely when their namesakes emerged unscathed from that fiery furnace. Grams finished and closed the book with a punctuating deep sigh.

"Praise the Lord," she added, still in her low reading voice, as she carefully stored the Bible away. Then she turned toward the Crimson Man and asked, "Do you happen to know what the word *satrap* means?"

He thought a moment, searching his memory, before suggesting, "I think in those times it meant a minor official, but one who is maybe a little too taken with himself."

"Makes sense." She turned to her grandsons and announced, "Bed time for you growing boys."

They obediently climbed bootless into their bedrolls, fully clothed, and were soon snoring.

Grams and the Crimson Man silently watched the fire die down for maybe another fifteen minutes, then they both turned in, too. He was tired, and drifted right off himself.

⁂

The Crimson Man awakened with a start.

He blinked, and found himself staring into the barrel of a rusty shotgun. Meshach was on the other end of the weapon. To his right stood Shadrach, also holding his shotgun on the Crimson Man. Just beyond them, Grams stood fully clothed, hand resting on her holstered side gun. "Don't make us shoot you, Red Man," Grams said, all the kindness drained from her grim expression. "Lean up off that backpack."

He wasn't about to test their marksmanship or whether their rusty, decrepit weapons were loaded or even functional.

The older woman came around behind Shadrach, picked up, opened, and examined the DP's backpack.

"My goodness, you got an awful lot of stuff jammed in here," she announced in a slightly kinder voice, carefully removing items. "Oh my, looky what I found, boys." She held up the Shield scrip and Smoke capsules he'd stuffed at the bottom of the pack. The boys both took a quick peek, shook their heads admiringly at her cleverness, and chuckled to themselves.

"We ain't taking none of your food, water, books, or other necessaries," Grams said in a benevolent voice. "But I guess we do badly need these here credits and Smoke. And we thank you kindly for saving them for us." She smiled down at the Crimson Man, then she turned to one of her grandsons. "Meshach, go get them horses hooked up to the wagon and bring it around here. Shad, you keep your eye on this red man, you hear me."

Both boys understood clearly.

In a few minutes, Meshach led the horses and wagon around.

Grams climbed up and took the reins. "Get in back, boys ... Red Man, you just stay put right there and relax. You follow us, one of my boys is going to have to fill you full of buckshot. You understand me?"

The Crimson Man nodded.

He watched as the driver deftly turned the wagon toward the northern lanes of the Black Desert. Apparently they weren't going down to trade hides at San Barboo after all. Probably weren't hide dealers—maybe there were no hides under that tarp. He should have felt elated that the thieves had missed his large stash of Smoke and credits in the pouch he kept tied to his back, but felt deflated that he had been so trusting. Their story didn't sound quite right from the start. Still, he'd gone to sleep and let two quasimodo boys and their old grandmother get the drop on him with perhaps nonfunctioning, unloaded weapons. He was disappointed more in himself than angry at the deceitful thieves. Should be thankful he was still in one piece.

He again faced the long, dirty, hot walk down the Black Desert to LA. Didn't think he'd be accepting any more rides even if offered, which was unlikely anyhow. He'd have to be more alert for

Desperadoes...or wolves in hide trader's clothing.

The Crimson Man sucked in a deep breath, pulled his blanket over himself, and went back to sleep

12

THE BLACK DESERT

The next five weeks of ambling along steadily in the muggy heat under the Curtain were monotonously dull, the days blending together into a shimmering blur of glaring sameness. The Crimson Man occasionally saw a 'skimmer or wagon in the far lanes of the Black Desert, and a few of the conveyances or men on horseback passed him in the southern lanes. *No* one stopped, bothered him, or offered a ride. He found wells and cache sites frequently enough to replenish his canteens and shrinking food supplies. Safe, boring, and sweaty. He broke the loneliness at night re-reading the paperback books he carried.

He'd finished *The Razor's Edge* and *The Catcher in the Rye* back-to-back. As he carefully wrapped Salinger's book in plastic and slipped it back into his pack, he wondered if his father, sometime pre-Collapse, had ever assigned the two books to be read together and compared and contrasted the protagonists. Larry Darrell from Maugham's novel and Holden Caulfield from Salinger's were both misfits, kind of anti-heroes turning away from conventional society. Darrell had forsaken wealth, a good marriage, and established family ties for a lifelong spiritual quest—his goal not ever easily defined.

Holden, perhaps less mature, may have taken that path himself after the end of *Catcher*. He'd debated with his sister, old Phoebe, about doing that very thing. There were some definite similarities in the two books, but there were significant major differences in the main characters, too. Darrell was mature, confident, and more directed in his search for an inner sense of salvation; presumably he found it, and the book ends with him driving a cab in NYC. Holden was much younger, obviously disturbed, not really self-confident yet, and cynical about society—at least overtly. But the characters were at different stages in their development in their explorations of their beliefs. Maybe Holden would also someday come to terms with himself, find a measure of inner peace, and perhaps end up contentedly driving a taxi in NYC. Maybe tell his curious fares where the Central Park ducks went when the lagoon froze over in the winter. The Crimson Man chuckled at the last fanciful thought and tucked himself into his bedroll. Before he drifted off, he wondered if either writer had read the other's book. He thought *The Razor's Edge* came out a number of years before *The Catcher in the Rye*, but the two writers' careers had overlapped in the 20th Century.

After hiking six days from San Barboo Cache Site #20 to #21, the Crimson Man spent an extra full hour veering westward off the super-highway and carefully circling widely down and around, finally coming back across all the multiple lanes and approaching from the south to the targeted green spot near the rest stop on the median strip. Drooping willows, a towering black oak, and a small stand of eucalyptus trees screened the likely watering hole from the nearby rest stop graveyard of collected derelicts—hundreds of rusting cars, SUVs, RVs, and pickups. A hot, dry wind from the southwest had come up as dusk descended. The Crimson Man crept through the large rest stop, muffling his approach to the cache site hummerpad located just east of the trees and well.

A horse snorted, drawing his attention to the pair of riders on their mounts, hidden back in the stand of gum trees. His careful indirect approach had paid off. He crouched on the westerly side of the grove, making sure he hadn't been spotted. The two bundled-up, masked Desperadoes were fortunately facing away from him, gazing at the southerly lanes. Occasionally one or the other looked over his shoulder to inspect the more distant northerly lanes. Neither glanced in his direction.

Won't be using that cache any time soon, the Crimson Man thought. He slowly eased back from the trees, well, and cache site, and continued down the median for a mile or so before he figured it safe to cross the open Black Desert.

He continued walking until long after midnight, putting a few extra miles between himself and the two bandits.

The next morning he was up early and again headed south, hurrying along, hoping to make up some time, and reach the next cache location #22 in a shorter period of time than the distance between the last two sites, #20 and #21—six days.

Sixty or seventy miles south of the outskirts of fabled LA, he lost a full day searching for the exit signs to old I-15. He finally found the downed and shot-up, faded remnants of a green Freeway sign announcing the east I-15 turn-off. The underpass to the easterly freeway was completely collapsed, possibly by an earthquake.

Glancing back after he finally stood on the graying blacktop of I-15, he was forced to admit to himself that the two horsemen were following him. He'd first noticed them behind him about a week ago, barely in view. It had to be the same trailing pair, because one rode a distinctive dapple-gray. During their seven or eight days of tracking him to the I-15 turnoff, they *never* once drew any closer than a mile or so. There wasn't much he could do about it. He ignored the trailing riders and soldiered on.

After sixty-five ten- to twelve-hour days of long, sweaty, and mostly uneventful walks, the Crimson Man arrived at the desert trade-off beside I-15. He hadn't seen the two riders tracking him for the last two days. Maybe he'd been wrong. He hoped so.

13

SHAKESPEARE

The trade-off near the I-15 rest stop a few miles north of the Barstow Ruins was an isolated, dusty, dry place, and almost vacant of vendors, unlike the bigger trade-offs the Crimson Man had seen up North. And this was at dusk on a Friday night.

There couldn't be over forty people total, which included two small family groups eating barbeque meat and beans picnic-style on blankets on the ground near the one open food stand.

A Freemen was bargaining at a spirit vendor's small stand. A few other people were engaged in some kind gambling at a table under the lonely oak—swearing loudly whenever their cards turned out bad. The rest were milling around several small corrals, looking over the stock—a few steers, several head of sheep, but mostly horses. There would be an auction tomorrow at noon, with more folks appearing in the morning.

Most of the buyers and the few sellers were Freemen, but the Crimson Man was surprised to see there were also *two* other DPs wandering around the trade-off: an amber man, and one dyed a shade of light blue. Even more surprising was that the Freemen seemed to pay little attention to the DPs, and there was certainly no noticeable hostility toward them.

After watching curiously for several minutes, the Crimson Man wandered to the wine stand.

He waited until there were no customers and said, "Hello."

The spirit vendor glanced his way and nodded, his bared features unguarded and pleasant.

"I'm looking for a Freemen who visits this trade-off on weekends."

Still the vendor didn't say anything, only nodded, but continued to look at the Crimson Man in a friendly manner.

"He calls himself Shakespeare. Do you know if he's here?"

The wine-seller glanced around the trade-off and shrugged. "Nope. I don't see him."

"Would you know if he'll be in tomorrow?"

The vendor shrugged again and said, "Sorry, I don't know."

The Crimson Man stood there for another few moments, then asked, "If I come back tomorrow morning, and he's here, would you mind pointing him out to me? Maybe even tell him I'd like to speak with him if you get a chance?"

"Sure, I can do that."

"Thank you kindly."

The Crimson Man turned away from the wine stand, looking about, his gaze finally resting on the food stand. The smell of roasting meat made his nostrils flare, his mouth water. Digging in his backpack, he decided to squander some of his hoarded scrip for a plate of barbequed meat and beans, *if* they would accept SF Shield credits so far down here. He didn't want to trade a cap of Smoke— too high a price for dinner.

They eagerly accepted his scrip.

⌁ – ⌁

The trade-off was much busier late the next morning, more Freemen kicking up a constant cloud of dust, but mostly around the stock pens sizing up animals slated for bid at the auction. The animals had numbers freshly painted in whitewash on their sides. A gravelly-voiced auctioneer climbed onto a little wooden stand and began his spiel, warming up the crowd. The first lot up for bid would be four sheep—a ram and three ewes, numbers 1, 2, 3, and 4, all recently sheared.

The Crimson Man turned away from the noise, dust, loud bidding, and moved closer to the wine stall—

A tall, lean Freemen stepped into his path.

"You looking for me, Crimson Man?"

The man wore an unusual neatly trimmed gray goatee—full beards the more commonly worn facial hair in all of Cal Wild. He was dressed in a well-fit mahogany duster and matching wide-brimmed Stetson, his pants tucked neatly into the tops of well-worn but freshly brushed cowboy boots. He stared steadily at the Crimson Man with a neutral expression.

"I guess I am, if you're Shakespeare?"

"That would be me," his tone perfectly matching his lack of facial expression.

The Crimson Man shrugged his backpack around and dug into it, producing the note of introduction from H.

Shakespeare read the note carefully, then looked up and shook his head. "Afraid I don't recognize this signature... Henry or something like that, right?"

"H, period."

Shakespeare shrugged and asked, "And you want from me...?"

"To discuss the whereabouts of a man you probably know as The Teller?"

"I see," the tall man said, scratching his hairy chin. He raised one hand and pointed at the noisy crowd pressed in around the auctioneer clear across the trade-off from where they stood. "Give me a few moments to check around with a few of my colleagues, see if anyone has heard of a person going by that name, okay?"

"Certainly."

Shakespeare strolled casually toward the area of loud, dusty bidding—

And that's when he spotted the dapple-gray tied to a post outside the horse corral. It was one of the horses that had been trailing him for over a week. But he couldn't separate and identify its owner from the group of Freemen clustered around the corral. Shakespeare made his way in that general direction.

Before the tall man reached the dapple-gray, the Crimson Man was grabbed from behind and jerked off his feet and slammed to the ground, knocking the wind out from him.

Regaining his breath and senses, he thought: *Companymen...*

But there was no come-along-stun forthcoming around his head. No, he was being rolled over and his arms were roughly pinned behind his back as his wrists were being bound together, someone else keeping his head forced to the ground so he couldn't look back. Nothing but heavy breathing as one of his attackers expertly bound him.

A hood was pulled over his head, his hands tightly bound.

Then he was jerked back onto his feet, at least two people clutching his arms firmly on either side.

Someone said in a surprisingly gentle voice, "We're going this way, Crimson Man."

After a walk of less than a minute, they stopped, and the same voice explained, "We're putting you in the back of a wagon. Lie down quietly until told to sit back up. It's going to be a long ride."

He was scooted into the bed of the wagon, where he remained down on his back, the blindfold preventing him from seeing his attackers or anything else.

"Geddy-up."

The Crimson Man couldn't tell which direction they headed. The road was bumpy and rough, almost jarring his teeth.

For the next hour, no one said a word as they bounced along.

Finally: "Whoa."

The wagon creaked to a stop.

Hands grabbed his legs and drug him from the wagon bed, his hands still bound awkwardly behind his back, and his head hooded. Then he was brought to his feet.

"Follow along this way," a strange voice said.

Others grabbed his arms under his shoulders and guided him forward. From the sounds of the footsteps, the Crimson Man guessed he was encircled by four or maybe five people total, including the two who gripped his arms so firmly.

They led him along passively for another few minutes until the whole escort party stopped.

A slight grating sound along the ground nearby ... something sliding along a metallic track—a gate, maybe, or perhaps a door.

Leading to where?

14

SANCTUARY

"Move."

They gripped him firmly from each side, compelling him forward again. He walked along as told, soon realizing from the sharp echoing sound of their footsteps and a cooling drop of temperature that they must be in a cave or perhaps a tunnel... Probably the latter as he could tell the floor was declined at a slight angle, and the loud echoes seemed to rebound from close by on either side. After another minute or so of noisy echoing footsteps, the group halted.

The hands gripping his arms relaxed slightly.

They had arrived at some sort of a destination ... somewhere underground.

The blindfold was removed and his vision returned in a dim flickering light. He glanced at the men still holding his arms on either side: the Amber Man on his left, the Blue Man on his right. The flickering light originated from several smoky torches on either side of a narrow tunnel at the widening mouth of a small, low-ceiling cavern.

In the center of the cave was a long, slightly crescent-shaped stone table, well-lit by lanterns at each end, with seven people seated behind it; at the center, apparently presiding, was none other than Shakespeare, smiling and nodding. He beckoned the Crimson Man to come forward.

Cautiously, he moved a few steps into the cavern, closer to the top of the table arc.

"Welcome to the Family," the man with the gray goatee said. "We are the currently presiding Council." He gestured to those sitting on each side. All appeared to be Freemen in conventional garb, except for a DP woman seated on the far right, dyed a deep shade of green.

Staring at the female DP, the Crimson Man realized he must be in the fabled sanctuary, the place the Lime Woman had talked about so emotionally two months ago before she died tragically. And he'd thought at the time that it was nothing more than a Smoke addict's pipe dream.

"We plan to offer you refuge from the Company, if you indeed come in peace with an open heart and mind," Shakespeare said. "Do you come to us in that condition, Crimson Man?"

He was more than convinced now. The Lime Woman's dream did really exist! This was her destination.

"I do," he said hoarsely after only a brief hesitation, still stunned that the fairy-tale hope of refuge from the Company and the possibility of avoiding wandering Cal Wild for life.

Shakespeare looked left, then right, each member of the Council nodding slightly.

"Good. Release his arms. Unbind his hands."

The DPs on either side released him. One leaned back and freed his hands.

He rubbed his wrists while glancing curiously over the Council. They appeared to be ordinary Freemen, except for the dyed woman; all shared a kind of serene calmness of facial expression, and with open, friendly smiles.

Almost like they had expected him. Was that possible?

"You have some questions, we know," Shakespeare said, as if privy to the Crimson Man's thoughts. He held his hand in the stop gesture. "But I'm sorry, they will just have to wait—to be answered soon enough. First there is another member of the Family who is anxiously waiting to greet you."

He was whisked off by the Amber Man into another larger tunnel that led off to a perpendicular angle to the cavern. A few steps into the dimness, they stopped at a cubicle and knocked at a rough-hewn wooden door.

"C'mon in," said a muffled but familiar voice.

The Amber Man opened the door and bid the Crimson Man enter.

He took one step inside, facing a man's dark-cloaked backside.

The inhabitant of the room turned about slowly. He wore an eye patch—

H!

"Welcome to the Family," he said, stepping forward to warmly greet the Crimson Man. "I know you have a dozen pressing questions," the old science teacher said, shaking his hand. "But, first, an apology for my being so secretive and evasive at the Monterey Trade-off, and then letting you go through the last sixty grueling days of … ah, well, I guess it's an initiation of sorts. We had to be one hundred percent convinced that you were sincere, and just as importantly that you were not leading any Companymen to our location here."

"Then the two horsemen following me the last week or so were your folks?"

H nodded. "That's right, but they've been following you for most of your long journey, staying well back out of your sight. Members of the Family. Part of the group of our members who live outside … He paused for a few seconds, then added, "Tomorrow morning you'll get the grand tour of the whole underground facility after a complete explanation of the Family's Cal Wild network, our general plans both short and long term, our aspirations, and such. Your questions will all be answered then, I'm sure—"

"Where am I right now?" the Crimson Man interrupted.

"Well, we are located over eight miles due east of the desert trade-off where you were first blindfolded, our location deep in the most desolate, dry part of the Mojave Desert, in a hidden refuge underground, far from any kind of Company scrutiny, even if a hummer happened to stray this far southeast searching with its infrareds. An asylum of sorts for all kinds of people … Rest assured, you are completely safe here."

A few moments of silence followed as the Crimson Man digested the information.

H waited patiently, peering at him with his good eye. Then his voice rose in pitch when he announced, "I have someone else for you to meet now, just a step over to next door." H gestured out the entry, and led the way out. "Our founder and leader's been impatiently anticipating your arrival for a week or more."

15

THE LIME GREEN WOMAN'S HOLY MAN

They walked down the tunnel toward another door, the Crimson Man noticing now that the hallway was dimly illuminated by a kind of luminescent lichen or moss that grew on the moist walls and even the ceiling of the tunnel. Many more cubicle doors ahead disappeared into the dimness.

H knocked.

"Come in," a barely-audible voice answered.

They stepped into the room, well lit by a pair of hanging lanterns—

The Crimson Man stared incredulously at the gaunt, slump-shouldered, almost bald elderly man sitting in a chair by a small table stacked high with books, next to a single bed. Even though the old man's features appeared heavily wrinkled and distorted, perhaps even partially paralyzed on one side, the Crimson Man immediately recognized the child-like, faded-denim eyes, which he hadn't seen for over thirty years.

The Holy Man was his father, Jacob Zachary.

"May I introduce The 'Teller, our esteemed founder," H said in a tone of almost reverence.

The ex-science teacher then backed a step toward the door. "I'll leave you two to get reacquainted." Before leaving, he leaned close and added in a whisper, "Four months ago he had a serious stroke, leaving his right side and face partially frozen, but he's regained most of his speech, although he sometimes talks haltingly, quietly, and a little hoarsely, especially when he's excited or overly tired. He's been so excited to see you that he didn't take his afternoon nap today. Therefore, I'm afraid that he must turn in fairly early tonight. I'll be back in an hour."

The Crimson Man nodded.

"Thank you, H," the older man said ever so softly. Then he said nothing more as he carefully struggled up from the chair with an obvious effort and held out his left arm.

Still trying to catch his breath, the Crimson Man embraced his father. So long he'd dreamed of this moment, so many nights. They clung to each other for almost a full minute before finally breaking apart. Both a little moist-eyed.

"It's good to see you again after so long," the Crimson Man said in a choked-up voice. "To find you alive and well ... in this unusual, secret place." He made a kind of sweeping gesture with his hand.

His father nodded, his smile warped by his partially stiffened features.

"My son."

The Crimson Man cleared the lump from his throat before speaking again.

"I have so much to say, but I'm not sure where to begin ... but sit back down, please."

The old man eased himself back into his cushioned chair.

The Crimson Man rubbed his scar, gathered his thoughts, and then finally said, "I guess the first thing I need to say is that I'm truly *sorry* for how we last parted. My adolescent and stupid behavior. I've regretted that moment in the mess hall at the med-camp many thousands of times over the last thirty years. I spent some happy years with MacKenzie, and early on she told me the extent of your relationship, and my stupid misunderstanding ... I always felt that you left the med-camp because of my hostility and rejection—"

"No," his father said, "You weren't wrong!" He swallowed after the forceful effort. "It's I who must apologize for abandoning you." He wiped his eyes with the back of his good hand. "I left you when you needed me most ... But you see, I was still grieving over your mother's horrific death ... And yes, I was deeply hurt by your unsympathetic attitude ... your poor judgment, the unnecessary and heartless slaying of the disabled man in the boxcar at the Iron Triangle, the sudden death of my friend, Leroy ... I guess I was only thinking of myself, overwhelmed by everything so violent happening so quickly after the Collapse, in such a relatively short period of time ... But mostly now I am ashamed for having left you—"

The Crimson Man slowly but forcefully shook his head. "*No*, you didn't abandon me. I intentionally turned away from you. I was traveling down a dark and questionable path with Shaw and the other young people, a course of which I knew you sternly disapproved, but I was stubborn and didn't understand your reaction. I'm sorry for being a major disappointment to you—"

The older man flicked his good hand, as if dismissing his son's explanation and apology as quite unnecessary.

"We can talk about responsibility, lack of blame, forgiveness, and what happened in the past, if all that's really necessary, perhaps sometime in the future." He swallowed with some difficulty before continuing. "How are you now? I must admit that I only barely recognize your voice ... You've changed drastically in so many ways ... Tell me about yourself."

The Crimson Man fingered his scar and touched his half ear.

"I guess I'm an intimidating, scary sight after all this time."

The old man cleared his throat again, and chuckled. "No, not to me. H and Shakespeare of course briefed me about you. What to expect concerning your physical appearance and all ... I must admit

I am slightly taken aback … I'm just glad you are still alive and well despite the color judgment and staining of your skin by the Company. I'd like to know why they did this to you, of course. But more importantly, I'm most concerned about your inner state—the real you?"

"Well, I'm—"

He stopped short of declaring his innocence; then he shrugged and smiled thinly before continuing in a heartfelt manner, "Although I was not guilty of the exact offense for which I was judged over a year ago, I've done so many, many dubious things during the last thirty years, many of them violent, some quite brutal, even a few really mean-spirited. Acts I haven't thought too much about until recently; but now I regret deeply … No, I've undoubtedly earned this crimson skin by past behavior. The color reaching much deeper than my skin, perhaps staining my very soul."

"No, that can't ever be," the older man insisted in a soft but confident tone. "A soul can never be blemished. Only a person's behavior is ever tarnished, which can always be changed. Forgiven even…Tell me a little about your life during the last thirty years."

The Crimson Man fingered the long facial scar. Then, as accurately and concisely as possible in the next half hour, he described to his father his adult years, focusing on the good times with Mac-Kenzie, but not brushing over lightly any of the years of violence with the Raiders during the Food Wars and afterwards…

His father took it all in, a thoughtful look on his partially paralyzed features.

"We must all atone for our past sins, but what we do now and in the future is what is significant in the final summing up of our lives…You understand we can't change the past; we can only learn from it …And then we modify our present behavior accordingly in a heartfelt manner."

The Crimson Man nodded at his father's succinct wisdom.

There were a few moments of silence, a natural period for reflection.

"Tell me about yourself. I've read a lot from your two journals, which I have in my possession. But there are important gaps."

"You have the first and second journals?"

"Yes, I found and bought them at different trade-offs."

The old man smiled as best he could.

His father briefly and humbly described the last thirty years of his spiritual search for redemption: his post-Collapse discovery of his true path—the reading of stories all over Cal Wild, the teaching of children to read, his attempt to establish schools, and finally the founding of the Family in the desert.

The door suddenly opened after a brief rap.

H poked his head in.

"It's getting late. You two can continue catching up tomorrow. You need your rest *now*." He gestured at Jacob, who nodded back with a reluctant shrug to his son. "We'll have breakfast with Shakespeare and begin orientation early in the morning."

"Okay," the older man said.

"I'm so glad the journals led me to you," the Crimson Man said and hugged his father.

"For the time being, you will live here, close to your father," H said, leading the Crimson Man out of the room and to a cubicle next door. "Get some rest, because tomorrow will be an important, busy day, with some surprises for you, I'm sure."

"Thank you."

16

THE FAMILY

Early the next morning, in a tiny communal dining hall, located in a smaller cave beyond the larger meeting cavern, almost as many children as adults ate breakfast. The Crimson Man pointed out this observation to his father.

"You're right, there are twenty-five children in dorm residence here, all attending school," the older man said in a less halting voice, his speech reflecting the energizing effect of a good night's rest after finally being reunited with his son. "They come mostly from around the general desert area—rancher's, herder's, and farmer's children. Some of the adults you see eating are teachers in training. We hope to eventually establish small covert schools all over Cal Wild, but especially near all the Shields. Educating children in the Company's shadow. Carefully and safely."

H added, "You'll get a chance to see the children in class and meet the ten teachers who are currently in training a little later."

"But first a brief orientation right after breakfast," Shakespeare said, spooning up the last of his oatmeal mixed with nuts and dried berries.

They took seats around a round stone table, a portable clean black-board behind where Shakespeare sat. He stood and wrote two words on the blackboard in caps: THE FAMILY. He turned.

"Jacob?" he said, handing the chalk to the Crimson Man's father.

The founder rose with an effort, took the chalk, and began his brief introduction to the orientation. "A little over four and a half years ago I realized the Company was probably intent on confiscating as many books as possible around Cal Wild. They actively closed down established schools, intimidating, brainwashing, and discouraging teachers … So, we started setting up a covert network to counteract these effects, a non-violent resistance, so to speak. By this time, I had many friends all over Cal Wild. Soon I recruited the core of what we now call the Family; and we set up headquarters and a governing council here in the desert…"

He handed the chalk he hadn't used back to Shakespeare. "You can best fill in the details, please."

Shakespeare drew a stylized map of Cal Wild from the Canadian border in the north to the Latin Confederation border in the south, designating a small circle near the southeasterly quarter; then he drew a series of intersecting lines that spiraled out and up, sometimes connecting like a spider web.

"Here we are at the heart of the Family, hidden in these caves and tunnels—we call it Central. About twenty adults more or less in permanent residence—drawing from a base of all kinds of people really, Freemen, DPs, even a few ex-Shield residents. We are the nerve center of the web, which extends across Cal Wild, north and south, to the very edge of the four Company Shields. A network designed for rapid communication, but also to provide tangible supply lines of people, food, and other materials."

He turned away from the blackboard and faced the Crimson Man.

"One short-term goal is to establish and supply an association of small schools, locations kept secret and protected from the

Company. Educate children at these sheltered locations. Currently, we have four established schools in addition to the one here at Central, and have plans for expanding to three more in the near future. We are also teaching teachers at Central to staff those and future schools. Another important goal is to provide refuge from the Company for those who need it. DPs mostly, but whomever. We also actively accumulate all kinds of books, not only for our schools, but also for our growing library here. Of course our long-term aspiration is that sometime in the future the Family will actively neutralize the influence of the Company outside their five Shields in Cal Wild. We call this The Cleansing. In the more distant future, we hope we will see the Shields age, shrivel from within, and die." He paused a moment. "Questions?"

"How many Family members total?" the Crimson Man asked.

"Nearly three hundred," Shakespeare said.

"A few of our operatives are so surreptitious, so far below the radar, we don't hear from them regularly and are unable to always include them in up-to-date accurate counts. Like the handful who live inside one of the five Shields, sporadically supplying vital information."

The Crimson Man shook his head in incredulous amazement. "Fascinating… And all this conducted completely outside of Company awareness?"

Shakespeare nodded. "We have to be discreet, especially secretive, and careful for now."

"I'm curious how you think I might fit in and help. I'm not a teacher. And obviously couldn't work underneath the Company's radar anywhere in Cal Wild, not while wearing this crimson color. They are probably actively searching for me by now, since I haven't palmed a cache site sensor for over a week. I'm a liability. Why did you invite me to be a Family member?"

Shakespeare chuckled. "I'm sure the Company is frantically wondering where you are. H, do you want to describe your next project?"

H nodded. "We've recently validated rumors about a skin clinic operating in Mazatlán in the Latin Confederation that has accidentally discovered a method of dissolving DP skin color. We are planning to set up an underground railroad along Cal Wild, eventually smuggling selected DPs across the border to Mazatlán for that skin cleansing procedure—" He interrupted himself, turning to address the founder of the Family. "You will probably want to talk more about this a little later, when you share your current … ah, special project with him."

The Crimson Man's father nodded, his frozen face not giving away anything about this endeavor.

"Any more questions?" Shakespeare asked.

"No, nothing pressing right now," the Crimson Man said, wondering what his father's special project might be.

"Let's take a tour."

For the rest of the morning Shakespeare and H showed the Crimson Man around the underground complex of three small caverns connected by four adjoining tunnels. The children's dorm, with the three small classrooms with students from five to fifteen, was in one cave. The children's mornings were spent in school, the afternoons topside, the younger kids in supervised play, the older students hiking and learning about ecological survival in the desert.

Then they spent some time watching a curriculum class in the meeting cavern, discussing effective methods for teaching reading to early readers.

The Crimson Man already knew about the long tunnel of cubicles, where permanent residents each had a small room, but they swung past these rooms on the way to the library at the end of the wing—the largest collection of books he'd ever seen in one place post-Collapse. They ended up meeting with the Governing Council in the dining hall, where he learned that elected members came from all over Cal Wild, each serving a staggered three-year term. They talked briefly about administration of the entire network, how decisions were always reviewed and approved in a democratic manner by the Council. But he also learned that H, Shakespeare, and Jacob served as permanent Central staff, in a capacity like advisors or consultants, to ensure a continuity of leadership.

Central was almost an underground utopia, with the long-term goal of spreading this ideal throughout Cal Wild. He was impressed. Of course he wanted to help in any way he could. He just could not see *how* at the moment.

When his father awakened after a nap in late afternoon, the Crimson Man met with him privately to discuss his special project, and to find out how he might fit into the Family's scheme of things.

17

THE THIRD JOURNAL

"You might want to travel south to the LC and have your skin's stain cleansed. We will be able to help guide you there safely—the crossing will be established in a few months from the San D Ruins across the border. Perhaps then you could come back and help Cal Wild in a number of ways...perhaps as a teacher. Or maybe working along the network in any number of capacities, capitalizing on your knowledge of Cal Wild...But if you don't want to go through that whole process of going to Mazatlán and removing the dye and training to work in the wasteland, there are a number of positions at Central that might interest you, or..."

The old man let his soft voice taper off, his eyebrows arched, a kind of playful twinkle in his light blue eyes.

The Crimson Man finished his father's suggestions: "Or there is something more specific you have in mind where I might help?" He nodded knowingly, remembering his father's past MO for subtly maneuvering students on a path already selected—allowing them to think they had many choices before making the actual judgment concerning their specific major or thesis topic or any number of other important academic decisions.

The older man shrugged. "Guilty as charged." His expression sobered. "Well, I do think I might have a personal long term project that you'd be interested in, because it's part of my own grand scheme of personal redemption. Something that may also provide an equally fulfilling opportunity for you to find your own inner sense of peace, while making a solid contribution to the Family and others living in Cal Wild, and perhaps the future."

"Okay," the Crimson Man said, his curiosity piqued.

His father dug out a journal from under the stack of books on his table—a black leather journal with the silver **JAZ** stamped on its cover in the right corner. It was the missing third journal, of course, one of the three the Crimson Man had given his father thirty-some years ago for his birthday.

"I want you to help me fill this journal with stories," the old man said, tapping the big book.

"Stories?"

His father reached for a typed manuscript resting on top of the stack of books. "About six years ago I met a young DP near San Fran Shield, dyed the severest shade of blue—indigo. He told me why he'd been dyed, a lot of what it meant to wander with the color, the devastation of the judgment on him personally. The loneliness of wandering as a DP. His guilt for his crime. So I wrote a kind of biography, taking a fiction writer's liberties and projecting him into the future as an old man thinking his skin color was finally fading, and developed a short true novel about his life, *The Burden of Indigo*." He handed the Crimson Man the manuscript.

"A true life novel?" he asked, not understanding how this related to him, or defined his future role in the Family.

"Read it. You are in a perfect position to judge what it says about being dyed. If the Indigo Man's personal search for redemption for his crime is valid ... Certainly you understand what a terrible punishment the Company is imposing when it dyes someone permanently and casts them out to wander Cal Wild like a leper. So read it, reflect, and tell me what you think. Let me know how I've done with this biographical novel."

"This is what you want me to do here at Central? Read this manuscript and comment on it?" He paused and shrugged, feeling more than a little disappointed. "Forgive me, that doesn't seem like something I'm uniquely qualified to do. There are a number of DPs already living with the Family, some who may've wandered with color much longer than me, who have perhaps given years of thought about what it all means—"

His father interrupted, holding up his good hand. "Yes, I understand all that, but I want you to read it, comment on it, and agree that it represents what the Company is imposing on DPs psychologically. But I also want much more from you than that." His crooked smile was warm and encouraging.

The Crimson Man arched his eyebrows.

His father held out his stiffened right hand. "You realize I can no longer type a manuscript, and obviously I can't write longhand anymore. Perhaps more importantly my writer's cognitive sensibility has also been damaged by the stroke, you see. I can no longer think of the precise words. My syntax is seriously affected. The words no longer make the text sing."

He held the third journal out to his son.

The Crimson Man took it and thumbed through the dated events, finally looking up, still puzzled.

His father nodded.

"I want you to fill this journal with stories of Cal Wild. Stories based on real people and real events—almost nonfiction. Stories that show it all: the aspirations and frailties of the Freemen, the sad plight of defectives, the directionless wandering of hopeless DPs. Stories that expose the Company and all its crimes of repression. The book a dramatic arc of beautifully written stories, spanning perhaps fifty or more years, stories with linking tight narration that deftly fit together all the tales into something like a novel. Carefully designed to inspire *all* the people of Cal Wild that there is a better near future for them without domination by the Company..."

He let his soft voice trail off for a few moments. Then he continued, "I'd outlined the first of these stories before my stroke, even know the title of the opening story. 'The Armless Conductor' is about a defective boy who lives down near the San D Shield. He's a rabbit trapper, and a great guide for DPs crossing the border—one of the most dangerous legs to freedom along the underground railroad..."

The old man sucked in a deep breath and shrugged almost sadly. "Of course, I can't write any of these true stories now, but I can mentor a good writer. I want you to be that writer. You were once a pretty good science fiction writer. We're living in a science fiction world now—"

He held up his hand to ward off any argument.

"Not just write them, but read them aloud, along with *The Burden of Indigo*, to those at Central, at first to the teachers-in-training, but eventually to every corner of Cal Wild, like I used to do, reading my stories for so many years."

"But I haven't written any fiction for thirty-some years."

The old man tried to grin, his frozen features almost a leer. "Well, then, I guess it's about time you got started, again, son. You have a lot of ground to make up in a short period of time. I'm not going to be around forever to keep you on the correct literary track. So you will have to practice, find the words, all the right words to make the stories truly sing. Compelling, exciting, relevant stories. And, like all great stories, ones that strike and resonate in the heart of the reader or listener. Like you were beginning to do with your SF stories so long ago. This will be our legacy to the Family and to Cal Wild."

After thinking it over for a few long moments, the Crimson Man smiled at his father. What a noble and unique goal, he thought. Of course he was apprehensive, not the least sure of himself, wondering if his father's trust was misplaced...

"Read the Indigo Man, and then decide," his father said. "We'll talk again tomorrow morning or when you finish."

That night he read *The Burden of Indigo* straight through before going to sleep.

His father had managed to tell the story almost perfectly—in short, accessible, lyrical sentences, almost like Ray Bradbury, one of his SF favorites. But the Crimson Man wasn't certain he could translate that vision into the book of *near future* ... and perhaps encourage and inspire a younger good writer to eventually do the *far future* stories his father wanted written for the grand story arc he envisioned.

The Crimson Man awoke in the morning with questions of his competence lingering on his mind, but feeling more confident about his new relationship with his father.

He decided he'd like to try writing a book of true stories ... to inspire Freemen and DPs and wasteland defectives to rise in rebellion against their mighty but evil foe; and perhaps his work inspire future writers to carry on. Maybe, just maybe. There was no question that he must try.

He met with his father at breakfast.

"What will we call these stories?"

"*The Cal Wild Chronicles*, of course," his father said at once, knowing his son was committed, knowing the stories would all be written one day, and that they would be wonderful.